I0635483

DECEPTIVE CADENCE

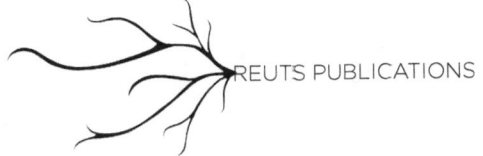

REUTS PUBLICATIONS

KATIE HAMSTEAD

DECEPTIVE CADENCE

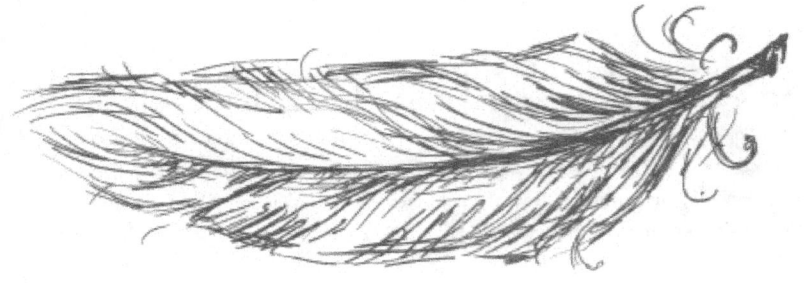

book 1

Deceptive Cadence Copyright 2015 by Katie Hamstead. All rights reserved. No part of this publication may be reproduced or transmitted in any form or by any means, electronic or mechanical, including photocopy, or any information storage and retrieval system, without permission from the publisher, except in the case of brief quotations embodied in critical articles and reviews.

Cover design by Ashley Ruggirello

ISBN: 978-1-942111-22-1

This is a work of fiction. Names, characters, places and incidents are either the product of the author's imagination or are used fictitiously, and any resemblance to actual persons, living or dead, business establishments, events or locals is entirely coincidental.

REUTS Publications
www.REUTS.com

For my daughters and husband, my hope for the future.
Also, this is for everyone who believes in second chances.

part one:
second chances

Chapter One

A steady beep brought me out of unconsciousness. My eyes felt heavy. I struggled to open them. The distinct aroma of cleaning products hung in the air. My brain switched on as I realized where I was and forced my eyes open. The beeping sped up. White walls encircled me in the hospital room; directly across from me was a closed bathroom door. I was completely alone. Where was my family? My husband? My baby daughter?

I tried to sit up, but my whole body writhed with pain. I moaned, and a second later, a nurse dressed in aqua scrubs burst into the room.

"It's all right. Just don't move," she said in a soothing voice.

I wanted to ask a million questions, but I couldn't form any words. She gently pressed me back onto the bed and checked me over. I watched her; she seemed to avoid looking directly into my eyes. As I followed her movements, I became aware of the cast on my arm. My right leg was bound and raised in a sling, and I appeared to have large bolts sticking out of my thigh.

"What happened?" I finally managed to utter.

The nurse slowed. "You have a fractured femur, ulna, and radius. You also sustained substantial head trauma, which is why you've been unconscious for the past few days."

"Few days?" I groaned. "What day is it?"

"Thursday."

"But how? The last thing I remember was . . . was . . ."

I didn't actually know. Monday was a haze. I'd come home from university and found my husband, Austin, had cooked dinner, and our eighteen-month-old daughter, Melody, was bathed and in her pajamas. I'd been so surprised. I kissed him, his dark scruff tickling my nose, and felt as if I'd never be happier. We'd sat and eaten together, enjoying our family time. Our little Melody rambled about this and that, while Austin told me about his day.

"There was an earthquake," the nurse said.

I snapped back into focus. "But we don't live near a fault line."

The nurse dropped her gaze. "It was an accident. Your leg was crushed under a ceiling beam, and your arm broke when you hit the floor."

"When I hit the floor?"

"You were found wedged between your bed and the collapsed wall and roof."

I tried to remember. Austin and I had put Melody to bed at her normal time, and a few hours later, we'd gone to bed. How had I ended up on the floor? I rubbed my forehead.

"Where's my family?"

"Your parents arrived yesterday," she answered.

"My parents?" I lived a long way from my parents, clear across the country, in Perth. For them to come last minute like that . . .

"Where's my husband?"

The nurse didn't answer.

"Where's my daughter?" My voice rose.

Again, no answer.

The beeping sped up. "Where are they?"

A doctor—wearing a white coat and carrying a clipboard—entered the room, my parents right behind him. Mum rushed forward and grabbed my hand. I felt sick. Before the doctor even said it, I knew what had happened.

"Your husband was found holding your daughter in her room. We believe it was fast . . ."

I couldn't hear any more. My ears buzzed. My heart ached.

"No." I pulled my hand free. "No! I don't believe it!"

"Cadence, honey," Mum said as tears streamed down her face. "Austin is gone. He died trying to protect you and Melody."

"Melody! Where's Melody?"

Mum sobbed uncontrollably. Dad stepped forward to grab her shoulders.

"I'm sorry, Cadence."

I gasped, feeling as if my heart had been ripped from my chest. "No! I don't believe you! I'm dreaming. This has to be a dream. It can't be real." I closed my eyes tightly. "Wake up, Cadence, just wake up."

Mum's hand squeezed my arm as she continued to sob. But I couldn't wake up from it. It was all real.

My eyes shot open, and I threw up. The nurse rushed to clean me, but I shoved her away. The beeping from the heart monitor increased.

"Cadence." Mum grasped my shoulder. "Breathe, honey."

"No, no!" I pushed her away, trying to pull free of my restraints. "I don't believe it. I want to see them, *now*."

"Nurse," the doctor said firmly.

The nurse grabbed my drip, and the next thing I knew, the world became hazy.

The drugs kept me relaxed as I drifted in a strange, semi-aware state. Mum's sobs echoed around me. I shut my eyes, willing for it all to end.

Austin appeared over me, his dark eyes sparkling as he smiled. "Good morning, gorgeous."

I glanced around. My belly bulged out, full of our almost-ready-to-emerge daughter as I lay in our bed.

"What day is it?" I asked.

"Saturday." He kissed me softly. "What do you think about heading out to Rottnest today?"

I groaned. "You're joking, right? The whales might think I'm one of them."

"It's the wrong season for whales." He wrapped me in his arms, kissing my temple.

Then, I heard a woman crying. I sat up, glancing around. "Who's that?"

Austin's smile faded as he sat up beside me, meeting my gaze. "Cadence, sweetheart, I have to go."

"What do you mean?" I grasped his bare, strong shoulder.

"I love you."

Fingers over mine dragged me from my sleep. Mum clung to my hand as Dad leaned forward and stroked my brow.

"Austin," I said weakly as tears rolled down my cheeks.

Dad brushed them away. "Do you feel up to seeing him? To say goodbye to him and Melody?"

Still weak from the drugs, I could barely move my body. But I had to see them. To prove they weren't dead. They couldn't be dead. So I gave Dad a nod.

He hurried out to get the nurse. They both returned with a wheelchair. I felt numb as Dad pushed me down the endless corridors to the morgue.

When they pulled out Austin's body from the cool room—his strong body covered in a white sheet—I shook my head. "That's not him."

Dad squeezed my shoulder. "Yes, it is, sweetheart."

"That's not my Austin." Tears built up in my eyes.

"It is. I'm so sorry, Cadence."

My tears burst out, along with sharp sobs.

"No!" I reached across and grabbed his hand. "No, no, no! Austin, if this is some sick joke, you better sit up right now!"

He didn't flinch.

I pressed his hand against my face. It felt ice cold. It never felt that cold, even after he'd been crazy enough to go diving in the ocean mid-winter. I trembled at the reality of his death. My Austin; my warm, loving husband.

Then, a tiny body was brought out and rested in my arms. I couldn't control my tears as I looked into my daughter's lifeless face. That little face that mirrored my own. I held her tightly against me as I wailed in agony.

Dad squeezed my shoulder, leaving me in peace to grieve.

I sat with them, talking softly and pretending they were just asleep. My heart ached. Austin was only twenty-five, the same age as me. Both he and Melody were too young to die. I longed for them to open their brown eyes and smile at me like they always had, but all that happened was that their pale skin grew wet as my tears soaked their lifeless faces.

I squeezed my eyes shut, trying to remember what happened. I remembered climbing into bed while Austin finished in the bathroom. As I'd tried to fall asleep, he'd climbed into bed and tickled me . . .

I struggled to fight free while he laughed. "Austin!"

"Shh, you'll wake Melody."

"Get off!"

He pinned me down and kissed me. I yielded, and his hands wandered. I knew exactly what he wanted. Without any resistance, I willingly gave myself to him.

After that, we'd fallen asleep, but nothing else . . .

Wait. A noise had woken me. He'd shoved me onto the floor. Then everything went black.

"Austin." I ran my fingers through his dark, thick hair. "Don't leave me. We need you. Melody and I . . ." My voice caught in my throat. Melody was gone too. "How can I go on without you? You're the calm to my crazy. I didn't even know what love was until you. Please, *please* don't be dead."

I brushed my fingers over his cheek, hoping maybe, just maybe, my touch would bring him to life. He remained pale, motionless.

"Austin." I pulled away, burying my face into Melody's soft blonde hair. "Couldn't I have at least kept you? You're barely more than a baby. I should have protected you."

The sobs came uncontrollably as my heart shattered. I couldn't see the point in living anymore.

Finally, my nurse returned and insisted I rest. She helped me up so I could kiss Austin on the forehead, and after I'd kissed Melody goodbye, the mortician took her from my arms.

Dad sat in the room as I entered, but I didn't acknowledge him. He helped the nurse lift me back onto the bed, then sat beside me, stroking my hand. I didn't care.

"Cadence, sweetheart." He lifted my hand to his lips, softly kissing it.

I drew a deep breath. "What happened?"

His chin trembled as he gazed up at me. "It was an accident."

"How can an earthquake be an accident?" I shot him a fierce glare.

He glanced away, squeezing my hand. "Let's not talk about it right now."

I pressed my head back against the pillow as my tears threatened to push free again. "Wasn't there something I could have done? Why did they die, but not me? I just want to be with them."

"I know it hurts, but don't give up."

I looked away, ashamed to let him see my tears. How could he know when Mum and his children were all alive?

"You know I loved Austin like a son." A warm tear fell on the back of my hand. I watched him out of the corner of my eye.

"And Melody was so beautiful, just like you." He hung his head as he slipped his hand into his coat jacket. "I found something in the house I thought you'd want to keep. It's perfect, and although we'll help you move on with your life, you shouldn't ever forget."

He opened my palm and pressed a photo into it. I glanced down, then stared. I'd taken the picture only a few months earlier and loved it so much that I'd insisted on having it printed and framed. But it seemed the frame was gone now, just like Austin and Melody.

"They'll always be with you."

Tears ran down my cheeks as I covered my mouth. The two grinning faces of Austin and Melody gazed up at me. So alive. So vibrant.

"Dad, how can I . . . ?"

He wrapped his arms around my head, letting me cry into his chest. "I'm here, baby girl. I love you so much."

I clutched the photo to my heart. If only my love could bring them back.

That night, I couldn't sleep. I lay awake, staring at the ceiling, unable to find the will to live. I set the photo aside and shut my eyes, trying to tell my heart to stop beating so I could be with my little family again.

"You don't want to do that."

My eyes shot open at the voice. There, standing at the end of the bed, stood a man dressed in white scrubs. He had cropped silver hair, a scruffy beard, and penetrating dark brown eyes. He ran his fingers along the foot of the bed. "Your time to die hasn't come yet."

"Get out!" I reached for my button and pressed it.

He came up beside me and sat on the chair. "Does that help?"

"Yes! The nurses will come in any moment and take you away."

"Will they?" He gestured toward the open door.

I looked out. The nurse at the desk stood motionless.

"Why don't we go for a walk around the ward?" He motioned beside him and I saw a wheelchair.

"Was that there before?"

He smiled. I blinked and found myself in the wheelchair. I glanced around in alarm, but then I sighed. "I'm dreaming."

"No, you're not." The man pushed me into the corridor. "This is very real. If it wasn't, would this hurt?" He reached down and pushed at the pin in my leg.

I screeched and slapped his hand. "You freak! Who are you? What do you want from me?"

He didn't answer. As we moved down the corridor, I stared at the frozen people we passed. I even touched the night doctor's coat. The man pushing my wheelchair leaned in close. "They're all frozen in time. I made it happen so we could talk."

A knot formed in my stomach. "Talk about what, exactly?"

"Your options." He turned me around, and we headed back to the room. "Hospitals are much nicer than I remember."

As soon as we passed through the door, I found myself in bed again as he sat beside me, making himself comfortable. The photo of Melody and Austin now rested on top of my belly.

My eyes narrowed on him as I slid the photo protectively under my thigh. "What are you?"

A wide smile spread across his face as he met my gaze. "Now you're getting the idea, sweet Cadence." He paused and leaned closer to me. "I'm a guardian angel, of sorts, here to give you some options on how you are to proceed."

"Options?"

He nodded. "Oh yes. Your first option is to continue your life as you're currently leading it, unaltered. The next option is a chance for you to change certain events."

I sat up. "Change events?"

He beamed. "I knew that would interest you. Would you like to go back and redo the events you regret?"

He had my complete attention. "Of course."

"Well, then, here's your chance." He gestured toward the bathroom door. "All you need to do is pass through and you'll go back to the year in which the course of your life changed to head down this particular path." He pulled out a notepad. "I believe you will find yourself in the second term of your ninth grade year."

"Ninth grade?"

He nodded. "You will be allowed to live your life normally, but with the knowledge and memories you currently have. The memories will often feel like a dream, and sometimes they will blur, but you will never lose them."

I stared at the door. "What's the con?"

"The con?" He grinned. "Good question. The only limitation is that you will not be allowed to warn anyone of the natural disasters, wars, terrorist attacks, and so on, that determine and shape human history. Those things are what we call 'fixed in time.' Events like 9/11, the Bali bombing, the tsunami in Southeast Asia, and Hurricane Katrina are fixed, unchangeable. If you try to prevent or change them, you will be brought back here to this moment and everything will return to the way it is."

I took a deep breath. It sounded too good to be true. To go back and be able to prevent my husband and child from dying was incomprehensible. I couldn't refuse such an offer. But I knew I had to be cautious all the same.

"Do I need to sell you my soul or something in exchange for this trip?"

He stood and I found us both standing beside the door, me with a crutch under my arm. I held tightly to the photo.

"No, no soul selling," he said. "I'm not one of the Devil's angels. This is an honest offer, a chance for you to change your life, save the innocent life of a child, and possibly help some people along the way. You have regrets just like everyone else, and this is an opportunity for you to change them for the better. You've lived a good life, Cadence Jones—or should I say Anderson, if you go back? —and you did the best you could, which no one can fault you for. But just imagine the possibilities. Friendships wouldn't be broken . . ."

An image of my best friend from seventh through tenth grade flashed through my mind.

"Painful moments could be avoided . . ."

I remembered a few breakups that left me humiliated and wishing they'd never happened.

"You could even save someone you didn't know."

I turned to face him. "Austin, he would be alive again. I wouldn't know him for a few years, but he'd be alive."

He nodded.

"And Melody, I could save her. My little angel." Tears burned in my eyes as I clung to the photo. "She didn't deserve to die. She'd only just begun living."

"Yes, Cadence, you could change whatever you wanted. But remember, events will start to change from the moment you arrive. The choices you make will be different, but some things will surprise you when they stay the same. Other people make their own choices too, so not everything you do will alter the events of your life."

"I don't care. As long as Austin's alive and I can save Melody, I'll be happy."

I reached across and opened the bathroom door. On the other side, I saw my bedroom at my parents' house in Sydney, set up like when I was a teenager. Everything was the same: the pale blue walls; my desk—straight in front of me—with my clunky old desktop computer on it and piles of school books and paper junking it up. Clothes, mostly my school uniform, lay strewn across the floor, with my two navy pleated skirts hanging over the back of my desk chair and several light blue blouses scrunched up on the carpet.

My closet doors hung open, shoes and clothes spewing out of it. I'd forgotten how much of a slob I was.

As I passed through the doorway, a numbness took the edge off my grief. I paused, surprised by the odd sensation, by the relief. I knew I felt sad, but the intensity had gone. I glanced at the angel.

"What happened?"

"You can't live this life properly if you are carrying around overwhelming grief," he said in a deep, soothing voice. "So, to assist you, the emotions will be dimmed."

Taking a deep breath to regain my composure, I finished stepping through the door and found it was night. My leg was no longer broken, and my arm was free of the cast. The hospital robe had gone, exchanged for an old set of teddy bear pajamas I hadn't seen in years. But the photo remained in my hand.

I rushed to the mirror on the wall beside my desk and stared at my fourteen-year-old self. I had thought myself chubby, but after school, my participation in sports had ceased and I'd gained some weight. Then, after having a baby, my body had become completely altered. I now stared at myself in awe. Setting the photo on the desk, I lifted my shirt and ran my hand over my stretchmark-free belly and sag-free abdomen. My waist was tiny and my boobs two bra sizes smaller, probably a comfortable C-cup.

I glanced up to see my face. I looked so young! I'd never noticed how different I'd looked from photos, but as I stared at my youthful face with my clear skin and shining dark blue eyes, I couldn't help touching my cheekbones and feeling the plump, soft skin. My mouth felt odd, so I pulled back my lips to see braces. I ran my tongue over them, remembering the relief I'd felt to have them taken off. I turned my attention upward, running my hand through my long hair and admiring the foils that appeared to be recently done. I'd always loved the golden blonde foils in my hair; they lifted the drab sandy color.

"I look amazing! How did I not know how incredible I looked?"

The man appeared in the mirror behind me and smiled.

"You were always humble, not to mention that the world around you told you that you needed to look like this." He gestured at a teen magazine on my desk. A skinny, blonde celebrity with a sexy pout and smoldering eyes graced the cover.

I dropped it in the trash. "I'm not going to fall for that crap this time."

He chuckled. "So you agree to this journey?"

I looked him steadily in the eyes. "I do."

He waved his hand, causing a contract to appear. "Read it carefully. You don't want any surprises."

I took it, grabbed a pen, and sank into my chair. I read it through, seeing the terms he'd told me about. I also couldn't tell anyone about what would happen to them in their own lives. When I read the next section, I paused. "I get one item to help me remember?"

He sat on the edge of my bed. "Oh, yes. Here."

He reached down behind him, and, as if out of thin air, procured a thick, spiral-bound black book.

I took it, opening it to the first page. It had my name in my handwriting, and the year: 2001. "What is this?"

"I guess you could call it a record, or a journal."

I flicked through the pages and photos appeared. School photos, photos with my old high school friends, with family . . . all alongside journal entries. "It looks like a scrapbook of my life."

Then, I flipped over to a picture of Austin at fourteen. "Or not . . ."

"Usually, it will show you your life, but if you really want to see someone, it will show them, too."

"Austin." I ran my fingers over the image of his chubby cheeks. "All of this . . . is it real? I'm not dreaming? Why me?"

He bowed his head. "Sometimes, we don't see how we affect the people around us. Sometimes, people need second chances to improve the lives of those around them. You are one of those people. But most importantly, a child needs you to save her, to give her the chance she was denied."

"Melody."

He nodded. "Good luck, Cadence Anderson. Make the most of this second chance. Not many people are given this kind of opportunity."

He stood and walked toward the doorway leading back to the hospital room. He stepped through and slowly closed the door.

I glanced around my room, suddenly apprehensive about my decision. To change my past could lead me down a completely different path. I flipped through the scrapbook and found that all the journal entries came from my journals, but times when I wasn't consistent with my entries were in typewriter print.

I opened to the first entry and found a note. It read: *To help you keep track of things. I'd recommend reading a week in advance.*

I turned to the first week. As I read through, I learned I was dating my first boyfriend, Tyler, and was about to start the second term of my ninth grade year. I planned on dumping Tyler sometime that week, and I would spend most of the week avoiding it.

I thought about what I remembered from that time. Tyler had been furious when I dumped him and refused to talk to me for the next few months. Although the least dramatic of all my breakups, I would do it with more grace and class this time around.

I also made the decision to have no boyfriends at all. I thought about all the boys I'd dated and knew I didn't want to date any of them again. I needed to remain faithful to Austin anyway, even if we weren't married yet.

I turned to Austin's picture again. He was so small. He hadn't hit puberty until the middle of tenth grade, so the Austin I knew hadn't surfaced yet. His dark hair was ruffled and scruffy, and he looked positively adorable with all his baby fat. I smiled and touched his face, knowing that if I *had* known him at fourteen, I wouldn't have paid any attention to him.

I plucked up the picture of him and Melody, and my heart felt heavy. My baby girl. Her golden locks looked just like mine when I was a child. How I loved her, and how my heart ached at the memory of her tiny lifeless body. More than anything, I needed to do this for her. She didn't deserve to die. I had to do this second chance right and prevent her death.

Sliding the photo into the scrapbook as a bookmark, I shut the book and slid it under the bed, covering it with a blanket and books. I climbed into my bed and sighed. As I drifted off to sleep, I felt hopeful again.

Chapter Two

"Cadence, it's time to get up."

I rolled over and pulled the blankets tighter around me. "Seriously, Austin, *you* can't complain about sleeping in—"

"Austin?" My younger brother Dusty burst out laughing. "Who's Austin? What happened to *Tyler*?"

Completely disoriented, I sat up and stared at him, gaping as his twelve-year-old self sprinted out of my room. How was he twelve again? Dusty was twenty-three and had just finished his bachelor's degree in architecture. I rubbed my eyes, confused.

Then, I remembered everything.

I leapt out of bed and shut the bedroom door. After scrambling to collect my uniform for the day and dumping it on the bed, I pulled out the scrapbook and found Austin's pictures. I found one with him at the beach with his stepdad. He'd lived on the West Coast his whole life, and I lived on the East Coast. I closed my eyes, longing for the day I could go to him, then shut the scrapbook and hid it away.

I rushed to the bathroom, pausing as my sixteen-year-old sister, Harper, stepped out. She glared at me and shoved me aside. "Move it, kid."

"Bite me, Harper." I had no idea why I said it—it just came out. I guessed some of my teenage traits would kick in on occasion.

"That was original." She twisted her long, dyed black hair into a bun.

I couldn't help staring at her. At twenty-seven in the past . . . future . . . she was married, had three kids, and had given up on dying her hair in her early twenties. I hadn't seen her hair in a color other than light brown in years.

"What are you staring at?"

"Nothing."

"Then get away from me."

I stepped backward into the bathroom and shut the door. While I took my shower, I wondered what I would face that day. There were so many possibilities, so many choices I could change, so many things I would and wouldn't do.

I dressed quickly, but couldn't help admiring my slim, athletic body. How I missed it! That was something I would avoid doing too—putting on weight.

As I entered the kitchen, I found Dad grabbing his lunch out of the fridge. Harper had inherited his light brown hair and eyes, and he stood tall and strong. I felt fairly certain he was a superhero. I smiled at him and kissed his cheek. "Hey, Dad."

He turned to me, surprised. "Good morning, sweetheart. You're rather chipper this morning."

I shrugged. "I'm going to make the most of my day."

"Good for you."

"What are you doing today?"

He raised his eyebrows. "I'm going into State Parliament."

"Oh, it's one of *those* days."

He grasped my chin. "Wow, you *are* different today. Since when have you cared what I'm doing?"

I hesitated. I needed to act more like a fourteen-year-old. My old fourteen-year-old self would have simply said, *"Hi, Dad, have a nice day. See ya later."*

I smiled back at him. "I gotta eat, you're in my way."

He stepped aside and I plucked the milk out of the fridge.

About twenty minutes later, Dusty and I walked together to the bus stop and, just as I remembered, Harper charged ahead. Once we arrived, she pretended we didn't exist.

"Harper's such a brat," I muttered.

Dusty snorted. "Yeah, so are you."

I punched his arm and he laughed.

On the bus, Harper hurried right to the back with her friends, while mine waved me over from the middle left side. I sat with the three girls I'd ridden to school with for years, staring at them. I hadn't seen any of them since I graduated, so it felt surreal to have them sitting right in front of me.

"Cadence!" Amy, one of the girls, slapped my shoulder. "What's up with you?"

"Nothing. Kinda tired."

"Well, you have maths first, so you can catch up on sleep then. We wanna know how things went with you and Tyler over Easter."

The other girls, Elise and Laura, grinned and leaned closer.

I hurried to remember. Tyler had taken me to the movies and kissed me. That was my first kiss, and my first make-out session. Nothing special . . . but then, I was fourteen.

"We, ah . . ."

"Did he kiss you?" Amy asked eagerly.

I thought hard about how I should react, then faked a blush and buried my face in my bag.

"No, Cay!" They all moaned and shoved my shoulders.

"I can't believe you chickened out *again*!" Amy whined.

"I didn't chicken out!" I hissed in a low voice.

Their attention instantly snapped into focus.

"Well?" Amy beckoned.

"Well . . . I don't wanna kiss and tell."

They groaned in unison. "Cadence, come on, give us something!"

Give them something? What had I given them before? "Well, it was actually kinda weird."

"How exactly? Did he slobber all over your face?"

I couldn't help giggling. "No. It was just . . . weird. I think he was way more into it than I was."

"Are you serious?" Elise said. "Tyler is adorable, and you weren't that into it?"

My cheeks warmed, really blushing that time. I buried my head in my bag again. "I just don't feel like we work. He hardly talks to me, and whenever I say something to him, he looks at me funny."

"Are you saying you're going to dump him?" Amy leaned closer.

And there was the first decision I needed to make differently. "I didn't say that at all."

They breathed a sigh of relief and sat back. First crisis avoided. The rumors wouldn't spread to Tyler before I had a chance to tell him myself.

We arrived at school and split into our different groups. I paused as I watched them go their separate directions and wondered how we could all be friends one minute, but then pretend to not even know each other the next.

I quickened my pace, heading straight to my group of friends. The group consisted of about twenty people, mostly boys. As I climbed the stairs from the lower quad to the upper level, I saw them gathered around a picnic table. I stopped to stare. There they were, my friends, half of whom I would somehow manage to offend and estrange before I graduated.

A curly-haired brunette burst from among them, heading right at me. I caught my breath, frightened for a moment that she would attack me, but instead she threw her arms around my neck.

"Hey, hey, Cay! I missed ya over the holidays. I believe we have some catching up to do."

As she linked her arm through mine, I couldn't help staring. Geri, my best friend from seventh grade to part way through tenth when we had a falling out, wanted to talk to me! I had no idea what happened. She just suddenly turned on me. I'd thought about it over the years, wishing I could at least know what I'd done.

"So, how did it go with Tyler?"

I glanced around, surprised to find us tucked away behind a classroom. "It went okay."

"Only okay? Didn't he kiss you?"

I gazed into her brown eyes, overwhelmed with joy to have her back. A tear streamed down my cheek and I threw my arms around her. "Geri, I've missed you so much!"

"Oh, hey . . . Cay, I missed you too." She pushed me back and looked into my face with concern. "Are you okay? Did he dump you?"

I shook my head.

"I think I'm going to dump him," I told her to cover my overemotional state.

"Damn, seriously?" She scowled. "He was *that* bad of a kisser?"

I chuckled at how simple she made it. "No, I just don't think I like him like that anymore."

"Sad. Well, I always thought you looked more like brother and sister than a couple anyway."

I smiled at her as my feelings over the loss of her friendship overcame me. I was determined not to let that happen again. She was the best friend I ever had, and I refused to blow it a second time. "Thanks, Geri. That makes me feel a little better."

She wrapped her arm through mine. "Good. That's what I'm here for."

We walked toward our friends, attached at the hip, just like old times.

Back at the group, I saw Tyler and his best friend had joined them. Geri's arm clenched mine and she whispered, "How are you going to do it?"

"I dunno."

"When are you gonna do it?"

"I dunno. Soon, I guess."

He looked across and saw me. He smiled and I remembered why I'd noticed him in the first place. Ahead of the game, puberty-wise, he stood taller and bulkier than most of the other guys. He had a wide, open smile with dimples in his cheeks, his best feature by far. But as I looked at him, I realized what Geri meant by brother and sister. We had the same color hair and eyes, the same athletic build, and even the same nose.

"Geri, I just saw what you meant by the brother thing."

She giggled. "Are ya totally freaked out now?"

"Yeah."

He met us eagerly and grabbed my hands. "Hey, Cadence."

"Hey, Ty."

He leaned over to kiss me, but I turned my face away. He kissed my cheek instead. "You look hot today."

Hot? Did he just say *hot*? "Ah, thanks."

Whatever happened to pretty or beautiful? Austin always called me beautiful or gorgeous, only calling me hot when he teased me or I practically begged for it.

The bell rang, and I looked around. "I gotta go."

"I'll walk you." Tyler smiled and slipped his arm between my backpack and my back. I glanced at Geri, who shrugged as she turned to head to her own class.

We walked in silence, just like I remembered. I glanced up at him, finding him content just walking beside me. "Ty?"

He looked down at me. He seemed startled that I'd spoken. "Um . . . yeah?"

"Why do you like me?"

"Huh?"

"Why do you like me? We never talk to each other."

He scratched his head. "Yeah, we do."

"No, we don't."

"Well, you're hot. I like that." He tried to kiss me again.

I raised my hand and pressed it against his lips. "What's my favorite sport?"

He grinned. "Soccer."

I shook my head. "I'll give you a hint. I play it on Saturdays."

"You play a sport on Saturdays?"

I raised my eyebrows. "See what I mean? Like most girls, I play *netball* on Saturdays. You could've just guessed it."

He shuffled closer to me, his brows furrowing. "I'll pay more attention from now on."

I sighed. Now was the time. I pulled him aside and we stood under a tree for some privacy. "This isn't working out."

"Huh?"

"You and me. We don't work. I'm sorry."

He leaned back as his eyebrows lowered. "You're dumping me?"

"Dumping sounds so harsh," I muttered, seeing the anger burning in his eyes. "I feel like if we don't end it now, we'll end up hating each other and I don't want that. I think you're a really nice guy, but—"

"Shut up, Cadence! I'm not going to let you dump me."

"Tyler—"

"Because I'm going to dump you. You're boring anyway. You're so uptight and never let me go in for a grope."

He marched away from me.

I turned and headed to my classroom. At least it wasn't a big scene like last time. He could at least walk away with his dignity intact.

I slipped into roll call just as the last bell rang, telling us if we weren't in class we'd be marked absent. I sank into my normal chair and an arm wrapped around my shoulders. "Hey, pretty lady."

I looked over my shoulder and smiled. My good friend Michael had always been there for me through thick and thin, and he'd never complicated things by developing a crush on me, which I appreciated more than anything. "Hello, handsome knight."

He chuckled and ruffled his white-blond hair. "I am the better looking of the two of us, huh?"

I giggled and elbowed him in the ribs. We fell silent while the roll was called, but jumped straight into a quiet conversation when study time began.

"You looked distracted as you came in," he said.

"Oh." I bit my lip. "Tyler and I just broke up."

His eyes widened. "No way!"

"Shh." I couldn't help smiling.

"That's okay. I always thought he was kinda stupid anyway."

I elbowed him in the ribs again.

He grabbed my arm and leaned closer. "So, since you don't seem too upset by it, I guess you did the dumping."

"Dumping sounds so horrible."

"That's a yes, then."

I sighed. "Yes, technically. But he's going to say he did it and I'm not gonna stop him."

He leaned back, stunned. "Wow, that's pretty mature of you."

Was I being too mature? I needed to think more like a teen. "Yeah, well, this way I'll get the pity votes, right?"

He rolled his eyes and smiled. "Yeah, Cay."

Most of the grade knew by recess. Tyler told everyone he could that he dumped me. I let it happen and didn't fight it. At lunchtime, people swarmed me, giving their condolences. I did the best I could to fake it, but Geri saw through me.

She eventually managed to pull me aside. "You *so* dumped him! I just know it! Why are you taking all this?"

"He was pretty angry, so I'm just letting him have this. Maybe it will die down faster this way."

She pursed her lips and folded her arms. Then, a light flashed in her eyes. "You've got someone else in mind already!"

Austin, yes, but to Geri, he would be an imaginary friend.

"No, I don't."

"You *so* do!" She slapped my shoulder with a grin. "I can see it written all over your face!"

"I really don't."

"Oh!" She leaned closer, her eyes sparkling. "It's some loser, huh? That's why you're afraid to admit it."

I huffed. "Yeah, it is."

She giggled. "Okay, you don't have to tell me. I *don't* wanna know."

She wrapped her arm around mine and we rushed back to the group.

I found the first week fascinating. Being among so many people I hadn't seen in years and reliving experiences I'd forgotten felt bizarre. But everyone thinking Tyler dumped me changed everything. By the end of the week, he felt as if justice had been served and wasn't angry with me. He was still upset, but unlike the first time around, he wasn't spreading vicious rumors about me.

Friday night arrived, and I felt pretty good about what I'd changed already. But I noticed that not everything changed. In fact, most events stayed the same. I still joined the same sports team, had the same conversations about the same guys my friends were crushing on, and during classes, I still became easily distracted. I had no idea why. High school classes seemed easy after finishing my bachelor's and starting my master's.

I was sprawled across the couch in my pajama pants and school blouse when Harper walked in. She tossed my legs off the couch, snatched the remote from me, and changed the channel.

I stared at her. Had she really just done that? I shook it off. "Harper, I was watching that."

"*Pft*, I don't care. I'm watching this."

"Are you serious?" It felt childish and stupid. I couldn't believe I was playing this game with her again. "Can't you just let me finish my show? It's got like five minutes left."

"Well, mine's just started."

I groaned and stood. I had no desire to argue with her, and since I knew how it always ended, it wasn't worth the fight. As I left the room, she sneered, "Yeah, that's right, you better know your place."

An overwhelming urge to smack her across the face hit me. Without even knowing it, I rushed at her. I grabbed her hair and yanked it. She screamed and shoved me off before she jumped on top of me. "You little brat! You messed up my hair. I'm going out in like ten minutes!"

"You're the brat! You're not even going to finish your show. You're so selfish."

We struggled on the floor before Mum rushed in and hollered, "That's enough!"

Harper leaped off me. "She started it. Look what she did to my hair!"

"Are you kidding me?" I cried. "Mum, she's—"

"I don't want to hear it. You're both grounded for a week."

"Mum!" we both whined in unison. Grounded? That *sucked*. I thought those years were long gone.

"Harper, you can go out tonight, but cancel the rest of your plans for the weekend."

Harper huffed and glared at me. "This is all your fault!"

"Me?" I gasped incredulously.

"Enough, Harper. Now both of you get to your rooms," Mum snapped.

We skulked to our bedrooms across the hall from each other. Before I turned to my door, I paused and looked at Harper. She was very pretty. She had long slender hands and legs, and she had light brown eyes rather than the blue that Dusty and I shared. With her hair dyed dark, she looked nothing like me. No wonder she pulled off being an only child at school. "Harper?"

She huffed and glared at me.

"I'm sorry I messed up your hair."

She rolled her eyes. "Whatever. Just don't talk to me."

She slammed the door in my face.

I slipped into my room and tried to recall when we stopped fighting. I was fairly certain it was after she graduated. I groaned, knowing I had to endure two more years of her sour demeanor.

I collapsed on my bed and huffed. I stared at my knees for a moment before lifting my legs. Unlike Harper's, they were short and stubby, but still slim compared to before I came back. I dropped them down and thought of Austin. He had great legs . . . he had great everything. While I was pregnant, I teased and said that I hoped our child would inherit his legs rather than mine.

He pinned me on the couch and ran his hands over my legs. "I love your legs."

I gazed into his brown eyes and stroked his cheek. He leaned over me and kissed me with such love I thought I'd melt.

Rolling onto my belly, I reached under my bed for the scrapbook. I pulled it out and opened to Austin's pictures again. I found one with him doing his homework, wearing the ugliest and biggest glasses I'd ever seen. I giggled at how goofy he looked. He'd worn glasses just for reading, but by the time I met him, he'd developed some sense of style and wore much smaller and fashionable ones. I pulled out the picture of him with Melody and placed it beside his to compare the two. I loved how their eyes matched.

Harper's door banged and she rushed down the hallway. She didn't even say bye to Mum when she called to her. I wondered if I could somehow change things with Harper, make her nicer earlier.

Mum's footsteps came down the hallway, so I slipped the scrapbook back under my bed. She tapped softly on the door. "Cadence, can I come in?"

I sat up. "Sure."

The door crept open. "Can I talk to you?"

I shuffled onto my pillows so she could sit on the bed with me.

As she sat, she sighed.

I looked her over, thinking about how much she had cried in the hospital. I had inherited most of my appearance from her, my sandy colored hair, my blue eyes, and my chubby legs. We'd always been close, which made many of my friends envious. But that day in the hospital haunted me. I'd never seen her cry so hard. With Melody being Mum's only granddaughter—Harper had all boys—she'd held a special place in Mum's heart. That, along with how close we were, meant she was easily just as devastated as me.

"Cadence," she said gently. "I know you didn't start that fight, but you should have been the one to end it."

My cheeks warmed. "I know."

"You know you're more levelheaded than your sister. I don't mean to expect more from you than from her, but I do."

I sighed. "I'm sorry, Mum. I'll try to do better."

"Thank you, sweetheart." She touched my face. "Now, come out and have dinner with us."

I swung my legs around and stood beside Mum. As she walked out, I wrapped my arm around her waist. She looked at me, surprised, but smiled and squeezed my shoulders.

At the table, I sat beside Dusty. He ignored me as he focused on the food. When Dad signaled for us to serve ourselves, he leapt up and dug in.

"I can't believe you're smart enough to be an architect," I muttered as I watched him.

Mum chuckled. "Architect? Wow, Cadence. I didn't realize you had that much faith in your brother."

"What's an architect?" Dusty muttered, his mouth full of food.

I raised an eyebrow. "How do you not know that?"

He shrugged. "Why should I care? I'm gonna be something where I don't have to do much to get there. Like a truck driver."

"Wow." I grunted, having forgotten how lazy he'd been.

"Anyways," Dusty said through his food, "I heard *you* got *dumped*."

I shrugged and focused on eating.

"Tyler dumped you?" Mum asked.

"Who's Tyler?" Dad asked, his voice rising.

"Tyler is the biggest hottie ever," Dusty teased, making kissing noises at me.

"You're so immature." I shoved his shoulder.

"You better not be kissing boys, Cadence!" Dad's eyes narrowed as he pointed his fork at me.

"Yeah, you're not allowed to do that until you're fifty!" Dusty laughed.

I scowled. "Dad, I'm not kissing boys."

"Hon, it's okay." Mum touched Dad's shoulder. "It was just a fling. It only lasted for about a month."

"A month!" Dad jumped to his feet.

"Dad!" I covered my face. So I hadn't blown his over-protective nature out of proportion.

"Cadence, I've told you, no boyfriends! You are fourteen years old and don't need them yet!" He sank back onto his chair. "You know what boyfriends lead to. Boys your age only want one thing."

"Gross, Dad," Dusty grumbled.

"Please don't start on the sex talk again." I groaned, remembering the thousands of times he'd climbed that particular soapbox.

"Oh, I will, Cadence. I don't want you getting pregnant before you're married, and sex, as you know, leads to getting pregnant. That's what sex is intended for, not for you and your friends to get their jollies off."

"Oh my gosh!" I covered my face as I turned bright red. *Did he seriously just say that?*

"You are not having sex until you're married."

"Dad, I'm not anywhere near having sex! It was just a thing. He liked me and I liked him, but it's over now."

"It better be over, or I'm going to go down to that school to castrate him and anyone else who looks at you!"

"Oh, for heaven's sake, David!" Mum grabbed Dad's arm. "You're being a bit overdramatic, don't you think? Cadence is a smart girl, and she knows what she should and shouldn't be doing."

I couldn't help smiling at her. I hadn't realized how lucky I was to have them both as a teenager.

Dad growled something under his breath, then pointed at me with his fork. "No more boyfriends. I don't want you turning out all foul and irritable like Harper. Don't think I don't know what she does."

A question that had bothered me for years, but that I'd always been too afraid to ask, bubbled to the surface.

I couldn't help blurting out, "Why do you let her go out and do things, then? Why are you so hard on me when you know she's the one who actually drinks and smokes and who knows what else?"

The table fell silent. They gaped at my outburst, and then Dad turned bright red with rage. "Go to your room!"

But I wanted to test this one. I had stewed over it for years as a teenager, but this time around, I wanted to know. "No! You know I would never do those things, but you're always on my case about it and never on hers."

Dad launched to his feet and pointed to my room. "Get to your room *now!*"

I scowled, knowing I wasn't going to get an answer. I stormed out and headed to my room. Once inside, I paced back and forth. My second chance suddenly didn't seem so appealing. Having to relive being under the rules of my parents, having to face injustices I'd managed to let go of, and the hormones, oh the hormones! Even with my rational, more mature twenty-five-year-old reasoning, the hormones seemed to thrust me into an emotional haze. It was ridiculous. How did I live with it the first time?

I stopped pacing and fell to my knees. I pulled out the scrapbook and read the next week's journal entries, reading clear into the following Sunday before I stopped and took a deep breath. I needed get control over my erratic emotions and focus. I needed to fix the things I had done wrong, not create problems that hadn't existed in the first place.

I flipped to the pictures and looked at Austin again. I found one of his sixteenth birthday. He stood beside his mother in the kitchen while she made her famous stroganoff, grinning from ear to ear.

I smiled and slipped out the photo Dad had given me in the hospital. Austin and Melody's matching wide grins and identical brown eyes gazing at the camera sent a chill through me. Melody loved her daddy more than anything. He was the only man in her world; she'd guarded him from her cousins jealously.

In return, he adored her and showered her with his devotion. I'd loved watching him rock her to sleep, then kiss her on the head goodnight, or play chasing games around the living room as she squealed with delight.

My throat clenched and tears filled my eyes. Forget everyone else. I needed to get this chance right for them. I closed the scrapbook and stashed it away, then leaned over to turn on the radio. I needed to remember the trends that year and focus on making sure I did everything just right.

Chapter Three

I woke up screaming. Mum burst into the room and shook me by the arms. "Cadence! Wake up!"

I cut off my scream and stared at her. "Mum! Oh Mum, it was so terrible! Austin and Melody were killed—"

"Honey, they're not real people. It was just a dream."

I glanced around and shook off my disorientation. My emotions swelled inside me as the images of them being buried alive burned into my brain. I threw my arms around her and cried.

"Sweetheart, it was just a dream." She held me tighter as I cried on her shoulder.

"Geez, Cadence, crying over nightmares is what babies do."

I looked up. Harper leaned against the doorframe with her arms folded.

"Leave me alone," I whispered.

"Oh, wah! You're such a pansy."

Mum let me go and turned on her. "Harper, if you can't say anything nice, then go back to bed."

"Whatever." She turned with a huff.

I remembered a time when she'd done the same thing. At the end of my ninth grade, she was about to start her Higher School Certificate classes. She'd come to my door while I worked on homework and said, "Why do you even bother? The system is rigged so we fail."

"Leave me alone," I'd muttered without looking up.

"Look at you, Miss I'm-So-Perfect. You need to face reality. You aren't going to succeed in life because you're not as special as Mum and Dad puff you up to be."

I'd set my paper down and turned to her. "No, Harper, you're the one who's going to fail because you don't care about anyone but yourself."

"Is that so?"

"Yeah."

She'd scoffed, rolled her eyes, and walked out. That night, she ran away.

I jumped off my bed and rushed over to her. "Harper?"

She looked down at me, scowling. "What?"

"You know that despite how mean you are, I love you, right?"

She gagged. "Gross. You freak." She shoved me and slammed her bedroom door behind her.

I walked back into my room and sat beside Mum. She stared at me with wide-eyed bewilderment. "Cadence, that was . . . very nice."

I shrugged. "Harper has pretty bad self-esteem. I figured she needed it."

"Wow, that's very mature of you." She leaned over and kissed my head. "Are you okay now?"

I nodded. "Thanks, Mum."

She stood and walked to the door. "I love you, dear."

"I love you too, Mum."

After she left, I scrambled back into bed. I pulled the blankets tightly around me before letting my tears fall.

Michael talked to me about his weekend while the announcements were read.

"Michael, Cadence?"

We glanced over at the teacher and fell silent.

"And student council is holding a school disco on the twenty-ninth," the twelfth grader read out.

Michael nudged me. "Here we go again. A chance for everyone to act like complete idiots."

I giggled. "I dunno, I kinda like going."

"You would." He grinned. "So, who do you have your eye on? Being dumped gives you the right to move on whenever you want."

I rolled my eyes. "No one. I think I'm done with guys for a while."

He raised an eyebrow. "Cadence Anderson, done with boys? No! Is the sky falling?"

"Mr. Allen!" the teacher snapped at Michael.

We turned and paid attention to the announcements.

Later, I met up with Geri as we entered the change rooms for PE. "Cay-Cay! It's disco time again!" She shook her hips at all the girls in the change room, but paused and turned away when she came to Melanie Gordon.

Melanie was the token outcast. She had drab brown hair that looked like she never washed, a face full of acne, and pungent body odor. She wore the boys' uniform—gray pants instead of the blue tartan skirt or black dress pants—and an oversized blue polo shirt.

I'd only spoken to her a few times during my school years. Despite her poor hygiene, she was nice, albeit a bit strange.

Melanie watched Geri as she walked away from her with a hint of pain in her eyes. As I pulled out my shirt, I paused to see what she would do. She shuffled into the corner and turned her back on everyone, while the girls nearby sprayed deodorant behind her. I felt a pang of pity for her.

Geri jumped into my line of vision and whipped off her shirt. "Do you like my new bra?"

"Geez, Geri!"

She burst out laughing and pulled on the dark blue sports polo shirt. "Well, I like it. It's got Playboy bunnies on it!"

I giggled.

"So . . ." She leaned in closer to whisper. "Who's next, huh? I've noticed Justin and Brian checkin' you out."

I shoved her shoulder. "Ew! I think I'm done for a while."

"Done? Ha!" She tugged her black shorts on under her skirt, then whipped the skirt up over her head. "You will never be done with boys. You like 'em too much."

"Maybe it's time for me to change."

She glared at me, then flicked my temple.

"Ouch!"

"Who are you and what have you done with the real Cadence?"

"Geez, Geraldine! Can't I have some time off?"

"What the hell, Cadence?"

I gritted my teeth. I didn't want to fight with her. "There's just no decent guys around."

A wide grin swept across her face. "Okay, yeah, you're right on that one."

We finished changing and headed out to the field, arms linked together. The teacher divided us into teams and, as usual, split me and Geri up. I found myself with Brian. He stood a head taller than me, with a skinny build and light brown hair. Kind of nice looking, but nothing outstanding.

"Hey, Cay," he said as I walked across to join the team. "I'm glad I'm on your team, 'cause you're seriously scary when it comes to playing footy."

I flexed my bicep. "I will destroy them with my awesomeness."

He raised his eyebrows and laughed. "Hey, that was funny."

I paused and realized what I said was *way* ahead of its time. "Yeah, I'm good at making up crap."

He grabbed me in a headlock and I shoved him off. Melanie walked up beside me. Brian cleared his throat and took a step back, but I didn't move. According to the social code of conduct, I should, but I'd noticed something I never had before. She was quite pretty. She had gray-blue eyes and a hint of a dimple in her cheek.

A ball smacked me in the face and everyone laughed. I glared at Geri, who bolted.

We lined up across the field. Geri and I positioned ourselves opposite each other, right in between some of the most athletic boys in our grade. She roared at me, which brought eye rolls from the boys around us. It was our thing, and I'd missed it. I scratched the ground with my foot and snarled at her. She chuckled evilly and bent over, waiting for the boys to pick the whistle from behind the teacher's back.

My team won and we walked to the try line. Once in position, Brian did the kick-off. As soon as his foot touched the ball, Geri came screaming at me. I charged right back at her, and somewhere in the middle, we collided. We struggled and wrestled with each other, yanking off our tags before I finally wrapped my leg around hers and knocked her to the ground.

The teacher, as usual, yelled at us as I climbed on top of her and held her down. She shoved me. "Just once, can't you let me win?"

"No." I grinned.

"Cadence!" The line surged up around me and Brian gestured for me to get up. "Are you done? We need a girl who can actually play."

"Miss Anderson!"

I swung around as the teacher yelled my name, but he faced away, toward the school buildings. Harper and her friends moved through the quad, openly smoking on the school grounds. I slapped my forehead. "Geez, no wonder she always got detention."

The teacher yelled for Brian to keep the game going, then stomped over to Harper's group, forcing them to hand over all their cigarettes. Brian tapped the ball and continued the game.

"Your sister's an idiot," Geri yelled at me as we jogged down the field.

"No kidding."

"That's your sister?" Brian asked as we lined up. "I never woulda picked it."

"Yeah, she claims she's an only child."

"My brother does that too," Melanie whispered. I glanced back at her, surprised. She'd told me once that she had a brother, but that hadn't happened in this timeline yet. It happened when we'd been assigned a biology assignment together in twelfth grade. She showed up late to meet me, explaining with embarrassment that she and her parents had had to bail out her brother after his arrest.

"Charming, aren't they?" I said to her.

She drew a sharp breath, apparently startled that I'd spoken to her, and dropped her gaze. As I turned to face forward, I saw everyone staring at me. "What?"

Brian stepped over and wrapped his arm around my shoulders. "Come on, hot stuff, let's keep this game rolling."

I shoved him off again, and he laughed.

When I arrived home, Mum was yelling at Harper. I slipped by, trying to blend in with the wall as I passed them, but Harper pointed at me accusingly. "You just want me to be her! Little Miss Goody-Goody. But I'm not her!"

"I know that, Harper! You and Cadence are very different, but that's no excuse for this behavior! Smoking on school grounds? Smoking *at all*?"

"It's cool, Mum. Get over yourself."

"Getting all kinds of cancer is not *cool,* Harper!"

"Whatever. I'm out." She turned to leave.

"No, Harper, you are locked in, all night and until the end of the month."

"What?" she hissed. "The school disco is at the end of the month!"

"Then I guess you're not going. This behavior has to stop! Your grades are suffering, you don't play the piano anymore, and your art is getting darker and darker!"

She scoffed and folded her arms. I edged away, hoping they wouldn't notice me, but Harper turned on me again. "This is your fault!"

"What?"

"Yeah, if your teacher wasn't so pissed off because you and your stupid friend always act like idiots, he wouldn't have turned us in!"

That made absolutely no sense, so I stared at her, utterly gobsmacked.

"Harper, go to your room!" Mum said harshly.

Harper marched to her room, slamming the door behind her.

Mum rubbed her temples, obviously frustrated. I dropped my bag on the floor and wrapped my arms around her. She gasped with surprise, but wrapped her arms tightly around me. Then, she cried onto my shoulder.

"It's okay, Mum."

She held me tighter. I'd never noticed how much Harper's bad behavior hurt her, but then, I'd always dashed away and hid when they fought. I'd wanted to stay clear of it, knowing Harper would do exactly what she just did—blame me.

"It's okay, Mum, you'll see," I whispered. "One day, she'll be married and have kids. She'll look back and say, 'I'm sorry I was so obnoxious to you, but I'm feeling the karma now with these wild boys.'"

Mum chuckled despite her tears.

"You're a good mum. Don't let her rebellious streak make you think otherwise."

She drew back and clasped my face, gazing lovingly into my eyes. "Thank you, Cadence. When I look at you, I can believe I'm not a complete failure as a mother."

I squeezed her tightly. "Never even think it."

I let go and leaned over to grab my bag.

"Cadence?"

I lifted my bag onto my shoulder and looked at her.

"Were you planning on going to the school disco?"

I nodded. "But if you don't want me to—"

"No! I just thought you haven't bought yourself new clothes lately. It might be nice if you and I go to pick out a new outfit."

I hesitated. Before, I would have told her to just give me the money and I'd do it myself, but this time, I sensed more behind her asking me. She wanted to spend time with me, to know she still had one of her daughters.

"Yeah, Mum. That'd be great."

Her whole face lit up. "Do you want to go this Saturday?"

"After netball?"

"Yeah."

"Sounds good."

"We'll get something really nice for you."

"Thanks, Mum." I turned and walked to my room.

Saturday morning, I awoke early, ready to go. I packed a change of clothes in my netball bag and met Mum to eat breakfast with her. Mum was more than surprised, but delighted, by my eagerness.

After my game, we walked around the mall, scanning different clothing stores, but in no rush. I enjoyed spending time with her after several years of living on opposite sides of the continent.

She seemed happy too. She picked out things which were so ugly I almost gagged with disgust, but I smiled and shook my head politely instead. I didn't want to ruin her fun.

Finally, I found the perfect outfit. I struggled to find something fashionable for the time, as my fashion sense was still eleven years in the future, but I found some cute jeans and a dark blue, striped satin blouse.

As we paid, Mum rested her arm around my shoulders. "I had fun with you today."

"Me too, Mum. It feels like forever since we've done something like this."

She beamed and pointed at the rack of jewelry. "Why don't you pick out something nice to wear with this?"

"Really?"

She nodded.

I rushed over and picked a gold necklace with matching earrings.

On the way home, I said, "Thanks, Mum. You really spoiled me today."

She smiled at me warmly. "You deserve it. You've been wonderful lately. You've been helpful and cheery, you've been nice to your brother, and you've even tried to be nice to your sister. I really appreciate that."

I grinned. Things were already looking up. My relationship with my mum had improved, and my good choices were paying off. If things kept going the way they were, there was no way anything could stop me from saving Austin and Melody.

Chapter Four

As I prepared to leave for the disco, Harper unleashed her fury on me. She stole my towel while I took a shower, trashed my room, and hid my makeup; she even tried to cut up my new clothes. Mum prevented her from destroying my shirt—she was about to put a pair of scissors to it—and Dad took her into her room for a sound scolding while I hurried to dress.

After I found my makeup and was ready to go, Harper popped her head out from her room and hollered, "Yeah, Mummy and Daddy's favorite better have fun tonight! I hate you, Cadence!"

Dad drove me to school. On the way, he cleared his throat and said, "Cadence, you look very pretty tonight."

I smiled up at him. "Thanks, Dad."

"Don't let any boys touch you."

I bit back a laugh. "Okay, Dad."

He glanced at me. "I mean it. It may be against the law to buy a gun, but I'm sure I could find one somewhere."

I couldn't help giggling.

He smiled at me proudly. "You're a good girl, Cadence, and I trust you. You have fun tonight, okay?"

"I will. Thanks, Dad."

We pulled into the front parking lot of the school. As I unbuckled, I paused to look at my dad. I'd always loved him. When he shed a tear at my wedding, and said how much he loved Austin in his toast, my love for him felt like it would explode out of my chest.

I leaned across and kissed his cheek. "I love you, Dad."

He blinked, shocked, but smiled. "I love you too, sweetheart."

I climbed out of the car with a goofy grin.

I lined up and presented my ticket at the door of the school hall. They wrapped a band around my wrist and I entered, making my way through the small crowd into the center of the hall. I smiled as my friends rushed toward me. School discos may have been the cheesiest events on the school calendar, but I had loved them the first time around, and I still did the second time.

"Hey, come on, let's get this party started!" Geri beamed.

I took her hand. "Let's do it!"

We found an open space and our group filled it as we jumped and danced around together. I had an absolute blast, although the amount of male attention I received surprised me. I didn't remember guys being so interested in me before, or maybe I hadn't noticed because I was so naive.

Tyler's best friend, Mitch, came up right beside me and grabbed my hand.

"Hey, how ya doin' tonight?" he yelled into my ear.

"I'm doing great!" I grinned, pulling my hand free.

"Ya look like ya are too!" His eyes did a quick dash down and up my body. *That was weird.*

I stepped back from him, but kept smiling. "Thanks! I love dancing."

Tyler came up beside him. Mitch turned his attention away from me, knowing if he continued hitting on me it would break the best friend code of conduct. I backed away, breathing a sigh of relief.

My friends and I decided to take a break and buy drinks. We stopped at the school canteen and each bought a soda before retreating to a nearby picnic table. We gossiped about who hooked up, who showed up drunk, and who would get dumped because they cheated. A group of our guy friends showed up. We made room for them, and somehow I found myself sandwiched between Brian and Justin.

"Hey," Brian said in my ear. "If there's a slow dance, we should dance."

"Ah . . ." I stared ahead at Geri. She raised her eyebrows. "Maybe, but they don't usually play slow dances."

"Sometime tonight, you and me will have to jam out or something."

Jam out? I thought that term died in the nineties. "Sure."

I tried to engross myself in the group conversation when Justin, who sat on my right, said, "Cadence?"

I turned to him and saw an odd look in his eyes. We were in the same main class in seventh grade, and had been friends ever since. Over the last few months he'd shot up and filled out, so he stood a good head taller than me. He was probably one of the better-looking guys in the grade, with strawberry blond hair, pale blue eyes, and a splattering of freckles across his nose.

"Yeah?"

"How are you doing since the breakup?"

I shrugged. "I'm fine. It's been a few weeks so, you know, I'm over it."

He grinned and leaned closer. "Ready to move on, huh?"

The way he looked at me made things awkward. I looked across at Geri. "Hey, I love this song! Let's go dance!"

She jumped to her feet. "Let's do it!"

We ran into the school hall and made our way to the back corner. She squeezed my hand and laughed. "Wow, Miss Popularity! I must say, if the guys weren't such dorks, I'd totally be jealous."

"Shut up!" I laughed.

"Maybe, since you're apparently in heat, you could work your magic and pick us up some real guys."

"I didn't know there were any at our school!"

She burst out laughing. "You have a point. But let's just see where your raging hormones take us!"

"You're so weird."

"That's why you love me."

We shuffled up the wall and attached ourselves to the edge of the crowd. I started to dance. Geri laughed. "You should be all sexy and raunchy!"

"What?" I couldn't help laughing.

"Go on! Like this." She raised her arms up and ran them down her body as she slowly moved her hips.

I laughed. "You look ridiculous!"

"I look hot! Shut up! It's what all the celebrities are doing. When was the last time you watched a Britney video?"

I pulled a disgusted face at her. "I'm not doing that."

"Come on, Cay! Do it for me! Please, please, please?"

I sighed. "Only if you give me five bucks."

"Done!" She pulled a five-dollar bill out of her pocket. "But I'll only give it to you after you do it for thirty seconds."

"Thirty seconds?"

"You heard me."

"Fine." I faced her in an attempt to look inconspicuous. I moved my hips with as much sexiness as I could muster.

She watched me, grinning mischievously. Her gaze suddenly lifted over my shoulder and she giggled. "Cay, stop!"

Turning, I saw a guy from the grade above us pull back and smirk at me. Behind him, his friends burst out laughing.

I grabbed Geri's arm and blushed. "Let's go somewhere else."

"Hey, where you goin'?" he called after me. "We just barely got started!"

His friends roared as Geri and I hurried away.

"What was he doing?" I hissed at her as we retreated to the back corner.

She giggled as she answered, "He pretended to spank you."

"Oh my gosh!"

Her giggling intensified. "Hey, at least he was hot, right?"

"That was James Gordon, Melanie's brother!"

"Melanie, as in crazy Melanie in our science and PE classes?"

"Yeah!"

"How do you even know that?"

I paused, and hurried to cover myself. "I just heard it around."

Geri shrugged. "Well, he may be hot, but he's in that group of pervs and potheads who hang out with Robbie Cluff."

I turned to see them all sitting along the wall, watching the girls pass by. "Gross."

I remembered that. I also remembered how they'd all turned out—on drugs and throwing their lives down the toilet. The last thing I'd heard of Robbie was that he'd ended up in jail.

We hurried away to find the rest of our friends. We re-joined the main group and again I found myself overloaded with male attention. I wondered if it had happened before, and racked my brain trying to recall.

After several songs of being tugged, pulled, and yelled at, I grabbed Geri's hand again and we rushed out. We hurried toward the bathrooms and burst inside, startling a group of girls from the grade above us who then gave us filthy looks. Geri and I rushed into a cubicle each to pretend to pee. One muttered, "Let's go somewhere else," before they all skulked out, banging the door behind them.

Geri opened her door and whispered, "Cay, come out."

I slipped out, relieved to find us alone. "I hate those girls."

"Yeah, me too. They're total dogs."

"They're all gonna end up pregnant and on drugs." I snapped my mouth shut.

Geri laughed. "Most likely. That blonde one, Carla, totally sleeps with Robbie all the time."

"Yeah, that will do it," I muttered, remembering she dropped out in the eleventh grade because she fell pregnant with his kid.

"Anyway, what's up with you tonight?" Geri grinned. "I'm not kidding when I say the guys are all over you!"

"I know. It's so weird!"

"I've always said you're a hottie."

"I'm so not." My cheeks rushed with heat. "Not compared to you anyway."

"I am pretty smoking." She flipped her brown hair over her shoulder. Then, she burst into giggles. "Justin totally wants to hook up with you!"

My eyes widened. Was it really *that* cisco? Justin had been my second boyfriend before, but I hadn't realized getting together with him had been so close to breaking up with Tyler.

"Oh my gosh, Cadence! You get all the luck. Tyler, Justin, Brian . . . who will be next?"

That was weird. She just listed my first three boyfriends in order, and I hadn't even dated most of them yet! "I don't want to hook up with Justin."

"Are you crazy? He's like one of the hottest guys in the grade!"

"Then he should go date one of the popular girls."

Geri scowled. "Hmm, I hate those girls."

"Everyone does, that's why they're popular."

She burst out laughing. "I love you, Cadence! But seriously, you should date Justin."

I shook my head. "No, I don't wanna date anyone for a while—"

She slapped my shoulder. "You're still harping on about that! Who *is* this loser you're into?"

I bit my lip, not wanting to lie to her. "You don't know him. He doesn't go to this school."

"Well, give me a name then!"

I took a deep breath. She couldn't look Austin up because there was no Facebook, Twitter, or any other popular social network, so even if she did look him up online, she wouldn't find much, if anything. "His name is Austin."

"Austin?"

"Austin."

She pursed her lips and narrowed her eyes. "Okay, kid, I'll believe ya. Where did you meet him?"

"He's my mum's cousin's son's friend," I lied.

"Wow, that's a doozy."

"What?"

"Okay, if you don't wanna tell me, that's fine, but I still think you should consider Justin. Come on, we'll go sit outside for a bit to give you a break." She grasped my hand and pulled me toward the door.

"Geri?"

"Yeah?"

"You know you're my best friend, right?"

She giggled. "Of course!"

I smiled, hoping I wouldn't screw things up between us this time around.

We burst out of the bathroom. James Gordon leaned against the opposite wall of the corridor, startling us. His eyes were barely visible beneath the matted mop of hair pressed over his face by a black beanie. He looked up at us and grinned. "Hey, we never finished our little dance."

I grunted, disgusted, as Geri and I dashed away. We found a quiet corner and sat together. She rested her head against my shoulder and I stroked her hair. I had missed her for so long. I spent so many years wishing I could take back whatever I had done that having her right beside me again felt like a miracle.

A teacher announced that the last three songs were about to play. Geri's head shot up and she looked into my eyes. "Come on, let's dance."

She jumped to her feet and offered me her hand.

"You know," I said as I took it, "you still owe me five bucks."

She grinned and pulled me up. "I sure do. I was hoping you'd forget."

She shoved the note down my shirt. I plucked it out and scowled at her. She laughed and we dashed back inside.

We rejoined our group and I cautiously kept myself among the girls. Geri stayed by my side the whole time as we danced around together. I did all I could to ignore the boys. When the end finally came and the lights turned on, I breathed a sigh of relief.

Geri and I walked out to the parking lot with the other girls, all singing and laughing together. Most of our friends' parents had already arrived, so they left us right away. Geri and I sank onto the asphalt by the wall to wait.

"I had fun tonight," she said.

I looked at her. "Me too."

"The best part was you making a total idiot of yourself."

I punched her arm as we laughed.

Melanie startled us by sitting beside me. I stared at her, surprised she was even there.

"Hey, smelly Melly," Geri said teasingly. "What are you doing here?"

She turned beet red and moved to stand.

I caught her arm. "She's just teasing, Melanie. Aren't you, Geri?" I glared across at Geri.

Completely thrown off guard, Geri nodded. "Yeah, that's how I show I care."

Melanie sank back beside me. "My brother wants to know your name."

"You know my name."

She huffed. "He told me to come over here and talk to you or he'd steal all my CDs."

I scowled. "Tell him bullies don't interest me."

She shrugged. "That's a good enough answer."

She climbed to her feet and walked around the corner.

"She's so weird," Geri muttered.

"She actually didn't seem that bad."

Geri's eyes widened with horror. "That comment stays between you and me."

I had the overwhelming urge to say, *"Don't be so immature, she has feelings too,"* but I held my tongue. High school was a game; say the wrong thing at the wrong time and lose in the most humiliating and cruel kind of way.

Geri stood as her mum pulled up. "Will you be okay? We can stay until your parents show up."

I shook my head. "There's plenty of teachers around. I'll be fine."

"Okay. See ya." She waved as she climbed into the car.

I rested my head back against the wall and shut my eyes. I had to be up early in the morning, so I wished my parents would hurry up. Someone approached, then sat beside me. I opened my eyes as Justin settled into the spot Geri had vacated. I did a quick double take and remembered we'd hooked up at this disco last time.

That night had gone very differently. I'd arrived in the same way, meeting my girlfriends soon after, and we'd danced. Tyler and Mitch *had* joined us momentarily, and thinking back on it, Mitch *did* hit on me. They fought for the following two weeks and I'd never known why, but now I did. How had I never noticed that before?

Geri and I did go out to get drinks and sit, and then Justin had moved in on me. Our conversation at that table had taken a different turn. After he asked if I was ready to move on, we'd engrossed ourselves in a deep conversation. I couldn't remember what we talked about, but we soon sat alone. He ran his hand down my back, telling me that he'd liked me for a while and wanted to see where things could go. I blushed, giggled, and dashed away in search of Geri.

When I found her, I told her about Justin and she had teased me like she always did. Then she saw him enter the hall and told me to dance sexy to get his attention. So, I did. He came right over, but before he joined us, James Gordon had pretended to spank me. I didn't know who he was then, though. I was stunned I hadn't remembered that.

Justin tailed me like a lost puppy for the rest of the night, and sat with Geri and me while we waited for our parents. Then, once she was picked up, he'd . . .

I looked at Justin.

He grinned. "Did you have fun tonight?"

"Yeah," I said breathlessly. I could see he wanted to kiss me; his gaze kept falling on my lips.

"You know, you look really hot."

Ah yes, a teenage boy's attempt at flattery. They never say beautiful, which, in reality, is all a girl really wants to hear. "Thanks."

He shuffled closer and I leaned away. "You know, I've liked you for a while—"

I raised my hand. "Let me just stop you there."

He stared at me, confused.

I sighed. "Look, here's the thing. I like you, but just as a friend. If we hook up, we'll have this huge, drama-filled breakup because we're both so hotheaded, and we'll throw around terrible things about each other and cause a huge rift between our friends. I really don't wanna do that."

His eyes darkened. "You don't know that. How can you even say that?"

I gnawed on my lip. I wasn't handling the situation well. "Look at what happened with Tyler. He hates me now, and he's fighting with Mitch because of me."

"He is?" Justin sat up.

"Yeah, but it only started tonight." I glanced around uncomfortably. "Maybe it's just me. Maybe I'm not ready for a new relationship."

He raised an eyebrow. "Cadence, I don't like being messed with."

"I'm not messing with you!" I grasped his shoulder. "Please don't be angry at me. I don't want to fight with you. You're a good friend, and I enjoy hanging out with you, but I don't feel ready to turn it into a boyfriend-girlfriend relationship."

He stood, dejection showing on his face. "All right, Cadence. I get it." He rushed away.

I sighed. At least it wasn't as bad as when we'd been together. What a loud and public breakup that had been! This way, neither of us had invested anything into each other emotionally, and he could walk away with his dignity still intact.

Laughter from farther down the building drew my attention. Robbie and his cronies hung around a car. I pulled my knees up to my chin, uncomfortable with them being potentially dangerous and acting like idiots so close to me. I glanced across, nervous that if I didn't watch the car, it would back out and hit me. I scanned the group of boys and noticed James staring right back at me.

My cheeks warmed and I climbed to my feet, wishing he would just forget my moment of humiliation and leave me alone. I walked around the corner of the building so I could still see the parking lot, but he couldn't see me.

Dad pulled up not long after that. I trotted over to the car, and once I climbed in, I looked across and saw James staring again. I dropped my gaze as I buckled the seat belt.

"Did you have fun?" Dad asked.

I smiled at him, loving how simple our relationship was before I'd grown up.

"Yeah." The whole ride home I told him about my night.

Chapter Five

"Justin is pissed," Geri said quietly as we moved down the hallway toward our lab. "He was convinced you'd go out with him."

I bit my tongue, knowing that in another time, I had. "I tried to be nice about it."

"That's not what he's saying . . ." She watched several eighth graders pass us by, then she lowered her voice even further. "He's saying you said you thought you were too good for him, and you pretty much think you're the hottest thing alive."

"What?"

We slipped into the classroom. Justin's friends' stares followed me as I walked to my seat.

"Skank," one said.

Geri glared at them as we took our seats. The class began, and after a few minutes, we collected our supplies for the experiment.

"I'll go," Geri whispered. "You set up."

I nodded and hurried over to our workstation. As soon as I arrived, one of Justin's friends leaned over. "Think you're hot stuff, huh?"

I bit my lip. This hadn't happened before. How should I deal with it? I felt like I was losing my adult reasonability and my mind grew hazy.

"Can't say anything?"

Two more boys joined in and leaned over on either side of him.

"Leave me alone," I whispered.

They "*ooed*" at me, and the first one grabbed my wrist. "You're not as hot as you think. Justin could do much better than you anyway."

I tried to pull away, but he yanked me back. I yelped, making the other boys laugh.

Geri appeared at my side. "Get lost, losers!"

"Shove it, Geri."

They pushed her away from me and pulled me closer, stretching me out across the workstation.

Brian broke in. "Hey, leave her alone!"

Again they "*ooed*" and one said, "Do you think you stand a chance or something?"

"No, but you're being bullies. I doubt she was as mean as Justin says. We all know she's not like that."

"Do we?" the one holding me sneered.

Something hit him, hard, and he let go. I looked across to see Robbie Cluff and James Gordon standing by the open window. James raised his arm and threw something at the boys.

Robbie laughed. "Hit him again, Jimmy."

The boys scampered away as a book flew at them. Geri and Brian grabbed me and tugged me behind the workstation as several more classroom items soared across the room.

"Robbie! James!" Our teacher's voice bellowed across the room.

We peeked over the desk as the teacher rushed to the window. Robbie and James hurried away. Our teacher slammed the window and glanced around. "Did anyone get hurt?"

The whole class shook their heads.

"Good. I'll be back. I need to find out where those boys are supposed to be."

He slipped out of the room.

I climbed onto my stool as Geri grabbed my shoulder. "Cay, they were out of line."

Brian grabbed my forearm. "Did they hurt you?"

"No." I pulled away. "Just leave me alone."

"I got it, Bri," Geri said gently.

Brian went back to his desk. Geri climbed onto the stool beside me and lit the Bunsen. "Wow. That was dramatic."

I huffed. "It's not supposed to happen like this. I didn't date him so I could avoid all this drama. I thought by making better choices, these bad things wouldn't happen."

"Huh?" Geri gazed at me with a confused expression on her face.

"Nothing. I'm just thinking out loud."

She flicked my hair back over my shoulder. "Did you get hit?"

"No. Why?"

"'Cause you're talkin' like a crazy person."

I shoved her shoulder and chuckled.

Melanie's head popped up from behind the workstation and we jumped. She glanced between us and waved a book. "It's mine. He stole it this morning."

She dashed away.

"Man, she's so weird," Geri whispered.

I scowled, but didn't say anything. "Let's do the experiment and forget all this stuff."

A few moments later, I noticed movement by the window. I glanced up to see James motioning to Melanie. I looked over at her as she shook her head. It seemed surprising people didn't know they were siblings. They looked remarkably similar, with the same chestnut brown hair and gray-blue eyes. They could almost pull off being twins.

They also looked just as shabby and dirty as one another. I wondered if their house had the water cut off. James always wore a stupid black beanie with his long scruffy hair sticking out under it, and it seemed they shared their school uniforms.

His gaze shot to me and I glanced away. Out of the corner of my eye, I watched him stand by the window before I dared to look over again. He stared at me with a ridiculous smirk, then waved and blew me a kiss. I rolled my eyes and tried to focus on my work. After a few moments he walked away, but Melanie appeared in front of us.

Geri reacted first. "Um . . . do you need something?"

She stared at me. "My brother wants you to thank him."

I raised my eyebrows. "What for?"

"For chasing those morons off you."

Geri chuckled. "Wow, they must be morons if she says they are."

Melanie scowled, but returned her attention to me. "He's been bugging me about you, all last night and this morning. He told me I need to make friends with you."

Geri laughed loudly. "Yeah, not going to happen."

"Geri," I whispered. "Don't be mean."

Melanie snorted. "Whatever. You guys are stupid anyway."

"Hey!" Geri moved to stand as Melanie rushed away, but I caught her arm.

"Don't worry about it. It's not like her opinion matters to anyone."

"Hmm." Geri sank back onto her stool. "Let's just forget about all of it and get this done."

I tried to keep a low profile for the next few weeks. It seemed to work, too, and soon all the vicious rumors died out. I kept myself going by staring at Austin and Melody's picture every night, just thinking about them. He wasn't into sports like me, but instead preferred gaming, reading, and when his stepdad took him to Rottnest Island—just off the coast from Perth—he went diving and snorkeling in his spare time. He didn't change when we married, either. I found comfort in his consistency and stability.

The winter holidays drew near, and things seemed to quiet down for me. I loved that I had managed to remove most of the drama from my life. Ninth grade suddenly seemed fun, whereas before, it had been one drama after another.

We were wrapping up our history classes so we could change to geography the next semester. My notebook lay open in front of me, but the teacher rambled all kinds of incoherent nonsense. I was glad it really wasn't just me being lazy the first time.

Brian sat next to me and nudged me. I glanced at him, and he handed me a note under the table. I opened it and read: *I'm so bored.*

I smiled, watching the teacher as I rested it over my notebook to write: *Ditto. I have no idea what she's saying.*

He smirked and slipped the note into his pocket. He leaned closer to whisper, "Whatcha doin' for the holidays?"

I shrugged. "Not much. Eating, sleeping, watching TV late into the night."

"So, I'm thinking of going ice-skating sometime. Do you wanna join?"

I loved ice-skating. I had gone many times with large groups of my friends, and I definitely didn't want to miss out on that. "Sure. When?"

He pulled the note back out and wrote down the details. "Do you need a ride?"

"No, my mum can probably drop me off."

"Cool."

"Does Geri know yet?"

He hesitated. "No . . ."

"Do you want me to tell her or do you wanna do it?"

"You can, I guess."

I grinned excitedly. "I love ice-skating."

Harper stepped out of her room just as I did. She scowled and folded her arms. "Geez, Cadence, it's not even ten."

I looked at her in her black pajama pants and tank top. "I'm going ice-skating. I guess you have no plans today."

She scoffed. "I wish. Mum and Dad have me under house arrest until the end of the holidays."

"I'm sorry."

She rolled her eyes. "I don't need your pity, kid."

I pursed my lips, my frustration rising. "You know, I'm just trying to be nice. We won't always be this close to each other. In fact, one day, we could live clear across the country from each other. So I'm trying to make the most of my time with you, but you're so pissed off at the world that you don't even care. I'm your *sister*, Harper. I hate seeing you so sullen all the time. I just wish you would remember how much fun we used to have together and stop being so mean and shutting me out."

Her eyes narrowed. Her hand slowly reached out and touched the hair hanging over my shoulder. I held my breath, hoping just maybe I had made some ground with her, but then she gave my hair a sharp tug.

"Ouch!"

"I hate you, you stupid loser. Stop trying to be my friend to win brownie points with Mum and Dad."

I pushed her off and rushed down the hallway toward the front door. I paused when I reached the living room and looked back. She was awful! How could I live with her until she finally grew up?

Geri's mum came to pick me up. On the way, Geri and I chatted excitedly about what we'd done so far and how the holidays always seemed to go too fast.

We hurried into the rink and rented our skates. As we made our way to the sitting area, we scanned the crowd.

"Are we early?" Geri asked.

"I guess so. I can't see anyone from school."

"There's Brian and Sean." She nodded across the ice. Her eyes widened and her jaw fell. "Cadence, I think this is supposed to be a date!"

"What?" I looked across at Brian and his best friend. "No way!"

It was too early for Brian to be making moves on me. We didn't get together until the fourth term. But then again, I had been dating Justin at this point before . . .

"Hey, Cadence." Brian grinned as he slid up against the wall.

I grasped Geri's hand. "Hey, Brian. Hey, Sean."

Sean seemed edgy. He definitely didn't want to be here, but he nodded and muttered, "Hey."

My hand tightened around Geri's as we headed toward the gate. The boys left us briefly, and I whispered, "Don't leave me for one moment."

She scoffed. "I'll do my best, but I'm fairly certain Sean's here so Brian can have some alone time with you."

I clenched her hand.

"Ouch! Cadence!" She tugged her hand free.

"Sorry."

We skated onto the ice and Brian came up behind me. "Wanna race?"

His hand pressed against the small of my back. I half-turned to face him. "Not yet. I gotta get my feet first."

His hand shifted to my elbow. "Do you need some help?"

"No. Geri and I will just be a few minutes. You and Sean go do your thing."

But he didn't leave. He hung off me, asking questions and constantly touching me. Finally, I needed a break and told Geri I needed to use the bathroom. We hurried in and I breathed a sigh of relief. "This is so awkward."

Geri scowled. "Seriously, why do all the guys like you?"

Her face showed a twinge of jealousy. It frightened me. I wasn't ready to lose her again. "I don't encourage it, if that's what you mean."

She huffed. "I know. It just sucks. I wish one of them would be interested in me for once."

I tried to recall when she'd had her first boyfriend. Then it dawned on me—it wasn't until after we stopped being friends. *That* terrified me. "I'm sure there's someone who's interested in you. After all, you're way cuter than I am."

She smirked. "Yeah, but you're blonde, aren't you? Guys prefer blondes."

"Oh my gosh."

She shrugged and folded her arms. "Whatever."

I sighed. "Geri, you'll always come first for me."

Her expression softened and she met my gaze. "Yeah, you too, Cadence."

I smiled and hugged her, relief washing over me when she hugged me back. "Come on, let's get this over and done with."

"Brian's not bad, you know," she said as we released our hug. "I doubt he'd be a jerk like Tyler and Justin."

"I know. Brian's a nice guy." My breakup with Brian had been the least dramatic, but I'd crushed him. He'd left me notes apologizing for not being a good enough boyfriend, begging me to take him back. The poor boy had been so smitten that when I moved on to my next boyfriend, he'd hidden in the boys' bathroom and cried. I had no desire to do that to him again. "That's why I can't date him. I don't want to ruin him."

Geri shook her head and twisted a curl around her finger. "Wow, Cadence. This Austin guy must really be special."

I grinned like an idiot. "Yeah, he is."

We headed out to the rink. Brian and Sean waited for us with food and drinks.

"Oh, geez," Geri muttered.

I dug into my pocket. "We can't let them pay for it."

"Why not? Free food!"

"Because he'll get the wrong idea."

She grumbled and pulled out her money. We tried to hand the money to them. Sean took Geri's without even batting an eye, while Brian flat-out refused to take mine. "No, Cadence. Really, it's on me."

"No, I don't want you to pay for me when I can pay for myself."

He pushed my hand back. "I mean it. It's fine."

When he turned to walk toward the table, I shoved my cash into Geri's pocket. She smirked and chuckled. "Thanks, Cay-Cay."

We sat to eat and had a great time chatting together. But I couldn't help noticing Brian shuffling closer and closer.

Sean sneered and nodded toward the entrance. "Look who's out of the loon house."

We glanced over to see Melanie and James walk in. I spun back around before they could see me.

"Why are they coming this way?" Brian asked.

I squeezed Geri's knee. She looked me over and scowled.

"Hey, Cadence."

I jumped at James's voice in my ear. My head smacked against his and I yelped.

"Wow, that wasn't the reaction I hoped for."

"Hey, leave her alone," Brian responded. He leaned closer to me and touched my head. "Are you okay?"

"I'm fine." But I didn't want to be there any longer. I jumped up and hurried back onto the ice with Geri rushing to catch up.

"Cadence." She grasped my elbow as we glided along. "What's the deal with Melanie and James? They're like creepy stalking you or something." She gasped, then giggled. "Maybe they're part of some weird cult where they don't shower, and they need a sacrifice."

I raised my eyebrows. "Wow, that's cruel."

She giggled harder. "I know, right? But seriously, what's their deal?"

"I dunno." It was all new to me. I'd barely interacted with Melanie before, and never even looked sideways at James. I wondered what changed.

Sean and Brian glided up either side of us. Brian took my hand while Sean took Geri's.

"Hey, Cadence," Brian began. "You wanna race now?"

I didn't. I knew he wanted to separate me from Geri, but racing was my thing. Just like in every other sport I played, I turned crazy when someone dangled competition in front of me. I couldn't refuse a challenge. "You know I'm gonna kick your trash, right?"

He laughed, surprised. "My trash, huh?"

Again with the terms a few years in advance. I grinned and covered. "Yeah! You'll be so humiliated because a girl kicked your butt that you'll jump in a dumpster to escape from the torment."

He burst out laughing. "The things you come up with." He tugged at my hand. "Come on, let me show you what real speed is."

I glanced at Geri and, seeing her roll her eyes, I grinned and let her go. Brian took me up to the far end of the rink, and we waited for a break in the small crowd going around and around.

"First one to that line on the hockey rink?" he asked.

I shook my head. "First one to the wall."

"Ah, no. You'll just crash right into it and hurt yourself."

I laughed. "Yeah, but I'll be the winner, won't I?"

He turned to face me. "So you'd rather win than avoid being in a wheelchair for several weeks?"

I leaned back as he advanced on me. "Always."

I hit the wall and he grabbed my waist.

"What if I don't let you?"

I didn't like the way he looked at me. I'd seen it before; he had every intention of kissing me. I pressed my hand against his chest to discourage him. "Ah, Brian, there's a break in the crowd. We should go now."

He ran his fingers through my ponytail. "It can wait."

I leaned back as he bent down closer to me. "Brian . . ."

Wham! He fell on the ground. A yelp tore from my lips as I grabbed onto the railing to stop myself from falling on top of him. A hand grabbed my arm to stabilize me. I looked up to see James. He glared down at Brian and snarled, "Hey, loser, she didn't want you to kiss her! What are you, stupid or something?"

He bent over and grabbed Brian by the shirt. Brian tried to escape, but James was much stronger. "I'm gonna kick your scrawny—"

"Stop it!" I yelled.

James looked at me. "What?"

"I said stop it! You're such a bully."

"He was practically forcing himself on you!"

"Like *you* actually care." I pulled his hand off Brian. "Come on, Brian. Let's get back to the others."

We turned away from James, but he followed. "You're not even going to thank me for stopping him?"

"Just leave me alone."

"You're such a dog!"

"Coming from the likes of *you!*"

"Hey, you don't even know me."

I swiveled to face him. "No, but I know enough about you to know I don't want anything to do with you."

"Oh yeah?"

"Yeah."

"What do you know then, princess?"

"I know you hang out with that Robbie Cluff and act like total jackasses. I know you do pot, and drink, and have sex with Carla and her cronies."

"Oh, you think that, do you?"

"Oh, I *know* that!"

"You are so wrong . . ."

"I know you scrape by in your classes barely enough to pass and move up each year, which is shocking considering you're never actually *in* class."

"Whatever." He scowled and skated away.

Brian grabbed my hand. "Hey, are you okay?"

I pulled my hand away. "You did try to force yourself on me. He was right about that."

His jaw fell. "Cadence, I didn't mean to—"

"Brian, this isn't going to work." I skated away.

I found Geri and dragged her out as fast as I could. We hurried to pull off our skates. On our way to return them, James intercepted us. "Cadence, you're going to talk to me."

"Are you insane?" Geri hissed as we shoved past.

"I don't have sex with those girls!" he yelled.

The people around us stared. Geri and I lifted our skates to cover our faces.

"I'm serious, Cadence! That's Robbie's thing," he continued to yell after us.

I turned on him. "Would you shut up?"

"No. Not until you hear me out."

I smirked as I dumped my skates on the counter. "Then you'll be yelling for the rest of your life."

Geri and I hurried out.

"When's your dad coming to get us?" she asked.

"Not for another half hour."

"See? *This* is why we need phones."

I chuckled, knowing that in about five years, every kid our age would have a phone. We sat against the side of the building to wait. She shuffled and pulled my money out of the pocket of her jeans. "Here, I don't need it. You've had a rough day. I guess it's not that great having guys into you."

I smiled and pushed her hand back. "No, really, keep it. I don't wanna feel like I owe Brian any favors."

"I saw what he did," she said softly. "I tried to get over to you, but Sean kept me back. You were lucky James came along when he did. I can't believe he would do that."

"Who? Brian or James?"

She paused and tapped her chin thoughtfully. "Both, actually."

"Cadence!" James burst out and fell to his knees in front of me. I pulled back in shock as he scrambled closer. "Just thank me."

"You're crazy!" I answered in a high voice.

"Fine, then let me kiss you."

"How is *that* any more likely than me thanking you?" His breath smelled rank, like he'd just smoked a box of cigarettes.

"I keep saving you, and you never thank me!"

"Get away from me!"

"But you're so beautiful."

My heart skipped and I paused. Not hot? Not cute? I looked into his eyes. "What?"

"You're the most beautiful girl I've ever seen."

I held his gaze, completely stunned.

Geri smacked him across the face. "Get lost and leave my friend alone!"

My daze broke and I snapped back to reality. "Coming from a guy who's probably high on something, that's not very flattering."

His eyebrows lowered in frustration. "I'm not high—"

"Hey!" We all jumped at my dad's booming voice. He leapt out of the car, his gaze fixed on James. "You stay away from my daughter!"

James backed away as Dad towered over him.

"Cadence, Geri, get in the car."

Geri and I scurried to the car as Dad stepped back to it, his fierce stare never leaving James.

"Did that boy try anything on you?" he snarled in the car.

"No, Dad," I answered.

"What did he want?"

I hesitated to answer. No matter which angle I approached it, he would get angrier. But Dad took my hesitance the wrong way.

"If I see him near you again . . ." His hands clenched the steering wheel. "He looks like he's on drugs or something. Cadence, you are not to hang out with people who use drugs!"

"Dad," I groaned.

"We weren't hanging out with him, Mr. Anderson," Geri said. "He was trying to make Cadence thank him for stopping another guy from kissing her."

I backhanded Geri.

"What!" Dad pulled the car over and turned to look at me. "Cadence Michelle Anderson—"

"He didn't kiss me!"

"I should turn this car around right now and—"

"Dad!"

"Cadence, you're not allowed to kiss a boy until you've graduated!"

"Oh my gosh!"

"Don't give me that! I won't have you turning into some drugged up, pregnant—"

"*Dad!*"

He clenched his jaw. He studied me, taking in every inch of my face. Slowly, his expression softened. "Cadence, I only want what's best for you. I don't want some boy to come along and ruin everything."

"I know."

He took a deep breath and rubbed his eyes. "Let's get you home."

He shifted the car into gear and we drove away. I glanced at Geri, who gave me an awkward look. She didn't have a father in her life, so she didn't know how to deal with my dad's protective streak. She always felt uncomfortable when he went on his rants, and she never quite knew what to say or do around him. I squeezed her hand and smiled.

She smiled back and mouthed, "Sorry."

I shrugged and leaned against her shoulder.

Chapter Six

Several weeks into the third term, the weather remained freezing. Even the layers of my school blouse, cardigan, and sweater, with my black scarf and beanie, and thick, navy tights under my skirt didn't seem to keep the cold away.

My teeth chattered as Geri and I huddled together under the small patch of sun peeking over the building. "I thought August was supposed to start warming up," she said with a stutter.

"Me too."

Brian walked over and wrapped his arms around us. I smiled gratefully up at him. After the ice-skating incident, he'd met up with me at school and apologized. We agreed to still be friends—just friends—and he didn't seem upset about it. At least one of the guys I dated the last time accepted my rejection and continued to be my friend. I had always liked Brian the most, so I was pleased I hadn't driven him away like I had originally.

He shuddered. "It's so cold!"

The bell rang, so we reluctantly let go and ran to our classes to try and warm ourselves. My classroom was colder than the air outside. I danced around on the spot beside Michael as he laughed at me.

"You're such a girl."

"Thanks, Captain Obvious."

The roll was called and the twelfth grader stood to make the announcements. "This term's disco will be on the eleventh of September."

I tensed. September 11, 2001? I glanced at Michael, feeling sick.

"Wow, that's late this term," he said.

I looked away and stared ahead at the announcer. September eleventh . . .

"Cadence? What's wrong?"

I turned to Michael in a daze. "September eleventh! It's the day before here, but still . . ."

"What are you talking about?"

"I should warn someone. Maybe I could . . ."

Everything froze around me. I gazed at Michael's face in surprise as he stared up at me, completely confused. I glanced around the room and saw a ball hanging in the air, a seventh grader leaning back precariously on two legs of his chair.

"Cadence."

I turned and saw the man with the silver hair and beard standing by the door. He wore white jeans and a white dress shirt instead of scrubs. "Cadence, follow me."

I trotted after him as we walked down the corridor.

"Do you remember the terms of your contract?"

I nodded. "It's getting a little hazy, though, to be completely honest."

"That's not surprising. Your mind will start confusing events, and you'll forget things here and there. You will soon be just like a teenager again, except it will feel strange because you will remember events from a previous life. But don't be afraid. You'll retain enough to know what you're doing and how to make better choices."

"I already feel like some of my other life was just a dream."

He smiled. "Yes, the more you change here, the less real that timeline will become."

I froze and caught my breath. "I don't want to forget Austin and Melody. I don't want them to be less real."

He turned to face me and covered my eyes. "They will always be vibrant and real to you because you hold them alive in your heart."

As he pulled his hand away, I found myself in a white room, with a window overlooking New York City and the Twin Towers. I gasped and stumbled back. "Why did you bring me here?"

"Why?" He gestured up at the towers. "In a few weeks, these buildings will fall, and there is nothing you can do about it." He plucked my contract out of the air and pointed to it. "You agreed that you wouldn't alter *fixed points in time*, which means you can't warn anyone about this."

I let out a desperate gasp. "Why? Even if I could just save a few people—"

"No, Cadence. This must happen. You know what happens afterward. This event changes the course of history."

I rubbed my eyes as tears burned in them. "But why? If you're an angel, why don't you stop them?"

He nodded thoughtfully as he stepped in front of me. "Mankind was given the right to choose by God himself. I have no right to take that away from any of them. When people make bad choices, they have to live with the consequences of their actions, not only in this life, but in the next as well. But, out of this horror, brave hearts will be ignited and selfless acts will inspire mankind."

"Wait." I shook my head. "By giving me a redo, aren't you interfering with that?"

He smiled again. "Not entirely. This was planned for your life. Without the understanding you would build, you couldn't do all that you need to do now."

I bit my lip and stared up at him. But I didn't want to press for more information and confuse myself further. I had this chance, and I didn't want to screw it up or lose it by asking too many questions.

He gestured toward a door behind me. I stepped over and pushed through. On the other side, I was shocked to find my classroom.

He stepped through behind me and shut the door. "Now, Cadence, you cannot tell anyone what is to come, or all of your hard work so far will be erased. I cannot stress enough that fixed points, no matter how horrible they may be, cannot be altered. Period. You must remember this, because if you try, you will return to the future you left behind and lose this chance to change your life."

I gazed around the room at all the faces I knew so well. In a few weeks, the room would be filled with dread, fear, and uncertainty. I looked up at the man. "I know that we might be clear across the world from it, but we felt it here. It was everywhere for weeks. You couldn't escape it or think of anything else. I remember feeling like the world was coming to an end. I don't want to have to feel that fear, that horror and devastation again. I don't think I could bear it."

He stared deeply into my eyes and slowly nodded. "That can be done. You are not meant to feel that grief again. When the time comes, the weeks following will skip over for you. The events around you will be changed to fit this new timeline, but everything you felt and every reaction you had will be the same in this timeline as the other. No one will know the difference, not even you."

I scanned the room, knowing each of the people had no idea what they soon faced, and selfishly felt relieved I didn't have to live through it again. "Thank you. So, when will the time skip? How will I know?"

He smiled warmly. "You will know . . ."

He faded before my eyes as the room awakened around me.

"Cadence?"

I jumped and saw Michael gazing up at me. He tilted his head, his eyebrows furrowed.

"What?" I asked breathlessly.

"What's so bad about the eleventh of September?"

I stared at him as I struggled to return to reality. "I have a geography assignment due that day. You know how much I hate geography."

He laughed, noticeably relieved. "Cadence, Cadence, Cadence. You had me concerned for a moment. You looked like the world was ending."

I sank into my chair and forced a smile. "Well, in my mind, it kinda comes close."

That evening, I pulled my scrapbook out to look at Austin again. I found photos of him at approximately that moment, and flicked through some of him at a school camp where he'd obviously had an absolute blast. I ran my finger over his dark hair and wished I could touch him again, could feel his warm body wrapped around me.

He seemed to be growing by that point too. He looked a little trimmer and an inch or so taller. I flicked over to my journal entries and found the picture of him holding Melody. My memories seemed to flood over me, things I had begun to forget.

I remembered that day at the park as she ran from him, squealing with delight. He laughed the whole time as she tried to hide, but she couldn't stop giggling. When he caught her, he tossed her into the air, and turned to me.

"Mummy, come here!" he called.

I trotted over and raised my camera phone. "Say cheese."

"Cheese!" they both said as I took the shot.

Once I lowered the camera, Austin tickled her. She laughed so hard I thought she might burst. He set her down, and she bolted across the play area. He wrapped his arm around my shoulders and sighed. "Life doesn't get much better than this."

I kissed his cheek. "It doesn't, does it?"

He grinned and kissed me softly on the lips. "Cadence, I love you so much, did you know that?"

I giggled. "You're such a sap."

He raised his eyebrows, feigning offense. "Sap?" His grip around me tightened and he tickled me. "Take it back!"

"No!" I forced out between laughter.

"Take it back!"

"No!"

I nearly collapsed, laughing so hard. Melody rushed over, thinking I was distressed, and wailed, "Mummy!"

Austin released me and plucked her up in his arms. "Mummy's fine. Do you wanna go down the slide?"

Someone knocked on my door. I jumped and snapped the scrapbook shut as Mum walked in. I stared at her in horror as she walked over and sat on the bed in front of me. "What are you reading?"

"What?"

She gestured at my lap, where the scrapbook rested in my crossed legs. "Is that a book for English?"

I looked down. The scrapbook had changed into a novel.

"Ah . . ." I lifted it up and looked at the cover. I recalled borrowing the title from the school library in my first timeline, but I'd neglected to borrow it this time. "No, this is something I picked out."

She patted my leg. "I'm glad to see you're still interested in reading, but it's time for dinner."

"Oh, okay." I set the book aside. Glancing back at it as I stepped out the door, I saw it had returned to being the scrapbook.

I sat in geography, so bored and so cold that my focus had vanished at least twenty minutes earlier. Shifting on the plastic chair, I tried to warm my hands under my thighs. I was glad I'd decided to wear tights, and had brought my coat to wear over my cardigan. I pulled my scarf tighter around me as Geri pressed up against my shoulder.

"Cadence," the teacher said, snapping me out of my daydream. "Can you open that window behind you?"

I jumped to my feet and pulled my chair over so I could reach the window latch. The weather outside was warmer than the classroom. Sometimes being at a public school really sucked, because it lacked heating in half the classrooms. But knowing warmer air would flow in, I was happy to fulfill my teacher's request.

As I stretched up, Robbie and his gaggle of morons walked across the quad outside. I tried to ignore them as I jiggled and yanked at the window before it finally jolted open.

The noise from me struggling with the window attracted their attention. Robbie yelled out, "Hey, isn't that the uptight little princess?"

I didn't react and climbed off my chair. As I straightened, one said, "Her name's Cadence, right?"

"Isn't that a musical term?" Robbie sneered. *Well, at least his brains aren't totally fried.*

"Cadence!"

Out of reflex, I looked up. James moved toward the window with a smirk on his face. "Hey, hot stuff. Why don't you come out here and join us? I'll let you suck on my—"

"James Gordon!" the teacher bellowed over my shoulder. "And of course, Robbie Cluff. Where are you boys supposed to be?"

"In Cadence's pants, miss," James sneered.

I stepped away from the window in disgust.

"You get to your classes right now and stop harassing my students!" she snarled at them.

They scoffed and swore at her before they moved away. I shuffled in beside Geri and covered my face as the whole class stared at me. The teacher turned and called on one of the students. "I'll be just one moment. Keep things under control."

She dashed out of the room, most likely to go find the head teacher or a vice principal.

Once she had gone, something small hit me in the back of the head. I grabbed my head and turned to see James climbing in the window.

"What the . . ." I leapt up and scrambled across the classroom as my classmates jumped to their feet.

He rushed after me and yelled at some of the guys, "Grab her for me, would ya?"

One of them snatched up my wrist and held me, while Geri ran across and caught my elbow. "Let her go!"

James grabbed me by the shoulders and pushed me up against the wall. "Cadence Anderson."

"Get off me!"

"You're even more beautiful up close."

I glared up at him, then glanced around to see the whole class watching. "You're making a scene."

"I don't care. I just wanna get your attention."

I shoved him in the chest and glared up at him. "Well, you have it, so what do you want?"

"I want you to date me."

I laughed. "You're insane."

"Come on, I've been watching you for weeks. You're a total prude, but you're hot."

I slapped him across the face. "Get away from me!"

As his gaze fell back on my face, a hint of pain reflected in his eyes. "So, you're rejecting me?"

"Um, yeah."

"Yeah, you wanna date me, or yeah, you're rejecting me?"

The teacher reentered the room with the vice principal behind her. "James Gordon! Get off Miss Anderson this instant!"

"Not until she answers me." He stared fixedly at my face.

The vice principal walked up beside James. "Mr. Gordon. My office, right now."

"I'm waiting, Cadence."

I met his gaze. "No. You're a bully and a pothead. I wouldn't touch you with a six-foot pole."

He pursed his lips and straightened, releasing me. "Is that what you think?"

"That's exactly what I think."

He glanced at the vice principal. "Well, Cadence, you're wrong, and I'm going to prove it to you."

"Go ahead."

His eyes narrowed on me as he walked out of the room with the vice principal. The teacher came over to me and spoke gently. "Are you okay, Cadence?"

"Yeah."

"Did you want to go to the nurse's office for a few minutes? You look a little pale."

I nodded, glad for an excuse to escape the stares fixed on me. Geri rushed up beside me and the two of us stepped into the corridor. We headed for the bathroom rather than the nurse, knowing we could huddle by the hand dryer to warm up.

We rushed in, checked we were alone, and then Geri pressed the button. We leaned against it as she spoke. "That was nuts."

"No kidding."

"What's up with him anyway?"

"I dunno. He probably just wants to see me naked."

She giggled. "I've never seen anyone do anything like that. Not at this school anyway. You know that's going to be all over the school by the end of lunchtime."

I huffed. "I think I might hide away for a few days."

"If only he wasn't such a jerk." She smirked. "But he's so hot! He has that bad boy look down. He's got that shaggy hair under his beanie, he wears that chain on his baggy pants—"

"Yeah, he looks like a total bum."

She laughed. "True. But he's still hot."

His face flashed before my eyes as his gray-blue eyes gazed down at me. Those eyes dazzled me. I couldn't deny that he had the potential to be hot, but his teeth were yellowing, his breath stunk, and he looked like he hadn't shaved or washed his hair in a month.

"Yeah, he could be hot, but he's not."

"Yeah." She sighed and pressed the button again as the air turned off. "The hot ones are always gay or destroyed by drugs."

I giggled. "Ain't that the truth!"

"But James Gordon?" She shook her head. "I never saw that coming."

"Me either."

A loud bang echoed around us as the last cubicle door burst open. We both gasped as Melanie stepped out, her glare boring into us. She watched us as we stood stiff while she washed her hands, then stepped over to us. "Move."

We stepped aside and she pressed the button to use the hand dryer. She glared at me as she dried her hands, and when she finished, she rested her hands on her hips.

"He looks like a bum, huh?"

I winced.

"Mmm." She turned to Geri. "My brother can definitely do better than one of you."

We stood frozen as she marched out.

"Oh my gosh," Geri said breathlessly.

I stared at the door Melanie just walked through. "I don't remember her ever being this testy."

"Yeah, well, suddenly her brother is interested in you, and she's so weird she probably has a Tasmanian-style crush on him."

"Oh gross, Geraldine!" I couldn't help laughing.

"At least she'll most likely tell him we were gossiping about him in a not-so-nice way and he'll get the hint."

"I hope so." I sighed and pressed the button again. "I don't want to go back to class."

She looked at her watch. "We'll give it another five, eh?"

I chuckled. "Deal."

Chapter Seven

The school disco came around again and, unfortunately, this time Harper could go. She insisted on driving, which I hated. She had to be one of the worst drivers ever. I had several near-death experiences as she mounted the curb and stalled mid-intersection.

"We're going to die!" I yelled as a truck rolled slowly toward us. It stopped, but that didn't matter—I just saw huge, bright headlights heading right for me.

"Shut up, Cadence!" Harper screeched.

"Stop it, girls," Dad said. "Harper, just lower the clutch and start the engine again."

Harper finally started the engine and bunny-hopped us out of the intersection.

When we arrived at school, I leapt out of the car and rushed inside, while Dad and Harper filled in her logbook.

"Be safe, Cadence," Dad called out.

I waved, having no desire to be around when Harper finally climbed out of the car.

Geri waited outside the hall and bounded over when she saw me. "Ready?"

I scanned the crowd waiting to go in, wondering when time would jump for me. "Yup."

We entered and, like the last time, our friends met us. We danced together for about half an hour before Geri and I decided to get drinks. After we ordered, someone stepped up beside me and placed two dollars down. "I got it."

I glanced up and couldn't help gaping. James looked down at me and smiled. "What?"

"Oh my gosh!" Geri gasped.

James had washed his hair, combed it back into a ponytail, and shaved.

"Do you like it?" He rubbed his chin.

I gave back his two dollars and paid for my drink before rushing away. I *did* like it, which I *didn't* like.

"Oh my gosh," Geri whispered. "He totally cleaned up for you!"

"Shut up," I muttered.

"He's *so* into you!"

"*Shut up.*"

She giggled. "Cadence, this is nuts! You should see where it could go."

I turned to her. "No, Geri. I like—"

"Yeah, yeah, that Austin guy. Whatever. *He's* not here, but James is, and James is *hot*!"

I scowled. "I have no desire to go out with James."

"Wow, you sound like a fifty-year-old." She glanced around and leaned closer. "He's watching you."

She nodded behind me. I turned. James leaned against the wall of the school's hall with his hands in his pockets, surrounded by Robbie and their friends. His friends acted like their normal drunk selves, with Carla's group mixed in among them.

James saw me looking and straightened, pulling his hands out of his pockets. I swung back around, grabbed Geri's hand, and dashed into the hall.

Michael met us as we hurried back in. "Did you hand that geography assignment in today?"

"Geography assignment?" Geri turned to me, confused.

I hurried to cover. "Yeah, I got the date wrong."

"Ah, so that's why the world hasn't ended yet."

I forced a smile as a pit formed in my stomach. "Yeah."

"Well, do you girls wanna dance with us?"

"Sure."

We joined him and four of his friends to dance. Three songs later, Robbie and his group pushed in nearby. Geri clenched my arm and met my gaze. We shuffled around so the boys stood between us and them and continued dancing. But when the next song started, an arm wrapped around my waist and pulled me away.

I gasped, frightened, but a hand clamped my mouth shut.

"Do you think you're too good for Jimmy?" Robbie's voice hissed in my ear. "Well, my frigid little princess, you're not, so get over yourself."

I leaned away as I got a waft of alcohol breath. "Let go of me."

He chuckled. "I can see why he likes you. You've got a bit of fire in you."

Michael pushed through. "Hey, let her go."

Robbie tossed me aside and grabbed him by the shirt. "Or what?"

"Or I'll fight you."

"Michael!" I gasped.

Robbie scoffed and raised his fist. James appeared, shoving between them and catching Robbie's wrist. He leaned in closer and spoke into his ear. He wasn't as heavyset as Robbie, but he stood taller, his nose level with Robbie's eyes. While James nudged Robbie backward, still talking, Michael grabbed my wrist and pulled me back to the group.

"Thanks, Michael," I said.

"Anytime, Cay. What did he want anyway?"

"He was just harassing me. You know how he is."

Michael glanced over and encouraged me toward the center of the group. "Stay with Geri, okay?"

"Okay."

Much later, near the end of the night, Geri and I rushed to the bathrooms. We chatted and giggled as we came out, and found ourselves face-to-face with Carla and her group of five girls.

Our giggling stopped instantly as they glared at us.

"Cay . . ." Geri grabbed my arm.

"Cadence Anderson." Carla scowled. "I thought you'd at least be cute, but look at you—no fashion sense and no clue. You're not even showing any skin."

She reached for my shirt. I pushed back her hand and tried to dart away, but the girls stepped in front of us.

"Where are you going, Cadence?" Carla asked.

"Please leave me alone."

She laughed. "*Please*? Since you asked so nicely . . ." They closed in around us.

"Hey! Get away from her!"

They turned, and Harper and her friends closed in. "Only I'm allowed to bully that brat."

Carla and her friends backed down from the older girls and hurried away. Harper walked over to me and rested her hand on her hip. "What are you doing?"

"I was just using the bathroom—"

"Blah, blah, stop giving me excuses. Those girls don't give a crap about anyone but themselves, so why were they so interested in you?"

My cheeks burned. "James Gordon likes me."

She leaned back, stunned, then burst out laughing. "James Gordon? Oh, Cadence, how did you manage that? He's a pothead, and you're, well, you're you."

My face felt so hot even my ears burned. "I dunno."

She patted my cheek. "Oh man, if Dad found out, he'd lock you up and ship you off to a convent." She laughed again and shook her head. "I'm gonna leave this one to you because it's just too funny."

She turned to walk away, but paused and looked at me. "If those girls try anything on you again, just let me know, okay?"

I nodded, shocked. She tapped my cheek again, then she and her friends moved off.

"Whoa!" Geri breathed. "Was she just *nice* to you?"

I nodded, speechless.

"That's so weird!"

"Yeah."

We headed back into the hall and stood at the edge of the crowd, scanning for our friends.

"They're right in the middle!" Geri hollered over the noise.

We pushed through the crowd toward them, but someone grabbed my hand and pulled me off course. I found myself in James's arms as he smiled down at me.

"Hi, beautiful."

I swallowed, dazzled by how good he looked. Up close, I saw he'd brushed his teeth, and he even smelled like men's cologne rather than the normal cigarettes. I couldn't help breathing in his scent as my eyes took in the rest.

He grinned. "Dance with me, just for one dance."

I nodded and he wrapped his arms tighter around my waist. I couldn't pull away. I couldn't even *look* away. Our eyes locked and he smiled.

"So, Cadence, your name's a little ironic. The only thing that comes close to musical about you is your hollering on the sports field."

I grinned. "I know. It's a family thing, musical names."

He leaned a little closer. "It suits you, though."

I held my breath and, without realizing, my gaze darted to his lips. He gave me a crooked smile and shifted closer. His nose brushed against mine and he paused, our lips not quite touching.

"Don't you dare kiss me," I said.

"Why not?"

"Because . . ." But his breath on my lips when he spoke pulled me in. I pressed my lips against his.

His right arm tightened around me as his left hand came up and caressed my face. My whole body tingled with excitement as I clung to him, our kiss intensifying. But when his tongue slipped into my mouth, I pulled away. "Crap!"

He pulled me back against him and planted his lips firmly against mine again. I melted into his arms as he clasped the back of my head.

Flashes of Austin and Melody burst into my mind and I pushed him off. "I told you not to kiss me!"

"You kissed me first."

"I . . . you . . ." I huffed and marched away from him, riddled with guilt. I didn't know how to feel. Was I cheating on Austin? Technically, no—I was only fourteen years old! But all the memories, our wedding vows, remained. I hated myself for enjoying how it felt to kiss James, and I hated that I wanted to do it again

Geri burst through the crowd, noticeably relieved to see me. "What happened to you?"

"I, ah . . ." I glanced back. James smiled and nodded to me. I swung around and leaned toward her ear. "James just kissed me."

"What?" she screeched excitedly.

"Shh!"

"Does that mean you and him . . . ?" She winked.

"No!"

Her face fell. "Cadence!"

"It was an accident. I'm not going to do it again. He's still him—a total jerk."

She rolled her eyes. "Whatever. You're totally getting into him." She squeezed my hand. "But, since you seem to be in denial about it, let's just have some fun for now."

We returned to dancing. About two songs before the end, James approached me again. My friends stepped back with wide, wary eyes as he wrapped his arms around my waist from behind and pulled me against him. "Are we dating yet?"

I pushed him off. "No."

"Do I need to be nice to your friends?"

"Go away!"

"Okay." He ran his hand through my loose hair.

I shuddered, but turned to face him. A crooked smile spread across his face. He had confidence, I'd give him that.

On the ride home, I was surprised, and relieved, when Harper didn't mention anything about James to Dad.

When we arrived home, we both trudged to our rooms, shutting our doors behind us. I hurried to change and before I turned out the light, I glanced at the clock.

Just after eleven.

I paused, frightened. I'd forgotten the significance of that night, and any minute I would jump in time.

Just as I thought it, the room fell black.

My eyelids felt heavy, but I forced them open. The past three weeks felt like a bizarre blur of events. I knew I hadn't experienced them, but yet, somehow I had. The memories from each timeline blurred, becoming one.

I rubbed my head, trying to regain my orientation. I knew we were in the second week of the spring holidays, but I couldn't recall much of what happened . . . yet somehow I could.

I swung my legs out of bed and made my way into the kitchen for breakfast. Dad had already gone, and Dusty sat playing a Mario video game. I stared at him and had flashes of memories as things settled down over the past week. I shut my eyes and rubbed them again, hoping the confusion would pass quickly.

"Hey, Cadence, wanna play me?"

I opened my eyes to see Dusty staring at me. "Sure, just let me get something to eat first."

I grabbed a bowl of cereal and sat cross-legged on the carpet next to him. He handed me a controller and changed the game to multi-player. He shuffled closer to me and leaned against my shoulder.

He would turn thirteen in January, but in so many ways he was still just a boy. I ruffled his dirty blond hair and his dark blue eyes turned up to me.

"Cadence?"

"Yeah?"

"You're pretty much the coolest sister ever. All my friends' sisters never do stuff like this. They're more like Harper."

"What did you say about me, loser?" Harper kicked him in the ribs as she flopped onto the sectional behind us and huffed. "You guys are so lame."

Memories flashed before my eyes. She turned seventeen on the fourteenth, and she'd continually called it "the suckiest birthday ever," which I found understandable. Only since school had gone out had she emerged from her bubble to interact with us in a *friendlier* way again.

"Hey, Cadence!" She snapped her fingers in my face. "What's up with you?"

I blinked and shook my head. "Ah . . . I have a bit of a headache."

"Take some drugs, you idiot, and stop staring at me."

I faced the screen to play with Dusty.

Several minutes later, Mum walked in and sat to fold laundry. Harper pulled her knees under her chin and said, "So what's the deal with you and that Gordon kid? Rumor has it you two made out."

I swung to her in alarm. "We did not!"

I glanced at Mum, who raised her eyebrows. "Cadence?"

"It's just a rumor, Mum."

"Well, no, actually." Harper grinned at me. "I saw you two at it at the disco. Carla and her cronies have been whining about how you stole one of their guys."

My cheeks burned. "I didn't! We're not going out."

"But he wants to, right? He's just been biding his time, making his way through all your friends and getting to know them—"

"Shut up!"

She chuckled. "You know I'm right." She glanced at Mum. "You know he just wants to have sex with you."

"Gross," Dusty muttered without looking away from the screen.

Mum cleared her throat to catch our attention. "Harper, I think that's enough."

Harper scowled and sat back. She folded her arms and pouted.

"Cadence?"

I looked back at Mum.

"You know I'm not going to lose it like your dad, so I wish you'd tell me things like this."

I hung my head. "I know, but it's nothing. He just kinda stole the kiss and—"

Harper scoffed. "No, he didn't! He put the moves on you and you kissed him!"

"Enough, Harper," Mum said sternly, then turned her attention back to me. "Cadence, it doesn't matter who kissed who, I just want you to know you can come and talk to me about these things. I will understand and not get angry at you. I want you to be safe and happy, okay?"

"But Dad will—"

"Leave your father to me. You're almost fifteen now, so he needs to accept that boys will be showing an interest in you."

"Although, I don't know why." Harper kicked me.

I scowled at her.

The phone rang and Mum went to answer it. Harper leaned forward. "Dad's gonna lose it."

I slapped her leg, but she just smirked.

"Cadence! Geri's on the phone for you," Mum said.

Relieved, I rushed to answer.

That night, Dad called me into his room to talk. I knew exactly what he would say before he even looked at me. Mum stood by the window to make sure he didn't lose it. He patted the bed beside him, and I tentatively sat. I tried to remember when we'd had this conversation before, but the memories were hazy. It might have been with my boyfriend in eleventh grade. Why was it so much sooner?

"Cadence, you know how I feel about you with boys," he said.

I slumped, my head falling. "I do."

"I just worry about you. You're a sweet, pretty girl who boys will try to take advantage of. You need to be smarter than them and see through to their true intentions. I know that I lose my temper whenever a boy is associated with you in any way, so I want you to know that you can go to your mother for help if a boy tries anything you know you shouldn't be doing. She can tell me, and we can deal with it together.

"You're a special girl, Cadence, and I love you very much. I'm only hard on you because I don't think there's a single boy out there who deserves you, and to find that some scumbag . . ."

He clenched the quilt on the bed. My gaze fixed on his hand as I held my breath, knowing how easily he could snap. "I can't stop you from making your own decisions, I just have to trust you and know that you're smart and capable of making good decisions. Just please, don't be afraid to come to us. We love you so much."

His hand released the blanket. I flinched as he raised it toward me. He wrapped it around my head and pulled me into his chest. I relaxed into his embrace, breathing in his familiar scent and loving him more than ever.

I wrapped my arms around Dad, wishing he'd never let me go, that I could tell him what would come in my life and that he didn't need to worry. I wanted to tell him about how wonderful Austin would be, and how much he would love him. But I couldn't, so I nuzzled into his chest and sighed, hoping he understood that I loved him too.

Chapter Eight

The weather finally turned warm, and the last term of school had begun. Ninth grade was almost over . . . again. I climbed off the bus and plodded up toward the area where my group of friends hung out, pleased with how things had gone this time around. I'd still encountered dramas, but nowhere near as bad; far less people had turned on me and ended up hating me for badly handling breakups and such.

Geri waved from her vantage point standing atop the picnic table. She leapt down, sprinting right for me. The whole group watched as she wrapped her arms tightly around my neck.

"Oh my gosh, Cadence! Come with me."

"Why?"

She tugged my arm. "Trust me."

"Can I at least put my bag down?"

"Sure, but hurry up!"

I dumped my bag on the table and glanced at everyone watching me. "What?"

The girls grinned and giggled and the boys turned away, pretending to be engrossed in conversations with each other. My eyes narrowed on them suspiciously.

Geri grabbed my wrist and gave me a sharp tug as we headed to the lower quad area. She darted around, glancing behind the gym and scanning the field.

"What are you looking for?" I asked.

"You'll know when you see it." She turned toward the art building and gasped. "Right there!"

I turned and saw Robbie and his friends huddled together with several groups of girls hovering nearby. "What am I looking at?"

"Oh my gosh, Cadence. Open your eyes!"

Robbie pushed off from the wall to grab one of the guys, and I saw it. I saw *him*. He was probably the hottest, sexiest guy I'd ever seen. He stood leaning against the wall, one leg bent up and his hands in his pockets. He wore the gray boys' trousers, perfectly fitted, with the pale blue dress shirt bearing the school emblem . . . also perfectly fitted to show his sculpted arms and chest. He had his chestnut brown hair trimmed and styled neatly.

"Who is that?"

"Are you kidding me?" Geri exclaimed with exasperation. "That's *James*!"

"Huh?" I squinted, then my jaw dropped. "No!"

She giggled and bounced up and down. "Yes! Rumor is that he heard the girl he likes thought he looked like a bum, so during the holidays, he got a haircut and pulled out his school uniform from the back of his closet."

I stared at her, completely stunned as she yanked on my arm. "But . . . he's not supposed to like *me*!"

Her giggling intensified. "But he does! Cadence, this is incredible. Guys don't normally do this."

Awestruck, I stared at him as he stood, calm and completely relaxed, listening to his friends talking.

Geri shoved me. "Go talk to him."

I shook my head. "I can't!"

"Why not? He's practically begging you!"

His head turned and he saw me. We looked at each other for a split second, then he pushed off from the wall to face me.

I gasped and tried to run, but Geri grabbed and held me. "No, Cadence!"

"I can't talk to him!"

"Stop it!"

We struggled against each other. When I saw him heading toward us, I pushed her off me and straightened. The groups of girls watched him, even gravitated after him as he crossed the quad, his gaze fixed on me. I held my breath as he paused in front of me, slowly looking me over.

"Hello, Cadence."

"Hermnm ah . . ." *Why am I acting like a love-struck idiot?* I thought I was over all this. But then again, I felt more like a teenager than a twenty-five-year-old, so I blamed my stupid body chemistry.

He smiled, and with his hair out of his face and his scruff gone, it just about made me melt on the spot. "You look good too."

"Your teeth are white."

Geri nudged me in the ribs.

He chuckled. "Dentist cleaned me up, and I quit smoking."

"Ah . . ." I couldn't stop staring at him, even though I probably looked like a fool.

His smile widened and I bit my lip, the urge to kiss him forcing itself to the surface.

He stepped closer to me. I tried to step back, but my feet felt like they had dissolved into the ground. He ran fingers down my arm and I swallowed hard.

"Are you speechless, Cadence? I didn't even know that was possible."

My gaze flashed up and met his. His eyes looked clearer, brighter, bluer. I looked down, not wanting to feel what he'd stirred up inside me.

His fingers brushed against my cheek, then pushed the hair from my half ponytail back over my shoulder. He leaned closer as he caressed my face. My breathing quickened, but I managed to regain a drop of sensibility as Dad's loving eyes flashed into my mind. I pulled back, just a moment before he kissed me.

"I told you not to kiss me."

Amusement flashed in his eyes as a wide grin swept across his face.

"Cadence!" Geri hissed.

I leapt back from James, pulling free of his touch. I turned away from him to regain my senses. This was madness! I loved Austin! I hurried away, my face burning.

Geri was hot on my heels. "Cadence! What the hell?"

"I couldn't, Geri. I just couldn't."

"Why not?"

The bell rang.

"Because I can't!"

She grabbed my elbow as she redirected us toward our bags. "Why not? He's changing for *you*!"

"But he's not supposed to."

She halted, staring at me. "What does that mean?"

I avoided eye contact. "I'm just not comfortable with it. I mean, is he for real, or is this just a thing to get into my pants?"

"You sound like your dad."

I turned away, ashamed of the feelings I struggled to suppress.

"Cadence, all this stuff he's doing is incredible! How many girls get to say a guy was this determined to have her?"

I reached the table and pulled my bag over my shoulders. "He's still *him* though, Geri. He still hangs out with the same group and is still a bully."

"No, he's not. He's been going out of his way to be friends with our group. Come on, Cadence!"

I huffed, knowing I wouldn't win this battle. "Fine. Look, I won't flat out reject him, but I'm not going to agree to anything either until I know he's not going to try anything on me."

She pursed her lips. She wasn't happy with my response, but was pleased I was willing to compromise. "Good, 'cause I think you'd be good together."

I sighed. "I don't wanna talk about this anymore."

"Fine."

We turned toward the building as James walked by with his friends. I gasped, still stunned by how good he looked. He grinned at me. I dropped my gaze and hurried toward the building.

But I couldn't escape him the whole day. He always hovered nearby, crossing paths with me so he could touch my hand and sneaking up behind me while I stood outside my classrooms. He'd whisper in my ear, making me jump, and I'd glance around to see everyone watching me.

By the end of the day, I couldn't escape the gossip about me and him, so I hid behind a tree while I waited for my bus. Dusty found me. He leaned against the tree, trying to look inconspicuous.

"Hey, Cadence."

I grumbled.

"I know, you had a bad day. Everyone's talking about it."

I huffed.

"He talked to me today."

I slapped my forehead and groaned.

"He told me to tell you it's his birthday tomorrow, and all he wants is a kiss from you. I told him he was gross and to stay away from you."

A smile curled at the corners of my lips. *Good old Dusty.* "Thank you."

He spun around the tree to look at me. "Cadence, am I smart?"

I blinked, surprised by the change of direction in our conversation. "Yes, you're very smart."

"Then why do all my classes bore me and the teachers yell at me?"

"Because you *are* smart, and the classes are too easy for you."

He tilted his head, surprised by my answer. "Really?"

I nodded.

"Huh . . ." He leaned against the tree. "So you think I could get good grades if I wanted to?"

"I know you can."

A smile flitted across his face.

James stood waiting as I climbed off the bus in the morning. My friends didn't disperse like usual, but hung back to watch as he walked straight toward me. I stepped around him as he tried to cut me off, but he followed. "It's my birthday."

"I heard."

"I'm sixteen now."

"I don't care."

"Sweet sixteen gets a kiss."

"That's *not* how the saying goes."

We passed through a gap between buildings and he grabbed my waist, spinning me to face him. "No one's around. No one will see. Let me kiss you."

"No."

I stepped back, but he kept after me. "Why are you making this so hard?"

"You're still, ah . . . you're, ah . . ."

He ran his hand down my arm again. I couldn't think. He caught my hand and pulled me closer.

"I'm a what?"

He touched my face and tucked my hair behind my ear. I looked up into his eyes, entranced by the intensity that burned in them.

"I'm not supposed to like you."

His arm wrapped around my waist. "But you do?"

"Mmm . . ." My gaze fell to his lips as they drew closer to mine. "Stop."

He paused, barely an inch away from my lips. "I'll never force you to do anything. If you don't wanna kiss me, I'll back away right now."

My heart skipped a beat as my eyes lifted to his. Then, impulsively, I grasped his face and pulled his lips against mine. It tasted delicious, warm, and made me dizzy with the excitement that shot through me. I wanted more. I wrapped my arms around his neck, holding him tightly.

He pushed me against the wall as his arms clamped around my waist. We kissed open mouthed, the intensity making my whole body tingle with excitement. His hands caressed my back, and his fingers ran through my hair.

We only stopped because the bell rang.

I pulled away from his lips, but didn't let him go. "Oh my gosh . . ."

A crooked smile flashed across his face. "Let's skip school today, just you and me, and we'll go hang out somewhere—"

"No, I can't." I stroked his cheek.

He softly pressed his lips against mine. "Why not?"

"I'm not like you. I want to get good grades. I want to go to class."

"Just once, that's all I'm asking."

I shook my head and forced myself away from him. "I can't."

"Cadence . . ."

"You got your kiss, James." I hurried away, heading straight for my class.

I flopped down beside Michael, but kept my head low. How could I have feelings for James? This was a totally new development, something that blindsided me.

"Cadence? Hello?"

Michael's voice startled me so much I almost fell off my seat. "What?"

"Where were you this morning?"

"At home, then here at school."

"No, I meant why didn't you show up at the table?"

My cheeks burned, and I turned away, raising a textbook in front of me to hide my red face.

"Did you hook up with someone?"

"No."

"You did!" He grasped the book and lowered it so he could look into my eyes. "Was it James Gordon?"

My face burned even hotter. "No!"

"Cadence, you did!"

I shoved his shoulder. "No, I didn't!"

"So, you guys are an item now?"

"No."

"Wow, you're making it really hard for him."

I leaned closer and whispered, "He wanted me to skip school with him. I can't date someone who'd want me to do that."

Michael's eyebrow rose. "You can't be serious."

"I am serious."

"What's happened to you, Cadence? You've always been a good girl, but you used to be daring, too. Over the last few months, you've become a real prude."

My mouth snapped shut as I stared at him in shock.

"Yeah, you heard me right. You're one of my best friends, but lately you've been pretty boring."

"Are you saying I should've skipped school with a guy I barely know and has a reputation for drug use and generally being a huge jackass?"

"That's exactly what I'm saying."

My eyes widened. "Are *you* serious?"

"Well, okay, realistically if he was still that way, I'd say no, but he's been changing to get your attention. Did you know he was even seen *in class* yesterday?"

I saw the odds piling up against me. Michael thought I should date him, and Geri did too, and if I was completely honest with myself, I wanted to as well. I dropped my head into my hands, trying to force my feelings for Austin to surface, but they seemed to be buried deep within me, lost in some abyss of alternate reality. What was happening to me? My feelings from that time seemed to be just labels attached to images in my head, not real at all.

"You should give James a chance," Michael said.

I gnawed on my lip. My feelings for James were so raw and real, but my feelings for Austin, try as I might, simply felt like a dream.

"I still can't believe you didn't just run off with him," Geri muttered during science.

"It's been two weeks, and you're still harping on about that?"

She flicked a piece of sheep's brain at me. "Yeah, because it would have been romantic, you idiot."

I brushed the brains off in disgust. "I just don't know if I could date him."

She scowled. "And you think I'm harping on? You've beaten that excuse to a pulp. You really need a new one."

Our teacher ordered everyone to clean up. We hurried to obey, then took down our final notes before the bell rang. Geri and I shoved our books in our bags and hurried toward the door. I paused when I almost ran into someone and was met by a pair of gray-blue eyes that caused me to jump.

Melanie gazed steadily at me with eyes identical to James's. "Stay away from my brother, Cadence. You've already ruined him."

Geri scoffed. "Um, hello? He's smoking hot now, and he's been going to classes, *and* he's stopped using drugs. How is *that* ruining him?"

She glared at Geri, then shoved my shoulder. "Of course *you* don't get it."

She skulked out of the classroom.

"Seriously? When did she get so surly?" I asked.

"As I said before—Tasmanian-style crush."

I glared at Geri, but giggled. As we passed out of the science corridor into the grounds, someone knocked me to the ground and tore my bag from my shoulder. They hit me in the face, causing my braces to tear my lip open. I spat at the taste of blood. A hand grasped my hair, yanking me backward, then smashed my head against the concrete.

Someone knelt on my chest as feet gathered around me. Finally able to register what happened, I saw my assailants—Carla and her cronies. The one sitting on me, Becca, flicked her long dark hair back and leaned closer to me, so our faces were only inches apart. "Stay away from James, you little slut."

I squirmed, and she smacked me across the face again. "Did you hear me?"

"Yes!"

She pressed her thumb into my cheek, causing my braces to cut into me. I hollered, which made her smile. "We can do so much worse than this."

The other girls fell around me, pulling at my clothes and hair. I screamed, having never been bullied so brutally before. What was happening? Wasn't my second chance supposed to be *better*?

One of the girls flew aside, soon followed by another and another. Harper, her face red with rage, plowed through to me. She knelt beside me and winced at the sight of my face. She softly touched my cheek, then launched to her feet and charged, screaming, at Becca.

Her friends fought with the other girls. I sat up as Geri rushed to me.

"Cadence!" She swore as she touched my face. "There's blood everywhere!"

Teachers rushed around, trying to break up the huge catfight. My head spun as I tried to stand, and I stumbled back onto the ground.

"Cadence! Oh, Cadence! Don't pass out on me!" Geri's voice sounded high-pitched and trembling.

I met her gaze. She looked more frightened than ever as her hands clenched my arm. Her eyes shot up and she gasped. I looked around just as James plucked me off the ground like I weighed nothing. He scanned the scene before hurrying me away.

"Geri," he said gently. "What happened?"

"Those girls just jumped her! She wasn't even doing anything!"

James looked at my face and took a sharp breath. "It will be all right. I promise."

"They told me to stay away from you," I said.

His arms tightened around me as fear filled his eyes. "You're not going to listen to them, are you? They're just stupid, jealous girls."

I didn't answer, which made him look at me with wide, fear-filled eyes.

We arrived at the sick bay. The first-aid lady gasped at the sight of me. "Lay her on the bed."

James gently placed me down and stepped back as the lady cleaned my face. I watched him as he stood beside me, tense and stiff while he chewed on his lip. I stretched out my hand and wrapped my fingers around his.

"Open your mouth, dear," the lady said gently.

I tried, but it hurt like crazy. I moaned. James's hand clenched mine as he looked away.

Geri rushed up onto the end of the bed and sat over my legs. "Cadence, your parents are coming."

"Dad too?"

She nodded. "He's leaving work to come here."

A knot formed in my stomach. "Let me see my face."

Geri tried to force a smile. "It's not too bad. Just a lot of blood, really."

A tear ran down my cheek. "I'm gonna be scarred, aren't I?"

"No," the lady answered. "But you will need to go to your orthodontist ASAP."

The lady gently slipped some wads of cotton in my mouth, and the separation of my cheeks from my braces was a huge relief. She handed me ice packs for my face and left us to fill out the paperwork.

With the cotton in my mouth, I couldn't say anything. I felt like an idiot lying there in front of James with my cheeks all puffed up. I looked away, not wanting him to see me like that.

His hand tightened around mine as he shuffled closer. "Cadence, I'm so sorry."

I nodded, but wished he'd go away until I didn't look so ridiculous.

Geri climbed off my lap. I looked up to see James mouthing something to her. She nodded and slipped out.

He shifted closer to me and brushed his fingers through my hair, pulling out my destroyed ponytail. "Cadence, this is my fault. I'll talk to them and the guys to make sure it doesn't happen again. I promise."

I nodded, too afraid to look into his eyes and see that he thought I looked ugly.

He took a sharp breath. "Please look at me."

I shook my head, ashamed.

"Cadence." He shuffled up next to me. He gently clasped my face and leaned over me. I shut my eyes as tears started to fall. "Cadence, please. Don't let them get between us. I'm trying so hard to convince you to be my girlfriend, and now I'm afraid they've screwed everything up for us."

My eyes shot open and met his. I didn't see disgust with me in them at all. Instead, I saw how deeply he cared and his concern for me. I clasped his hands resting over my ears, and nodded.

"Oh, Cadence." He leaned forward and kissed my forehead.

"Cadence?" Mum stood by the door with her jaw hanging. "Who's this?"

James leapt to his feet to face her. "I'm James. You must be Mrs. Anderson."

"I am, yes." She looked him over. "I've never seen you among her friends before."

"I'm in tenth grade."

"Oh." Then it dawned on her, and her face fell. "Oh . . . James Gordon?"

"Yes, I'm James Gordon."

"You don't look like a druggie."

He shifted uncomfortably and dropped his gaze. "I'm not anymore. Not that I was much of one before, just some smoking and beers every now and then."

That didn't please Mum at all and she scowled. "I think you should leave before her father arrives. He'll eat you for breakfast."

James glanced at me nervously, but shook his head. "I'm staying with Cadence."

Mum sighed. "Oh, wonderful." She looked out the door. "Geri, dear, come on."

Geri shuffled in and climbed on top of me, resting her head on my chest. I sighed and stroked her hair, grateful for her unwavering loyalty to me. I hoped I could keep it forever.

James sat by my legs as Mum stroked my hair. "How are you feeling?"

I nodded.

"What happened?"

I raised my eyebrows.

"Well, of course you can't answer." She smiled and touched my chin. "It's not that bad, don't worry. Nothing the orthodontist can't fix."

I nodded again.

James's hand rested on my leg. I was so glad I'd shaved that morning. With Geri and Mum focused on my face, his hand ran up and down my shin.

Mum suddenly stood, and he pulled his hand away. "I'm going to go talk to someone and find out what happened."

Geri's head shot up. "I can tell you."

I stared at James, who gazed back at me, his fingers barely touching the side of my leg.

Mum cleared her throat and I looked up at her. "Can I trust him if Geri and I step out for a few minutes?"

I nodded.

"Hmm." She shot him a warning glare as she and Geri slipped out.

James stood up and leaned over me. "Be my girlfriend."

I shook my head. I looked like a beaver! It wasn't the time for that!

"Why not? You want to. I can see it in your eyes."

I dropped my gaze.

"Cadence, you know I'll treat you right. You've been too much work for me to just screw things up."

I shook my head, but couldn't help the tear that ran down my cheek.

He ran his fingers through my hair. "Look at me."

I did.

"You're so beautiful."

I whimpered and grasped his shirt.

He grinned. "I'd kiss you, but . . . you know."

I let out a short laugh, but stopped myself because it hurt.

"Be my girlfriend."

I stared into his eyes, wanting to say yes, but hesitant all the same as my memories seemed to hold it back.

"What are you doing?" Dad's voice boomed across the room.

I jumped and shoved James back. Dad advanced on him, but James stood tall and firm. Dad was almost a whole head taller and twice James's width across his shoulders, but James didn't stand down as Dad towered over him.

"Who are *you*?" Dad asked.

"I'm James Gordon, sir." James raised his hand for a handshake.

Dad ignored it. "What makes you think you can be *that* close to my daughter?"

James took a deep breath, but didn't back away. "I care about her very much—"

Dad shoved him aside and sat beside me. "Who did this to you?"

I shrugged.

He touched my cheek. "Do you want me to press charges? Because I will. This is assault."

I shook my head.

He sighed. "I'm going to at least make sure they're suspended."

"Dad?" Harper stood by the door. She had a black eye and held an ice pack to the side of her face.

"You too?" He jumped up and pulled her into the room to look at her.

James stared at me and mouthed, "*Harper is your sister?*"

I shrugged.

"What happened to you?" Dad asked Harper.

"They were beating up on Cadence and I just kinda snapped," she answered, avoiding eye contact.

"You stood up for your sister?"

She nodded.

He wrapped his arms around her. "Harper, I'm so proud of you."

Harper flinched, surprised, but wrapped her arms around him and nuzzled into his shoulder. I smiled. That was definitely a drastic improvement over the last timeline. Even after she'd moved beyond her wilder years, she and Dad never became close, and would have *never* embraced.

Her eyes lifted and she looked at me. She blushed and mouthed, "*Shut up.*"

I nodded.

She saw James and an evil grin spread across her face. "Dad, he's the reason the fight started."

Dad had never moved faster. James scampered away as Dad hollered all kinds of profanity at him and chased him around the room. Harper laughed evilly as Mum burst into the room and yelled, "David!"

Dad spun to her. "Ooh, Harmony, I'm going to rip him to shreds!"

"You're so over-the-top! Leave the boy alone."

Dad pointed at James accusingly. "It's his fault our daughters look like punching bags!"

I slapped my forehead, utterly mortified.

Harper cackled and almost collapsed onto the floor. Mum glared at her. She forced her laughing to stop, but kept a smirk across her face.

"David, come with me."

Dad puffed up his chest and glared at James.

"*Now.*"

Dad watched James with narrow eyes as he followed Mum out. Geri slipped in once they'd gone, staring apprehensively at Harper, who had begun to laugh again.

She shuffled up beside me and pulled her curls back out of her face. "All the girls are in the principal's and the vice principal's offices. It looks like Carla and Becca will be suspended and the other girls are on probation." She glanced at Harper and leaned closer to whisper, "Including Harper."

I looked across at her as she sank onto a chair, tears of laughter streaming down her face. I shrugged. Geri gazed at me for a moment, then pulled one of her notebooks out of her bag and handed it to me with a pen. I scrawled down, *I don't think she cares.*

Geri smirked. "How are you feeling?"

I wrote, *Fine, considering . . .*

She nodded. "I know. Everything has been kinda crazy lately, huh?"

I nodded.

James shuffled up beside me and grabbed my hand. "I think I'll go before your dad gets back."

I sighed and wrote, *I'm sorry. He's overprotective, that's all.*

He nodded and smiled. "No kidding." He kissed my forehead and slipped out.

Geri grinned at me.

I glared at her.

She shrugged and slipped her book back into her bag.

Chapter Nine

For the next few days, my mouth felt sore and puffy. A few of my brackets broke off and my top wire snapped. Thankfully, I remained on track to have them removed over the Christmas/summer break.

James didn't approach me for almost two weeks, but tailed me everywhere. I wasn't sure if he did it out of guilt or if he was afraid to come near me after Dad tried to pull him limb from limb. Either way, I felt discouraged, like maybe he would decide I wasn't worth the hassle.

Our science teacher sent me and Geri to the library one Thursday afternoon. I'd spent all of lunch watching James from afar, trying to will him to look over at me. But he never did.

"Don't worry," Geri said. "Your dad's pretty scary. He's probably just afraid to come near you right now."

I huffed, wanting to distract myself. "It's so hot."

She shrugged. "Yeah, it's been worse."

I giggled as she pretended to wipe sweat from her forehead. We passed by a group of painters working on one of the buildings and hurried up the stairs to the library. Geri grabbed an armful of books and the librarian sent her back while she loaded me up.

On my way back, I passed the painters again and noticed the youngest painter staring at me. He looked to be eighteen, and fixated on me so much that he'd stopped painting. I hid my face behind the books.

I looked around as I approached a staircase, and glanced into a classroom window. Inside I saw a tenth grade class, and I scanned for James. To my delight, he sat in the back, looking very bored.

The boy next to him nudged him and whispered. James looked up at me. I flushed and hid my face behind the books, but knocked off the top two. Grunting, I set the pile down. A hand grasped one of the books. I looked up to see the painter smiling at me. "Hi."

"Ah . . . hey." I remembered in the last timeline returning to class without dropping the books, and Geri had gushed about one of the painters stopping her and asking about me. To have him actually talking to me made me uncomfortable.

He rested the book on top of the pile and lifted them for me. "I'm Blake."

"Uh . . . hi. Thanks for helping me." I tried to take the books from him.

"Aren't you going to give me your name?"

"Uh . . ." I tried to tug the books away. "I'm jail bait, aren't I?"

He shrugged. "You're cute."

"Can I have the books please?"

"Once you give me your name."

The window burst open, making me start.

"Hey! Give her the books!" James bellowed.

"Who are you?"

"I'm her boyfriend, moron!" James leapt out the window.

I jumped in front of him as he lunged at Blake. "James!"

"Give her the books," James snarled.

"Fine. Geez, settle down." Blake stretched out the books for me. James snatched them from his hands and placed them in mine. Blake shuffled off back to his work.

James turned to me. "Cadence, are you—?"

"Mr. Gordon, stop ignoring me and get back in here," his teacher bellowed.

"Yeah, one second," he yelled back.

"Thank you," I gazed at him through my lashes. "But I don't wanna get you into trouble."

He shrugged. "I'm always in trouble." He grabbed the windowsill.

"James?"

He paused and looked at me.

"Meet me after class?"

He raised his eyebrows. "Right here?"

I nodded.

"Okay." He jumped back in through the window, causing the teacher to yell at him all over again. I grinned, but felt a twinge of guilt for doing so.

I returned to class, still with a stupid grin across my face, and handed out the books. When I took my seat, Geri stared at me with a raised eyebrow. "Okay, kid. Explain yourself."

I shrugged.

"Uh ah, no! You don't get to do this to me!"

I met her gaze. "I saw James."

"*And?*"

"He's going to meet me after class."

She shrieked and bounced around, drawing everyone's attention. I grabbed her arms.

"Shh!" I hissed with a grin.

"Are you gonna kiss him?" Her cheeks flushed.

"No!"

"You so are."

I grinned sheepishly. "Well, maybe."

She shrieked again and ran around in a circle.

"Stop it!" I laughed.

"Girls!" our teacher said, scolding us.

Geri froze and bit her lip, but her grin never disappeared.

After class, as everyone rushed to the bus bays, I slipped away in the other direction to meet James. He stood waiting for me as I reached the stairs. Careful not to make a sound, I stared at him, admiring him.

He sensed my movement and looked down at me. I smiled and my cheeks warmed, which made him grin.

"Hello, beautiful."

I giggled as I reached the top step. "Why do you call me that?"

"Because that's what you are."

I dropped my gaze.

"So, you wanted to see me?"

I nodded. "I wanted to know why you're avoiding me."

He let out a long breath. I looked up at him and he examined my face. His hand reached up and he ran his thumb over my cheek. "I thought maybe your dad told you to stay away from me."

I shook my head. "He's been too focused on getting those girls disciplined."

His gaze fell to my lips. "And I thought maybe you blamed me for what happened."

"It wasn't your fault."

His free hand lifted and he grasped my waist. "So, you're not mad at me?"

I smiled up at him as our eyes met. "No."

He exhaled. "Cadence, that's such a relief."

I wrapped my arms around him, sliding them between his body and his bag. "You called yourself my boyfriend."

He grasped the back of my neck. "I did."

"Why did you do that?"

"Because I wanna be."

I smiled and stretched up to kiss him.

"James!"

James jumped and looked over my head. "Melanie?"

"Her? Seriously?" Melanie rushed over beside us and glared at me. "You *know* what she and her stupid friend did to me."

I turned to her, confused. "What did I—?"

"It's your fault everyone hates me!" She pressed her hands against her hips. "Or don't you remember back in seventh grade, when you told everyone I was a boy?"

I gasped, suddenly remembering. Geri and I had honestly thought she was a boy for about a month. "Melanie, we didn't—"

"Shut up, Cadence!"

"Cadence?" James looked at me with his brow furrowed. "Did you really do that?"

I pulled away from him. "It was an accident. We didn't intentionally—"

"See?" She turned to him.

He ran his hand through his hair. "Cadence?"

"She wore the boys' uniform, and was so tiny and had that short haircut, we honestly thought she was. When we found out she was a girl, we stopped and felt really bad about it."

"You felt bad about it?" she said sarcastically. "That didn't stop everyone teasing me about it all year and making me the grade joke."

James kept looking from me to her. He obviously had no idea what to think, and was torn between his loyalty to his sister and his feelings for me. I dropped my gaze and started creeping away from them. "I'm really sorry, Melanie, *really*."

I turned to rush away, but James caught my arm.

"Cadence." He pulled me under his arm. "Melanie, I know enough about Cadence to know she wouldn't intentionally do something like that. I'm sorry she hurt you, and I really hope you can forgive her."

Melanie turned red. "Seriously, James? You're going to let her 'I'm so sweet' façade trick you?"

"It's not a façade, Melanie—"

She rolled her eyes. "I thought you'd be smart enough to see that she's a great big *fake!*"

She spun on her heel and marched away.

He rubbed the back of his neck. "That's going to be a huge fight when I get home."

"I'm sorry," I said. "Maybe I should go. I don't want to . . ."

He pulled me around into his arms. I held my breath as our noses touched. "You wanna finish that thought you were having earlier?"

I giggled as butterflies filled my belly. I pressed against him and softly brushed my lips against his.

He shuddered as I pulled away. "Don't tease me like that."

"Like what?"

He grasped the back of my head and pulled me in for a long, deep kiss.

I ended up missing my bus.

James stood waiting for me as the bus pulled up. As I stepped off, he shoved his hands in his pockets, grinning from ear to ear. "Hello, beautiful."

I flushed as all the girls around me "*awed*" in unison.

He walked up beside me and took my hand. "So, am I your boyfriend now?"

I took a sharp breath. After I'd finally arrived home the day before, I'd spent the evening flicking through photos of Austin, trying to force my feelings for him to surface. I still felt a glimmer of pain for Melody, but nothing remained for Austin. I wished that I could *feel* them again, and not just *know* I had them. The problem was, I felt them for James instead.

"I don't know," I answered, avoiding looking at him.

He let out a long sigh. "Really?"

I wove my fingers between his. "I'm sorry, I'm just unsure about a couple of things."

"Like what?"

I gnawed on my tongue. *Like that I remember being married with a child, but can't feel that love anymore because I've been stuck as a teenager for too long.* "Just stuff."

"It's your dad, isn't it?"

"Yeah."

"I get it. You're his little girl. Harper's a huge brat, so he doesn't want you turning out like her." He lifted my hand and kissed it. "But I'm not going to do anything to ruin you."

My heart fluttered. "James—"

"You know, I've kinda picked up that this isn't going to lead to sex, so he doesn't need to worry about that, and neither do you."

I pulled my hand free. "Excuse me?"

"I mean, it would be nice, but I'm fine with not going there. I'd just be happy to be with you."

I had to admit, I wasn't listening to anything he said. My brain caught on the word *sex*. "You just wanna have sex with me? Is that all this is about?"

"No, I just said that—"

I marched away.

"Cadence!" He rushed after me. "Cadence—"

"Get away from me, you perv!"

He swore. "No! You totally misunderstood what I'm saying."

"You haven't changed at all, have you? It's all just a thing to get into my pants!"

"Are you kidding me? This . . . *you* have been way too hard to get to be a quick shag!"

I swung around to slap him, but he caught my wrist. "Cadence, this is ridiculous. What's really going on?"

I pulled my hand free as tears burned in my eyes. "Nothing."

"Geri told me you've mentioned liking some other guy called Austin."

I gasped and leapt back from him. It felt like a slap in the face. I couldn't work out if I was betraying Austin or not, especially because I couldn't feel that love anymore.

"Cadence, tell me what's going on."

My chin quivered as I fought back my tears. "No, James. I need to work this out myself."

He followed me as I tried to walk away. "How long will it take you?"

"I don't know!"

"Well, I'll wait as long as I need to. You're worth it to me."

I covered my mouth as a sob wrenched itself free. Flashes of Austin's face burst into my mind, but they seemed faded and distorted. In contrast, James's face came through clear and vibrant, his gray-blue eyes piercing right through me.

Chapter Ten

*H*e gave me space for the next few weeks, but stayed nearby, waiting patiently. When I'd caught him talking with Geri and Michael several times, they'd clammed up as soon as I approached them.

Then, my birthday arrived.

I chatted with my friends during lunch, standing and leaning over the table. With the sweltering December heat, I did all I could to cool down.

Geri squirted me with water. "Ha ha! Happy birthday, Cay-Cay!"

"Oh! I'm gonna kick your butt!"

She screeched and sprinted away. We charged across the lower quad out onto the football field, right through the middle of a cricket game. The boys hollered at us to get lost, so she turned and headed back toward the buildings. We sprinted through the corridors with the teachers yelling at us to stop running inside, and she burst into the school hall.

I charged in after her. She danced around in circles.

"Geri, we're not supposed to be in here!" I laughed.

"I know, but it's actually a little bit cooler in here."

I glanced back toward the door to the administration offices, hoping no one would look in and see us. "We could get detentions for being in here."

She stopped mid-spin, ran up the stairs onto the stage, and disappeared.

I climbed the stairs and peeked through the door to the dark stage. "Geri?"

"I'm over here."

"Geri, we're gonna get so busted for this."

Her giggling darted across the darkness.

I stepped through the door and shut it behind me. At least no one could see us if they passed by. I walked out onto the stage, my hands outstretched, feeling for the curtains and any desks or chairs lying around. My fingers found a curtain and I followed it out onto the stage. Then I felt a shirt and warm, firm abdominals. I pulled back, startled.

A pair of hands clasped mine and placed a small box into them. I held my breath as I opened it. Blue light burst out, and inside, a crystal sat on top of a light. Round, but with grooves cut along it, the light distorted and burst out at different angles. The light faded to purple, then red as the hands that given it to me wrapped around mine, blocking the light. James moved closer; I knew just by the smell of him. His hands found my face and he pulled me close.

"Happy birthday, beautiful."

"James . . ." My heart tore apart.

"I have something special for you for Christmas, too, if you'll agree to be my girlfriend."

I ran my hand over his chest, just to feel his presence, but I paused over his heartbeat. I held my hand there as it pulsed steadily. He was so alive. I took a deep breath and shut my eyes.

What should I do?

I thought about Austin and Melody, and everything that happened. The last time I saw them, they were dead. I'd been shot back in time to save them, but Melody hadn't even been born yet, and Austin was miles away and didn't even know I existed. I'd had boyfriends the last time and it hadn't harmed our marriage . . . then it struck me.

I wasn't *married*.

I was a teenage girl again, with a second chance to live life exactly how I wanted. I would be with Austin again eventually, and we would have Melody and I would save them, but right now, I could be with James if I wanted. I could see what lessons he had to teach me. I could feel something with him that I'd never felt with any of my other high school boyfriends.

I slid my hand up onto his shoulder. "James?"

"Yes, Cadence?"

"Why do you like *me*?"

He chuckled. "Because you're incredible."

I wrapped my hand around the back of his neck and stroked his hair. "James?"

"Yes?"

"Be my boyfriend?"

He let out a short laugh. His arms wrapped around me and his lips slammed against mine. I kissed him openmouthed and with passion, my heart pounding as a rush of excitement surged through me. I couldn't get enough of him as I ran my fingers through his hair and over his face. Being so engrossed in each other, we didn't hear the bell ring.

"Cadence!" Geri's voice echoed around us.

I pulled away, startled by being brought out of such a passionate kiss. "Geri?"

"The bell went. We have to go."

I stroked James's face in the darkness, wishing I could see it. "James, I wish you could come with me."

"Let's just leave, right now." He stroked my cheek.

"No, I have to go to class."

"I know. You're such a good girl." He ran his hand through my hair. "But you're my good girl now."

I giggled and gave him a quick kiss. "I'll see ya later."

"Okay. Goodbye, beautiful."

I pulled away hesitantly, and Geri and I slipped out the backstage door. We hurried to PE as she rambled about how she and Michael had helped plan the whole thing. I giggled at her excitement. My butterflies rushed out of my stomach and tingled all over my skin. James was my *boyfriend!* How could a guy I'd never known before be constantly on my mind, making me feel things I hadn't felt until I was twenty?

Outside the change rooms, Geri swung to face me. "Okay, we have to stop talking about him now because Melanie will freak out."

"Huh?"

"Yeah, James told me what she did. She's less than happy about the prospect of you and him."

"Oh." I scowled, lifting the little box in my hand and opening it. It didn't seem so vibrant and beautiful in the sunlight, but I still smiled as it changed color.

Geri giggled. "Cadence, I've *never* seen you this into a guy. It makes me so happy!" She threw her arms around my neck and squeezed. "I love you, Cay-Cay. You're the best friend ever. When it's my turn, you better return the favor."

I laughed as she let me go. "Deal."

We rushed in to change. I set the box on top of my bag to pull off my shirt and laughed when Geri poked my belly button. As I lifted my dark blue sports shirt, I jumped at someone pressing against me.

Melanie stared intently at the box. "Where did you get that?"

Geri snatched it up and shoved it in my bag. "It was a birthday present."

"From who?" Melanie's eyes narrowed on me.

"Me and Michael," Geri answered, a little too quickly.

"Let me see it." Melanie lunged toward my bag.

"Hey!" Geri grabbed her hand. "You can't just go through people's bags."

"Let me see it!"

I yanked on my shirt and grabbed my bag to hold the zipper together. Several more girls rushed in. Melanie screamed and tried to wrestle my bag out of my and Geri's hands.

One of the female PE teachers burst in at the sounds of a fight and blew her whistle. The piercing sound echoed around the tight change room, making us all jump and cover our ears.

"What's going on? Who started this?"

Everyone pointed at Melanie except me.

"Melanie Gordon." She scowled and rested her hands on her hips. "I would expect this from your brother, but not you."

She turned bright red.

"Miss," I said, wanting to try and make amends with Melanie. "It wasn't her fault."

The teacher raised her eyebrows. "Oh?"

"No, it was my fault."

"Cadence!" Geri grabbed my elbow.

The teacher looked me over and placed her hands on her hips. "I doubt that, Miss Anderson. But since you owned up to it, I'll need you to come with me, too."

"No!" Geri shot in front of me. "She didn't do it, miss! Melanie was being a jealous brat and tried to steal something from her bag."

"Geri!" I grabbed her shoulder.

"It's true," one of the other girls piped in.

"Yeah, she tried to rip Cadence's bag open," said another.

All the girls murmured in agreement. Geri opened my bag and pulled out the box. "She wanted this. It's a birthday present."

The teacher looked at it with a scowl, then looked at me. "Cadence?"

I looked at Melanie, who stared at her feet. "I . . . ah . . ."

What could I do? Everyone accused Melanie. But I couldn't get her into trouble. That would just make things worse. "She was confused. I should have just shown her. So it's still my fault."

"No, it isn't, Cadence," the teacher answered. "She shouldn't have tried to go through your bag. That's a very serious issue." She looked to Melanie. "Come with me, Miss Gordon."

Melanie shuffled out after the teacher as the rest of the class went about their business as if nothing had happened. No one cared what happened to Melanie. She was nobody.

I hurried onto the field with the rest of the class and set up the cricket stumps. Brian came up beside me and shoved the last stump into the ground. "Happy birthday, Cadence."

"Thanks." I forced a smile on my face, but couldn't help feeling guilty about Melanie.

"So . . ." He scratched his head. "Did you get your special birthday present?"

"Huh?" I rested the wicket on top of the stumps.

He cleared his throat.

"Michael told me that, ah . . ." He grinned sheepishly.

I giggled. "Oh, *that* present." I walked away from him.

He stood beside me as teams were divided. "Well?"

Geri walked up beside him and punched his shoulder. "Well what?"

I giggled, enjoying the game.

"Are she and James together?" he asked in a loud and exasperated voice.

Geri burst out laughing.

The class tried to look indifferent, although they were obviously listening. I tugged on Brian's sleeve and he bent down so I could whisper in his ear.

"Yes."

A smile flashed across his face, but he suppressed it and glanced around. He whispered, "Where's Melanie? Is that why you're being so quiet?"

I shrugged, then heard my name called for a team. As the teams split up, I thought about Melanie. I needed to do something to try and get along with her. I didn't want to cause James grief and drive a wedge between him and his sister.

Melanie eventually returned to class and stood on the outfield a long way from everyone. I watched her during class and tried to approach her several times, but when she noticed me creeping closer, she'd dash across to the far end of the field.

Determined to talk to her, I hurried to change after class to follow her out. She changed quickly too, so I had to finish buttoning my blouse as I ran out after her. "Melanie!"

"Get away from me," she responded.

"Please hear me out."

"No!"

"I don't know what you want me to do!"

She swung around and glared at me. "Stay away from my brother."

I stared at her in frustration. "Really?"

"Yeah. He can do *way* better than you." She headed toward the front of the school.

"He's my boyfriend now."

She flinched and clenched her fists, but kept walking. "Then dump him."

"I don't want to. I really like him."

She gagged. "That's disgusting." She rushed through the main building to the parking lot and paused, glancing around. "You're disgusting. You're not even pretty. I don't see why everyone thinks you're so wonderful."

"I'm sorry you got into trouble."

She scoffed and folded her arms. "No, you're not. It just made you look even better because you tried to take the blame. *Saint Cadence* tries to save the day."

I forced my anger aside. "I don't want to fight with you."

Her eyes narrowed on me. "Then stay away from James."

I groaned, exasperated.

James walked up behind her. He glanced at me, then rested his hand on her shoulder. She jumped and turned to him.

"Hey, Mel."

She flushed and bit her lip.

"Why are you being like this? We've talked and yelled about it, but you're still holding on to this. I'm going to date Cadence whether you like it or not, so just let it go."

She slapped his chest. "She got me a detention! Mum will be here any second and will yell at me because they called her and told her I tried to steal something from *her* bag!" She pointed at me accusingly. "I hate her, James! All she ever does is make everything worse for me!"

James looked at me. "What happened?"

"Don't ask *her*!" Melanie shoved him. "She'll do her sweet girl thing and make me look like the bad guy!"

James glared at her. "You're doing a really good job of that all on your own."

She slapped his shoulder and opened her mouth to speak, but then a car pulled up. They both turned to face it as an auburn-haired woman dressed in a tight, black A-line skirt and ruffled blouse jumped out. She was slender and didn't reach my shoulder in height.

"Melanie!" she called with a hint of frustration in her voice. "Stealing? What's going on?"

"Mum, I wasn't stealing." She glanced at me, and I knew she wished I would just vanish into thin air.

"Then why did I get a call saying a girl stopped you from taking a birthday present from her bag?"

James's gaze flashed to me before he glared at Melanie. "You tried to take the present I gave Cadence, didn't you?"

I started backing away.

"You're such an idiot sometimes!" Melanie yelled at him.

Their mum gasped. "Melanie!"

They seemed unaware of me creeping away as they squabbled between themselves. I'd almost made it back inside the door to the main building when James said, "Cadence! Where are you going?"

I flinched as they fell silent, staring at me.

"That's Cadence?" their mum asked. "Well, James, introduce me."

James motioned for me to come over. I took a step forward as Melanie glowered at me.

"Ah, I'm going to miss my bus," I said.

James shot Melanie an icy stare. "You have a few minutes."

"We can take you home." His mum had a gentle smile as she gazed steadily at me.

"No, it's okay. I don't want to inconvenience you," I said.

Melanie scoffed. "Let's just go."

Her mum ignored her and walked toward me with her hand outstretched. "I'm James and Melanie's mum, but you can call me Karen."

I took her hand. "Hi."

She held on to my hand firmly and pulled me toward their car. "James has told me a lot about you. I've been eager to meet you."

"Oh?"

James ran his hand over my ponytail. I looked up at him and he smiled warmly.

"Yes," she said. "Anyone who could get him to cut off that horrible hair is a winner in my book."

I couldn't help giggling.

James laughed and rested his hand on my waist. "Yeah, well, I liked it."

"You look much better now." She tapped his cheek fondly.

He looked down at me. "I think so, too."

My cheeks warmed.

Karen chuckled. "For someone who told him what-for so often, you're very quiet."

"Oh, ah . . . sorry." I had no idea what to say. How could I respond to something like that?

"She's just nervous." James wrapped his arm around my shoulders.

Her gaze darted to his hand resting on my shoulder and a smile curled the corners of her mouth. "Well then, all the more reason for us to take you home. You should feel comfortable with us."

"No!" Melanie moaned.

James shrugged. "She's probably missed her bus by now."

"There we go. It's settled. We'll take you home."

"Mum!" Melanie whined.

Karen turned to her. "Melanie Gordon, you're in enough trouble as it is. Now get in the car."

James guided me to the back door and opened it for me as Melanie climbed into the front and sat pouting. I shuffled in behind her and she pushed the seat all the way back. I gasped and pulled in my legs. As James climbed in the other side, he reached across and smacked her in the back of the head. "Mel!"

"I needed more room!"

"No, you didn't!"

She shoved her backpack in front of her feet and folded her arms.

Karen climbed into the driver's seat and scowled. "Melanie . . ."

Melanie huffed and pulled the chair forward.

On the ride home, Karen talked endlessly. She asked about my schoolwork, my hobbies, my family . . . . I thought it would never end and struggled to interject directions into the conversation.

James's hand drifted down and caught mine. I smiled as Karen talked about something or another. Looking at him, my heart fluttered as he grinned at me and leaned closer. He grasped my chin and pulled me closer. "She likes you."

He kissed my cheek.

I squeezed his hand. When I glanced up, I saw her in the rearview mirror smiling at us. I blushed.

As we turned onto my street, my stomach did a somersault. I hoped more than anything Dad hadn't come home early to celebrate my birthday.

Mum lifted groceries out of the back of her car as we pulled up. She paused, surprised by the unfamiliar vehicle parking in front of the house. Before I had a chance to get out, Karen leapt out and waved. "Hi! You must be Cadence's mum."

Melanie slapped her forehead as James and I hurried to climb out of the car.

Mum looked startled by the strange woman approaching her and glanced at me rushing up behind her. "Yes, I'm Harmony Anderson."

Karen stretched out a hand. "It's nice to meet you."

Mum took it, her gaze darting to me. "You too."

I hurried over and stood beside Mum. "This is James's mum."

Mum flashed me a confused look. James stepped up behind me.

"Oh! James!" A smile spread across her face as she looked back to Karen. "So what brings you here?"

"Cadence missed her bus, so I told her we could bring her home."

Mum gave me an odd look. "Again?"

"Ah . . ." It looked suspicious, I had to admit. "I got caught up."

Mum's gaze lifted to James. "With what, exactly?"

Karen smiled. "With me. I was interested to meet her, since James is forever talking about her."

James's arm wrapped around my waist just as Mum looked back to me. Her gaze fell to his arm, then flashed back up to meet my eyes. "Oh, good heavens. Your father isn't going to be impressed."

"Mum," I muttered, embarrassed that she would say something like that in front of James's mum.

She sighed and turned back to Karen. "Thank you for bringing her home."

"You're very welcome," Karen said. "She's a lovely girl. You've done a wonderful job with her."

Mum smiled at me. "Yes, we're very proud of her."

"Thanks, Mum." My gaze fell to the ground.

"Mum!" Melanie groaned from the car.

"Well, I'd love to stay and chat, but I have a daughter to ground." Karen flicked her short hair back out of her face. "It was nice to meet you."

"You too." Mum took Karen's hand again.

"Mum, can I stay?"

We all turned to face James. I subtly shook my head, but he just grinned at me.

"Well, honey," Karen began. "I don't think I'm the person to ask."

James's gaze shifted to Mum. "Mrs. Anderson, would you mind if I stayed? I'd like to help celebrate her birthday."

I turned to get a read on Mum. She looked agitated, her eyes fixed on James. "Ah, we were going to go out for dinner—"

"That's all right. I can cover myself."

Mum's eyebrow twitched. I knew if Karen wasn't standing right beside her she would snap at him and send him away. But she was not one to be rude. "Cadence, what do you want?"

Great, she dumped it all on me. I turned back to James. His gray-blue eyes gazed steadily into mine. I just about melted.

His hand came up and touched my cheek. "What do you want?"

I took a deep breath to compose myself. I caught his hand and pulled it away. "You can't do that when my dad gets here."

A wide grin spread across his face.

"Does that mean he stays, dear?" Mum asked.

"It does."

She sighed. "Okay, help me with these groceries, then."

James rushed over and grabbed several bags, then headed to the front door. Mum watched him, her eyes wide with shock, and Karen chuckled.

"Yes, he's been full of surprises lately." She reached across and squeezed my hand. "It was nice to finally meet you, Cadence. Please feel free to come by our place sometime. I'd really like him to do things like that for me more often."

She nodded toward James as he waited for the door to be unlocked.

I smiled at her. "Okay. Thank you for the ride."

"No, Cadence, thank *you*." She waved to James as she walked back to the car, then drove off.

Mum's arm rested around my waist. "He's the boy the fight was about, right?"

I nodded.

"Great. Your father's going to be a nightmare." She pulled me around to the groceries. "So, he's your boyfriend now?"

"Yeah. He's persistent, Mum. He's completely changed from what he was before."

She grabbed a couple of bags and pulled them into the crooks of her elbows. "How so?"

"At the beginning of the year, he smoked, drank, and acted like a total rat bag, but now he's going to classes and cleaned up his act."

She straightened. "That explains his mother's thank you."

My cheeks warmed. "Yeah, I told him I'd never date him how he was, but now . . ." I trailed off as we turned toward the house and looked at him. "Mum, he's actually pretty nice underneath all those bad choices."

We walked toward the door while she dug for her keys in her pocket. "Okay, Cadence. I can see you've thought this through, so I trust you."

We approached James and fell silent as she unlocked the door. James held the door open as we slipped inside and set the groceries down in the kitchen.

"Thank you," Mum said.

"Do you need help putting everything away?" James asked.

Mum chuckled. "No, thank you. Stop trying so hard to impress me. Save it for her father." She rested her hands on her hips and looked him over. "So, James, do you intend on wearing your uniform out to dinner?"

He looked down at himself and brushed some dirt off his sweaty shirt. "I guess so."

"No. I doubt Dusty would have anything big enough to fit you, but my husband might have something small enough. Just give me a minute."

She hurried down the hallway into her bedroom.

James turned to me and grinned. "So, where's your room?"

I scowled. "No."

"What?" He laughed.

"Just no."

He grabbed me by the waist and lifted me over his shoulder.

I screeched and slapped his shoulder. "James! I'm wearing a skirt!"

He ran his hand up the back of my thigh. "I know."

I kicked and he rolled me off his shoulder. He caught me as I almost landed face first on the floor and pulled me up to face him.

"You idiot!"

He grinned and kissed me. I tried to push him off, but I couldn't. I was too enraptured by his kiss.

"Oh gross!"

James pulled away, and we looked across to see Dusty entering the house. He walked up to me and shoved my shoulder. "You left me to walk home alone."

"I'm sorry."

"Yeah, you better be." He turned to walk toward his room.

"Why didn't you walk with Harper?" James asked him.

Dusty let out a sarcastic laugh and looked at me. "Cadence, do you like dumb guys or something?"

I rushed at him. He darted down the hallway to his room.

The front door banged and Harper came at me, her eyes on fire. "Are you kidding me? What's *he* doing here?"

"Hey, Harper," James said.

She raised her hand and covered his mouth. "Shut up. I'm talking to my sister."

Her glare burned into me, waiting for me to answer. I shrugged. "He's coming with us."

She stepped back and folded her arms. "Dad's going to lose his mind." A smirk spread across her face. "This is going to be the best family thing yet."

Mum appeared beside her and handed James some clothes. "Leave him alone, Harper. I hope these are okay,

James. They might be a bit old-fashioned. I'm fairly certain they're from the seventies."

James opened the gray trousers and cream-colored shirt to look at them. "I think I can work with them."

Harper scoffed. "Yeah, he's definitely worn worse."

"That's true." James looked down at me. "Show me to your room so I can change."

Mum grabbed his arm. "Ah, no. You can use the bathroom."

Dusty sprinted through the house with an armful of clothes. "No! I'm using the shower first!"

He slammed the bathroom door behind him and started the shower.

"I guess you'll have to wait," Mum said. "Go watch TV or something for a while."

James glanced down the hallway, obviously wanting to see my room.

"No boys in the bedrooms," Mum said as she turned to put away the groceries.

James slumped, but let me guide him to the living room.

He sank onto the sectional and pulled my hand so I'd sit beside him. I sat stiffly, feeling weird for having him there. I remembered visiting my parents with Austin when we were engaged and making out on the sectional, but I shook off the memory. That was still in the future. I needed to focus on the now.

James ran his fingers through my ponytail. "Why so tense?"

I forced myself to lean back into the couch. "You're the first guy I've had here."

He reached across and pulled my legs over his lap. His arm wrapped around my waist and he pulled me against him. "I've never gone to a girl's house before. Not like this, anyway."

"What? With your hand creeping up her skirt?"

He pulled his hand back. "No, I mean as a boyfriend."

"Have you ever had a girlfriend before?"

He shrugged. "Not technically."

I raised my eyebrows. "What does that mean?"

He stroked my cheek. "Have you had a boyfriend before?"

"Yes, one, but that's not what we're talking about."

"Who?"

"Tyler Hansen."

He laughed. "That guy's an idiot. You seriously went out with him?"

I slapped his shoulder. "Shut up."

"He looks like he could be your brother."

I grunted. "That's what Geri said."

I tried to pull away, but he held me tightly and kissed my cheek. "Cadence, stay here with me."

"Then tell me what 'not technically' is supposed to mean."

He sighed. "I don't wanna talk about my indiscretions. I just wanna focus on you."

I looked in his eyes. "Indiscretions? Geez, James! If you wanna date me, you need to come clean."

His gaze fell onto my lips. "I don't want you to dump me."

"Really?" I shifted up onto my knees beside him. "When you first started hitting on me, you stunk from smoking pot, and at the disco, I'm fairly certain you were tipsy. But that was before. What's important is what you do now."

"Wow, you *are* amazing." He turned to face me directly and lowered his voice. "I'm not a virgin."

I sighed. "I kinda figured that."

"It wasn't the best decision I've ever made, and was more of an 'everyone telling me to do it' thing rather than me being into the girl."

"Who was it?" I let slip.

He rubbed his neck. "Carla."

"Oh gross."

He groaned. "Shut up. It was Robbie's idea."

"I thought she was his girlfriend."

"Eh . . ." He waved his hand. "Kinda sorta, but nothing serious. She'll put out for anyone, and he's happy to take advantage of that."

"That's sick."

James shrugged. "What can you do? To each their own, I guess."

I slumped back onto the couch and folded my arms. I wasn't sure how I felt about him telling me that. My gaze fell to his lap before I caught myself and looked back up to his face.

His eyebrows furrowed as he watched me with concern. "Cadence, it meant nothing."

I gnawed on my lip as tears burned in my eyes. *Why did it hurt so much?* I knew what he was like before, so why did it feel like he'd ripped my heart out of my chest?

"Cadence." He shifted closer and caressed my face. "Don't cry, please."

"Why are you still friends with them? I don't want you to go near her."

He fought to hold back a smile. "You're jealous."

"No."

"Yes."

"No."

He pulled my face in and kissed me.

I grabbed his shirt and pulled him closer, desperately wanting to claim possession over him. Breaking away, I looked into his eyes. "Okay, maybe I am."

He grinned and leaned in. He lifted me onto his lap and stroked my face as our kiss deepened, giving me butterflies.

The front door slammed. I pulled away from James to see Dad standing, stiff and red, glaring at us.

I jumped to my feet and rushed over, grabbing his clenched hand.

"Dad . . ."

But he didn't look away from James. James sat frozen. Dad's clenched fist tightened under my hand.

"Dad."

"Is that the boy who turned you into a punching bag?"

"Dad, he didn't do that."

"But he's the reason those girls attacked you."

"It wasn't his fault."

His arm wrapped around my waist. "Why's he here?"

"He's . . . he's coming with us."

Dad's gaze finally pulled away from James and fell on me. "What?"

"He's . . ." I sighed. He would find out eventually. "He's my boyfriend."

A crazed rage flashed into his eyes. He released me and charged toward James. I darted across and jumped between them before Dad could grab him. "Dad, don't!"

"I'm gonna rip him apart!"

"Dad, stop it! Please!"

"He was all over you in *my* house! He's *never* going to touch you again!"

"Dad!"

Mum rushed into the room and grabbed Dad's arm. "David! Stop it right now!"

"He had his hands all over Cadence! I'm not going to stand for it!"

Tears burst from my eyes. *Stupid hormones.* Being a teenager again really sucked.

Mum pointed at me. "Look at her!"

Dad glanced at me. "Those tears are *his* fault!"

"No, David, they're your fault! You need to control your temper. Can't you see she really likes him? Why can't you just trust that she can handle herself and knows her boundaries?"

Dad grabbed me and pulled me under his arm. "I trust her, I just don't trust *him.*"

"Oh, for heaven's sake!" She gestured for James to stand up beside her. "He's going to be in our life for a while, David, and I know for a fact that she's made it very hard for him to catch her. He's not going to do anything to ruin his efforts."

James stared at her, gaping. She pushed his mouth closed.

Dad's arm wrapped around me again. "She's only fifteen!"

"Yes, David, she's fifteen, not five."

His arm tightened and he looked down into my face. He looked into my eyes and his expression softened. He gently wiped my tears away. "Cadence, do you really want this? Do you really want him around?"

I nodded.

He groaned and glared at James. "You! If I so much as see you *think* about touching her in a way I don't like, I'm going to cut off your hands!"

James nodded. "Yes, sir."

Dad grumbled something under his breath before walking me toward my room. "Cadence, if he tries anything, you tell me right away."

"Okay, Dad."

He kissed my forehead and lifted my bag off the floor in the hallway as we passed. "I wish you could stay a little girl forever."

I giggled. "I'll always be your little girl, even when I'm thirty!"

He grinned and we entered my room. He set my bag on the chair by my desk. "I love you, Cadence. You know that's why I can't stand boys around you."

I sighed. "Yeah, Dad."

The first time around, I probably would have lost it with him for humiliating me like that, but I knew better. He did love me, and I knew it wasn't about embarrassing me.

He kissed my head. "Get ready to go while I interrogate him."

"Be nice, Dad."

He shrugged as he walked out the door. "Don't worry. Your mother won't let me be too cruel."

I shut the door behind him and rushed to pull out the scrapbook. I opened to the photos of my wedding day to see the way Dad had looked at me. I found one of the daddy-daughter dance, and stared at his face. His brown eyes reflected such a deep love that goose bumps rippled over my body.

I scanned through some more and found one of him hugging me goodbye as Austin and I left for our honeymoon. A tear ran down his cheek as he clung to me. He was happy I'd found Austin, whom he loved, but a hint of sadness showed on his face too. His little girl had grown up.

I flicked to the next picture. Austin held me close, gazing into my eyes. There was so much love between us. I closed my eyes and took a deep breath, having flashes of when I'd first met him.

I had just finished my first year of university. My friend, Tara, invited me to a Christmas party before I headed back across the country for Harper's wedding. He had been there—Tara was one of his high school friends. I'd noticed him right away. He was handsome, with his thick dark hair and wide smile.

"Who's that?" I asked Tara.

She turned to me, surprised. "That's Austin Jones. Why?"

"Is he single?"

She laughed. "I believe so, yes."

I met her gaze. "Is he straight?"

She laughed harder. "Yes."

I looked him over again, liking his solid, strong body.

"Do you want me to introduce you?" she asked.

I ran my fingers through my hair. "He wouldn't wanna talk to me. If we meet, then we meet. I won't force it."

She shrugged. "Suit yourself."

I'd watched him all night, but he never once noticed me. It wasn't until we returned to university that I saw him again. I'd gone out with Tara to a club for her birthday, and he was there. But that time, I was determined to catch his attention. I felt confident and cute, so I danced and whispered to my friend Lyla that I was interested. Finally, it got back to him. His head shot up, and he looked me over.

I pretended not to notice him as I danced with as much sex appeal as possible. I felt his eyes on me, and as one song mixed into another, I turned to face him. Our gazes met and he smiled. He liked what he saw. I smiled back.

He stood up and pushed through the crowd toward me. I turned and grinned to myself as he came up behind me and rested his hands on my hips. "Hey."

I looked at him over my shoulder. "Hi."

"Can I dance with you?"

I nodded.

We were attached the whole night. He even drove me home, and we made out in his car. The next day, Saturday, I woke to a knock on my flat's door. I answered it and found him smiling sheepishly at me.

"I hope I'm not being presumptuous, but I just couldn't stop thinking about you."

I giggled. "Really?"

"Yeah. You're just so beautiful. I really wanna get to know you better."

I bit my lip and pulled my robe tighter around me. His gaze fell onto my lips as I released the bite. I smiled at his obvious attraction. "Do you wanna take me out?"

His gaze met mine. "That's why I'm here."

I stepped back to let him in. "Watch some TV or something while I get ready . . ."

Someone knocked on my door, and I snapped the scrapbook shut. "Yes?"

"Shower's free," Harper said. "Unless you wanna share it with your *boyfriend*, then you'll need to wait until he's finished getting grilled."

I rolled my eyes. "Thanks, Harper."

"You're welcome, brat-face."

Chapter Eleven

James used his charms shamelessly. He sat beside me as we ate and probably contributed to the conversation more than I did. Dusty loved him and watched him in complete awe. Harper pretended to be disinterested, but fought back a smile when he cracked jokes. Mum was the chattiest with him, and I could see she liked him, too. Even Dad seemed to soften toward him.

As the night progressed, his hand came from holding mine hidden under the table, to being rested around the back of my chair. I watched Dad carefully while he watched James. He wanted to hate James, but he just couldn't. James was too friendly and gentle with me.

When the cake came out and everyone sang "Happy Birthday," James was bold enough to kiss my cheek. I blushed and looked into his eyes as he smiled down at me. As I turned away, I saw Dad pursing his lips with wide eyes, but he didn't say anything.

We drove James home, and as we pulled into the driveway, his home surprised me. It sat on the end of a cul-de-sac with tall bushes out front to block the windows, and a short stairway leading to a small patio by the front door, located just beside the garage. It looked like a nice house. I'd expected something rundown, considering the way both he and Melanie dressed.

James thanked my parents for letting him come along, and as he opened the door and wished me a happy birthday, a man appeared beside him.

James jumped. "Geez, Dad, you startled me."

His dad bent over to look into the car. He saw me, then turned to Mum in the passenger seat. "I'm John Gordon."

A large man, similar in size to Dad, he had the same chestnut brown hair as James. James looked remarkably similar to him, except his dad's eyes were hazel.

"It's nice to meet you," Mum answered, offering him her hand. "I met your wife earlier."

John smiled. "Yes, she told me. I was surprised to find my son wasn't home, when he's grounded."

James grabbed his hair and grunted.

Harper laughed. "Good job, loser."

Dad leaned across. "Grounded? For what?"

"Dad, don't." James grabbed his elbow.

"There was some fight at the school he was involved in a few weeks ago. I believe your daughter was at the receiving end."

My head fell into my hands. *Here we go . . .*

Dad leaned closer. "So he *was* involved?"

John nodded. "They were some of his girlfriends. They weren't too impressed with a newcomer."

"Gah!" James punched his dad's shoulder. "Dad, stop it!"

"Girlfriends?" Dad turned to look at me with alarm. "As in *plural?*"

John sighed. "Yes."

"No, Dad! None of them have ever been my girlfriend!"

Dad clutched the steering wheel as he glared across at James. Harper chuckled beside me, while Dusty kept whispering, "Dad's about to lose it!"

I had to do something or the whole situation would explode. I unbuckled and jumped out of the car.

"Cadence!" Dad said.

I ignored him and grabbed James's hand. "Mr. Gordon?"

He turned and looked me over with narrow eyes. "Can I help you?"

"Please don't provoke my father."

Harper burst into fits of laughter. Dad's anger seemed to fizzle, and he shrank back.

John rested his hands on his hips and stared at my hand around James's. "I think you should go home now, sweetheart."

The front door banged and Karen came charging out to us. She bent over at the car window and smiled. "Hello again, Harmony."

"Uh, hi." Mum smiled hesitantly.

Karen straightened and looked her husband dead in the eyes. "John Martin Gordon, what do you think you're doing?"

"I'm trying to keep our son on track. He's just barely cleaned up his act, and I don't want some floozy screwing it all up."

"*Floozy?*" Dad lost it and jumped out of the car. *Shoot! That's not good.*

Mum shot out and intercepted him. "David!"

"He called Cadence a floozy! No one calls *my* daughter things like that!"

John faced Dad with a smirk. "Don't like it when someone points it out to ya, huh?"

Dad roared and tried to push by Mum.

"John!" Karen snarled. "This is embarrassing!"

It fell silent . . . other than Harper's laughter from inside the car. Finally, James cleared his throat. "Dad, Cadence is the reason I cleaned up my act. I thought you knew that."

Everyone faced him.

"James," John said with a scowl. "Melanie told me what she's like, and I don't—"

"Melanie doesn't like Cadence because *I* like Cadence. She's not the best source of information for this."

"John," Karen said gently. "Cadence is a good girl. She keeps James on track."

John glared at me, then turned to Dad. "Are you okay with this? My son has used drugs and gotten drunk at parties. Surely, since she's a 'good girl,' you wouldn't want her around *him*."

Dad's chest rose as his glare burned into James. He surprised me when he said, "He knows I'll kill him if he does those things around my daughter."

I couldn't help grinning.

He saw it and nodded to me. "I trust my daughter."

Harper's laughter stopped abruptly.

John stared at me. "Well then, Cadence, since your family has been able to spend time with James, I expect to see you here over the holidays so we can get to know you. Does that sound fair?"

I took a deep breath. "It does."

He folded his arms as he looked me over again, then turned to Dad. "I'm sorry to insult you, but I can tell that you know how it is. My son has proven to be more of an idiot than a saint over the last year or so, so I had to be sure."

Dad's jaw fell, stunned. *I* was stunned. What a complete one-eighty. Dad scratched his head, perplexed. "Yeah, sure."

Karen pushed John toward the house. "Say goodbye, James. It's time to come inside."

Mum and Dad slipped back into the car as James turned to me. "Well, you can't say your birthday was boring."

I smiled. "Nope."

He stared at his feet. "Sorry about my dad. He's overly strict. It drives me crazy."

"I know how that is."

He gazed into my eyes, smiling. "Yeah, you do. Maybe there's hope for me after all."

"What I've learned is that they do it because they love us, so I've learned not to fight against it."

He raised his eyebrows. "Huh. I'll have to try that sometime."

"Maybe he'll loosen up."

"Maybe."

He touched my face and leaned in for a kiss, but Dad cleared his throat loudly. James paused, and planted the kiss on my cheek. "I'll see ya tomorrow, beautiful."

He stepped back and waved to the car. "Thanks for having me. I'll wash the clothes and get 'em back to Cadence as soon as I can."

Mum smiled and nodded. "Thank you. It was nice to meet you, James."

He looked at me one more time, then lunged forward and smacked a quick kiss on my lips before darting toward the house.

Dad grumbled under his breath as I climbed back in, but I didn't care. I stared out the window the whole way home, lost in my daydreams.

I grinned as the bus pulled up and I saw James waiting for me. My friends chatted excitedly before Amy said, "Are you an item yet? Seriously, how long are you going to string him along?"

I giggled and jumped into the aisle. The three of them gasped in unison.

"No!"

"When?" Elise asked.

"Yesterday." I shrugged.

"Is that why you missed the bus?"

"Kinda, yeah." I shuffled forward as the line started to move.

"Cadence, you are seriously the hardest person to gossip with."

I laughed.

He saw me moving through the bus and stood waiting for me as I stepped out the door. "Hey, beautiful."

I couldn't help giggling as he took my hand. Seriously, the giggling thing when I was nervous needed to stop.

He pulled me under his arm as we walked through the school to my friends. Everyone stared at us as we passed by, and when I glanced up at James, he looked mighty proud of himself. As we turned the corner and my group came into view, Geri's head popped up by the table. She came screeching over and threw her arms around me; I would have hit the ground if James hadn't caught me.

"Cay-Cay! I'm so excited! You and James are *finally* together after months of you dodging your feelings for him." She shook her head. "My little girl is all grown up."

I laughed. "You're ridiculous."

James lifted my bag off my back and set it on the table, then went around greeting my friends. I watched, amazed that he seemed to know all of them. He really *had* worked hard to catch me.

He returned to my side, wrapping his arm around my waist as I talked with Geri and Michael.

The group fell silent.

I looked across to see Robbie and five other boys approaching us. I pressed against James, remembering my last encounter with Robbie.

He shoved Michael aside and grinned at James. "Hey, mate. So you finally got your girl."

"Yeah, it's pretty sweet, huh?" James reached out and they shook hands.

"So, will we be seein' ya get back to your old self soon?"

"Nah, mate, her dad would kill me."

Robbie's gaze flashed to me. "Daddy's girl, huh?"

"Yeah, big time." James laughed.

I elbowed him in the ribs.

He looked down at me. "What? You are, and you know it."

"Why are you being such an ass?"

His friends "*ooed*" mockingly at me. He glanced around at them, agitated. "Cadence, stop being a—"

"You better watch what you say!"

His friends scoffed, and Robbie said, "Bit of a ball crusher, ay Jimmy?"

James glanced at Robbie and rubbed the back of his neck. He grabbed me and pulled me in. "Cadence, please don't embarrass me in front of them."

I gasped and pushed him off. "Seriously?"

"Cadence—"

"James, just don't." I marched away from him as his friends cackled.

Geri was right at my side as we hurried away. A moment later, James rushed in front of me. "Cadence, they're my friends!"

"They're not very good friends if they make you turn into what I just saw."

He swore.

"Hey!"

"Cadence, come on! I've made friends with all of your friends. You could at least give them a chance."

Geri sneered. "Your friends are jerks, James, and you turn into one around them. Cadence is the same no matter what."

He growled in frustration. "You are so high maintenance!"

I stopped dead in my tracks and folded my arms. "Really? So that's it, huh? Months of chasing me and you're done after a day?"

His eyes widened as fear spread across his face. "No! Cadence, don't do that."

"Okay, James, how about this? Show me you can be the same no matter what, and I'll try to get to know your friends."

He took a deep breath. "Okay, I can handle that."

The bell rang.

James glanced around, then grabbed my arms. "Don't dump me."

"I'm not."

He sighed, relieved. "Good. Let me get your bag for you."

He dashed away as Geri and I watched him. "You're seriously going to give those jerks a chance?" she asked.

"Yeah, I guess."

She turned me to face her. She looked worried. "They're not good people, Cadence. If your dad finds out you're hanging with them, he's gonna flip."

"What am I supposed to do? If I just keep it to when we're at school, I should be safe."

James approached and helped slip my bag on my shoulder. He smiled at me and gave me a kiss. "I'll see ya later."

"Bye."

Geri and I watched him head around the corner to his class, then started walking to our own.

"It makes me nervous," she said. "Those guys are bad news."

"Hmm." I rubbed my arm, knowing exactly what they would turn into. "But James turned out okay," I said, trying to convince myself I'd be fine.

"Yeah, well, he better protect you, 'cause if I find out he pressured you into doing drugs because of his stupid friends, I'm gonna kick his butt."

I smiled warmly at her and wrapped my arm through hers. "You're the best."

Chapter Twelve

I sat on my bed cross-legged, catching up on my journals. I'd fallen three weeks behind, so I flicked through as fast as I could. Brian breakup . . . he cried . . . my birthday . . . Harper ran away . . . *wait!* I backtracked. I read slower over the page where I talked about Harper running away, and realized it should have been two days earlier.

I leapt up as she yelled at Dusty about something or other and rushed to the door. She jumped as my door flew open and snapped at me. "Cadence, you and Dusty are serious pains in my butt! Why can't you both just—"

I lunged at her and wrapped my arms around her. She flinched, but touched my hair just before she pushed me off. "What are you doing, you freak?"

"I love you, Harper."

She rolled her eyes. "You're so weird. Did you and your pathetic boyfriend have a sappy conversation on the phone, and now you feel the need to spread your disgusting sap all over me?"

"No."

She folded her arms and scowled. "Whatever. Just get out of my face."

She spun on her heel and slammed her bedroom door behind her.

I returned to my room and sat on my bed, staring at the journal entry. What was different? I tried to think back to everything that had happened this time around and scanned back through the journal entries. I couldn't figure it out.

Mum called us for dinner and we made our way to the table. As we sat and ate, I watched Harper. Then, I noticed it. Dad leaned closer to her and said something about her earrings looking pretty, just like her. She smiled at him and touched her left earring. She and Dad were getting along.

As I stared, a smile crept across my face. Somehow, somewhere along the way, my choices had made a difference in their relationship. She'd never been able to see eye to eye with Dad, even as an adult, but somehow, it had changed.

That night, when Mum came in to say good night to me, I asked her when things had changed between Dad and Harper. She shut the door and sat beside me on my bed.

"Ironically, it was that fight," she said. "She did something selfless in protecting you, and he respected that. He could see that she isn't just a surly teenager. There's some of the little Harper he always loved still inside. Harper made some bad choices that broke his heart, but seeing her stand up for you made them all go away. His two little girls, standing side by side."

I smiled and flicked at a crease in my sheet. "He really loves us, doesn't he?"

"More than you know." She leaned forward and kissed my head. "Good night, sweetheart."

The last day of school arrived, and hardly anyone showed up. It surprised me when James did, since most of his grade stopped coming after their School Certificate exams.

"I had to bring you your Christmas present," he told me with a grin. "And I needed to give you the chance to give me mine."

I laughed. "How presumptuous."

He handed me a small box with a set of diamond stud earrings. By the jewelry store emblem on the case, they had to be expensive. "James! This is too much."

"No, it's not." He wrapped his arm around me and kissed me.

"My present seems so stupid after this."

He grinned. "I doubt it."

"To be honest, I wasn't sure what to get you, so . . ." I pulled out his present. He hurried to unwrap it. "It's just a wallet. I noticed yours looked worn out."

He faced me with a wide grin across his face. "It's perfect."

I smiled and leaned against his shoulder. "James?"

"Yeah?"

"I'm gonna miss seeing you every day."

He ran his fingers through my ponytail. "Me too. So we'll need to see each other as much as possible over the holidays. Next week is Christmas, so I don't think we'll be able to do anything then, but how about New Year's?"

"I'd like that."

"Good, 'cause I wanna kiss you into the New Year."

Christmas, like always, just flew by. When James came to get me for New Year's, he sat in the driver's seat with his mum beside him, which surprised me. He jumped out and rushed to the door to meet me.

"Got my learner's," he said as he flashed his permit in front of me.

"Nice."

"Once I'm driving, you and me are gonna have a lot of fun."

Dad stepped up behind me and scowled.

"As in driving places," James hurried to say. "And *never* in the back seat."

"That's better," Dad said as he walked away.

James took my hand and we rushed to the car.

"Hi, Cadence," Karen said in a chipper voice. "It's nice to see you again."

"You too."

She turned her focus onto James as he concentrated on putting the car into gear. I tried not to smirk as he ground the gears and stalled twice before we took off.

"I can see you in the mirror," he said.

I giggled.

"Yeah, just wait 'til you start driving."

Finally, we arrived—alive—at his place. I stepped out of the car and looked up at the house again, while James and Karen filled out his logbook. I liked the look of their home. It felt comfortable and welcoming in the quiet neighborhood, until Melanie stepped out.

She stood on the porch with her arms folded, glaring down at me. I took a deep breath and walked toward her. I needed to try to get along with her and away from school, where no one wanted to judge her, seemed like the perfect place to start.

She watched me with narrowed eyes as I walked up and stood in front of her. "Hey, Melanie."

She rolled her eyes.

"Hey, could we at least try? For James?"

"I hope he dumps you."

"Melanie, please, I'm trying."

"Oh yes, of course you are. Little Miss Perfect with your Barbie doll hair, perfect clothes, and winner's attitude," she responded sarcastically.

I looked down at my trendy denim capris, flip-flops, and purple striped polo, compared to her baggy gray T-shirt and bright red boys' basketball shorts. She had tied her hair in a ratty ponytail, while mine hung loose, freshly highlighted and straightened. I touched my hair self-consciously. "Melanie, I—"

"Shut up. I don't wanna talk to you."

James rushed up behind me and wrapped his arm around my waist. "Mel, you're a brat."

He tugged on my waist to pull me around her.

Inside, we stepped into a bright living room with pale green walls and a dark green feature wall behind the couch and two armchairs. Through an archway to my left lay a dining room, and behind that, an entry to the kitchen. Straight ahead, an archway led to a family room that had a glass sliding door leading out the back, and stretching to the right, a hallway led to the bedrooms.

I smiled at how cozy it felt as James led me through to the family room. His dad sat at a desk using the computer. He glanced up at me with raised eyebrows as I entered. "Hello, Cadence."

"Hello, Mr. Gordon." I offered him my hand.

He looked at it with a raised eyebrow. Karen tapped his shoulder. "Be nice."

He took my hand. "Call me John. Mr. Gordon is a bit stuffy, don't you think?"

I smiled as a grin spread across his face. "Okay."

Melanie retreated to her room as I sat and talked with James and his parents. I liked them both right away, and we even played a few rounds of cards. After beating them all three times in a row, John nudged James. "Looks like you've finally got a winner here, boy."

I flushed as James grinned at me. He stroked my hair and shifted closer.

"Oh, look at the time!" Karen said. "It's time for you both to go."

Confused, I responded, "I thought we were spending New Year's here."

"That would be nice." She stood. "But one of James's friends is having a party. Didn't he tell you?"

I glanced at James. He shrugged. "I guess I must have neglected to mention it."

I tried not to feel sick, but forced a smile, knowing I needed to at least try with his friends. "Yeah, it would've been nice to know."

"Well, you look perfect, so it doesn't matter." He stood and squeezed my shoulder. "Come on, let's go."

"Can I use the bathroom first?"

He nodded and pointed down the hallway. "The first door on the left. Don't mistake it for the right, 'cause I don't want you to see my trashed room."

I smiled at him and hurried away. I shut the bathroom door behind me and took a deep breath. I was terrified. James's friends were rude enough at school, but to spend the evening with them, where they'd likely be drinking and smoking and, worst of all, doing drugs and having sex . . . I rushed over to the sink and tried to hold in the contents of my stomach.

Dad would kill me if he found out. But James would be devastated if I didn't at least *try*. I shut my eyes and concentrated on my breathing. I'd never been in a situation like this before. But the muffled sound of James's voice made my heart skip a beat. He would look out for me. He would keep me safe.

I reached across and flushed the toilet to hide that I'd just been standing there, then washed my hands and dabbed water on my face so I wouldn't mess up my mascara. I stepped out and found myself face to face with James as he shut his bedroom door behind him.

"You ready?"

I nodded, and he took my hand.

He drove again, which didn't help with the sick, nervous feeling in my stomach. When we arrived, the house looked perfectly normal and quiet. I waited for James to fill out his logbook and come around to get me.

He rested his arm around my shoulders as we walked to the door. "I can tell you're freaking out, but it'll be okay, I promise. I'll stay with you the whole time."

I forced a smile. He kissed my head.

He knocked, and one of his scruffy, cigarette-stench ridden friends answered. "Jimmy! Dude, you're late! Come on, we're all out the back."

As we walked through the house, I scanned for adults, hoping they would keep the illegal activities to a minimum, but there weren't any. I pressed against James. "Where are the parents?"

He shrugged. "Not here."

"I don't know about this."

"Cadence, you'll be fine." He smiled down at me.

I whimpered, but didn't protest. I knew better. Every instinct screamed at me to run, but with his arm around me, I just couldn't.

We stepped onto the back porch, and his guy friends hollered to him as they raised their beers. I hesitated, but he coaxed me forward.

The girls glared at me as I sat beside James. Becca's stare bored into me; I just knew she wanted to attack me again and rip my eyes out.

I clung to James's hand and shuffled closer to him. He lifted my hand and kissed it, giving me a reassuring smile.

The first hour or so wasn't bad. I kept quiet as the boys made crude jokes and the girls gossiped quietly together. Occasionally, they'd throw me an icy glance, but I tried to ignore them and focus on James.

The darker it became, the more drunk they grew. To my relief, James only sipped at one bottle so he could keep his wits about him. I didn't want him drunk and leaving me exposed to anything. I carefully drank from unopened bottles of water. I didn't want to risk someone taking advantage of me.

Just after ten, Robbie walked over to Carla, whispered in her ear, and they disappeared inside. I felt sick. I pulled my chair right against James's and leaned against his shoulder. He wrapped his arm around me and stroked my hair. "Hey, it's okay."

"I don't wanna be here anymore."

"Nothing's happened. You're fine."

I looked up into his eyes and saw him pleading with me. I nodded toward the pool. "Maybe I just need a break to recompose myself."

He nodded and stood.

We walked over, and he leaned against the fence, pulling me into his arms. I rested against his chest and sighed. I felt safe there, and loved the sensation of his fingers running up my back.

"How was your Christmas?" he asked conversationally.

"Good. Harper actually smiled a couple of times."

"Wow, there are such things as Christmas miracles." I giggled.

"Hey, James." I jumped and turned to see the group of girls approaching. I clung tighter to him, hoping they wouldn't try to attack me again as Becca's glare burned into me.

"Hey, Cadence," she said as they stopped in front of us. "I think we started off on the wrong foot. I'm Becca." She stretched out her hand.

My hand trembled as I took hers. "Hi."

"I thought you were trying to pull something on James before. After months of him chasing you, you can understand how I came to that."

"Oh."

Several boys approached and one wrapped his arm around Becca's neck. "Cadence, right?"

I nodded.

"You're very quiet."

"I, ah . . ." I clung to James.

"She's a little nervous, guys," James said.

"Aw, how sweet," one of the other girls—Sally?—said teasingly.

James's arms tightened around me. "Don't be like that, Sal. She's a bit sheltered, but that's nothing to make fun of."

The guys laughed.

"I guess we'll have to do something about that!" one said.

"Has she ever even got drunk before?" said another.

"Or stoned!" said another, and they all laughed.

I pressed against James, trying to edge behind him.

"Guys, stop it," James said.

"I bet she's still a virgin!" Sally sneered.

The guys stared at me. I caught my breath. "James . . ."

"A virgin, huh?" One of the guys grabbed my arm and wrenched me away from James. "You better do something about that, Jimmy."

"Guys, stop it. You're freaking her out," James said.

"How about a beer first?" Another guy shoved a bottle under my nose. "To help you relax a bit."

He shook the bottle and beer splashed all over me. I pulled back and whimpered as they laughed. Dad would kill me—I couldn't explain that smell away.

"Hey, seriously, stop it!" James raised his voice.

But the group ignored him and closed around me.

"She's so boring," one of the girls said. "She's not showing any flesh. She could probably pull off cute if we could see some."

"I can fix that." One of the guys rushed at me and grabbed my shirt. I screeched as he pulled it up to expose my midriff. The laughter rose around me, and my arms were grabbed from behind. The guy lifted up my shirt past my bra.

"Oh, look at those abs!" one of the boys jeered. "You can tell she plays a lot of sports."

"Forget that! Look at her rack."

"James!" I screeched, terrified.

"Oh, James!" I heard echo mockingly around me.

But something inside James snapped at my distress. His arm wrapped around the neck of the boy holding up my shirt, and he squeezed. "Let her go!"

The group fell quiet with surprise. The guy turned red. James shoved him aside and punched the guy holding me in the face. He pulled down my shirt and wrapped his arms around me, rushing us toward the house.

"James!" one of the guys bellowed.

He ignored him and pushed me through the door. Inside, we came face to face with Robbie and Carla.

Robbie looked from James to me. "What's going on?"

"We're leaving," James replied.

"What? Jimmy!"

"I'll talk to ya later, Rob."

"Hey!" He left Carla and rushed after us into the front yard. "What's going on?"

James turned to Robbie. "They were getting on Cadence's case."

Robbie's gaze fell on me. "Ah . . . well, she needs to loosen up a bit."

James pulled me closer. "She's fine how she is."

Robbie glared at him. "*You* changed for *her*. The least she could do is give you a little bit back." His eyes took in my body.

James pulled me away from him. "She's mine, Rob! Don't look at her like that!"

"Oh, come on, Jimmy! We all share our girls around. I let you have Carla—"

"Don't even think about bringing that up! Cadence is different. She's actually my *girlfriend!* And she's—"

"A total bore! Geez, James! I thought maybe you were working hard to get her because you knew she'd put out. But apparently not. All she's done is turn you into another clone because you're so whipped! Get out of my face until you can bring my best friend back."

James glared at him. "Gladly."

He hurried us down the street.

I didn't dare say a word. I could his anger as he marched, jaw clenched. We turned the corner, then another, and slowly, he relaxed. His face softened as we walked and distress filled his eyes instead.

We made it to a service station and he called his mum to come pick us up. We sat on the gutter to wait. He pulled his knees up and rested his elbows on them. His head fell into his hands.

I wasn't sure what to do, but I did want him to know I was grateful he'd stood up for me. I shuffled closer and rested my cheek on his shoulder. "James?"

"Mmm?"

I couldn't get the words out. They felt fickle after he'd just walked out on his friends. His head turned and he looked at me, waiting for me to speak.

"What are you thinking?" I asked.

He rubbed his eyes. "You don't wanna know."

I pulled away from him and wrapped my arms around my knees. "You're wondering if I'm worth ditching your friends for. That's okay, I get it, and I'd understand if—"

"Cadence, no!" He grabbed my face. "No! You are worth it. I'd do it a hundred times over, because what they just did to you was wrong, *so* wrong."

My emotions bubbled up and tears welled in my eyes. I cursed my hormones again.

"Oh, Cadence, don't cry." He brushed my cheek to wipe away the tear that fell. "I was just thinking that I should have noticed sooner, and I wondered if I'd done things similar and *not* thought it was wrong. I'm also wondering what's gonna happen when we go back to school. I'm not gonna have any friends."

"You'll have me."

He smiled. "I will."

"And I have some friends in your grade that would probably be happy to help out."

He wrapped his arms around me and pulled me against him. I nestled into his chest as he sighed. "Thanks, Cadence."

I looked up into his face. The pain in his eyes broke my heart. He'd done the right thing, and I wanted him to know that and not feel guilty about it. I sat up and caressed his face before I kissed his cheek. He leaned into me, sighing as I softly pressed my lips against his.

He shuddered. I paused, surprised by the effect I had on him, then kissed him firmly. He pushed into me as our mouths opened and his tongue slipped into mine, stroking my lips.

I wrapped my arms around him and pulled him closer as our kiss deepened. We were so enthralled in each other, we didn't notice the car pull up in front of us.

"Herm. James?"

I jumped and looked around to see Karen looking down at us.

She chuckled. "Do you want to drive?"

James shook his head and examined my face. "No, I had something to drink." He helped me up and opened the door for me.

On the way to his home, he held me close as he stroked my hair. Several times, Karen looked in the mirror at him with concern.

"So, James, is everything okay?"

James pulled me closer and kissed my ear, but didn't say anything.

Karen sighed and looked disappointed. A hint of my motherly instincts kicked in and my heart broke for her. "Karen, James was really brave tonight."

Her eyes met mine in the mirror. "He . . . what happened?"

"Nothing," James replied.

"It wasn't nothing, James," I said, looking into his eyes. "What you did was one of the hardest things you could ever do."

"Standing up for you isn't hard."

"But standing up against your friends is." I ran my fingers through his hair. "You're so brave."

He took a sharp breath as total adoration gleamed in his eyes. My heart pounded in my chest. I loved how expressive his eyes were, and I gazed into them, reveling in his feelings for me. His gaze flashed to my lips and I smiled. He smiled back, picking up on my cue, and softly kissed me.

After he pulled away, I looked forward again to see Karen smiling at me in the mirror.

At their house, John and Melanie sat watching the TV. Melanie was curled up on the couch, while John halfheartedly read the newspaper on the furthest arm-chair. They both sat up as we entered, obviously wanting to know what happened.

James didn't say anything. He took me over to the couch and sat in the middle, pulling me down beside him. He rested my head on his shoulder and stroked my hair as he stared at the TV.

Melanie stared at him, gaping slightly. She touched his arm and he pulled away. Her gaze flashed to me as she stared with suspicious eyes. She blamed me—that was obvious.

I looked away and saw John watching us over the newspaper. Karen hung up the keys and dumped her bag on a small table by the door. A brief moment of eye contact passed between her and John before she said, "Cadence, would you like to help me bring some snacks and drinks out?"

"Sure." I moved to stand, but James pulled me back down. I turned to him, startled, but he drew me back into his arms and stared ahead.

"James."

He looked into my eyes and allowed me to peel his hands off me. I stood, and his gaze never left me as I walked out of the room.

In the kitchen, Karen turned to me, wide-eyed. "What happened?"

I glanced toward the living room and lowered my voice so it wouldn't carry. She listened intently as I explained everything. When I finished, tears filled her eyes.

"I didn't know they were that bad," she said softly. "I knew they weren't the best influence on James, but they always seemed polite when they came here."

She sighed and wiped her eyes. "Cadence, you have no idea how grateful I am that he found you. Ever since he looked at Melanie's grade photo after that disco, I've noticed changes in him for the better. But I hadn't realized how bad it was. He used to be so closed off from us, and although I knew he smoked and drank, I struggled to do anything about it. I'd ground him, and he'd just run away. I'd say no to going to parties, and he'd just sneak out."

She glanced toward the living room. "Don't tell him I told you this—he'd be very embarrassed—but since you came along, everything's changed. He's so completely smitten with you that impressing you is all that's mattered for months."

Heat flushed my cheeks. "I don't know what to say."

She wrapped her arms around me. "Nothing. I'm just grateful for you, and I'm grateful you gave him the courage to stand up against his friends and cut them off. This is all I've hoped for."

Touched, I hugged her back. I wondered what had happened to James in the other timeline. Had he ever moved on? He was smart enough. Maybe after high school, he'd found new friends and became the James I knew.

"Karen?" John slipped into the kitchen.

Karen let me go and smiled up at him. "I'm fine, John."

He looked down at me with concern. "What happened?"

Karen took his arm. "I'll tell you later." She handed me a bowl of chips and a bottle of soda.

I walked back into the living room and saw James had gone. Melanie stared up at me as I set the chips on the coffee table.

"Where'd he go?"

"He didn't wanna see you anymore."

I sighed and decided to try his room. I was right. As I cracked the door open, he sat up on his bed. "Cadence!"

"Can I come in?"

"Ah . . ." He glanced around the room and hurried to pick up several things. "Okay."

I entered as he closed the lid to his laundry hamper. I scanned the room, interested to find a poster of a rugby player over the head of his bed; several shelves full of books hung above his desk to my left. I turned to the shelves and examined them. "Sci-fi, huh?"

"Yeah . . ." He rubbed his neck, looking terribly embarrassed. "It's a new thing."

"All the *Dunes*, *Star Wars*, *Hitchhiker's*, *Battlefield Earth* . . ."

He dashed in front of me. "Yeah, it's nerdy, I know."

"No, it's not." I pushed him aside. "These are all sci-fi classics, except . . ." I slipped out *The Count of Monte Cristo.* He snatched it out of my hand. "It was for English."

I laughed. "No, it wasn't. Don't worry, it's a good one. Sword fights, intrigues . . ." I smiled at him. "Romance."

He flushed and shoved it back on the shelf.

"James! Are you blushing?"

"Shut up."

I laughed. Looking around the rest of his room, I saw a large collection of CDs. I headed over, surprised to find them alphabetized. His taste in music surprised me even more.

"This is all techno," I said. "I woulda picked you as a heavy metal guy."

"Nah, I get enough of that around the guys." He sank onto his bed. "Well, at least I did."

I stepped in front of him, resting my hands on his shoulders. He gazed up at me, wrapping his arms around my waist and pulling me onto his lap. I curled up in his arms as he sighed.

"James?"

"Yeah?"

"It'll be okay. I promise."

He lifted my chin and kissed me.

"James." His dad's firm voice came from the door. "No girls in your bedroom."

"My dad has a similar rule," I said to John as I walked out.

Back in the living room, we resumed our previous positions, with Karen in the second armchair. James seemed to cheer up as we chatted. He kept his arm around me, running his fingers through my hair.

Melanie seemed less than impressed. She pulled her knees up and rarely spoke, but every time James smiled at me, she threw me a filthy look.

Finally, the countdown came, and James sat up. "Mum, Dad, just as a heads-up, I'm about to kiss Cadence."

Melanie gagged, John shrugged and looked away, and Karen chuckled as she stood and walked over to John.

When the countdown hit one, James grabbed my face and turned me toward him. He leaned in, and our lips had barely touched when everything froze.

Chapter Thirteen

I pulled away from James and glanced around. Everyone sat completely stationary. His parents were kissing, and Melanie had the most vicious look in her eyes as she glared, arms folded, at me and James.

"Cadence."

The man in white stepped into the room, dressed as Father Time. He definitely seemed to enjoy his job.

"How festive."

He shrugged. "New Year's is a big night for me." He tilted his head so I'd follow.

We walked out the front door, where we stood in the middle of the quad at school. I saw myself with Geri by the table, talking with our heads close together.

"This was your first day in this timeline," he said.

I stared up at him. "Did I do something wrong?"

He shook his head. "This is customary. I will visit you every year as the clock hits midnight, when time is in limbo between each year. We will evaluate what you've done, and all your lost memories and feelings will be restored so you can make decisions for the coming year."

He touched my shoulder and a wave of emotions and memories hit me—Austin smiling at me with our newborn baby in his arms, our first night together, our wedding night. I felt the love again and I gasped, shocked by its intensity. Then I saw his cold, stiff face in the morgue and Melody lying limp in my arms.

Melody.

I had thought so little of her because her memory seemed more like a dream. Guilt consumed me and I fell to my knees to cry.

"Cadence, why do you weep?"

I looked up at him and tried to compose myself. "I saw Austin and Melody, and felt everything they were to me. I'd begun to forget. I feel so . . ." I trailed off as tears streamed down my face.

He smiled. "Yes, you will feel that each time we do this. That's the reason *why* you chose this path, so it will always be the first thing that comes back. But don't worry— it will fade away again once we return to time in motion."

"What if I don't want it to fade?"

"Oh, you do, sweet Cadence. Those feelings are distractions from what you need to do before it arises in the future. Look here."

Time fast forwarded. We turned to the hall behind us and saw the disco in full swing. He led me inside. We passed like ghosts through the people milling around and dancing, and stopped right in front of James.

With his shaggy, greasy hair, baggy and ripped cargos, and black T-shirt with stains all over it, he looked terrible. But he wasn't paying any attention to his friends—he stared off into the crowd.

"What's he looking at?" I asked.

"Follow his gaze."

I bent down beside him and saw Geri and me toward the back. We talked frantically, and I knew what had just happened. "He watched me after that spanking thing?"

The man in white nodded. "Up until this point, the two timelines were mostly running parallel. But this night, some crucial choices were made by you which veered this timeline in a completely different direction."

He waved his hand and everything froze. The room seemed to split. I saw two Jameses sitting and staring ahead at two versions of me and Geri. Geri's clothes were the same in both timelines, but mine were different; in *this* timeline, Mum took me shopping, but in the original one, she hadn't.

Then, as if watching a video on a split screen, everything started to move again as I stood stationary. In both timelines, Geri and I moved up toward our group of friends, and James craned his neck to watch.

In the first timeline, Justin moved in on me, and I let him, while in the second, I was showered by male attention. James's response in both interested me. He leaned over to Robbie and said, "Hey, who is that girl?"

Robbie scoffed. "I dunno, some do-gooder ninth grader."

James straightened and continued to watch me. After a few minutes, he stood. "I'm gonna get a drink and pee."

"Whatever, dude," Robbie replied without paying much attention.

James moved around the hall to get closer to my group. He stayed completely fixated on me, and grew irritated when someone got in his way.

Then, in the second timeline, Geri and I split from the group and headed to the girls' bathroom, while in the first one, Geri left with one of the other girls, leaving me with Justin.

James continued to watch me in the first, and even moved close enough to hear Justin talking to me. "You're cute, you know that?"

I giggled. "I most certainly try, but I've never really been sure if I succeed."

"You most certainly succeed."

"She's beautiful, you moron," James said.

That shocked me. I'd never known.

Meanwhile, in the second timeline, he followed Geri and me to the bathroom and stood waiting outside. Carla and her friends came out first and saw him. Becca moved in and leaned against him. "Hey, Jimmy."

"What's up?" he responded distractedly.

"I'd like to see you up," she answered seductively.

He scoffed. "Yeah, maybe some other time."

"Too bad." The girls made their way back into the hall.

Not long after that, Geri and I burst out. He shot upright as our eyes connected. He looked eager, hopeful, but I blew him off and dashed away. He slumped.

"Fascinating, isn't it?" the man in white said. "How small choices make such a big difference?"

The night fast forwarded again in both timelines. Geri and I sat waiting for our rides, but in the first timeline, Justin sat with us too. In both, James came around the corner of the building and saw me. He watched me as he followed his friends across the lot. He leaned against the side of a car and, while his friends acted like idiots, never stopped staring at me.

He noticed Melanie and waved her over. "That girl there, she's in your grade, right?"

Melanie followed the direction he pointed and scoffed. "Yeah, she's a real piece of work, too, especially when she's with that friend of hers."

"What's her name?"

Melanie scowled. "No, James. Just no."

"Go talk to her for me."

There the two timelines differed again. In the first, her response was, "No, that Justin kid pisses me off," and she walked away, but in the second she said, "Seriously, James?"

"Yeah. Go or I'll smash all your CDs."

She groaned and walked over to us. When she came back, she growled, "I hate her and her stupid friend. If you even think about dating her, I'll disown you." She walked away.

Then, Geri left.

"Watch closely now," the man in white said. "This is the moment that changed everything."

In the first timeline, Justin leaned over and kissed me, while I rejected him in the second. James's reaction drew my focus. In the first timeline, he swore and turned away, pulling at his hair. But in the second, as Justin stood and walked away, his face lit up. He was in the running.

"Now, watch this." The man grabbed my shoulder and we stood in James's house, still the same night of the disco.

James burst in. He marched in with anger on his face in the first timeline, but in the second, his whole face was lit up, eager, excited. Both times, he headed to a bookshelf in the family room and pulled out Melanie's ninth grade photo. In the first, he pulled out a black marker and scribbled out Justin's face, then tossed the photo in the trash; in the second, he scanned the photo until he found me. He stared at me with a crooked smile, then read the names at the bottom.

"Cadence Anderson," he said quietly to himself. "Cadence."

He glanced around and slipped the photo under his shirt, then dashed into his room and closed the door.

The man in white stepped in front of me. "And just like that, everything changed." He waved his hand and I saw James pluck out a note I'd tossed in the trash to read the details for my ice-skating trip with Brian. I watched him tail me and write down my class schedule. I saw Melanie tell him to get over me because I thought he looked like a bum. He went home and tossed out all his ripped and worn out clothes, then stared at himself in the mirror for an hour.

During the school break, he shocked Karen by asking her to take him for a haircut and to pick up some new school uniforms. He started going to class and reading.

"All of this because I didn't date Justin?" I asked.

The man in white nodded. "He gave up because you were taken, and when you and Justin broke up, you went straight on to Brian, then Flynn, then—"

"I get the picture." I sighed. "But I made it nearly impossible for him. I told him flat out *no* several times."

"But you were always available, so he always had hope. Especially after this." The room transformed into the third term's disco in September. James had me in his arms and I stared up at him. The scene froze as the man led me up beside us.

"We're about to kiss," I said. "Of course that would give him hope."

"Ah! But see the way you're looking at him?"

I looked at myself and in my eyes I saw awe, attraction, and, most significantly, adoration.

"Yes, Cadence, he saw the way you looked at him and he knew he had you. The kiss was just a test to make sure. After that, he knew if he just tweaked his appearance and showed you he could go to class and do the right thing, he'd have you." He turned and walked toward the door.

"Why is James so important?" I asked as I rushed to follow.

"James was the most significant influence that you had with the different choices you made. Yes, Harper and your father's relationship was altered for the better, but that was through a choice which, ultimately, *she* made."

We stepped through the door back into James's living room on New Year's.

"Now, Cadence, tell me." He tilted his head. "What do you intend on doing this year?"

I looked down at James. "Is it wrong for me to be with him? I mean, now that I remember everything with Austin, I feel like I've betrayed him."

"No, Cadence. This is a *second chance*. This life you are living now should be lived like it was your first. You should do all you can so your future turns out better. Don't feel guilty about giving people around you second chances too."

I sat beside James and grinned at his face locked in an unreciprocated kiss. I touched his cheek. "Okay, I'll see where this takes me. This year, I will explore our relationship."

I tried to remember my tenth grade year. I looked up at the man in white fearfully. "I lose Geri this year! I'm not going to let that happen. I'm going to find out what I did, and I'm going to prevent it. Losing Geri was one of the worst things that ever happened to me."

"Very good, Cadence. Now you're thinking like someone with a second chance." He gestured at James. "You better lean in and kiss him."

I shuffled back into his arms and pressed my lips against his. Instantly, his lips moved over mine and his arms tightened around me. The emotions and memories drained out of me and I returned to the hazy blur of what was to come. But I felt reassured that being with James was the right thing for both me and him, and I wasn't betraying Austin in any way. I kissed James with all my feeling, until John cleared his throat, signaling that we'd had enough.

part two:

james

Chapter Fourteen

W e had our school swimming carnival the first week back, like always. Geri stood waiting for me when Mum dropped me off. She grinned as I approached. "There's a hot new guy in our grade."

"Oh, that would be Flynn," I said without thinking.

"You've met him already? Cadence! Holy cow!"

I realized my mistake and quickly covered. "Yeah, he's in my maths class."

"Oh!" She grinned from ear to ear. "Talk to him for me."

"Ah . . . okay." We walked to the gate and paid for entry. Flynn would have been my next boyfriend, but even without dating James, I wouldn't have gone there again. After we graduated, he came out as gay. I'd been his only girlfriend, and I wasn't sure whether to be flattered that he'd considered me, or insulted because it implied I was masculine.

We found our group and I pulled off my shirt. I had every intention of competing in every event like I always had. As one of the biggest jock chicks in the grade, it was almost expected of me. I'd done some training over the summer and realized just how much I'd missed swimming.

Geri leaned closer and pulled down my bottom lip. "Let me see again."

I pulled my lips back to show my braces-free teeth.

"My gosh! I can't believe how straight your teeth are now, and that huge gap between your front two is just *gone!*"

I smiled. "That's the point." I'd had my braces removed a week earlier, just before school started. Going through that twice had sucked, but I liked the slick, slimy feel of my teeth once they came off. Geri lost her mind with excitement when she saw them gone, and James snuck me behind a building so he could "see how different it felt" to kiss me.

As I rubbed in my sun lotion, a new pair of hands rested on the exposed skin of my back. I jumped and turned.

"James! You startled me."

"I hope no one else is touching you like that." He frowned, but a hint of a smirk curled the corners of his mouth.

"Hey, Cadence, there he is!" Geri whispered in my ear.

Flynn walked shirtless toward the starting blocks. He did look good. He wasn't tall—he and I had stood eye to eye—but he was built for a tenth grader, and his sandy blond hair was thick and luscious. I remembered why I'd been attracted to him in the first place.

"He's so hot!" Geri said in a high-pitched voice.

"What, that guy?" James nodded at Flynn. "He's totally gay."

I stared at James, surprised, but Geri slapped his chest. "No, he's not! Why do all guys think that other guys who are better-looking than them are gay?"

I giggled. "I don't think I'd say he's better-looking than James."

"Thank you, Cadence," James responded, puffing out his chest. "We could test it." He looked down at my rack. "Cadence, your boobs look outstanding in that swimsuit—"

I slapped his chest and folded my arms around myself.

He laughed. "No! I mean, they would make any straight guy take a quick look, so go shake 'em in front of him and see what he does."

"You're such a perv," Geri said.

"Fine. I'll go bend over in front of him and see what he does." He moved to walk away, but Geri and I caught his arms.

"James." I giggled. "Leave it alone. If he is, he is, and if not, then Geri can have some fun."

"I'm telling you, he is!" James grinned.

Geri pouted and marched away.

"Geri!"

She ignored me and kept walking. I shoved James and ran after her. "Geri—"

"You know, Cadence, just because you have a hot boyfriend doesn't mean you can treat my interests like they're stupid!"

"Oh, Geri, no, that wasn't what I was doing—"

She turned on me. "Oh yeah? Why don't you go shake your boobs in front of him and find out?"

"Well, *you* could do it instead. Your boobs are equally as—"

"See? You're doing it again!"

I stopped, my panic rising. I had to diffuse the situation. "I'm sorry, Geri. I didn't mean to tease you."

She pursed her lips and looked me over. She sighed. "I know. I guess I'm just a little jealous 'cause you and James are so cute together, and I'd really like something like that. But unlike you, I'm not blonde and pretty—"

"Geraldine Turner! You're gorgeous!"

"Fine, I'm not blonde then." A smirk spread across her face.

I smiled and wrapped my arm around her shoulders. "Come on, let's go see what kinda weird crap we can convince James to do."

She giggled and wrapped her arm around my waist. "Cay-Cay?"

"Yeah?"

"How's he doing? You know, with being cast out by his friends."

"Okay, I guess. Better than I expected. Luckily, Julz's group took him in for me. He seems to really be getting along with Tom and Sam."

"Yeah, I didn't realize James was a science geek. He's doing chem and physics, as well as PE, which is almost the same as bio."

I shrugged. "He's a smart guy."

"Yeah, but he wouldn't have done it without you showing him."

I felt someone behind me. "Slut."

I didn't dare turn to look at Robbie, just picked up my pace.

"When are you gonna give my boy his balls back, huh?"

"Leave me alone."

"Ooh, *leave me alone*. What's that, your catchphrase or something?" He grabbed my arm and swung me around. "I want my best friend back you little—" His gaze lifted over my head.

James pulled my arm free. "Rob."

"Jimmy, she's ruined you! Look at you. You're such a poof now."

"Come on, Cadence." He rested his arm around my shoulders and turned me around.

"Jimmy! Bros before hoes! What happened to that?"

James pulled me closer. "Hey, they called your first race."

"Oh!" I dashed toward the starting area to be given a starting block.

As I stood in line, I watched James walk back to his new group of friends with Geri. I smiled, relieved they'd taken him in so willingly when they knew what he'd been like before.

"Hey, you're Cadence right?"

Turning my head, I found Flynn beside me. I remembered this—I'd flirted shamelessly with him. This time, I wouldn't. "Yeah, and you're the new guy. Flynn, right?"

I thought about what James said and wondered if he did have a bit of attraction to girls. So, I picked at my swimsuit just under my arms. His gaze fell at the movement, but he didn't check out my boobs. James was right.

"Yeah. I think I'm in your maths class."

I smiled. "You sat with my friend, Brian."

He grinned, and I found myself struck by his deep dimples. *Crap, he's hot.*

"Brian told me *a lot* about you." He winked.

Great, Brian still has a thing for me. "We've been friends for a while. He's pretty cool."

The person in front of me stepped aside. I gave the teacher my name, and she gave me my block number and race. A few moments later, Flynn rushed up beside me. "So, what kinda fun stuff is there to do around here?"

I paused, recalling where this was headed. "Well, James and I like the movies, but we've also done some laser tag. I think that's just 'cause he can whoop me, though."

He laughed. "This James is your boyfriend?"

I pointed toward the group. "He's the one in the green and blue board shorts and dark blue beater."

James noticed me pointing and rushed over.

"I can see that," Flynn said. "You guys make a cute couple."

Holy cow! What straight guy says that?

"Hey." James wrapped his arm around my shoulders. "I'm James."

"Flynn."

Then James deliberately knocked my towel off my waist. He bent over, turning his back to Flynn, and Flynn looked. I felt like such an idiot for not noticing the first time around. James wrapped the towel back around me and kissed my neck.

He grinned. "Cadence here is crazy when it comes to sports."

"So I've heard."

James smacked my butt, earning him a glare. "Your reputation precedes you, Cay."

"You're a jerk," I said.

Flynn smiled. "Well, if you don't mind, would I be able to hang around with you guys? I heard you were nice, so . . ." He shrugged.

"Sure," I answered before James could say anything obnoxious.

Noticing my race coming up, I bent over, flipped my hair up, and pulled my cap over it. As I straightened, poking the stray hairs underneath, I glanced at James who, by the smirk across his face, had enjoyed the show.

I rolled my eyes and glanced at Flynn . . . who stared at James. Good heavens, I'd been an idiot.

My race was up. James kissed my head. "Kick some butt for me."

"You know I will."

"That's my girl." He backed away and, with a wink, turned and headed back to our group.

My stomach filled with butterflies as I mounted the block. Years had passed since I'd swum a race. Well, mentally, anyway. Physically, it had been just before I'd entered this timeline. The horn sounded and I entered the water. I remembered why I loved swimming so much. Under the water, only the sound of my strokes and breathing broke the silence. I felt so strong, so lightweight.

I glanced down the line and saw I needed to pull ahead. I kicked harder and pulled the water with my arms. I surged forward, and a moment later, my hand hit the wall. I looked up as everyone else surfaced and was handed the second place stick.

Second. I always got second, even when I'd go on to zone competitions and place ahead of whoever beat me at school. I *always* got second at school.

I took a deep breath. Oh well, it kept me humble, right? I ducked under the lane ropes and James met me at the stairs, holding my towel. I think he enjoyed the swimming carnival more for the scenery than anything else. His eyes took in my exposed body as I stepped out of the water.

"I think I could die now and be happy," he said as he handed me my towel.

"Perv."

He went in for a butt grope, but I blocked him. He laughed and walked me over to the winners' table to check in my time and place. As we wandered back to the group, he leaned closer to whisper, "Was I right? Because he was the only guy who *didn't* look when you did that hair flipping thing."

"Oh my gosh!" I shoved him in the chest, my cheeks burning.

"Did he look at my butt?"

"Seriously, James?"

"Come on, Cadence. Was I right?"

I glared at him. "Don't tell Geri."

He burst out laughing. "Okay, I won't. I just like being right."

Harper walked into my room and slapped my leg. "Hey, I need your nerd power."

"Huh?"

"Do I have to spell it out to you? I need help with English."

"Ah, twelfth grade English is probably a bit advanced for me."

"Blah, blah, blah. Shut up and help me."

I followed her into her room. I'd never been in her room after she turned twelve, so I felt a little excited and nervous all at once. Inside, her paintings covered the walls. They were deeply moving too; some were dark and sad, and others were bright and joyous. The half-finished painting on the easel had a lion devouring her school books. I grinned.

"So, I'm supposed to analyze this stupid poem," she said as she sank onto her desk chair, "but it might as well be in Latin to me."

I leaned over. "Oh, I know this one."

She raised her eyebrows. "Wow, you really are a nerd."

"'The Road Less Taken' is one of the most famous pieces of poetry in the world," I answered hurriedly. I remembered studying it in the eleventh grade though. I guess they shifted the curriculum around between now and then.

She frowned at me impatiently. "So?"

"Give me your assignment sheet."

I sat on her bed and we dissected the poem piece by piece. She stood and huffed several times, cursing the teachers, the school, and the Higher School Certificate. Then, she sank back down and typed out several lines of almost perfect work. I was impressed, and proud of her.

Finally, we finished and she hit print. "Thanks, Cadence. This was really sucking big time."

"No worries. Anytime." I made my way to the family room to retrieve her paper from the printer.

When I came back, she slipped it in her folder and filled out the cover sheet. "Cadence, do you think I'm smart?"

"Well, yeah." I shrugged.

"No, really. Because I don't think I'm gonna pass this crap."

"You'll be fine. You'll go on and paint marvelous nude portraits, marry a dreamy Italian, and have lots of kids."

She burst out laughing. "Seriously? Your imagination is as bad as mine."

She waved her hands around at her paintings. "I wish I could paint for the rest of my life, but realistically, that's not a job that will keep me alive."

"I dunno, there's probably lots of things you could do. Have you looked into the art degrees at all the universities?"

"University?" She gave me an incredulous look. "Cadence, I'll be lucky to graduate high school."

"You're smarter than you think. You're just hotheaded and impatient. I just sat and watched you write that thing almost entirely by yourself." I nodded at her assignment on her desk.

She looked at it, flicking through the pages. "I did, huh?" She turned and narrowed her eyes on me. "When did you get so wise, missy?"

I shrugged. "Not wise, just an outside perspective."

"Hmm." She stood and walked around the room. Then, she spun and pinned me onto the bed, tickling me. I screeched through my fits of laughter and she laughed at me. When she drew tears and I begged her to stop, she collapsed on the bed beside me and we stared up at the ceiling. "Cadence?"

"Mmm?"

"I hate my name. What's with the musical crap anyway?"

"It's tradition."

"Well, it's something I'm not going to do. I'm going to give my daughters real names, like Elizabeth and Susan. Just nice, ordinary, boring names."

I giggled and rested my hands on my belly. "You know, you should paint the ceiling."

"Random."

"I'm serious! It's the only white thing in here."

She stared up at it, contemplating my suggestion. "What would I paint?"

"Whatever you wanna wake up and see every day."

She paused, then said, "You don't think Dad will flip out?"

"He might, but remind him that once you move out, he just needs to buy white paint and rollers and it's fixed."

Her fingers wove through mine. "I might just do that."

Chapter Fifteen

"Caaaadence!" Geri rushed at me, jumping on me and pinning me against the table. "Cadence, Cadence, Cadence—"

"What, Geraldine?"

"Flynn *talked* to me."

"Oh."

She jumped off my back. "Oh? Is that all I get? *Oh?*"

"Oh, ah . . . let's go over there and chat."

She grinned and dragged me away from the group. Once out of earshot, she did a crazy little dance on the spot. "Cadence, it was awesome! He just came up and sat beside me in English, and was all, 'Hey, you're Cadence and James's friend, right?'" I giggled as she lowered her voice in an attempt to mimic him. "And I was somehow all cool about it, and was all, 'Yeah, I'm Geri.' Then he was all, 'Cool, they're pretty cool.' And we talked through the *whole* lesson! Oh Cadence, do you think I should ask him out? Or should I wait and see what happens?"

I paused, unsure how to answer. So, to deflect my thoughts, I sat her on a metal bench. "Okay, let's analyze this."

She nodded and grasped my knees in anticipation.

"He came up to you, right?"

"Yeah, I was already sitting down, and he just sat right next to me."

"Okay, so what kind of things did you talk about?"

"Well, he asked me what kinda stuff I like to do, so I told him about the book I just finished reading and about my recent shopping trip and—"

James climbed between us. "Hey, this looks like an intense conversation. Fill me in."

"Ah, James, maybe not now." I gave him a warning look.

"It's okay, Cadence." Geri shrugged. "I'm just telling Cadence about how Flynn and I flirted together in English, and she's helping me decide if I should ask him out or wait for him to ask me."

"Geri." James grabbed her shoulders and looked her dead in the eyes. "The dude is gay."

She shoved him off. "No, he isn't!"

I grabbed James's wrist. "Geri, why don't you ask him if he wants to go see a movie or something?"

"Seriously, Cadence?" James groaned.

"Only if you double with us," Geri said.

"*Oh my gosh!*" James stood and turned to face us. "Cadence, if he looks at my butt or squeezes my biceps, I'm out."

Geri glowered at him and stormed away.

"James, that wasn't very nice," I said as he watched her leave, his jaw hanging.

"She needs to know so she doesn't embarrass herself."

"Maybe she needs to find out for herself. I need to support her, and you should, too, considering all she did to help us get together."

He sat back beside me. "Fine. But only if you kiss me, now and on that date."

I grinned and clasped his face, softly kissing his lips.

James wasn't happy about the seating arrangement. As the movie began, he leaned over to me. "Why didn't you and Geri sit together? How did *I* end up next to him?"

"Shush, James. Just watch the movie."

"Can we swap places?"

"Are you serious?"

"Yeah, call me a homophobe, but *yeah*!"

I groaned and we switched places. I ended up not minding—it gave me a better vantage point for what was happening with Flynn and Geri. It turned out very similar to how our first date did in the other timeline. He was sweet and charming, and even held her hand. I nudged James. He looked across and rolled his eyes.

The next Monday, Geri rushed at me as I arrived. "He asked me to be his girlfriend!"

I paused. "Who? Flynn?"

"Yes, Flynn! Gosh, Cadence, sometimes you really are blonde."

It had gone just as it had with me, but I wrapped my arms around her and we bounced around with excitement together.

"He's obviously in denial, or trying to hide it, or something," James said later as he walked me to my maths class, which was located near his economics one.

"James, let Geri have her moment. She's really into him."

"You're going to let your friend get hurt?"

"No." I frowned. "I'll keep an eye on it. But if I keep harping on about it like you, all it will do is make her mad at me."

"Whatever." He paused outside the door and glanced in. "Hey, am I still coming over on Wednesday? I really need some help with memorizing the bones and muscles."

I knew he wanted to change the topic, so I didn't push it. "Yeah, Mum's picking us up and everything. Dusty's stoked."

He grinned and clasped my face to kiss me. "Catch ya later, beautiful."

That night, I went through my journal entries to see if my memory about me and Flynn was right. Yes, everything he did with Geri he'd done with me. I turned to the next week, and saw the fight.

I'd written that I was so confused. Geri had come at me in a fit of rage, hollering all kinds of accusations at me. She'd called me a slut, a user, and a selfish whore. She'd said she was tired of looking at my Barbie doll hair and stupid, dopey eyes, and she no longer wanted anything to do with a backstabber like me.

When she'd marched away, I'd cried in Flynn's arms.

That was it! I flicked back and read over everything she'd said. I'd ignored her when she'd expressed her interest in Flynn and gone after him myself. She'd watched me go through three boyfriends the year before, while she still hadn't had her first.

I rubbed my eyes at the realization of how awful a friend I was. I hadn't even seen it because I'd been so enthralled with my own thoughts and feelings. I dashed into the kitchen and snatched up the phone. I retreated to my room as the phone rang. Her mum answered.

"Hey, it's Cadence. Can I speak to Geri?"

"You sure can, hon. Just one second."

Ruffling noises came down the line as she handed over the phone, then Geri said, "Hey, Cay-Cay. What's up?"

"I just wanted to tell you how awesome a friend you are."

She paused, then giggled. "Cadence, you can be so weird sometimes."

"No, really, you're my best friend, and I really wanna make sure you're always happy."

Another pause. "Did James dump you or something?"

I giggled. "No."

"Ah, okay, because this is weird. You know that, right?"

I sighed. "Promise me we'll always be friends."

"Now you're starting to scare me. Are you dying?"

"No! I've just been thinking. James and I haven't been really supportive with the whole Flynn thing, and I wanted to make sure you know that I do support you, and I love you, and I'll be here for you no matter what."

Pause. "Oh, Cadence, that means everything to me. I really thought you were with James on this, and I was worried you'd abandon me."

"Oh my gosh! Geri, no! I'll never do that. I promise you, no matter what, I'm here."

"Cay, you're the best."

"No, Geri, I could never reach your standard."

"Now you're getting all sappy on me."

I giggled.

"Okay, well, I better go. Mum's got dinner ready."

"Okay, see ya tomorrow."

I sprawled back on my bed. I felt relieved to reassure her, and hoped more than anything it would be enough. Now that I knew what had happened, I would do everything I could to make sure we stayed together. Only time would tell.

James waited for me outside my classroom after school. His face, as always, lit up when he saw me. I loved that. I grinned back as he kissed my cheek and wrapped his arm around me.

"I'll see ya tomorrow!" Geri waved.

We both waved back, and he kissed my cheek again. "I missed you."

"It's been like an hour and a half!" I giggled.

"So? I was in English. It was the longest hour and a half of my life."

"English is easy."

"For you!"

I laughed and we headed toward the parking lot to meet my mum.

"So, does your dad still hate me?" he asked.

"I think you're growing on him. He doesn't call you 'that useless meathead' anymore. He usually just refers to you as 'that boy.'"

He smirked. "That *is* a drastic improvement."

"Hey, meathead." Harper slapped him across the back of the head.

James rubbed his head. "I guess I'm not growing on everyone."

I chuckled. "From her, that's a term of endearment."

Dusty appeared in front of us, grinning up in complete awe at James. James was like the brother he'd always wanted, so he would hover and ask James about everything. "Hey, you're coming over today, right?"

"Right." James grinned.

"Cool. I should show you what I made in woodwork. It's really cool. It was—"

"Dusty, he doesn't actually care," Harper said.

Dusty glared at her, but when he opened his mouth to continue, Mum pulled up. James whipped out a flower and handed it to her. She chuckled and shook her head as we climbed in.

Back at the house, James asked, "So . . . do I get to study in your room?"

I laughed. "You really wanna go in there, huh?"

"Ah, yeah. You've seen my room, it's only fair."

"Well, yes, we are studying in my room. But we have to keep the door open, and you have to stay sitting at my desk."

He followed me eagerly to my room. I'd cleaned it up the night before, knowing he would see it. I didn't want him to think of me as a slob. As he entered, I smiled at my made bed and clear floor and desk.

"Oh, boy bands!" He rushed to my NSYNC and Backstreet Boys posters. He pointed at them and laughed.

"I really need to take them down."

"Boy bands are so three years ago," he said, teasingly.

"Shut up."

He laughed and scanned the room. "Stuffed toys? Cadence, how old are you, really?"

I growled and sat on my bed to pull my school books out of my bag. He walked over to my drawers and grabbed the top one. I leapt to my feet and shoved his hand away. "James!"

"Oh! That's your underwear, isn't it?"

"Get away!"

"Let me see."

He reached around me, but I grabbed his hand. He simply redirected his focus and wrapped his arm around my waist, pulling me against him. I caught my breath as I felt his on my lips. He stroked my hair before resting his hand on my neck as his thumb stroked my cheekbone. "You're so easy. Just one touch and you're gone."

"Shut up."

He smiled and kissed me. I clung onto him as he shifted the kiss into an open mouth motion and our tongues touched. His arm around me pulled me closer.

"Cadence." I jumped and pulled away at Mum's warning tone. My cheeks warmed as she shook her head at me. "Aren't you supposed to be studying?"

"Yeah." I pushed James off.

"James."

He cleared his throat, hurried over to my desk, and sat.

We ran through all the bones and major muscle groups. He kept ruffling his hair as he struggled to remember the muscles. "How do *you* remember all this stuff?"

My area of study at university had been Sports Science, so bones and muscles came easily for me.

I shrugged. "I dunno. I just like PE, I guess."

"PE for you is kicking a ball around, with the occasional sex ed and drugs class. I wish I could do sex ed again."

I giggled. "Did you even go to those classes?"

He scoffed. "Yeah, we liked to steal the condoms. It was one of the few classes we actually wanted to go to."

"Condoms, huh?"

We turned to see Dad scowling by the door. I glanced at my clock. Six thirty. "So, you have a collection, do you?

I hope you don't intend on *using* them any time in the near future."

"Crap." James lowered his head.

"Yeah, boy, you better watch it." Dad rested his hands on his hips. "I thought you were supposed to be studying."

"We are," I answered, waving James's textbook in the air. "We're just talking about the difference between my PE and his PE."

Dad's eyes narrowed on James. "Dinner's ready."

James shot out the door. Dad waited for me as I packed up.

"Dad, why do you have to make him so uncomfortable?" I asked.

He walked over and kissed my head. "I'm just keeping his boundaries clear."

I wrapped my arm around his waist and nestled my head onto his chest. "Did you have a good day?"

He touched my hair. "I am now."

I smiled and squeezed him.

At the table, Dusty sat right beside James, so close he practically sat on his lap. He rambled on and on as James listened patiently. I sat beside James and his hand rested on my knee. I looked into his face and sighed. Things couldn't be much better. My family was all getting along, and I had an amazing, incredibly attractive boyfriend. If only I'd known the first time around what I was missing out on.

Chapter Sixteen

I pulled up my hockey socks. Second term had begun, and I'd just tried out for the girls' field hockey team. I'd get in even though I didn't play outside of school. The teachers loved having me on their teams because of my aggression on the field.

We used a public hockey field down the road from school, but since the tryouts had been after school hours, I stood waiting for James and Karen to pick me up. I tugged at my black sport shorts, hating how they only came halfway down my thighs. I was glad the dark blue hockey socks came to my knees so I felt a little covered.

I glanced back and saw the teacher still in the team box with some of the younger students. She wasn't paying attention to much as she made notes on her clipboard.

A car pulled up in front of me. I turned, thinking James had arrived, but several sets of hands grabbed me and pulled me inside. Robbie held me down and covered my mouth.

"Hello, Cadence."

I struggled against him, but he straddled me to keep me down. Several of the boys sat in the car, glaring at me.

"We've decided something," Robbie said. "We're going to strike a deal with you. We want James back, and you, well, I'm sure you don't want that little friend of yours hurt, do you? What's her name again? Geraldine?"

They snickered as my eyes widened. I struggled, but he shoved me hard into the seat.

"So, princess, here's what's gonna happen. You dump James so I can have my best friend back, and I'll let you keep *your* best friend. Fair's fair, right?"

He released my mouth so I could speak. "What are you going to do to her?"

He smirked. "There's lots we could do to her. We could beat her and her boyfriend, we could follow her home and leave little messages for her—"

"Okay, I get it."

"So we have a deal, then." His smirk widened. "Good. I expect James back with us by the end of the week."

He opened the door and shoved me out.

I hit the edge of the gutter and ripped the skin off my knee. Wincing, I turned to look at it as they drove off. Once they'd gone, I allowed my tears to fall. I didn't want to break up with James, but I couldn't let those boys bully Geri.

I pulled my water bottle out of my bag to wash my wound as I sobbed. How could I choose between my two best friends? How could I drive James away and back to that life with those boys? What could I do?

I rubbed my eyes and tried to force my adult sensibility to surface. What would I have done when I was twenty-five? I definitely wouldn't allow those boys to bully me. Would I tell the cops? No, that was so lame. This was teenage drama.

A car pulled up in front of me. I recoiled, afraid that Robbie had come back for a second round of threats. Instead, James burst out. "Cadence! What happened to you?"

I pulled my knees up and tucked my face away. I didn't want to look at him, knowing I might have to hurt him soon.

He sat beside me and wrapped his arm around my shoulders. "Come on, talk to me."

He knew I wouldn't cry over a grazed knee. I'd held back tears over much worse. I shook my head, afraid I'd just blurt out something I'd regret.

He took my arm and helped me into the car. I sat in the back while he drove, staring out the window, my emotions in turmoil. No one would get physically harmed if I chose Geri, but James would be devastated. I couldn't do that. I pictured the pain in his eyes if I did that to him.

He had become more than a boyfriend—he was my best friend too. But so was Geri, and I kept running through every terrible thing they could possibly do to her.

We arrived at James's house. Karen took me in to clean up and cover my wound. I sat in the family room with her beside me as I stuck a large square Band-Aid over it. She ran her hand over my ponytail as she watched me.

"Cadence, honey, you know you can talk to us if you need to. Especially James. He cares about you very much."

A sob wrenched from my chest and I started crying all over again.

"Cadence, what happened?"

I shook my head and stood up. "I can't."

James walked in from his bedroom. In his eyes, I saw his concern for me, and more than anything, how much he cared about me. I turned away, unable to face him.

He grabbed me by the waist and clasped my chin, forcing me to look up into his eyes. *Oh those eyes!* So intense, so perfect. Tears streamed down my face as I shut my eyes, unable to look into his.

"Cadence, talk to me." He had so much pain in his voice that my heart tore apart.

I threw my arms around him and sobbed into his chest. "James, I don't want to end it with you. But if I don't, they'll go after Geri and she'll get hurt and it will be my fault!"

Karen gasped as James's breath caught. "What are you saying?"

"James, you mean so much to me, but I'm scared. I'm so sorry, but they'll only leave her alone if I—"

"Who's *they*, Cadence?"

I swallowed hard and clung onto him. "If you don't go back to them, they'll hurt Geri."

He clasped my face and forced me to stare him in the eyes. "Are you talking about Robbie?"

I closed my eyes again, the pain in my heart too strong.

"Mum, call the school," James said. "Tell them that Geraldine Turner has been threatened by Robbie Cluff and they need to keep an eye on her."

Karen leapt to her feet and rushed to the phone.

James softly kissed my cheek. "I'll take care of this. It's me they want. They're just blaming you."

"They told me I had to break up with you."

"Don't you even dare." He held me tightly as he kissed my head. "I promise you, Cadence, I'll take care of you and Geri. They won't touch either of you again."

Geri rested her head on Flynn's shoulder. They had been together longer than he and I had, probably because she was far more into him than I ever was. I'd broken up with him just before the end of first term, but she was still going strong with him. She even told me she'd had her first kiss with him a few weeks earlier. She'd gone on and on about how perfect it was, while I smiled and forced aside how awkward I remembered it being.

"Cadence."

I blinked. "Huh?"

"Stop staring at me like that."

I giggled. "Sorry."

She smiled, but then her face fell. She straightened and leaned back. "Cay . . ."

A hand wrapped around my braid.

"We had a deal, princess," Robbie said with a hiss in my ear.

I whimpered, glancing around for James. Instead, Robbie's cronies closed in behind Geri and Flynn. One grabbed Geri by the hair and lifted her off the chair, while another shoved Flynn and forced his face onto the table.

"Geri!" I cried as they pulled her away.

"Shut up!" Robbie said. "We gave you fair warning."

Flynn tried to force himself free, but another guy rushed over to hold him down. Geri screamed. Tears burst out of my eyes.

But then, Robbie's hand on my hair jolted.

"I told you to leave them alone," James said in a low voice. "Now let my girlfriend go."

Robbie's hand released my hair, but Geri screamed again.

"Tom!" James yelled.

"I'm on it." James's new best friend dashed away after Geri.

"Robbie, we've talked about this."

"No, we haven't," Robbie responded. "You're so blinded by this stupid girl you're not seeing things clearly. You abandoned your best friends for a *girl*, and a stupid little do-gooder at that! We shared everything, we were practically brothers!"

"Cadence is the best thing that's ever happened to me. But you, all *you* were doing was dragging me down!"

Robbie swore at him and spat out all kinds of foul names for me. In return, James lost it and punched him in the face. Robbie stumbled onto me, pinning me against the table, but James wrenched him off and tossed him into the dirt.

"We're *done,* Rob! Done! Unless you change your ways, I'll never go back to you guys!"

Turning, I saw James standing over Robbie with his fists clenched, his ears reddening with rage. Robbie stared up at him, gaping, but then his expression darkened.

"No one does that to me!"

He launched up and grabbed James. I screeched as his fist struck James's face. Robbie forced him to the ground beneath him, but James matched him in strength and he hit him across the jaw, knocking him to the side.

The sounds of struggling broke out behind me. I swung around to see Flynn hit the guy holding him while Brian and Justin dragged off the other guy. Tom shoved Geri down beside me as he rushed to James's aid.

"Geri!" I turned her to face me. Her hair was messed up, but apart from that, she looked unharmed, just shaken. "Are you okay?"

She shook her head. "They forced drugs down my throat."

I gasped. "Geri! Oh my gosh! We have to get you to the nurse!"

Her lip quivered. "I don't even know what. What if they overdosed me? What if . . . ?" She turned green.

Realizing what was about to happen, I jumped back just in time to avoid having her lunch dumped all over me. Among the vomit lay three little white pills. Cringing, I plucked one up, grabbed her hand, and sprinted her away from the fight.

Geri lay on the bed in the sick bay while I dropped the pill into a Ziploc bag and washed my hands. When I came back to her, she had her hands over her face as tears streamed down her cheeks. I rushed to her side and dabbed at her tears with a tissue. "Geri, I'm so sorry."

She didn't pull her hands away, but her lip trembled.

"It's my fault. I should have warned you after they threatened me. But when James confronted them and his mum called the school, I thought you'd be safe." I stroked her arm. "Please look at me."

She parted her fingers and one brown eye, all blood-shot from crying, stared up at me. "Is Flynn okay?"

I nodded.

"Do you know what they gave me?"

I shook my head. "But the first-aid lady took it to get looked at."

Her fingers closed over her eye. "I'm gonna get sick, aren't I? Or start hallucinating or something."

"I think you threw them up in time."

She bit her lip and clenched her face.

"Geri, I feel like this is my fault. If I'd just dumped James like they said, maybe—"

Her hands flew off her face and she shot up beside me. She grabbed my wrists and stared fiercely into my eyes. "No, Cadence! You and James belong together. If you dumped him because of me, I'd hate you!"

I leaned back, startled. We stared into each other's eyes for several moments, exchanging something, but I wasn't really sure what. "This wasn't your fault," she said softly. "That Robbie is a giant jackass. If he's really James's best friend like he says, he would leave you alone and be happy for you like I am. That's what a *real* best friend does."

Tears burst from my eyes and I threw my arms around her. "I love you, Geraldine Turner."

She clung onto me and buried her face in my hair. "I love you too, Cay-Cay."

A tap on the door brought us out of our moment. We let go and turned to see Flynn, his hair tussled and his shirt half-hanging out. He scratched the back of his neck. "Hey, I just wanted to check on you guys. Your mum's been called, Geri, and she's coming to pick you up and take you to the hospital."

He walked over and kissed my head before softly kissing Geri on the lips. "The fight just got broken up. All of the guys have been dragged into the rooms down the admin hallway. I just got let out with a warning."

"As you should!" Geri folded her arms. "You didn't do anything other than defend yourself."

"Yeah, but it's not looking so good for James. Plenty of people are saying he started it."

I bit my lip, wanting to go to him, but not wanting to leave Geri.

She sensed it and squeezed my hand. "Go, Cay."

I looked into her eyes. "No, I should stay with you."

"Get out of my sight, woman! I'm fine. Flynn's here, so I won't be lonely."

I stood hesitantly. "But I—"

She slapped me hard across my rump. "Go!"

I winced and grabbed at it. "Okay! Geez!"

I hurried into the hallway and turned toward the admin offices. Immediately, I saw several of my guy friends sitting, lining the hallway. I folded my arms around myself, nervous and frightened for James. I stopped in front of Brian and Justin, staring down at them. Their eyes lifted and they both climbed to their feet.

"Cadence! Are you okay?" Brian asked.

"I'm fine."

"Your boyfriend is getting grilled right now," Justin said, tilting his head toward the vice principal's office. "It doesn't look good for him. All those guys said he swung first."

"What are you guys saying?" I asked, glancing desperately between them. They both dodged my gaze.

"To be honest," Brian began, "none of us actually saw. Flynn said he heard Robbie charge James, but his face was pinned to the table, so he couldn't see."

I gnawed on my lip, clinging tightly to myself. "He could get expelled."

Neither of them responded.

I faced the vice principal's closed door. I had to do something. James had stood up for me and protected me again, as well as Geri. He hadn't gone looking for the fight—he'd tried to prevent it. Robbie and his cronies deserved to be expelled, not James.

I took a deep breath and shut my eyes to muster up the bravery I needed. Then, I charged in.

The vice principal stopped talking abruptly, startled by my intrusion. James leapt to his feet. "Cadence—"

"It wasn't James's fault!" I blurted out, my adrenalin pumping through my body. The same crazy aggression I felt while playing sports surfaced and I talked fast and in a near yell. "It was Robbie Cluff! He threatened me and made his moron friends force drugs down Geri's throat. James protected me! If it wasn't for him, Robbie would've really hurt us. And it was *Robbie* who swung first. I saw it! James pulled him off me, and Robbie charged him."

I surged forward and slammed my hand against the desk. "You should be after him, not James, because James did the right thing. They wanted him to go back to them and their self-destructive lifestyle, but he told them no, so they were pissed and tried to force him back by taking it out on two innocent girls!"

The vice principal scowled. "Miss Anderson, isn't it?"

"Yes."

"As much as your outburst was highly inappropriate, I appreciate your input. I'd noticed the absence of Mr. Gordon here in my office of late, *and* the improvements in his grades and attitude in general. I was going to give him a suspension because I didn't want to discourage whatever it was that changed."

"No! He doesn't deserve—"

"Miss Anderson, let me finish." He stared me down as I clamped my mouth shut. "But, with what you've said, I'm inclined to give him some leniency."

I smiled and relaxed. "Really?"

He nodded. "I didn't want to believe what those boys said, but none of your friends knew what happened. Maybe next time you could approach me in a more appropriate way—but I hope there isn't a next time."

I turned to James, who had sat back down. "I told ya, Mr. T."

He nodded calmly. "So you did, James."

"She's a nut, but she keeps me in line."

"And I'm glad to see it. Now get out of my office. I have at least ten more boys to see."

"Aw, I thought we'd catch up. How's the wife?"

The vice principal cracked a smile. "Get out, James."

James jumped up and wrapped his arm around my shoulders as we headed out. In the hallway, everyone had heard me explode at the vice principal. My friends all smirked, while Robbie's friends scowled, knowing I'd turned the tables on them. I didn't care. James was safe from being unjustly disciplined. I squeezed his waist and leaned against his shoulder as we walked away.

We headed to the sick bay. He stopped us outside, turning me to face him. I noticed his split lip and swollen left eye. I gasped and touched his cheek. "James!"

He shrugged. "It's nothing. I've definitely had much worse. You should see Robbie. Phew-ie! I got stuck into him good!"

"James, that's not funny."

He sighed and pushed me against the wall. Our foreheads pressed together. "As long as you're okay."

"Thanks to you."

He stroked my cheek. "When I saw him grab you . . . oh, I just lost it. I told him very clearly to stay away from you."

"I'm sorry, James."

He leaned down and kissed me, but winced and pulled away. "Stupid lip."

I pulled his head down and softly kissed his left eyelid. "Does that help?"

"Mmm." His arms wrapped around me. I giggled and kissed his eye again.

Geri and I sat in the admin offices, completely stunned. "Ecstasy? Cadence . . ."

I grabbed her hand and squeezed it. "Lucky you threw them up."

She shuffled closer to me and leaned on my shoulder. "I'm glad they let you come with me."

I pulled at one of her curls, watching it spring back up when I let it go. "I'm glad you wanted me here with you."

She smiled. "Of course I would. I swear, sometimes it sounds like you think I'm gonna ditch you."

I forced a giggle. My nerves about our fight had died down, but I remained completely focused on *not* offending her in a new way.

"Let's not talk about this," I said. "We've been allowed to take this period off, so let's go hide in one of the library study rooms."

We hurried to the library, where we picked out a couple of novels each, then slipped into a study room. She closed the blinds and the room fell dark for a moment before she switched on the light.

"I love these rooms." She locked the door. "Complete privacy."

We dumped the books and our bags on the desk and sat on the floor together.

"Got any food?" she asked.

"Yeah." I opened my bag and pulled out a packet of chips.

"Sweet."

We sat and munched in silence for a few minutes before she sighed. "Cadence, I think Flynn is losing interest in me."

I stopped munching. "What makes you say that?"

She shrugged. "I dunno. He seems more interested in hanging out with the guys than spending time with me, and he doesn't look at me the way James looks at you. In fact, usually I feel like he's looking straight through me."

"Oh, Geri." I rested my hand on her knee.

"I think I'm gonna break up with him. Our relationship just depresses me, because I'm not getting what I want out of it."

"What do you want?"

She met my gaze. "I want what you and James have. I want a guy to look at me like I'm the only girl in the world and hang off my every word. I want a guy who can be my best friend *and* a boyfriend, so we don't have those awkward moments between us when we feel pressured to do or say something."

I dropped my gaze. "I hope I don't—"

She squeezed my hand. "Hey, there you go again. Cadence, you're my best friend. You're always there for me, and I'll always be here for you, okay?"

I smiled. "So, what are you going to do?"

She leaned back onto her arms. "I'm going to break up with him. I figure it's better if I just cut it off before we can't even be friends anymore."

"Okay, Geri. I'll do anything you need to help you out."

She smiled at me as she lay back on the floor. I shuffled down beside her, our heads touching. Her hand wrapped around mine. I smiled, relief filling my heart.

Chapter Seventeen

The announcement board was boring. I lifted my hand to check the time on my watch. James would be out of detention soon, along with my other guy friends. Across the quad, Melanie sat on the stairs with her back to me as she read. She completely blew me off when she saw me waiting for James by retreating to the stairs, and she hadn't looked around since. I considered going over to sit with her, but I knew that wouldn't end well.

"Hey, Cay." Brian came and stood beside me. "Anything interesting?"

I shook my head as I turned away from the notices. "Same old boring."

"Yeah, that's life." He shifted closer to whisper. "So, out of the five guys in Robbie's group, three were expelled, including Robbie. Apparently, it was the last straw for them."

My stomach flipped. "Are you serious? Over a fight?"

"Nah, it was the drugs on school grounds. When the test came back with what they forced into Geri . . ."

He did a kicking motion.

"Oh my gosh!"

"I know, eh? James found out during detention. He's a bit torn up about it. You might wanna give him a shoulder to cry on."

Justin and Michael emerged, and both acknowledged me before James stepped into the circle. The three of them said a quick goodbye before leaving us.

"James . . ."

But before I could say anything more, his arms wrapped around me. He clung onto me, smelling my hair, stroking my back, and generally reveling in my presence. "I'll never regret choosing to be with you."

I wrapped my arms around him and grasped his shirt. I never wanted to let him go; his soft kisses on my ears sent goose bumps down my body.

"When I heard they got expelled, my only thought was that if it wasn't for you, it could have been me, too."

I clung tighter to him, knowing that wasn't the case. Without me, he still would have graduated somehow, but I understood what he meant. I stretched up and kissed his neck, making him shudder. He dropped his gaze to meet mine.

"Oh gross! Could you guys just stop?" Melanie scowled. "I wanna get home."

James grinned at her. "Mel, you should be nice to Cadence. Without her, I would have been expelled."

Melanie rolled her eyes. "Give up, James. I'm not going to like her, *ever*."

An idea struck me. "Melanie, would you like to go out to the movies sometime with Geri and me? I'll pay if you want."

She scoffed. "That's probably at the bottom of my list of 'must dos' in my lifetime."

"I think that's a good idea," James said. "I'll come along too, just so it's an even number."

"Ah . . . no." Melanie folded her arms.

"Done deal." James wrapped his arm around her shoulders and dragged us away under his arms.

At his house, James and I did our school work as fast as possible before rushing out into the living room and curling up on the couch to watch TV. I sat on one end and he sat on the other. We played this game regularly. He'd start by touching my ankles, and I'd do all I could to ignore him as his hand crept up my leg; once he reached my knee, I'd always shove him off and he'd grab my hand to pull me against him.

He'd rested his hand on my ankle, his fingers creeping up my leg, when Melanie walked in. She groaned and walked back out. James grinned at me and shifted closer, his hand running up my shin.

"Cadence?" Karen walked in and James's hand pulled away. "Would you like to help me bake some chocolate chip cookies?"

"Mum, she's not eight years old!" James said.

The thought of freshly baked cookies after dinner made my stomach growl. "I'm in."

"Aw, Cadence!" James grabbed my hand as I rushed by, but I pulled free with a giggle.

Karen and I got along like a house on fire. We laughed and had a great time as she made dinner and I threw together the cookies. When John came home, he smiled warmly at us. Melanie met him as he walked down the hallway and followed him into his room.

"Why doesn't Melanie give me a chance?" I asked. "I try so hard."

"Don't mind her," Karen said. "She's just moody, and very jealous of her brother's time. They've always been close, being only sixteen months apart. She wasn't really impressed when he changed his ways for you. She thought he was selling out."

"But he's still essentially the same, isn't he? I mean, he just cleaned up his act a bit."

"Yes, and no. He's always been good at heart, but now he doesn't need *her* as much."

I stared into the bowl, my mind ticking it over. *She sees me as a thief . . .*

Karen's hand rested on my back. "It's good for her. She needs to make friends other than her brother."

A door slammed. I looked up as Melanie stormed down the hallway and slammed her bedroom door behind her. James's head appeared through the archway before he trotted away and slipped into her room. After a few moments, she yelled, "She's gonna dump you soon anyway! You've been together for what, six months? Your expiry date is coming up, James! Most relationships at our school are lucky to get past the six-month mark, so I *refuse* to be nice to her! She doesn't deserve it."

"You're so selfish!" James's voice echoed down the hallway. "You used to be cool! Me and Cadence, we're going strong, and all I want is for you to accept her. Her family accepts me, so why is it so hard for you?"

"Because *she* doesn't deserve you! She's a manipulative, backstabbing whore!"

"Don't talk about her like that!"

The yelling continued for several minutes, while I bit my lip out of guilt. Karen watched me, and, noticing my distress, left dinner on the counter and headed down the hallway. The volume increased when she opened the door, but then it fell silent.

James burst out of the room and rushed straight to my side. He kissed me quickly. "Let's go somewhere."

"Where?"

"I dunno. It's not like we can go far. Let's try the park around the corner."

"Okay."

He tugged my hand and we hurried out of the house. We walked to a small play area behind a rugby field. He led me to a bench and sat me down. He paced, running his hand through his hair over and over.

"Today hasn't been a good day for you," I said.

He scoffed. "No, it really hasn't."

"I'm sorry."

He paused and stared down at me with such an intense gaze I stopped breathing. "Cadence, we're all good, right?"

"Yeah."

"You're not bored of me or interested in someone else?"

"No."

He ruffled his hair and fell to his knees in front of me. "Promise me we're fine."

"James, we're more than fine. Being with you makes me so happy."

He leaned over and clasped my hands between his and kissed them. I bent over, lifting his face so I could kiss him. He eagerly reciprocated and sat up on his knees. I wrapped my arms around his neck, leaving his hands resting on my knees. His hands opened around my knees and slowly crept under my skirt.

I gasped and broke away from the kiss, but his hands wandered higher as he leaned in and kissed my neck. Intensely aware of his fingers on my thighs, I held my breath as they found their way to my underwear.

"James . . ."

"It's okay. I'm not going to take them off."

His hands moved on to the insides of my thighs, making me flinch away. His hands retreated from up my skirt and he clasped my face to kiss me again. He climbed up beside me on the bench and pulled me onto his lap as we made out.

Eventually, we stopped and sat gazing into each other's eyes.

"We should go back."

"Mmm." He stroked my face and his gaze followed his finger over each curve and contour. "You're so beautiful."

I broke into a wide grin, giggling and blushing as I buried my face into his shoulder. His arms tightened as he laughed softly at my reaction.

I held Geri's hand as Flynn approached the group. She took a deep breath as he paused to greet the guys, then stood.

"I'll be here when you get back," I said.

She squeezed my hand as she stepped out from the picnic table. She made her way to Flynn and pulled him aside to talk. Michael took her spot. "Hey."

"Hey." I wasn't paying attention to anyone other than Geri. Flynn had his back to me, so I couldn't see his reaction as she spoke to him.

"Disco is tomorrow," Michael said. "Are you going?"

"Hmm?"

"Cadence!"

I turned slightly. "Sorry. It's just . . ." I gestured to Geri and Flynn.

"Oh." He sighed. "Oh well, it was kinda coming. They don't spend much time together anymore."

"Mmm."

He wrapped his arm around my shoulders. "Cay, are *you* okay?"

I tilted my head to face him and rested my cheek on my hand. "Melanie's kinda getting to me, that's all. She's dead set against me and James, and they had a huge row last night about me while I was there."

"Oh, bummer."

"Yeah."

"Why does she hate you?"

I twisted my loose hair around my finger. "She thinks it's my fault everyone hates her." I went on to explain everything to him.

When I finished, he paused thoughtfully, then said, "Why don't you try to make people like her then?"

I raised my eyebrows. "People don't like her 'cause she's weird."

"Everyone thought James was a total druggy loser." He shrugged. "Geri's coming back."

And with that, he left.

Geri sank down beside me and rested her head on my shoulder. "That's it."

I stroked her hair. "How'd he take it?"

"Surprisingly well. He didn't say anything until I finished explaining myself. Then he said, 'Okay, I understand,' and offered me his hand and said we could still be friends."

"How about you?"

She sighed, but didn't answer. I stroked her hair, knowing she felt hurt. But she had been brave and had done the right thing, and I'd done right by her this time around.

"Where's James?" she asked.

"He said he had some catch-up work to do or something."

She shuffled closer to me. "The second term disco is tomorrow." She lifted her head with a crooked smile. "Where you and James first met last year."

"Don't remind me. He was a jerk back then."

She giggled and rested her head back on my shoulder. "Yes, but it changed everything, didn't it?"

I smiled. She had no idea.

"Yeah, it did."

Getting ready at James's house felt odd. He watched me wash up in the bathroom, and stood by his door without a shirt on when I came out, again watching me. He eyed me over slowly as he pulled on a white, pinstriped shirt and started buttoning it.

I went to get my hairbrush from my bag. His hand came down and grabbed my butt as I passed. I swung around and slapped his arm.

He grabbed me and pulled me in. "You look incredible. What else am I supposed to do?" His hand ran over my butt again in my tight, black flared pants.

I tried to pull his hands off me. "Seriously, stop it."

He smirked and lifted his hands onto my waist. "I can see why I couldn't resist you last year. You scrub up really nice."

I giggled. "I wish I could say the same about you that night, but it wasn't exactly . . . you know."

"Uh huh. You're so superficial."

I giggled as he kissed me.

"Ugh." Melanie dashed back into her room.

I remembered what Michael said and dashed in after her.

"Get out!"

"Why don't you join us tonight?" I asked.

"Ew, no."

"Melanie, come on. You'd be pretty if you wanted to be. You just don't seem to want to try. Surely there's some guy you've got a thing for. We can scrub you up and catch his eye."

She glared at me. "I don't want a makeover. I'm not desperate like my brother."

I pulled her hair out of her messy ponytail. "Brush it."

"Get lost."

"Just brush it or I'll do it for you."

She scowled, but lifted a hairbrush to it. Her hair looked quite healthy and had a beautiful chestnut color, just like James's, but the ends were ratty and split.

"James?"

He popped his head in.

"Are there hairdresser scissors around somewhere?"

Melanie swung to me with alarm. "You're not cutting my hair!"

"It won't be much. Just to here." I did a cutting motion on her shoulder.

"No!"

James appeared at my side, holding out a pair of scissors. "Do as she says, Mel. She's trying to be nice."

"She's trying to turn me into a clone!"

While they argued, I snipped off her ratty ends and evened it out. "Done."

"What?" She sprinted down the hall to the bathroom. She gasped. In her absence, I dropped her hair in the trash.

James poked his head out the door. "I don't know if she's freaking out or not."

"I'd say she is," I answered calmly.

Finally, she plodded back into the room and James whistled his approval. Her hair had completely transformed into a healthy glow around her face. The ends curled neatly under, but she kept her eyes down as she returned to the chair by her desk. I stepped up behind her and ran her brush through it one last time to tidy the ends. Then I turned to her wardrobe and flung it open.

"Hey!" She leapt to her feet.

"Geez, are these all hand-me-downs from James?"

"Get out!" She rushed at me, but James caught her and held her back.

I pushed through and found a pair of cargos that could be considered fashionable, and a smaller white T-shirt. "Put these on."

"No!"

I tossed them on the bed. "I could make you wear this if you want?" I tugged at my pink and red tank top.

She glared at me. "Fine. Get out so I can change."

When she opened the door, she growled. "This shirt is too tight."

But it wasn't. "You're just used to baggy shirts. It looks completely normal. In fact, I can see your waist, and it's so tiny!"

She flushed and slammed the door shut. James threw it open again. "Melanie, you actually look like a girl! You're staying as you are."

He grabbed her wrist and pulled her out of the room. I grinned as I hurried to finish getting ready.

As we climbed out of the car together, the reaction to Melanie's transformation was immediate. Guys stared at the girl who'd been hidden under oversized clothing and ratty hair. She wasn't comfortable with it and ducked behind James.

She tried to disappear into a corner, but James caught her and forced her to join our group.

Geri's jaw dropped when she saw her, and she rushed over to me. "What did you do to Melanie? She looks like a *girl*! And a pretty one at that!"

I glanced over as Brian leaned in and said something to her. She blushed, which made him grin.

"Wow, that was quick," I said.

James looked over and laughed. "Nice!"

Later that night, while James and I sat outside having a drink, Melanie and Brian slipped around a corner. James shot to his feet and yanked me after him. We peeked around to see them kissing.

James pushed me back with a huge grin. "Finally! She's totally liked that guy for ages!"

"Brian? Seriously?"

"Yeah."

"Maybe that's why she didn't like me, 'cause he's liked me for ages."

He clasped my face. "Who cares? She'll get off our case now!" He smacked a kiss on my lips. "Let's party."

Later, as we stood around waiting for our parents, Melanie hung back with Brian to say goodbye. Geri came up beside me, nudging me. She nodded toward them just as they kissed. "Wow, didn't see that coming."

"I know. It's great, huh?" James grinned. "I have the best girlfriend ever."

Brian's ride arrived and once he'd gone, Melanie came over and stood beside James with a giddy grin across her face. She glanced across at me. Her grin fell slightly, but she didn't say anything. By the look in her eyes, I knew things would be different between us from then onward. The next day, she wore the girls' uniform to school.

Chapter Eighteen

The rest of the year seemed to soar by. Before I knew it, September arrived and so had Harper's graduation. She ended up getting very good grades—much better than the first time around—and even applied for several arts degrees. All she needed was to sit the exams to know if she'd get in or not.

The night after her graduation, she called the whole family to come to her room. She stood outside, holding the door shut with a nervous smile. "I wanna show you guys something, and Dad, in case you flip out, it was Cadence's idea."

She opened the door and led us in. We glanced around, wondering what was new. She gestured to the ceiling. Mum looked up first and gasped, causing us all to look up. Above her bed was a painting of us. Mum and Dad gazed into each other's eyes, while Dusty and I sat laughing with our arms around each other, our matching sandy blond hair blending together where our heads touched.

"Harper!" Mum said breathlessly as a tear ran down her face.

Harper shrugged. "It's what I wanted to wake up and see every day."

Mum threw her arms around her as she sobbed. Harper looked at me with alarm, and I mouthed, "*They're happy tears.*" She smiled and clung tighter to Mum.

Curious to see their reactions, I turned to Dusty and Dad. Dusty stared up at himself, tilting his head back and forth, unsure whether he liked it, while Dad fought back a scowl. I stepped over and wrapped my arm around him. "Dad, it's a really nice gesture."

"I know, which is why I can't be mad." He rested his hand around my shoulder. "But the ceiling? We buy her enough canvases and art books."

"You can just paint over it when she's gone."

"That's the thing. I like it, so I don't want to."

I squeezed his waist and rested my head on his chest. "You're the best, Dad."

He rubbed my back, kissing my head.

James was stressing out about his end of year exams, so I spent almost every afternoon at his house working through his notes. He grew short-tempered with me when I knew things I shouldn't. One day, as we studied his PE notes for his exam the next day, he lost it.

"How do you know all of this? Are you taking extra classes I don't know about?"

"James, I've been studying with you all year!"

"That doesn't explain how you know all this new stuff!" He tossed his book across the room. "Geez, Cadence, you're such a little know-it-all! Why don't you just sit the exam for me? At least then I know I'll pass."

"James!"

"I'm tired of it. You're such a brainiac, and I'm so stupid!"

"You're not stupid!"

"Compared to you I am!"

I jumped to my feet. "This is stupid. I don't wanna argue about this."

"See? You just said I'm stupid."

"No, I didn't! Argh!" I marched out of his room to find Melanie.

"Get back here, Cadence!"

"Not until you're done being a jerk!"

I found Melanie in her room, studying with Brian for our exams. I stood with my arms folded as we listened to James rant on about being too stupid to pass, until he finally fell silent. I waited a few moments before I returned to his room.

He lay on his bed with his earphones in. He saw me come in and rolled onto his side, facing away from me. I hesitated. Biting my lip, I quietly shut the door.

I sat on the bed beside him and touched his shoulder. He pulled away. I sighed and lay beside him, wrapping my arm around him. It felt right. I'd done it to Austin when he was upset, so my instincts told me it would make James feel better too.

James's breath became shallow as he felt me curl up beside him, and it only took a moment for me to feel his hand on mine. I shut my eyes and snuggled up to him. He turned off his music and set his earphones on the bedside table. He rolled over to face me and gazed into my eyes. He stroked my face, making me smile.

"Cadence?"

"Yeah?"

"I'm sorry I yelled at you."

"I know, and I'm sorry I irritated you."

His arm wrapped around me and he pulled me in for a kiss. The kiss was long and passionate, sending my whole body into quivering excitement.

When he pulled away, he pressed his forehead against mine. "We fight a whole lot."

I giggled. "Yeah, but making up is nice."

He softly kissed me. "Yeah."

The weekend before our School Certificate exams, Geri, Melanie, and I decided we needed a break from studying. They came to my house, and we sat in my room playing cards.

Melanie was kicking our butts when Dusty walked in and sat on the bed beside me. He leaned against my shoulder and watched us play in silence.

"Dusty, why are you here?" Geri asked. "Why don't you go play a video game or something?"

"Because I wanna hang out with Cadence," he answered.

"You're so weird, kid. What thirteen-year-old wants to hang out with his sister?"

Dusty sat up straight and looked her firmly in the eyes. "Me. I like Cadence."

"I like hanging out with my brother," Melanie said nonchalantly.

"Yeah, but James isn't a little dweeb." Geri scowled. "James is a hottie, and he's cool."

"Ew. He's my brother."

Geri turned to face her. "Oh, so you *don't* have Tasmanian-style feelings for him?"

She stared at Geri, confused, then she scowled. "Are you implying I have a crush on my brother? Geri, seriously, you have some messed up ideas."

I giggled at the playful banter they tossed between them. Melanie remained surly and sarcastic, but she'd really opened up to Geri and me. Although the Gordon kids had been closed off and rebellious in the other timeline, they held big hearts inside them that they wanted to give away.

"Brian, Brian, Brian, Brian . . ."

"Shut up, Geri! You're such a weirdo."

I returned to reality and intervened. "So, James is getting his Ps today, right?"

Their heads snapped around to look at me.

"Yeah," Melanie said. "If he passes the driving test, he's gonna pick me up."

"I can't believe he's seventeen!" Geri exclaimed, leaping to her feet. "That means that right now, he's two years older than you, Cay! Two years!"

I laughed. "That's not how it works."

She ignored me. "Soon, you'll be dating a twelfth grader! Holy cow!" She pulled at one of her curls and stared off with a dreamy look in her eyes. "That's so old!"

"Geri! We're going to be eleventh graders soon, and I'm sixteen in a week. You're totally blowing this out of proportion."

"No, I'm not. Just think about it. We were in the ninth grade when you started dating him, and now, he's almost in year twelve!"

"But he was a tenth grader."

"Don't use that logic on me, missy."

Melanie threw a card at Geri's face. She grinned as Geri glowered at her.

"So, talking about James," Melanie said without looking away from Geri, "he's got a huge thing planned out for your one year anniversary. Hopefully he'll get his license, or it will all be ruined."

Geri scrambled back onto the bed, getting right in her face. "What's he doing?"

Melanie smiled, but didn't say a word. Geri squealed with delight and danced around the room. "It's so romantic!"

She hurried over and turned up the music on my computer to dance. She pulled me to my feet so I'd dance with her. We laughed and spun around my room before she fell into my arms in a giggling fit.

"You guys are weird," Dusty said.

Someone knocked on the front door. Geri gasped, her whole face lighting up as she gave me a mischievous grin. But Melanie reacted the fastest. She shot out of my room, while Geri screamed and hurried after her. They tussled all the way to the door before Geri answered it.

"Hey, James!"

"Hey, Geri, Mel."

I hurried down the hall with Dusty at my side as James came through the door. Dusty rushed at him and rambled about being the only guy in a house filled with crazy girls, but James only had eyes for me. His whole face lit up when he saw me and my heart skipped a beat. My cheeks warmed, making his smile widen. He pushed through the three of them to meet me.

"Hey, beautiful."

It amazed me that after so long, those two words could still make my heart flutter.

He dug into his pocket and pulled out his license. "I got it."

I grinned and wrapped my arms around him, kissing his cheek. He sighed and held on to me.

"That's still gross," Melanie said.

"No, it isn't!" Geri shoved her. "It's so cute."

"No, I agree, it's gross," Dusty said.

The three of them argued as James and I smiled at each other. He bent down and softly kissed me.

Exams came to an end. The day of my birthday, I arrived at school feeling giddy with anticipation. James had something big planned that everyone kept whispering about. As the bus pulled up, my stomach filled with butterflies. James was waiting for me, his hands in his pockets.

He rushed at me as I stepped off the bus, scooping me up and spinning me around. He kissed me over and over before he set me down. "Today, it's just you and me."

He dragged me over to his bag and pulled out a pair of my jeans and a pale pink polo shirt. "Hurry up and get changed so we can get out of here."

My heart pounded. I'd skipped school in the first timeline, but only one class at a time, and never the whole day. But as I looked at him, his eyes bright with excitement, I couldn't refuse. I snatched my clothes and hurried to his car.

I changed in his backseat as he stood outside with his back pressed against the window. When I finished, we both climbed in the front. He grinned and kissed my hand. "Are you ready?"

I nodded, my stomach doing somersaults.

He started the engine, and as we pulled out, he pumped up the music. As we drove, I had to yell over the music to talk to him. He found it highly amusing, and turned it louder when I started to talk, yelling, "What?"

After half an hour driving, I grew curious and turned off the stereo. "Where are we going?"

He grinned, but didn't answer.

"Seriously, where are we going?"

"I'm going to throw you off the harbor bridge."

"You're hilarious," I responded as he smirked. I turned and saw his bag sitting on the backseat. He had to have some hint in there, so I lunged at it.

"Hey!"

He tried to stop me, but I was too quick. I pulled it onto my lap, and even with his hand trying to grab the zippers, I managed to open it. "My swimsuit and board shorts? And your board shorts too? James! Are we going to the beach?"

"You need to stop being so nosey." He pulled his bag out of my hands and tossed it into the back. But he wasn't upset—he wore a wide grin.

I giggled. "My first beach trip for the season and it's with you. I'm so excited! James, you're the best boyfriend ever."

His smile widened as he gave me an adoring glance.

We arrived at the beach and found it surprisingly quiet. A few groups of teenagers hung around, also skipping school to avoid the holiday rush, but aside from that, only one small family knelt in the sand, building sandcastles together.

James guided me straight to the change rooms to put on my swimsuit, then we ran into the water. Still being early in the season, the water felt like ice. I shrieked and pulled back. He laughed and lifted me off my feet, walked out until the waves crashed around us, and dropped me.

I sprang out and clung onto him. The freezing water made my heart pound, but my momentum, along with a wave crashing into us, knocked us both back in. He wrapped his arms around me and pulled us back up. As we resurfaced, he burst out laughing. "You're such a girl!"

"Shut up!"

He held on to me as he walked out beyond the break. We stayed out there and talked for an hour. The cold soon seemed to be not as bad as we swam around in circles. He slowly moved closer to me until our faces almost touched. His gaze fell onto my lips as I talked, making me pause. He didn't even notice I'd stopped talking as he stared at my lips, so I kissed him.

He clasped my face and kissed me eagerly. Despite the cold, his lips against mine filled me with warmth and excitement. I ran my hands down his back, and noticed something. I pulled back and looked at his chest. "Wow, you've filled out."

He grinned and flexed. "I know. I did weight training, remember?"

I ran my hands over his chest and shoulders. He'd always been toned, but he'd bulked up, making him look like more of a man and less of a teenager. How had I not noticed it before? I bit my lip, feeling more attracted to him than ever.

He watched my face as I ran my hands over him. "You like it, huh?"

"Mmm." My breath caught as his pectorals twitched under my touch.

He pulled me closer, my sudden awareness of his muscular arms making me gasp before he kissed me. We fell into a long kiss, so much feeling from both of us pouring into it. I couldn't believe how crazy I was about him, and how much I'd missed out on the first time around.

When he let go, he said, "Cadence, you're the best thing that's ever happened to me."

"Oh James." I stroked his face as I stared up at him, my heart pounding.

"Every day, when I see you, I wonder how I got so lucky." He rested his forehead against mine. "This year has been the best year of my life."

I stroked his cheek. "James, you've made this year so much better than I could have ever hoped."

He smiled and let out a long breath. "Happy birthday and anniversary, Cadence."

"You too, James."

We made our way out of the water and found a fish and chips shop. We took the paper package to a picnic table overlooking the beach by his car. As he set up, I rushed to my bag and pulled out my present for him. I handed it to him as we sat to eat.

He opened it eagerly. "A gift card for Pavarotti's Pizza! Perfect! You know me too well!"

He leaned over and kissed me.

After we'd eaten and he'd tried to make a seagull eat a Panadol pill to see if it would explode, he pulled out a present for me. "I hope it's okay if I combined three presents in one."

I opened it and stared in awe at a gold necklace with an intricately woven heart pendant. Inside the heart sat a small, clear diamond. "James!"

"Is it okay?"

"James! How do I even . . ." I ran my fingers over the heart. "This . . . it's beautiful!"

"Just like you."

My heart melted. I leapt up and jumped onto him, kissing him passionately. His hands found everything on the table somehow, and he packed up without breaking away from me for a moment. He guided me over to the car, tossed everything in the front seat, and pushed me onto the backseat.

He climbed on top of me, pulling the door shut behind him. He had his hands all over my face. It felt so intense, so intoxicating, that I couldn't resist him. I wrapped my legs around him as he pressed down on me.

"Cadence!" he moaned excitedly. "You're driving me wild."

"Shut up and kiss me."

He rubbed up against me, our board shorts sticking and pulling together. I stroked his bare back, enjoying the feeling of his muscles flexing as he rubbed up against me.

"Cadence?"

"Yes?"

"Are we . . . ?" He pulled away and stared at me. "Shoot! Not here!"

He jumped off and climbed out of the car, slamming the door. I sat up, breathless, and watched him sprint to the beach and jump into the waves.

Then I came to my senses and slapped my forehead. *Crap!* We'd been leading to sex! And worst of all, in the back of a *car*. A freaking *car*!

As James walked back, I bit my lip. He was so attractive, and every inch of me screamed to have him. I cursed my raging teenage hormones. It wasn't hard the first time around because I hadn't cared about someone like I did James. I hadn't desired someone like I did him.

But I had to resist. Austin needed to be my first and only, even if I couldn't feel anything for him yet. I knew I would eventually.

James opened the door and squatted in front of me. "That was intense."

I ran my fingers through my damp hair, avoiding his gaze.

"Are you okay? You look a little rattled."

"I, ah . . ." I looked into his eyes. "I wanted it, really bad. I can't do that again."

He nodded and clutched my hands. "I know, I understand." He shifted up onto the seat beside me, then lifted my chin. "It's going to be harder from here on, but I will do all I can to respect you. You mean too much to me to mess things up like that."

"Thank you, James." I snuggled up into his arms. We sat in silence, just enjoying being together.

We returned to school so we could pick up Dusty just as the end of day bell rang. We sat in the car together, feeling something different between us. It wasn't just him who wanted more, but both of us. But that *more* was off limits.

He stroked my leg, staring at his hand as it made its way up and down my thigh. His desire for me poured out of him, but he held it in. I appreciated that, knowing what it meant.

Geri leaned over and pounded on my window. I opened it as she grinned. "How was it? Man, I wish I could have gone to the beach today. It's been so hot!"

James grinned, all the pent-up tension instantly disappearing from his face. "It was great. I love seeing Cadence in her swimsuit."

Geri laughed. "You perv!"

He shrugged. "Would you like me to look at you instead?"

She leaned in and punched his shoulder. "You're creepy! Cadence, he's creepy. How have you put up with him for a year?" Her face was right next to mine as her eyes twinkled.

"I dunno." I sighed. "He's kinda cute, I guess."

Geri squeezed his shoulder, giving it a good feel. "Oh, yeah, okay, I'll give you that."

"Cadence." James grunted. "Your friend is feeling me up."

Geri smirked and her hand wandered onto his chest. He shoved her off and she burst out laughing. She pulled out of the car and winked at me. "He's only getting better with age. Love ya, Cay-Cay!"

I waved as she ran off, and turned to see James staring at me with that same intense desire. My breath caught as I gazed into his eyes. Finally, I managed to say, "Don't let my dad see you looking at me like that."

He blinked. "Huh?"

"Tonight, at dinner? He'll kill you."

"Oh." He rubbed his face. "I think it'll be easier once Harper is whining in my ear."

A moment later, Dusty burst in and started rattling off his day to James. James glanced at me as he started the engine and mouthed, "*That'll do, too.*"

Chapter Nineteen

Mum and Dad agreed to let each of us kids have a couple of friends over for New Year's. Somehow, I managed to weasel my way from two to four, so I could have Melanie and Brian with us. That also meant Dusty and Harper complained and ended up with four, too.

Harper and I sprawled on the couch, watching the clock tick by on the wall.

"This is the longest hour of my life," she said.

"Longer than your exams?"

"Yeah. At least I had something to do." She shifted and pulled at her black tank top. "It's so hot."

"Harper, do you think you'll move out when you go to uni?"

"Wow, segue." She flipped over to look down into my face. "I dunno. I guess it depends on which school I get into. I mean, Newcastle or Charles Sturt would definitely mean a move, but the Sydney ones, maybe not."

I remembered she'd moved out as soon as she'd lined up something in the city the first time around. She'd met her future husband with some friends during that first year, and I wondered if going to university instead would prevent her from meeting him. I hoped not. Daniel had been great for her, and still would be.

"I hope I stay local," she said. "I'd like to stay at home and mooch off Mum and Dad."

I giggled.

She smiled and brushed her fingers through my hair. "Cadence, thanks for not being such a brat this year. It's nice to have you to talk to, like when we were little."

I didn't want to say her attitude made all the difference and make her angry, so I just smiled. "It's been nice to have you to talk to as well."

For a moment, her whole face lit up, but then she flicked my cheek. "You're such a sap."

Movement outside the front window made us both sit up.

"Who do you think that is?" I asked.

"I hope it's Loz," she responded, referring to her best friend. We both leapt to our feet when the doorbell rang, but she shoved me back onto the couch as she rushed to the door. She opened it and looked noticeably disappointed. "Oh, it's you."

"Shut up, Harper," Geri responded. "Let me in."

Harper moved aside. Geri opened the screen door and grinned at me. She rushed over, grabbed my arm, and pulled me into my bedroom. She sat me on my bed, then flopped beside me. "Okay, so, I know it's been a few weeks, but I could tell something happened on your birthday with James."

My stomach knotted. "What?"

She sat up, her eyes wide. "I'm right, aren't I? Cadence!" She rushed over and shut the door. She shot back to my side and grabbed my hand. "Did you guys . . . you know?"

My cheeks burned. "No."

"Really? I kinda got that vibe from him over the last few weeks. He's been staring at you really intensely."

I glanced toward the door, hoping Dad wasn't listening on the other side. "We didn't go that far. Things heated up a bit, but we stopped. We agreed that we're not going to go there."

She stared at me, her mouth hanging open. "Really?"

I nodded. "I don't want to have sex yet. I wanna be an adult first so I can be smart about it, and not do it just because I can."

"But you've been with James for a year, and you're sixteen now, too. Cadence, I'd even say he's in love with you.

He's the perfect guy to be with. He's not going anywhere, and he'll be gentle with you."

I glared at her. "I don't need to have sex, Geri."

"I'm not saying that. I'm just saying you and James work. I think if you were both five years older, he'd totally wanna marry you. So, if you were to do it, I would totally understand."

I scowled and turned away from her. I wrapped my arms around myself. "I'm not ready."

"Is it because of your dad?"

I turned to her, alarmed. "What?"

"I'd be scared to do it, too, if I had a dad like yours."

"No! That's not it at all! I mean, I respect my dad not wanting me to, but this is my decision. *I* don't want to."

"Okay, okay." She leaned back and stared up at my ceiling. "But if something does happen, know I'll be here for you and I won't tell anyone."

I rested my head on her shoulder. "I know, you always are."

Later that night, we all crammed into the living room, talking loudly while the TV played to itself. Dad watched me closely with James. It made me uneasy. I felt like he knew what had happened, and it riddled me with guilt.

"Cadence!" Harper yelled. "It's your turn to fill the punch bowl!"

I jumped up, pulling free of James's arm around my shoulders, and dashed into the kitchen with the bowl. I took a deep breath to calm my nerves, but then Dad came up behind me. I jumped and turned to face him. I found him smiling.

"Cadence, I must say, I've been very impressed with James of late."

"Oh?" I tilted my head, hoping my guilt wasn't written across my face.

"Yes. Your mother told me about the gift he gave you, and he's been very respectful to you. It seems my initial concerns were unnecessary."

I forced a smile. "He's good to me. I really like him."

He touched my hair. "I know you do, and I can see he really likes you, too. I'm proud of you, Cadence, for being so careful who you date and sticking to your boundaries. You are such a good girl."

I almost burst into tears and confessed everything when he wrapped his arms around me, holding me in a tight embrace. But I couldn't tell him. He would forbid me from seeing James and would never look at me the same way again. I shut my eyes and squeezed him, swearing I'd never go that far with James again.

I returned with the refilled punchbowl, and as I set it down, I instantly felt James's hands on my waist.

"Hello, beautiful," he said in my ear. "Since that kiss worked perfectly last year, I have every intention of taking it again." He softly kissed my ear, making me smile.

Melanie shuffled up beside us and sighed. Something was wrong with her—I'd sensed it all night. She was quiet and closed off from Brian, so he'd spent most of the night talking to Geri instead.

"Hey, Mel," I said gently.

She grunted her response, then shoved food into her mouth.

"Is everything okay?"

She shrugged, but didn't look up at me.

James let go of me and took her arm. "Hey, come with me."

She let him lead her away. I scanned the room, looking at our friends. Harper's friends had been with her as long as I could remember. They were good and loyal, and stuck with her no matter what.

Dusty's friends were typical little eighth grade boys—a hint of nerdy about to step into the awkward 'trying to be cool and notice girls' stage. I noticed one staring at one of Harper's friends, obviously already entering that stage.

I looked at Geri and Brian. They'd known each other since kindergarten, and were comfortable just chilling out together. They talked casually, not really paying much attention to anything else. I smiled, feeling lucky to have such good friends.

I sat beside Geri. Brian sat up straight and looked me over. Was he *completely* mad? He was with Melanie, and I was clearly tied to James.

In the middle of Geri's sentence, he said, "Hey, Cadence."

Geri paused and raised an eyebrow. "Dude, I was *talking.*"

"Sorry, I just didn't want her to think we were ignoring her."

"I'm fine, Brian," I responded. "Go on, Geri."

She continued talking and I closed my eyes, just enjoying listening to her voice.

"Are you tired, Cadence?" Brian's voice cut in again.

I opened my eyes. "No, I'm fine. Stop interrupting her."

Geri huffed before she continued. A moment later, James came over and shoved himself between me and the arm of the sectional. Geri raised her eyebrow, but didn't miss a beat. Melanie slipped in and sat in front of Brian, but apart from shifting his legs to give her space, he didn't even react.

I stared down at Melanie, realizing the source of her somber mood. Brian was blowing her off. I threw him an icy glare and found him staring at me. He flinched at my look and turned his attention to Melanie, softly touching her hair.

Was he *crazy*? Melanie was *way* prettier than me. To make him stop screwing up his relationship, I leaned back onto James's chest. James's arms wrapped around me and he kissed the top of my head.

Brian saw the exchange of affection and sank back into the sectional.

James shifted my hair so he could whisper in my ear. "Why did you invite Brian tonight?"

I sighed. "For Melanie."

"Is that the only reason?"

"Of course."

His right arm tightened around my middle while his left came up and touched my jaw so he could pull my ear closer. "I remember you went on a date with him. There's no lingering feelings between you, is there?"

I turned to look into his eyes. I saw a hint of jealousy, but mostly pain. "No. The only person here I have feelings for is you."

The pain and jealousy vanished in exchange for adoration. "I thought so too, but Mel is pretty upset and says he still likes you. She believes he took the invitation as a hint that you were maybe interested in him."

"That's crazy!"

"I said that too, but . . ." He sighed. "You should talk to her before we leave tonight."

"I can do that."

Geri shrieked as Dusty dumped a cup of water over her. He swung around, startled, having no idea he'd done it, and she stood and ripped into him. He stepped back and stared up at her, wide-eyed and frightened.

"Geri." I reached for her arm. "It was an accident."

"Stupid little brat should be paying more attention and not flinging his arms around wildly!" Geri hissed into his face.

Dusty looked to me for help.

I jumped up and pulled him away, taking him back to the safety of his friends. There, he turned to me and said, "I didn't mean to. Geri's totally nuts."

"Don't worry about it," I said. "She's just wired from all the sugar."

"Hey! The countdown is about to begin!" one of Harper's friends called out.

They hit ten, and I turned to see James leaping to his feet and looking at me. I rushed across the room, unable to look away from his smile. As they hit two, I jumped into his arms, and he kissed me.

One . . .

Freeze . . .

Everything fell silent. I pulled away from James and saw everyone frozen in time. I'd forgotten about this. The man in white hadn't come to me once all year.

Looking around, Geri grinned up at James and me, and my parents had their lips pressed together. Everyone else stared at the TV with anticipation as the fireworks from the harbor were about to ignite.

Except Melanie. She stared at Brian with a sad longing in her eyes as he stood beside her, apparently watching the TV, but really watching me and James out of the corner of his eye. I glared at him, rested my left hand on my hip, and slapped him across the face.

"You jerk."

"Cadence."

I turned at the voice. The man in white, again dressed as Father Time, stood by the front door. He stepped over to me with a scowl. "Was that really necessary?"

I looked back at Brian. "Yes, it was."

He bowed his head. "If that's how you feel."

He reached out and touched my shoulder. Like the previous year, my feelings and memories of Austin and Melody overwhelmed me—her tiny hand wrapping around my finger as she nursed, his eyes watching in total awe and devotion at the sight of his little family when he arrived home from work.

I stumbled back onto the couch as my heart swelled with love, grief, pain, and a new feeling . . .

I looked up at James, again locked in a kiss, and felt . . . torn.

"What's happening?" I tugged at my hair.

"Things are changing," the man said. "This time-line has strayed a long way from your original past, and now it's not just a few people who are affected." He gestured to the people in the room. "Everyone here has been touched by the different choices you've made. Harper is happier, and so her friends aren't as weighed down by her bad mood. Dusty has an older brother figure, so he feels bolder around his friends and is becoming the leader of their little pack."

He turned me and led me to my parents. "Their marriage is stronger because they aren't so burdened by Harper's bad choices, your string of boyfriends and social dramas, and little Dusty being bullied."

He stretched out his hand and motioned to Melanie. "And Melanie Gordon has discovered she is likeable. She looks in the mirror and sees she is not a nobody. She has even started to believe that maybe she might be pretty to someone."

"Melanie is beautiful." I stepped in front of her and looked into her gray-blue eyes. "I wish she could see it. She fights it so much, but I truly feel that if I continue being her friend, maybe she'll finally see what I see."

He leaned in behind me and spoke softly into my ear. "Very good, sweet Cadence. Do you want to know what happened to Melanie in the other timeline?"

"You can do that?"

"Oh yes. Follow me."

He led me out the front door and I found myself standing in Melanie's room. She was in the twelfth grade, with a pile of books on her desk. But she wasn't looking at them. Instead, she sat on her bed, cutting her wrist open. By the bandage on her left arm, she had no intention of killing herself, she just wanted to cut.

I gasped and collapsed onto my knees in front of her. "Oh no! Melanie!" I tried to grab her hand to stop her, but my fingers went straight through.

"This is just a shadow," the man said. "The only way to avoid this outcome is by you making different choices. All she wants is friends and to feel cared about. She cuts to relieve the pain of rejection by her peers."

He waved his hand and the room changed to several years later. She must have been about twenty-two and wore more feminine attire. But she was packing her bags. She was going somewhere, and fast.

"What happened?" I asked.

"James isn't in her life anymore," he said. "He was the only person she believed ever cared about her, so without him, she wants to run away and start over fresh."

I stepped over to her desk and saw a plane ticket to London Heathrow resting open on it. "She's running clear across the world? Is there really nothing here for her? What about her parents?"

"She doesn't want to have anything to do with them. They remind her of James."

I watched as she zipped up her two full bags and grasped her ticket. Then, the scene changed, but we were somewhere else completely. We were back at school earlier that year. I glanced around, confused by the sudden change, and asked, "What are we looking at now?"

"This is about Geri now. This is the day you and she fought."

Like the last time, the scene split in two so I could watch both timelines. In the first one, I saw myself holding Flynn's hand and gazing into his eyes with a flirtatious smile. In the new one, I sat with James at the table while he drew something on my hand.

Both Geris left the main building and headed right for me. She sat beside me in the new timeline, grinning at me even though I didn't even acknowledge her, and sighed before pulling out her food.

In the first, she paused and her face fell. Her fists clenched, and she stormed over to me. "Cadence!"

I turned to her and smiled. "Hey, Geri."

"Why . . . you . . . and . . ." She turned bright red. "I hate you! We're over! You are the worst friend ever, you backstabbing slut! You think you're so wonderful, with your perfect blonde hair and your flirty eyes! But you're not! You're selfish and . . . and . . ." She shoved me. "We're done! I did *everything* for you, and you . . ." She glanced at Flynn before pointing at my chest. "I hope you rot in hell!"

She marched away while I stared after her, gaping. Then, I said something that made me cringe with shame.

"What's her deal? Whatever, she'll get over it."

The scenes froze.

I covered my face in utter horror. How could I have never seen that? How had I never known?

"Cadence." The man took my elbow and led me over to the second timeline. I didn't want to look, I felt so ashamed of what I'd done. I'd hurt my best friend so badly, and in my ignorance I'd never known why. I'd just grieved for her loss and wondered where it had fallen apart.

"Cadence, look."

I shook my head. I didn't want to see. I wanted to curl up in shame and hate myself for hurting Geri.

"Cadence."

His stern tone made me open my eyes. Geri sat, watching me with James.

"Look at her eyes."

I bent over to get a better look. In them, I saw devotion, love, and above all, fierce loyalty. "It wasn't about Flynn. It was about *me*. She'd been there for me for everything, and she loved me like nothing else. The one time she'd wanted me to do the same for her, I threw it in her face and stole her chance. Her strongest trait, her loyalty, was betrayed by the one person she'd given it all to. But it was different this time, because I wanted to *be* that friend for her. I wanted to make sure it worked out, so I was conscious of her feelings. It didn't matter what happened with Flynn, as long as I was there with her."

"Very good, Cadence." He bowed his head. "You're a fast learner. Geri mourned the loss of your friendship every day until you graduated. She watched you and missed you, but never dared go near you again. When she saw people turn against you, she wished she could trust you enough to support you, but she always felt a hint of justice in your loss of friends. After all, she'd learned that you weren't a very good friend at all."

A sob wrenched free from me as I fell to my knees beside her. How could I have been so blind? Why had I never gone to her and apologized, admitted my ignorance, and made amends? I truly was a terrible friend, and I wished more than anything I could take it back.

But, then again . . .

"I've made up for it, haven't I?" I asked. "I did everything I could to be a good friend this time. She'll never know what I did to hurt her, but I'll always remember and will never do it again. She means too much to me."

He touched my head and the scene fell dark. As light returned, I found myself kneeling in the middle of my living room on New Year's Eve again.

"Now, sweet Cadence, what are your plans for this year?"

"I . . . I don't know." I wiped my tears. "Eleventh grade was fairly uneventful, and the few things that were bad I've already eliminated by still being with Geri and not having so many boyfriends."

"Think about where things are going for you in this timeline." He gestured around the room. "Harper is about to venture off into the adult world, you have a second chance with Geri, you know what could happen to

Melanie, and you cannot forget your continued relationship with James. Things are very different for you now, so you will need to rely entirely on your own good judgment rather than memories of what happened before."

I examined the people in the room. "I don't want Melanie to hurt herself, so I'll do all I can to make sure she knows she has friends and people who care about her. Harper and Geri? I'll still be there for them no matter what, and James . . ."

I looked into his face, my torn feelings resurfacing as Austin's face flashed into my mind. "James I will need to resist. I need to remember Austin somehow and all he means to me so I can keep my virtue intact for him. I care about James so much, but I'm not going to marry him. I need to keep that in mind."

"They are good goals. Now, do the best you can."

I turned to him. "Wait!"

He paused as he rested his hand on the door frame.

"Don't you have a name?"

He smiled. "You can call me Angel, if you like." He nodded toward James. "Quickly, or he'll be one very confused boy."

I rushed over to James, resumed my position in his arms, and pressed my lips against his. As the scene reanimated, cheers arose around me as James clung onto me. From behind me, Brian muttered, "Man, I feel like someone hit me."

Chapter Twenty

Harper sat at her computer, hitting refresh over and over. I sat on her bed, my knees shaking in nervous anticipation. She growled, then something finally popped up. I leapt to my feet and stood behind her to see her results.

"What is it?" I asked. "What do you need?"

"Shh, Cadence!" But then she gasped. "No way!"

"What, what, what?"

"I got high enough to go to UNSW! Oh my gosh, I could really get in!"

"Harper! That's amazing!"

She grabbed her hair. "I . . . how is this even possible?"

I wrapped my arms around her neck and kissed her cheek. "Because you're an amazing artist, and you deserve it."

The University of New South Wales was right in the heart of the city, right near where she'd met Daniel with her friends. Maybe she *was* meant to be with him. Maybe, despite a different path to get there, it was still meant to happen.

I squeezed her. "Harper, you're going to be so happy. I just know it."

"Thanks, Cadence."

Mum and Dad rushed into the room to see her results, and they were just as excited as us.

The last week of the summer holidays arrived, and soon we had to go back to school. James's parents insisted I be with them to help him learn how to maintain the car in case we ever got stuck somewhere. I changed the tire, checked the oil, refilled the wiper fluid, and checked the battery without even batting an eye.

"Wow," John said, looking me over with a nod. "Your parents taught you well."

I smiled at him while James huffed. "Yeah, she got her learner's without even studying too, and she's never once stalled a hill start. How is that even possible?"

I shrugged and bent over the car to avoid answering.

"Seriously, Cadence, sometimes you freak me out with things you seem to just *know*."

"I don't mean to *just know* them, I just do."

"No, I'm fairly sure you look things up and study things you know I'm going to come across just to freak me out."

"You sound paranoid."

"So you don't deny it!" He waved the oil stick in my face. "You have some kind of ninja skills so you can get to me!"

I rested my hand on my hip. "Ninja skills? Really?"

"Yeah, like that song from that album I bought *the day it came out*. You sang it like you'd known it forever! How is that even possible?"

I turned away from him. "We've been through this, James. I'm fairly sure it's a remake."

"Ah!" He shoved the oil rod back into its slot. "But I looked it up. It's completely original! You are some kinda psychic or something."

"James—"

"Leave the girl alone, son." John interrupted. "You're just jealous that she's better with the car than you."

James muttered under his breath as he leaned over the engine.

Movement from down the street caught my attention and I glanced up. Melanie marched our way, apparently coming back from the bus stop around the corner. I nudged James. "Hey."

"What now? You see rainstorms coming for us this evening?"

"No. Look."

He straightened to see over the car. "Mel? But she's supposed to have a ride home, and not for a few more hours."

John looked over too, and the three of us watched her approach. She came up my side of the car and jumped when she suddenly noticed us. She flushed, seeing our eyes on her, and turned toward the house.

"Mel!" I called. "Wait."

She swung around and glared at me. "Shut up, Cadence! Not everyone cares what you have to say. Not everyone worships the ground you walk on."

"Melanie!" James surged toward her.

"You can shut up as well!" She shoved him. "I'm tired of your ridiculous obsession with her. She's not that great, and she's definitely not that pretty. She's just got that perfect hair and those giant boobs!"

"Melanie!" John pointed at her. "You do not speak to or about people that way."

Melanie snapped her mouth shut and ran inside, slamming the door behind her.

I moved to rush after her, but James caught my arm. "I got it. Why don't you clean up and go help Mum in the kitchen?"

I nodded, and we went inside together. I ducked into the bathroom while he hurried into her room. The bathroom, being right next door to her room, made a perfect place to eavesdrop on their conversation. I turned on the shower and pressed my ear against the wall.

"Melanie, talk to me," James said.

"Go away. All you'll do is take *her* side."

"Mel, come on. I really wanna know what happened. It has something to do with Brian, right?"

She burst into tears. I held my breath, startled by her sudden change in emotion and desperate to hear the reason why.

"Yes," she answered. almost too quietly for me to hear. "He dumped me. He said he just wanted to be friends because he can't feel as strongly for me as he wants. When I asked him what he meant by that, he tried to blow it off, but when I pressed him, he yelled at me and said he's into Cadence!"

"What an idiot."

"I know! She's so horrible."

"No, don't say that about her! He's an idiot for not seeing how great you are."

"But even you think Cadence is better than me. I hate her! She's so . . . so . . ." There was a long pause. "So *fake*! She pretends to be everyone's friend so everyone loves her, but it's totally self-serving. She just wants to be worshiped."

"Melanie! That's my girlfriend you're talking about, and she's not like that at all. She's been nothing less than a good friend to you—"

"Yeah, so she can please *you*! So she can keep her social-climbing stepping stone on the leash. She never cared about me. It's her fault this happened. If she'd just left me alone, I'd never have dated him and I would never have felt this way!" Her sobs lifted again.

My heart broke for her. She'd put herself out there, been with the guy she'd liked for a long time, only to be dumped for another girl . . . her brother's girlfriend . . . me. My anger at Brian bubbled over for doing that to her, and I felt angry at myself for not intervening sooner.

Then James spoke. "But aren't you glad you did put yourself out there? You went from no friends to one of the biggest groups in your grade, and now you have great friends who love you. Cadence loves you, Mel, and as much as you hate her now, you really don't want to lose your friendship with her. I've seen you with her and Geri, and you love being part of their little circle. Forget that loser and look at what you've got."

She didn't say anything as she continued sobbing. Then, "I don't want to be friends with her anymore. I refuse to let her use me for her own selfish agenda. I don't even want to see her ugly face again."

"Geez, Mel! Well, you're gonna have to because *I* want her around. So you're just going to have to deal with it!"

"Get out!"

"Gladly!" He slammed the door behind him.

I stepped away from the wall, shaken and concerned. If Melanie turned her back on me, she'd have to turn her back on the rest of our friends as well, and that thought sent images of her cutting herself through my mind.

I sank onto the tile and silently cried. Stupid Brian! Why did he have to ruin everything by pining after me? I'd been with James for over a year and wasn't showing any hints of ending it with him, so how could he think he stood a chance?

Poor Melanie. I really was the bane of her existence.

Someone tapped on the door and it cracked open. James's head popped in, and he saw me on the floor.

"James!" I jumped to my feet. "I could've been naked!"

He slipped in and shut the door behind him, then rushed to me. "I knew you'd be listening. I also knew you'd be sitting on the floor, crying."

"No, you didn't."

"Yes, I did. I know you, and I know you care too much *not* to do those things." He wrapped his arms around me as I cried. "Melanie's just hurt right now. She'll get over it. She'll see sense and come around. It's not your fault that idiot would think he stood a chance with you when you're taken. It's not your fault he couldn't see the great thing he had right in front of him."

"I make everything worse for her. I don't mean to, but I do."

"No, don't think like that." He stroked my hair and kissed the top of my head. "You've made everything so much better for her. Those things are because other people are stupid. They're not your fault."

I nuzzled into his chest, more grateful than ever to have him. He let me cry in his arms, his warm presence soothing my anguish. He was right, and I loved that he stood by me so firmly.

There was a tap on the door. "James?" Karen's voice echoed into the room.

James reached across and opened the door. "It's okay, Mum. We're not doing anything."

She looked at me and, seeing my tears, rushed over. "Cadence, honey."

Her hand rested on the small of my back.

"It's okay, Mum, really." James nodded toward Melanie's room. "Go talk to her. I've got this."

She nodded and hurried out as James let me go. "Now, seriously, take a shower. You smell like oil and sweat."

I giggled as he brushed the tears from my face.

Geri stood beside me in the line to enter the pool with her arms folded and her jaw clenched, absolutely livid. "I'm gonna kick his butt. What an idiot!"

"Maybe you should focus on Mel," I said. "She's not talking to me, and she needs someone."

"I hate drama."

I giggled. "You love it."

We paid and entered the pool area. Most people had already arrived, so we rushed to the tree where our group had set up. As I set down my bag and squatted to pull out my towel, Brian appeared at my side. "Hey, Cadence."

I tried to ignore him.

"Do you need some help?"

"No, I'm fine."

"How do you think you'll do today?"

I huffed. "Same old, I guess."

He snatched the sun lotion from me as I pulled it out. "I can help you with this."

I snatched it back. "No, I've got Geri or James to help me."

He leaned closer. "Hey, I don't wanna freak you out or anything, but there's a rumor going around that James is gonna dump you."

My heart stopped and I froze. But then my logic kicked in. "James and I are fine. It's just a rumor."

He lowered his voice. "But I heard he's done because you won't put out."

I threw him an icy glare, furious he would even say that. "Get away from me."

I leapt to my feet and rushed to the starting line to check in for the first race. I'd put my sun lotion on later. I lined up and a moment later, Flynn wrapped his arm around my shoulders. "Hey, kid."

"Hey, Flynn," I answered flatly.

He looked into my face. "Oh man, is the rumor true? Did James dump you?"

I turned on him. "No! Who's saying that?"

He pulled back, startled by the venom in my voice. "I just heard it around. Everyone's talking about it. And just so you know, I respect that you don't wanna have sex. I mean, we're still young, so how do we know—"

"Oh my gosh!" My face and neck burned. "Everyone needs to mind their own business."

Flynn saw my embarrassment and changed the subject. We checked in for our races and stood at the starting line together. I wondered where the rumors had originated. I certainly hadn't told anyone—other than Geri, but she wouldn't say anything—so I wondered who James had told. Tom and Sam maybe? But they wouldn't say anything either.

"Hey, beautiful."

I flinched at the sound of James's voice. Despite how unlikely, I still felt concerned that he might break up with me. After all, I didn't know what the outcome of this relationship would be.

"Hey, are you okay?" He touched my back softly. "You seem . . . jumpy."

"I . . . ah . . ." I had no idea what to say. The way he looked down at me with such devotion washed away all my doubt, and I felt foolish.

Flynn answered for me. "There's a rumor going around that you're going to dump her."

James rolled his eyes. "Seriously? Do people have nothing better to do? Well, maybe this will kill it off."

He spun me around and smacked his lips against mine. What a fantastic kiss! Openmouthed, he bent me into a dip as I caressed his face. We only stopped when one of the teachers yelled at us.

We straightened as he pulled away and I stood, dazed. *Wow!*

He grinned. "Well then, I don't think either of us is quite ready to break up any time soon."

"Mmm." I flushed again.

Flynn chuckled beside me. "Nope, it certainly doesn't seem like it."

James kissed my cheek. "Get your head back in the game. I wanna see a first place stick today. You need to break that second place curse."

I watched him as he walked away. He had his shirt off, and his shoulders looked better than ever. I bit my lip and tilted my head, unable to look away. Flynn nudged me and laughed when I blushed from being caught ogling.

After the race, I filled Geri in on what I'd found out. She instantly began scheming up a plan to find the source. It took me several minutes to veer the topic onto Melanie.

"She's still pretty mad," Geri said. "It was near impossible to get her to talk to me, 'cause you and I are best friends. But I managed to get a little bit out of her, and she just wants to be left alone. She's pretty beat up about it . . . stupid Brian." She shot his back a filthy look.

"I guess we need to be patient and keep trying."

She nodded. I watched her glare burn into Brian as he walked away. I smiled at her, loving her fierce loyalty. I knew, just by the twitch of her eyebrow, she was imagining ripping his eyes out with her nails.

During the lunch break, James and I walked to the shop to buy food. He made it a point to be affectionate with me and never stopped touching me in some way or another.

"James," I said quietly as we walked back with our food. "Did you tell anyone what happened . . . you know, on my birthday?"

He shook his head. "Not really. Just Tom. But he wouldn't say anything."

"Where do you think the rumor came from?"

He grunted. "I don't know, or care, to be honest. People are stupid and are just trying to sabotage us."

"Sabotage?" I hadn't thought about that angle. But who would want that? Brian? No, he wasn't like that. He may still like me, but he wouldn't stoop to that. Melanie and I had started getting along, so she wouldn't have done it. I wondered if I'd offended anyone that I hadn't realized. Apparently, I was good at that.

I waited for my first race after lunch. My gaze wandered over the students lining the grassy area beside the pool. I saw Dusty and a group of his ninth grade friends watching girls walk by. I grinned at Dusty's dazed face as he tried to work out what exactly he was supposed to do.

Then, a group of twelfth grade girls walked in front of them. Their wide-eyed stares followed the girls, but the girls didn't pay them any attention. A thought hit me. There *was* a group of twelfth grade girls who would want James and me to break up—Carla and her following.

They'd been quiet since Robbie and the other two boys were expelled, so I'd forgotten about them. But they'd want me gone—I would still be considered the reason why James left them.

Throughout the race, my mind ticked over those thoughts. It had to be them. No one else would think that would be the reason why he'd break up with me. I felt so angry that I took it out on the water, kicking and pulling at it with all my strength.

When I hit the wall—which startled me because I wasn't paying attention to the line on the bottom—I glanced around to see a good quarter of the length of the pool between me and the next person. The teacher handed the first place stick to me, and I stared at it. I *never* won first.

James's face appeared above me with a wide grin spread across it. "Wow, Cadence! You just broke the school record! You just flew on that second lap!"

"I did?" I watched as the rest of the girls finished the race, then made my way to the side of the pool.

James wrapped my towel around me and kissed me. "You're amazing!"

I giggled. James's eyes captivated me. Nothing mattered aside from the adoration I saw there.

He walked me to the winners' table, where the teacher announced my new record over the speaker. As we walked back to our group, everyone showered me with congratulations for my swim. James and I headed to a tree nearby, where we sat on the ground, him leaning against the trunk of the tree with his legs and arms around me as I leaned against his shoulder.

I shut my eyes and breathed in the smell of him. Although tainted by the smell of chlorine from our lunchtime swim, his usual scent was there all the same. His fingers stroked my arms, making me smile. But then the thoughts that had plagued me while I swam rushed into my mind.

I lifted my head so I could look at him. "I think it was Carla or one of those girls."

His eyes narrowed. "Huh?"

I explained to him my theory. He listened quietly, his lips pursing tighter and tighter until they were a thin, white line. When I finished, he grasped my waist and encouraged me to my feet so he could stand.

"I'll see if this is true. I've heard rumors Becca still likes me. I should find out so I can end it. This has hurt people other than us, especially Mel, and no one hurts Mel without having to face me."

And with a squeeze of my hand, he left. I returned to Geri, who stood talking with some of the girls, and wrapped my arm through hers to listen. I scanned the group for Melanie. She sat by the fence, half-tucked behind a tree. She wanted to be close to us, but she didn't want to be part of us. I took a deep breath and walked over to her.

Her glare flashed up when she noticed me coming, but she turned away. I sank onto my knees on the grass beside her. "Melanie, I'm really sorry about what happened. I understand if you don't wanna be my friend anymore, but don't close off everyone else. We've enjoyed having you with us, and I'm not going to tell the others to stop talking to you just because of this. Please, just blame me, not them."

She pulled her knees up and buried her face into them. "Go away, Cadence." She hissed my name with venom, making my heart ache. "Stop trying to be the hero."

I sighed and stood, brushing the mud off my knees. "Okay, Melanie. Just know that you have friends when you're ready."

Her arms tightened around her legs as I walked away.

I had no idea why, but Community and Family Studies was extra boring that day. Geri sat beside me, staring off with her jaw hanging. If she faded any further, she would start to drool.

For the first time since seventh grade, we had a nearly identical schedule. We'd elected all the same classes but one—I chose Food Technology while she chose Drama—so those classes, along with different English classes, were the only two periods we had separately. Amazingly, nursing and sports science had very similar requirements.

A loud *bang* echoed in the corridor that made everyone jump. I looked toward the doorway just in time to see Becca toss a water bomb at my face. It hit with force, stinging my eyes and making my cheeks burn from the impact.

"Get back to your classes!" the teacher yelled.

They moved down the corridor, but by the soft whispering I could still hear, they'd stopped in the stairwell.

Geri's eyes met mine with alarm. I nodded. "We'll go the other way and hope they don't notice."

"Why don't we hang with the teacher?" she asked quietly. "They won't get us if we stay with her."

"You want to tail the teacher and make us look even more like a pair of goody-goodies? They'll get us worse for that when they have the chance. No, we'll use the crowd for cover and make a run for it."

She nodded and pulled out a packet of tissues. "You're all wet."

I glanced around, my cheeks warming when I noticed people cautiously watching me. My stomach flipped as I tried not to panic.

The bell rang, and we waited to be in the middle of the rush for the door. Then we ran in the other direction. We jumped down the stairs and into the school grounds, running around the building to the quad. Unfortunately, when we stepped into the quad, the girls stood huddled together, watching the door, waiting for us.

We hightailed it out into the middle of a soccer game where Justin and Tyler were playing.

"Hey!" Tyler yelled at us. "You're interfering with our game!"

I spun around and hid behind him, using his bulk as a shield.

"Cadence! What are you doing?"

"Move it, loser!" Becca snarled at him.

Justin ran over to us, pulling Geri behind him. "I don't like to hit girls, but for you, I'd make an exception."

"Gross, nerds," Carla groaned.

"Stop protecting them," Becca said. "Everyone knows she hurt both of you. We just want some justice for turning James into a pansy and getting Robbie, Kev, and Greg expelled."

Tyler tilted his head back. "Cadence, where's James?"

"I don't know. He was supposed to have physics." I popped my head up over his shoulder to scan the quad. He should be around somewhere . . .

Becca charged. I pulled back, but just as Tyler caught her, her nails found my face. I touched my cheek to check for blood. Luckily, nothing.

I glared at her. "Why won't you just leave us alone? I get that you still have a thing for him, but he's *not interested*. He wasn't before, and he isn't now. Even if we did break up, do you really think he'd go for this crazy-person thing you have going?"

She glowered at me, pushing Tyler off. "I guess I should try a different approach." She folded her arms, slowly looking me over. "But that will—"

James shoved past the other girls and swung her around. "You spoiled, selfish whore! Just so you know, Becca, and know it clearly so you don't have any more wild, fanatical aspirations, *I don't like you*." He spoke the last few words clearly and slowly, making sure each one sank deeply into her brain. "I never did, and I never will. Now leave my girlfriend and her friends *alone*."

Her lip quivered, but she didn't dare cry. She hurried away with her friends rushing after her.

I stood, stunned, as I thought about James's words. In the other timeline, he and Becca had had a brief fling about this time. Had he not liked her then, and it had been a thing of convenience? I shook off the thought, not wanting to think about James that way.

Tyler stepped aside as James rushed over to me. "Cadence! Wow! I heard what you said. That was pretty bold."

I shrugged. "I'm tired of her bullying me."

"Yeah, well, I think they've got the idea now. Plus, Carla's pregnant, and without their leader, they're not anywhere near as brave."

"Carla's what?" Although later than last time, her pregnancy had still happened. I paused, realizing that there were things that wouldn't change, because other people still had their own choices to make. I couldn't save everyone.

"Yeah, Robbie's such a moron. He never used protection, the cocky SOB."

"What's going to happen?" I asked breathlessly.

James scratched his head. "Well, according to her mum, who's friends with my mum, she almost aborted it, but her mum stopped her. Robbie has no intention of being a father, so they're going to arrange an adoption."

"Are you serious?" I shook my head in disbelief. "She's so brave."

"Who knew, right?" James tried to look optimistic, but as he slowly looked me over, I sensed uncertainty and apprehension. He didn't want that to be *me*.

He wrapped his arm around my shoulders and nodded his appreciation to Justin and Tyler for looking out for me. He tilted his head for Geri to follow, and we walked back to have lunch on the quad.

Chapter Twenty-One

"Cadence!" Harper screamed through the house.

I dropped the half-taped box and ran out to her. "What?"

She stood in the driveway, her arms full of boxes.

"Don't *what* me! I invited your stupid boyfriend so we could have some muscle around here, but where is he? Nobody knows!"

"Dad took him to get—"

"Blah, blah, blah! Dad better hurry up, because my arms are killing me!"

I giggled as I rushed back inside to tape down the last box we had left. We hadn't realized how much stuff Harper had and so didn't save up enough boxes for packing. It didn't help that each painting had to be packed with an inch of padding on either side. Dad and James went to get more boxes, and Harper had been griping about having to carry her own stuff into the trailer ever since.

When they arrived, she gave James a piece of her mind. He stood and patiently took it before sighing and lifting the boxes out of the car. I couldn't help laughing as she tailed him up into the house, never stopping her stream of nagging.

Finally, we'd packed everything and her room lay bare. She and I stood in the doorway looking it over.

"I'd forgotten the walls were cream," she said.

"Yeah, it looks weird without the assault of colors everywhere."

She nudged me in the ribs and giggled. Her gaze lifted to her painting on the ceiling. "I'm gonna miss waking up to that."

"It's a good painting. Even Dad likes it."

"No, not just that. Those people."

I turned my head to look at her. She stared up at it with tears in her eyes. She rubbed her left eye with the heel of her hand and grunted. "Look at me. You've turned me into a sap."

I wrapped my arms around her waist.

Later, at her apartment in the inner suburbs, she rushed inside, leaving Dad and James with all the heavy lifting. She dragged me behind her and showed me around. She would be sharing with three other girls, only one she actually knew.

We dumped her bags in the wardrobe and paused to assess her room.

"It's small," she said with a sigh. "But it will do. I'm close to school, and there's plenty of places to get a job around here." She looked into my eyes, and I saw in them what she wanted to say, yet couldn't—*but it's not close to you.*

I looked away, not wanting to get emotional. "So, grand tour!"

She pulled me around the apartment while Mum set her things up in the kitchen, and James and Dad brought her furniture in with Dusty guiding them. When the bed and her desk were in, we retreated to her room to set up everything.

We didn't talk much—just a few "where do you want this?" questions—but when we finished, and Mum announced it was time to leave, Harper jumped up and clung onto me.

"Cadence, why don't you stay the night with me?"

"I can't. I have school tomorrow."

She let out a sharp sob, but fought it back down. "You stupid kid. Hurry up and grow up already."

I wrapped my arms around her and rested my face on her shoulder. "I'll miss you too, Harp."

She took a sharp breath, but refused to allow herself to cry.

The first game of the netball season arrived. James loved coming to my games to egg on my crazy aggression. He laughed maniacally when I knocked other girls to the ground, and yelled at me to give them what-for if they tried to push me around. The year before, my coach told me to stop bringing him, it became so bad. So, as he came along for a new season, I set up some rules.

"No swearing."

"That's a given," he answered.

"No yelling at me to break their nose."

"Aw, but I wanna see blood."

"No abusing the umpire about being prejudiced."

"What if they are?"

"And when you get told by anyone to stop, you *stop*. I don't want you getting banned again."

"I didn't even know you *could* get banned at these things, but I guess it's apparently so."

I slapped his chest and laughed. "Just behave."

He sat with Mum as I joined my team to warm up. One of the other defenders looked over and said, "Cay, you're still with that guy?"

"Yeah." I'd been with the same group of girls for the last three years. They all knew me well and had liked having James there at first, until he opened his mouth.

"Did you tell him to keep his mouth shut this season?"

"I most certainly did."

"Good." She trotted up beside me and we looked him over. "Wow, you've been with him for ages."

"Just under a year and a half."

"What, are you gonna marry him or something?" She tilted her head as she looked him over. "He's pretty hot, so I can see why you keep him around."

I laughed. "That's just a bonus."

The coach called us over, and soon the game began. She stuck me in the goalkeeper position first off, down at the spectator end. Thankfully, James behaved himself. I only heard one comment about my legs in a miniskirt.

Afterward, we went to his soccer game where I sat with his parents. Karen squeezed my hand as I settled into a camping chair beside her.

"How'd it go?" she asked.

"We won, but barely."

"No deaths today?"

I grunted. "Apparently, I'm gonna kill *James* for telling everyone I'm crazy."

She chuckled.

John was the one who spouted off the abuse during James's games. Karen and I kept a safe distance from him so we weren't associated. He yelled all kinds of obscenities, usually at anyone who came near James, and Karen and I ducked down. It amazed me how a sports game could turn people into savages . . . but I wasn't one to talk.

"How's school?" Karen asked during a lull.

"Good. Just cruising along."

We both flinched as John bellowed.

"How's your sister doing?" she asked with her face covered.

"Good. She's really enjoying her course. I don't think I've ever seen her happier."

She squeezed my leg as the ball approached the goal. We leapt to our feet and yelled in excitement as James appeared and lined up for the pass. He received it perfectly and shot a brilliant goal.

James pulled his shirt over his head and ran around in a circle, then pulled it back down and ran to John for a chest bump.

"Good heavens." Karen covered her face.

James looked at me and blew me a kiss. "That's for you, baby!"

Karen rolled her eyes as I giggled.

Afterward, as we packed up James's car, he glanced around. "We're the last people to leave."

"So?" I slipped the camping chair in the back.

"So . . ." He grabbed me and turned me to face him. "I'm gonna kiss you."

He shut the back door and pinned me against the car, clasping my face and placing a kiss firmly on my lips. I melted into it, loving how easily his lips glided over mine and how familiar it had become.

"Jimmy."

James swung around, pulling me behind him as he shifted me toward the passenger door. "Robbie!"

"Still playing soccer, I see." Robbie's gaze drifted over James's shoulder and onto me.

"Yeah. I feel like I need it now more than ever with the HSC coming up."

Robbie's eyes narrowed on me as he shoved his hands into his pockets. "Still at school then, huh?"

"Yeah."

Robbie scoffed.

"I don't wanna waste my life, Rob," James said. "I feel like I'm on track, you know? I'm working toward getting into uni to do a bachelor's in science."

Robbie scowled and stepped toward him. "I've got a job, good one too. You don't need a degree to get a good job and do well in life."

"No, but that's what I want because I know I can."

He sneered and looked over at me. "She's filled you with crazy notions of grandeur. I can't believe you're still with her. According to the girls, she doesn't even put out."

James clenched his right fist while clutching my shirt with his left. He struggled to hold himself back.

I grabbed his hand on my shirt. "James, let's go."

Robbie burst out laughing. "Yeah, James, go with your little princess. Leave your best friend since you were ten for some pathetic child."

"At least I didn't get her pregnant!" James responded with passion. "Unlike you! And even if anything did happen with us and she fell pregnant, I wouldn't abandon her like you did. You're such an ass!"

Robbie stepped back, his jaw clenched. "It was her fault. She can deal with it."

"See? This is exactly what your problem is. You can't take responsibility for anything."

"I didn't come here to fight with you! I came to see if you wanted to make amends. You and me again, Jim, like old times. Forget all this and let's go hang out—"

"No, I'm done with all that." James opened the door for me. "We're leaving. If you wanna be friends, you're the one who needs to change. You were dragging me down, and now I'm up again, I wanna stay here."

I sat in the seat and he closed the door. He hurried around to the driver's seat as I buckled my seat belt, but the door flew open. I didn't have a moment to react before Robbie grabbed me and dragged me out of the car.

"I can't believe I encouraged you to go after her!" he yelled at James. "She's ruined everything! She ruined *you*!"

James rushed back around, his fury exploding from him. "Let her go!"

Robbie wrapped my ponytail around his hand and wrenched my head backward. I screamed and tried to grab his hand to make him stop. His other hand grabbed my throat and he squeezed. "I'm gonna get rid of her for good."

"No! Cadence!" James sounded desperate, making my fear surge through me. I couldn't speak or scream. Robbie's hand clutched me so tightly I couldn't breathe. I clawed at his hand, desperate for relief, desperate for air.

"Stupid bitch."

I saw stars, the world began to spin . . .

Thwack!

I fell to my knees as Robbie stumbled back and James grabbed his neck. "I swear, Robbie, I *never* want to see you again! *Ever!* If you come near her or me ever again, I will hand you over to the cops for everything I know you've ever done. All the drugs, underage drinking, robbery, assault, vandalism—do I need to go on?"

Robbie's eyes widened. "You wouldn't dare! You were usually doing it along with me."

"And I'll go down, too, if I need to. I'll do anything to protect Cadence from you." James tossed him back.

Robbie stumbled, but managed to stay on his feet. He gave me one last long, icy glare before he turned and marched away.

James fell onto his knees beside me and pulled me against him. "Will this ever be over? Why won't they just leave us alone?"

To my shock, a tear ran down his cheek. I scrambled forward and kissed it away. "James, you're so brave."

He scoffed. "I'm an idiot, that's what I am. I screwed up my life and now I'm living with the consequences. I just wish they didn't affect you."

"Oh, James." I stroked his cheek and ran my hand back into his hair. "Your life is so much better than it would have been if you'd stayed with them."

He smirked. "Another one of your 'premonitions,' huh?"

"Stop that," I said, trying not to smile. "I just know the path you were on. I will deal with anything that gets thrown at me because I care about you, James, so nothing can stop me from being with you."

His gaze lifted and met mine. His eyes looked bluer than I'd ever seen as they pierced into my soul.

"You mean more to me than anything."

He kissed me softly. When he pulled away, he helped me to my feet and we climbed into his car. We remained silent during the drive to his house, allowing him time to process his feelings.

At the house, he held my hand as we walked in, but retreated straight to the shower. I felt terrible for him. He was so forlorn and heartbroken. I went into his room and sat at his desk, flicking idly through the pages of *The Hitchhiker's Guide to the Galaxy*. A thought popped into my mind. I glanced into the hallway to see if anyone was nearby before I whispered, "Angel? Angel, can you hear me?"

The sound of the shower ceased. I turned around and saw the man in white sitting on the windowsill. "You called, sweet Cadence?"

I gaped at him for a moment, struck by a strange familiarity. I shook it off. "Yes. I have a question."

He walked up beside me. "And what might that be?"

My lip quivered. I wasn't sure if I wanted my question answered. I knew what the answer could be, and it frightened me. But I took a deep breath and asked, "What did happen to James, in the other timeline?"

The man smiled gently and gestured for me to follow. We walked out of the room and, to my surprise, I found us walking down James's street toward his house. It seemed odd, considering we'd just been *in* his house.

"James barely graduated in this timeline," the man in white said. "And he never went off to university or any forms of higher education. He settled for a mediocre life with a mediocre job."

We walked in silence down the driveway and up the stairs. The man pushed the front door open and we stepped inside.

"Any money he earned he used to feed his party lifestyle. Gambling, clubbing, alcohol, and especially drugs burned his money up faster than he could bring it in. By the time he reached twenty-one, he had a $35,000 debt hanging over him, without anything to show for it."

We paused outside James's closed door. The man touched the door as he gazed into my eyes. "When he was twenty-three, he overdosed on a cocktail of drugs that landed him in the hospital, and he ended up like this."

He pushed the door open and I stepped through. James sat in a wheelchair by the window. I rushed over and looked into his face, but it hung limp and his eyes were dull.

"Is he . . . dead?"

The man shook his head. "He's a complete vegetable, as you would say. Not dead, but not alive either. The incident tore his family to shreds. His father left, unable to deal with it, and his sister ran off to England. Only his mother remained . . ." He trailed off as Karen slipped into the room and sat beside James.

I watched her as she spoon-fed him, but he didn't even move. Not even his eyes registered her presence.

"James." I reached over and touched his face as I cried. "All of this because I wasn't in his life?"

The man gave me a slow nod. "You made him leave his friends and clean up his act. Because he had to prove himself to you, his life was set back on course."

My head fell onto his lap as I sobbed. "I'm so sorry, James. If only I'd known . . . this shouldn't have happened to you."

As I wept, the light in the room faded, and I found myself leaning over the chair by the desk. I cried harder as guilt overcame me. How could I wipe that from my memory? How could I live with the knowledge that without me, James would have become *that*?

Karen burst in. "Cadence What happened?"

"It was . . . and James, he . . ." I couldn't think of anything to say. I couldn't tell her what I just saw. I swallowed hard and thought about what made me want to know in the first place. "Robbie was there before we left. He grabbed me and tried to strangle me, but James protected me. He's done so much for me, he deserves better than that."

She pulled me into her arms, not realizing the *that* I was talking about was a brain-dead James. "Sweetheart, you and James have gone through so much together, and all it does is make you stronger. He's lucky to have you with him through all this. You mean the world to him."

James walked in with just his jeans on, his hair wet and ruffled, a confused expression on his face. Seeing him so strong and alive set me off again as the image of his glazed eyes burned in my memory.

He sank down beside Karen. "What . . . ?"

"James, we need to do something about Robbie," she said firmly. "He has gone too far this time."

"Mum, I told him I'd hand him over to the police if he shows up again. Egging my windows and leaving threats for me is one thing, but as soon as he laid his hands on Cadence, he took things to a level I won't tolerate."

She stroked my hair. "I'm sorry, sweetheart. You didn't deserve that. But let's not dwell on it. Let's have a pleasant afternoon together."

I nodded and climbed to my feet. She slipped out of the room first, and I threw my arms around James. I clung onto him, trying to force the images of his limp face out of my mind. More than ever, I felt grateful he'd pursued me so determinedly, so he wouldn't have to face that reality. I wanted to tell him everything, to explain that his choice to change his life was the right thing, but I knew I couldn't. If I did, everything would return to how it was.

I couldn't risk it. More than ever, I realized so much was at stake if I slipped up and told someone their future. It wouldn't just be Austin and Melody gone, it would be Geri from my life, Melanie would be broken, James might as well be dead, and his family would be destroyed.

"Hey, Cadence, you're crying again," James said softly.

I looked into his eyes and took them in, making his vibrant, living eyes wipe away the memory of his dead ones. "I'm sorry. Maybe I'm PMSing or something."

He smirked. "That would do it."

Chapter Twenty-Two

Geri and I stood together in the bus bays after school. Mid-winter made it cold again, so we wrapped our arms together and huddled up. Her teeth chattered as we stood, temples pressed together.

"Where's your boyfriend when I need him?" she asked. "He's like a pre-warmed blanket, and he has a car."

"They're going to his grandparents' for the first few days of the holiday, and they live up at Coffs," I replied. I couldn't believe we'd reached July already, and we were about to start our winter break.

"What's the point in going to Coffs? You can't go to the beach 'cause it's freezing cold."

I shrugged. "There's a giant banana."

She burst out laughing. "A giant banana? Oh yeah, that's something he wants to think about when you're not around."

I slapped her shoulder.

"Hey."

I grinned up at Dusty. He'd sprouted almost overnight and now stood a whole head taller than me. He loved that he stood eye to eye with James—it made him feel like more of a man.

He scratched his sandy blond mop of hair and looked down at Geri. "You're not coming to our place, are you?"

Her gaze turned up to him, her surprise about his sudden height written all over her face. "Holy cow, kid! Did someone trade out your legs?"

He smiled his wide grin that looked so similar to mine. "Nah, growth spurt. About time too."

She grabbed his chin. "Cadence! Does your little brother have . . . facial hair?"

"A little, yeah." I laughed.

She tapped his cheek. "How did I not notice this happening?"

Dusty smirked. "Well, it sounded something like"—he cleared his throat to put on a higher voice—"Cadence! You're bratty brother is hovering again. Cadence! Watch him, he's trying to steal all the good food. Cadence! Doesn't your brother understand personal hygiene? Cadence—"

"Yeah, yeah, I get the point." She scowled.

"If you like what you see, we could go out sometime?" He winked at me.

Geri gagged. "That's disgusting. You're a ninth grader, and you're . . . well, you're you."

"Aw, come on," Dusty said, enjoying taunting her. "You always go on about how pretty my sister is, and I look just like her in boy form, so *obviously* you find me attractive."

I burst out laughing. This was the Dusty I knew as an adult. Cheeky and a giant tease, but clever as a whip.

Geri elbowed me in the ribs as she turned on Dusty. "You're so full of yourself. And no, I don't think you're attractive at all."

He shrugged. "Pity. I think you're pretty cute for an old bat."

He walked away from us as Geri smoldered.

My bus pulled up and I gave her a quick hug. "He's just playing with ya, Geri. I'll call you, okay?"

"Yeah, you better," she said as I turned and walked away. "I expect as much time as James gets!"

James was gone longer than he expected, so I spent most of the winter break between Geri and Harper. Harper, hungry for my time, had me stay overnight on several occasions. On the last Thursday of the break, she convinced me to stay over again, and once our parents left, she whipped out a fake ID for me.

"Harper . . ." I pouted.

"Oh, come on, Cadence," she said with a huff. "We'll be with my friends the whole time, and I won't let any guys hit on you. It's just a club. Come on, we'll go dancing and—" She paused. "Okay, maybe we'll skip the drinking part, but I *really* want you to come."

I sighed. "Mum and Dad will kill us if they find out."

She shrieked with delight and threw her wardrobe open.

An hour later, I somehow managed to pass as a believable eighteen-year-old and found myself dancing with Harper's high school friends. Although surprised to see me, they didn't make a fuss.

I stuck close to Harper, convinced someone would point at me at any moment and say, "Hey, she's only sixteen!" and I'd be tossed out, my parents called, and end up grounded for a year.

Then, I saw him. Daniel. I paused, startled to see him after so long, and to see him so *young*—only twenty-one. Being Italian, he had olive skin, dark hair, and dark eyes—and those eyes were fixed on Harper.

I looked at her. She hadn't noticed. I wondered what to do—point it out or just let it happen? I couldn't believe I was going to be there when they first met!

One of her friends noticed him and subtly pointed. I held my breath as she turned around and laid eyes on him for the first time. He smiled a cautious smile as their gazes met. She smiled and blushed before turning away. I bit my lip as he straightened and locked his focus entirely on her.

He finished his drink, then handed the empty glass to one of his friends. He made his way through the crowd on a beeline for her. I couldn't help myself. I tugged on her arm. "Harper, there's a guy coming over."

Her hand clamped on my arm as her eyes widened. "That tall, dark, and handsome one?"

"That's a pretty good description."

"Oh my . . ." She took a deep breath to compose herself. "Is he headed for me or someone else do you think?"

"I, ah . . ." I hesitated as he appeared behind her. He looked her over before touching her shoulder.

She turned with surprise and he gave her a coy smile. His hand rested on the small of her back. "Hey, I'm Danny."

Direct and to the point. No pickup lines. I always knew I liked him.

She blushed and bit her lip. "Harper."

"Harper? That's unusual. Unless it's a cover name because you think I'm a creep."

And he just killed it.

"No." She smiled. "It's my real name, and this is my sister, Cadence. All the girls in our family are given musical names." She grabbed my arm and pulled me forward.

He looked at me with a hint of confusion. "You're really sisters?"

"Yes, we're twins," Harper answered, a little too quickly.

"You look nothing alike."

"It's the hair," I answered. "When she's her natural color, we actually look related."

She dug her heel into my toe.

But he smiled, amused by our playfulness. "Well, then, musical twins, may I borrow Harper to dance?"

Wow, so formal. He asked permission in a club where people usually just jump right in.

Harper didn't seem to mind, and she eagerly took his arm.

I watched her from among her friends, delighted to see her and Daniel getting along perfectly. Both flirted like crazy, and slowly, they danced closer and closer together. Then it happened. He kissed her. I bit back a shriek of delight. I witnessed Harper falling for Daniel!

On the way home, she talked excitedly about him, and I encouraged it. I wanted to know everything she'd never told me and to feel the excitement of her fresh new love. I knew it would be another two years before they were married, but the beginnings felt exciting and intoxicating.

In her room, I faded to sleep while she continued talking about him, and my dreams were filled of things to come for her.

James picked me up from my netball game covered in mud and sweat. He'd had an early game, and with the rain we'd had on and off through the break, the ground was slick and easily churned up by the cleats.

I sat and before I had a chance to buckle, he grabbed my arm and pulled me in to kiss me. My elbow hit the center console and I slipped, causing our teeth to knock. I pulled back and touched my mouth. "Ouch."

"Sorry." He clasped my face and held it firmly while he gave me a long kiss. When he pulled back, he said, "I can't believe they extended the trip *three times*! So much for just the weekend, try almost two weeks! I missed you like crazy."

I smiled as my heart fluttered, having not seen him in so long. "I missed you, too. But I have so much to tell you, starting with what happened with Harper on Thursday night . . ."

I monopolized the conversation all the way to James's house, filling him in on everything that had happened with Harper's blossoming relationship with her future husband, and occasionally throwing in something about Geri and Dusty.

When we arrived at his house, he turned on the TV for me so he could take a shower and rinse off the mud. I flicked through the channels and paused to watch the last of the Saturday morning cartoons.

When he came out, he tossed a towel at me and I hurried to shower off my sweat. When I'd finished and dressed in jeans and a comfortable T-shirt I'd packed in my sports bag, I found him in the kitchen making canned pumpkin soup for lunch.

I walked up behind him and rested my head on his shoulder. "Where are your parents?"

"Grocery shopping and such. I think they said something about visiting my aunt."

I took a deep breath to smell his freshly showered fragrance.

"You're smelling me again, aren't you?"

I giggled as I stepped around and leaned against the kitchen counter. "Maybe."

A flattered smile swept across his face. I stared at it while he mixed the soup. He was hot beyond reason, and I couldn't believe I'd never noticed him the first time around.

"I love this stuff." He flicked the spoon at me, spraying my face with orange goop. He laughed as I scowled and wiped it off. "It's perfect for a lazy Saturday afternoon."

"How was your soccer game, by the way?"

"How was your netball game? Did you kill anyone today?"

I giggled and his smile grew. I almost melted. "You know, I don't *usually* maim people."

"Every game I've been to you have."

"Ha ha," I said sarcastically.

He grabbed two mugs and poured the soup into them. "We won, like usual. The wind was pretty intense though. My lips got pretty chapped."

"Maybe I'll just have to kiss them better."

He looked at me with a grin and leaned in. "That would be nice."

I touched his cheek and softly kissed his lips. He wrapped his arm around my waist and pulled me closer. "That wasn't a kiss! Come on!"

I giggled and kissed him open-mouthed. He held tightly to me and pulled my hair out of the ponytail so he could run his fingers through it. I wrapped my arms around him, loving the way he felt—his warmth, his strength. He pushed me against the counter as his hand ran down my neck and over my shoulder.

I pulled away. "James?"

He knew he had pushed his limit and sighed. "Yes?"

"Your soup is getting cold."

He grinned and kissed my cheek. "But things are just starting to heat up."

I giggled as he kissed my ear. "Seriously, stop."

He huffed and pulled back from me. He reached across so his whole arm and shoulder were right in my face. I gnawed at my lip, trying to force back my intense desire to jump him.

He handed me a mug, and we walked into the living room to sit on the couch. He turned on the TV again, and I snuggled up against him as he flicked through the channels.

"Nothing," he said. "Well, it *is* Saturday. We could watch rugby or AFL?"

I shrugged. "Whatever."

"Don't 'whatever' me." He pushed me off and scanned the DVDs. "You'd probably know who wins all the games today anyway." He turned and gave me a sly look, which earned him a scowl. He chuckled and turned back to the DVDs. "There's some girly flicks here, if you want? I know you love that crap."

"You're hilarious."

"Hey, look! Titanic! 'Oh, don't let go, Jack!' Pft, stupid movie." He bent over, and I forced myself not to stare at his butt. "Now, this is a movie I can do. 'Bond, *James* Bond.'" He flexed his biceps. "It must have something to do with the name."

"Ah, he's way smoother than you."

"He wishes he was as smooth as me."

Again, he bent over and my gaze lingered over his butt. I forced myself to look away. He sat beside me and pulled me closer to him. He shuffled up against the arm of the couch and lifted his leg behind me so he could hold me against his chest. Completely wrapped in him, I relaxed, having missed him over the past two weeks.

At first, we watched the movie as he slowly stroked my arms. But then, he moved my hair and started nibbling on my ear.

"James, I can't focus on the movie."

"Good."

His arms fell and wrapped around my waist as his lips drifted down my neck. I shut my eyes as my heart rate jumped. His right hand came up and stroked my hair as I leaned back, enjoying his affection after being separated for longer than I was used to. Then, his hand slid down my chest, into my shirt, and under my bra.

I gasped with surprise, but his arm around my waist held me against him as he lifted his lips. "Cadence, I've missed you."

My breath grew sharp and shallow. Adrenalin pumped through my body, causing me to feel lightheaded and giddy. His hand shifted and slipped around my other breast; I bit my lip to hold back a nervous whimper.

When his hand withdrew, I felt breathless, my heart pounding so hard I thought it would leap from my chest.

I watched his hand move away from my chest and return to my waist.

I pressed against him. "James?"

"Yes?"

"Don't ever go away for so long again."

He chuckled and his hand slipped up under my shirt while his other hand grabbed at the button on my jeans. When he undid the button, I panicked and pulled away. "No, James."

He sighed, but in his eyes I saw the intensity I'd seen in the car on my birthday. He desired me, and he was fighting to keep a handle on it.

I pushed off him. "James, we can't have sex. I don't wanna have sex until I'm engaged or something."

"We don't have to have sex, you could just let me—"

"No. That leads to sex. And my dad, oh my gosh, my dad! He'd kill you."

James winced. "Ah . . . yeah . . ."

"I think we should set up some boundaries. No more touching under the clothes and no groping."

He scowled. "Are you serious?"

"Yeah, very serious. My dad would kill you. He'd drive you out to the middle of nowhere, hack off your head, and bury you in a shallow grave."

He grasped his neck. "Wow, that was way too well thought out for my comfort."

"And as I said, *I'm* not ready for it. I'm still just a kid. I need to at least graduate, but I want to be older and in a committed, marriage-type relationship."

"Okay, Cadence."

I looked at him.

He grasped my arms. "I want you to be happy and to know you're safe with me."

I leaned against him. "Thank you, James."

Chapter Twenty-Three

September arrived. With James's graduation being family only so they could fit everyone in the hall, I waited in the lobby just outside. I didn't mind—it meant I could read a book through the boring speeches and special awards. But when they started calling names, I listened until they reached the Fs. I jumped up and pressed my nose against the window on the door.

James lined up on the far wall. I watched as he slowly crept forward and disappeared backstage. They called his name. I leaned against the door to watch him walk across the stage and shake the principal's hand before heading off again.

I grinned and returned to my chair, so proud of him. He'd received an early placement into Macquarie

University's science program, so his exams in a few weeks were just a formality. There would be no real pressure.

The door opened, and he stood in his navy blue gown, grinning at me. I jumped up and rushed into his open arms. He lifted me off my feet and kissed me over and over.

"I couldn't have done this without you," he said.

I flicked the tassel on his cap. "I'm so proud of you."

"I'm so excited. Next year is going to be awesome. Tom, Sam, and I are gonna find a place together closer to the city, and Mum and Dad are gonna help me find my own car. None of this would be happening if it hadn't been for you."

I softly kissed him. "I'm so proud of you, but I'm gonna miss you being here with me every day. It just won't be the same without you."

He tucked a stray hair behind my ear. "I'll make sure I see you."

James claimed the Saturday after my birthday. As our two-year anniversary as well, we had a romantic lunch at a lookout where he whipped out a box.

"I saw it, and it reminded me of your eyes," he said in my ear.

Opening it, I gasped. "James!"

He slipped the sapphire ring on my right ring finger. He'd done his research too. He knew what size it needed to be.

I lifted my hand and rested it on his chest to look at it. He smiled proudly. "I'm glad you like it."

"I love it," I said breathlessly as his lips brushed against mine.

After finishing our picnic, we went to his house to drop off the left-over food. When we arrived, James searched the house. "Hello?"

When he came back, he shrugged. "No one's here."

"I'll put the leftovers away." I headed into the kitchen to unpack the basket.

He followed me and reached out to get a free butt grope.

"James!" I laughed, pushing him back.

"What? It's so . . ." He wrapped his arms around me to grab it again. As he did, he buried his face into my neck, kissing it.

It felt like he'd flicked a switch, putting my hormones into overdrive. I pushed him away. "Why don't we put some music on instead?"

I hurried away, hoping that leaving him alone would help him to control himself. But once in his room, I paused to control my own desires. Two years of being so intimate with him emotionally, my physical needs were starting to flow through. I leaned over his CD stack and took several long, deep breaths.

His footsteps headed toward the room. I straightened and grasped for some CDs. It didn't matter which ones, I just needed to have my hands full.

His hands ran over my waist and hips as his breath caressed my neck. I clung to the CDs as his body sharpened my senses and threw me into a frenzy. "What are you doing?"

"Enjoying your company," he responded. He kissed my neck again as his hands slipped under my shirt onto my belly.

I shuddered as goose bumps rippled over me. I set down the CDs as I rested back into his arms. "James . . ."

"Shh." He brushed my hair away from my neck and softly kissed behind my ear. I shuddered and rested my hands over his as he ran them over my waist and hips again. "You're so beautiful."

My heart fluttered. His hands came around me and held me closer as he ran them over my belly. He nibbled on my ear. I bit my lip to suppress a giggle. His hand came up to my face and he turned me to face him.

I gazed up into his gray-blue eyes, fascinated by how he made me feel. I felt so drawn to him that I couldn't break my gaze.

He clasped my face and kissed me. I threw my arms around his neck and kissed him back. He wrapped his arms around my waist and pulled me closer. His kisses felt eager, excited, like he couldn't get enough of me. To be honest, I felt the same way about him.

His hands wandered under my shirt. I pulled away from his kiss and gasped, but he held tightly onto me. "Cadence."

I looked into his eyes and again found myself spellbound. I moved closer to his lips until I could feel his breath on mine. My breathing grew sharp and shallow as his fingers ran up the skin on my back. "What's happening?"

"Shh." He softly kissed me.

I moaned, energy surging through his kiss. I ached for him to kiss me more. Without me realizing, he had my bra undone. I gasped and tried to pull back, but he held onto me.

"Cadence."

I met his gaze again. "James, I'm nervous."

He stroked my neck. "I won't hurt you, Cadence. I promise."

He pulled me in and kissed me again. I fell into the kiss, completely lost in him.

It took me a moment to realize he was fondling my breasts. But I didn't stop him. It felt good. I wanted him to do it. His thumbs stroked me, sending a shudder over my body as I clung to him, unable to control my desire.

He broke away from the kiss and pulled my shirt and bra over my head. I jumped back from him, startled by my sudden nakedness, and wrapped my arms around myself. "James . . ."

He rushed at me and kissed me firmly on the lips. I stumbled back against the wall as he slipped off his shirt. Groaning with desire, I pulled away from his kiss and looked down at his chest and arms. They couldn't be more perfect.

He took my hands and rested them on his chest. I ran my fingers over his pectorals as his found my breasts. I shut my eyes and shuddered at his touch. He pressed against me, pinning me against the wall as he nibbled on my neck.

He drove me wild as he reignited sensations I hadn't felt in a long time. He bit my neck. I grunted as goose bumps rippled over my body. I grabbed the button on his jeans and pulled it open.

His breath quickened as I slid my hand down his pants. He felt hard as I ran my fingers over him.

He returned to kissing me as he swung me around and tossed me onto the bed. He removed his pants, and pulled mine off just as quickly. Giggling softly, I shut my eyes as he moved down to kiss my bare skin. His hands ran down the inside of my thighs, encouraging them to open for him.

He moved back up and kissed me on the lips as he lowered himself over me. I shuddered at the new, yet familiar feeling. He paused when I gasped at the sharp pain, and he watched my face before carefully pushing into me again.

"Oh, Cadence," he whispered.

I clung to him as he moved rhythmically over me. When he sat back and pushed harder, I moaned and squeezed my legs tighter around him. It felt so good, so exciting.

He withdrew, rushed over to his drawer, and slipped on some protection. I sat up, and as I scanned the room, I began to realize what I was doing.

"Oh, crap . . ."

He rushed back to me and caressed my face. "Cadence, it's all right. It's me. Just let me be with you."

I gazed into his eyes as his tenderness and adoration poured out of them. My resolve faltered. I wanted his body around me, his affection flowing over me.

"James . . ."

He planted a firm kiss on my lips and pushed me back down onto the bed. I was completely lost in him, in the moment. My heart raced as I ran my hands over his chest and shoulders, feeling their strength and marveling at his reactions. His muscles twitched under my fingers and he sighed, gazing down into my eyes. I became lost in those eyes. Nothing else in the world mattered as I saw that he truly believed I was the most beautiful girl he'd ever seen.

I shuddered as he pushed deeper. I shut my eyes as my feelings intensified. "Oh James, don't stop!"

In response, his left hand came up and grabbed my breast as he kissed my cheek. "You are incredible." He sat back and grunted as he shuddered.

He leaned back over me as we both caught our breath. His hand came up and stroked my hair. "Open your eyes."

I opened my eyes and looked into his. He smiled gently down at me, then softly kissed my lips. I sighed and ran my fingers down his back. He smiled again and kissed my cheek before he rolled beside me.

I lay on my back as he stroked my belly. I looked over my shoulder at him. His eyes closed, and a contented smile spread across his face. As I gazed at him, it dawned on me that Austin would have the same expression on his face after we made love for the first time. I rolled onto my side and covered my mouth.

What had I done?

I'd only ever been with Austin, and I had been proud that I'd given him my virginity. But I'd screwed up.

I leapt to my feet and grabbed my clothes, rushing to the bathroom.

"Cadence?"

I ignored James and locked the bathroom door behind me.

"Cadence?" He moved toward the door. "Cadence, let me in."

"No."

"Cadence . . ."

"Leave me alone." I turned on the shower.

I stepped in and sobbed. How could I have done that? What would I tell Austin? I scrubbed every inch of me, wishing I could wash the moment away.

When I finished and dressed, I stepped out into the hallway. James stood in the laundry, in just his jeans, shoving his bedding into the washer. I gasped and covered my mouth in horror.

He turned and dropped everything. "Cadence . . ."

I sprinted out the front door and into the street.

"Cadence!"

I ran to the nearest bus stop and sank into the chair. I proceeded to cry harder than I ever had before. I couldn't believe what I'd done. I felt like I'd betrayed the world and screwed up my second chance worse than I'd screwed things up the first time around.

But the part that I hated myself for the most was that I'd enjoyed it. I'd betrayed Austin in the worst way, and I'd enjoyed doing it. James had been so perfect, so tender, so gentle, and I'd succumbed to my desires for him.

Glancing around, I called out, "Can't you zap me back or something? This wasn't supposed to happen!"

My head sank as I held myself tightly. Then, to my surprise, someone sat beside me. I jumped and shuffled away, but as I glanced up, I saw my angel beside me. He wore a white business shirt and white pants, making him appear casual and relaxed.

"Take me back," I said. "Make it so this didn't happen."

He looked at me with piercing dark brown eyes. I saw pity and sorrow, and I knew he felt my pain too. "I can't do that. It's done now. This was your second chance, you don't get a third."

"I thought God was supposed to forgive unceasingly."

"God does, and he'll forgive you for this, and everything you do, if you let him, but chances are a horse of a different color."

I glared at him. "What do I do then? I've screwed things up much worse than before."

He leaned closer to me, his gaze cutting into my very soul. "Have you?"

He vanished right before my eyes. I blinked, stunned.

I heard a car coming. It pulled up in front of me and Geri burst out. She rushed straight at me and knelt in front of me, clasping my knees. "Cay, come on, let's get out of here."

She took my hand and guided me to the car. She sat in the back with me while her mum drove us to their house. I leaned against her shoulder as she stroked my hair. I felt so lost, and every time I shut my eyes, James's face turned into Austin's.

We arrived at her house. She guided me to her bedroom and shut the door. She sat on her bed while I stood well clear of it and leaned against her desk with my arms folded around myself.

"Cay," she said softly. "James called me and told me what happened."

My tears burst out again. I sank onto the floor.

She scrambled over to hold me. "Cadence, it's okay."

"No, it's not."

"Why?" She pulled back and made me look into her eyes. "Did he *make* you? Because if he did, I'm gonna—"

"No, he didn't make me." I grabbed her balled fist.

"Then what's wrong? You guys have been together for ages, and you're crazy about each other."

"I wasn't supposed to give him my virginity. I was supposed to give it to my husband."

She let out a long breath. "Oh, Cadence."

"I'm such a slut."

"Oh my—" She grabbed my arms and squeezed. "No, you're not! You are far from that. Carla and her posse, *they* are sluts, but not you. The fact that you're so upset about sleeping with your boyfriend of two years proves that. Cadence, please don't cry."

But I did, as hard as I could. I still felt him in me. I still felt him touching me with such tenderness my heart soared.

But my guilt overwhelmed my emotions for James.

I didn't notice it happening, but the next thing I knew, Geri held me in her arms as we curled up on her bed. "Cadence, you stay here. I'm gonna get you some hot chocolate and a giant bowl of ice cream."

She rushed out of the room. While she was gone, I shuffled into her bed and pulled the blankets over my head. Maybe I could just hide away from the world and stay there forever.

When she returned, my crying had turned to a quiet snivel. She touched my hip, and then felt for my shoulder. "Cadence? I brought comfort food."

I peeked out from the blankets. She set the bowl and mug on the bedside table. "Geri, did you know you're the best friend in the whole world?"

"I love you, too, Cay." She sat on the edge of the bed beside me and pulled the blankets back. "Now, sit up and eat some chocolate."

A short laugh burst from me as I sat up. I devoured the ice cream, then slowly sipped at the hot chocolate.

Seeing I had calmed, she reached over and tucked my hair behind my ear. "Cadence, talk to me."

I sighed and took another sip. It was done, and I couldn't do anything about it. I needed to accept it.

"It just . . . happened," I said quietly. "We just kinda lost control. I can't believe I did it, Geri. I mean, James is wonderful, but . . ." I took a deep breath. "It wasn't supposed to be him. He wasn't supposed to be my first. I feel so guilty, like I've betrayed everyone. Except, at the same time, I can't forget how good it felt, how wonderful he made me feel."

I bit my lip as I stared into the half-drunk hot chocolate. "What am I going to do? I don't know if I can even look at him again. I feel so ashamed, but yet . . ."

The words lingered in the air between us as she stroked my hair. Finally, she said, "I understand that you didn't want this, but it's done now. I don't want you wandering around blaming yourself for this mistake. James is wonderful, and he cares about you so much it makes every girl in school green with envy. This could've been worse. Forgive yourself for it, and if you want, just don't do it again."

I nodded slowly. I definitely had no desire to do it again. I didn't even want to see James again. I couldn't go out in public with him knowing what we did. "I . . . I think I should end it with him."

Geri gasped. "No! Oh, Cadence, no!"

Tears streamed down my face again. "Yes. I can't do this again."

"Then don't! But don't end it with him. He's your Romeo, your Jack, your—"

"Their loves came to tragic ends."

"Okay, well, how about your Tom Hanks in *Sleepless in Seattle*? Or Prince Henry in *Ever After*?"

I smiled. "I love those movies."

"See?" She giggled and stroked my cheek. "James is perfect for you. He's fought so hard for you. Don't end it. You know it will only make you both miserable."

Geri's mum tapped on the door and peeked in. "Geri, phone for you."

Geri jumped up and took it, shutting the door. "Hello?"

"Geri! Is she with you?" James's muffled voice came through. He sounded tense and anxious.

Geri gave me a side glance. "Yes, but—"

"Let me talk to her."

I shook my head and crawled under the blankets.

"She doesn't want to right now."

He swore loudly. "Please, Geri. She doesn't have to say anything. I just want her to hear me out."

Geri sat on the bed beside me and pushed the phone under the blankets. She peeked under and lined the phone up with my ear. "She's listening."

"Cadence?" James's voice came through clear and tense. "Cadence, what happened between us was amazing. I don't want you to be afraid or ashamed. It meant so much to me. I don't want you to be hurt because of it. Please come back so we can talk about this."

I pushed the phone away and wrapped the blankets back around me.

"James, she heard you," Geri said.

"Geri! What's she doing?"

"She's hiding in my bed." Her footsteps moved out of the room and she shut the door behind her.

I pulled the blankets back so I could listen to her.

"James, she just needs some space for a while . . . . No, I can't do that . . . she just . . . No! . . . . Look, I want that too, but she needs to do this in her own time . . . . It'll be okay, I promise . . . . All right, bye."

I threw the blankets back over myself as she reentered the room. She sat back beside me and rested her hand on my hip. "You need to talk to him."

"I can't face him."

She sighed. "All right. But it's getting late, and you should get home. I'll tell my mum not to say anything to your parents, if you want?"

My head shot up and I pulled the blankets back to stare at her. "My parents? Dad's gonna kill me and slowly torture James to death! They can't know. Promise me you won't tell them!"

"Okay, okay, I know how your dad is. I'll say nothing."

I swung my legs over the edge of the bed and ran my hands through my hair to flatten it down. I rushed into the bathroom and washed my face. Then, it occurred to me that I'd left my handbag at James's house.

I poked my head out the door. "Geri?"

She rushed over. "What is it?"

"I left my handbag at James's house. We have to go get it."

A glimmer of hope flashed in her eyes. "Will you talk to him?"

The very thought made me sick, so I shook my head. "Can you get it for me?"

She sighed. "Okay. But you know you can't avoid him forever."

We pulled up to his house, and he burst out. I ducked down and shoved Geri. She jumped out and ran between him and the car.

"Let me see her, please!" James grasped her shoulders, looking toward the car.

"No! We just came for her bag." She tried to shove him backward.

"I have to see her."

"She doesn't want to right now!"

He bent over himself as he grasped his knees. He straightened and grabbed his hair, pain written all over his face. "She doesn't want to see me?"

"Come on, show me where her bag is."

He took her inside, but he burst back out of the house again and sprinted to the car. He wrenched my door open and grabbed my hand. "Cadence! Please don't be like this. Let me talk to you."

I fumbled to unbuckle my seatbelt and shuffled over in the seat, but he followed. "Please, I know you're freaking out, but don't shut me out."

I found the door handle and stumbled out of the car. James retreated back out the door and hurried after me. "Cadence . . ."

I swung on him and stared him down. He paused and leaned back, startled by my ferocity. "Just leave me alone," I said in a whisper, but so full of animosity he winced and staggered back from me.

"Cadence, I don't—"

Geri snatched my hand and tugged me toward the car. "James, give her some time, okay?"

As we drove down the street, I watched him as he bent over himself and held his head in his hands.

Chapter Twenty-Four

On Monday, James showed up to drop off Melanie. He tried to meet me at the bus, but I blew right past him and hid among my group. He got the hint and stayed back, but waited again outside the gates that afternoon. The scene repeated every day as he bided his time.

The guilt consumed me. Even Dusty noticed I had become withdrawn. On Thursday night, he slipped into my room and sat on my bed while I tried to focus on my homework.

"Cadence, did you and James break up?"

I gasped and froze. "No."

"But he usually comes around on Tuesdays and Thursdays, and everyone has noticed that you're not talking to him when he shows up. It's easily the biggest piece of gossip flying around school right now. You guys have been inseparable for so long, it's like the world has flipped upside down."

I bit my lip as tears burned in my eyes. "We just had a fight, okay? But we're . . . we . . . I need some time to deal with it."

"Mum and Dad have noticed too, and are really worried. Dad's about to go down to his house and ask him what he did. You know Dad—no one messes with his Cadence."

I groaned and covered my face with my hands. "That will make things worse. James will freak out, and Dad will freak out, and it will really be the end of everything. I don't want James to . . ." I trailed off and lifted my head. I didn't want James to end it with me.

Then why had I pushed him away?

I forced myself to assess my feelings. Where did my guilt come from exactly? I turned to Dusty. "Go tell Dad not to harass James, and I'll deal with it. I just need a moment."

Dusty hurried from the room, closing the door behind him. I scrambled to pull out my scrapbook from under the bed. I hadn't looked at it in a while, so I had to dig through some dirty laundry to get to it.

I pulled it out, rested it on my bed, and opened to Austin's pictures. I found one of him out with some friends and his first girlfriend . . . and they were kissing. I bit my lip as jealousy flared inside me, but I forced it down. I was being ridiculous. I knew he'd had girlfriends before me. Heck, I knew he'd had sex with two other girls before me.

I ran my thumb over his cheek, able to see the nineteen-year-old I'd first met. He wasn't as solid across the shoulders yet, but he was burly and strong and growing in dark sideburns. My guilt stemmed from my feelings of betrayal for a guy I technically hadn't met yet. But James, oh, my feelings for James were so intense that I was . . . I was . . .

I shot to my feet, slamming the scrapbook shut. I was in love with James! Everything about him made me love him more and more. The way he smiled at me, the way he looked at me with that gleam in his eyes, the way he smelled. I loved the way he ruffled his hair when he was frustrated and confused, and the way his breath on my skin always sent chills all over my body.

He was gentle and loving and fiercely protective of me. He was funny, charming, goofy, and embarrassing. He knew me so well and saw through everything I did, but still he wanted to be with me, despite how much I put him through.

I felt guilty because I loved someone other than Austin.

The first day all week that James didn't show up was the one day I was ready to talk to him. I scanned for him as I climbed off the bus, but he wasn't anywhere in sight. I surveyed the school as I walked to meet up with my friends, but there was still no sight of him.

The bell rang. I walked to class and sat beside Michael with a sigh. He flicked my shoulder and I looked across at him.

"You look better than you have all week," he said.

"Wow, I must have been super depressing."

"That's an understatement."

I bit my lip. "Have you seen James today?"

"I thought you weren't talking to him right now."

"I wasn't, but now I need to."

He leaned closer to me to whisper as the teacher read out the roll. "Melanie rode the bus to school today."

I slapped my forehead. "Crap!"

"I could text him, if you like?"

"No . . ." I paused to answer my name being called. "I'll let him have his day."

I walked to my classes feeling sick. I'd hurt James and blown him off for too long, and now he needed to get some space and recuperate. Slowly, through each class, I convinced myself he wanted to dump me the first chance he got. At the end of school, I fought back tears as I left my classroom after everyone else to walk to the bus bay.

"Cadence?"

I jumped and swung around at the sound of James's voice. I glanced around the corridor. We were alone. He pushed off from the wall and stepped toward me. My heart filled with fear, so I hurried away from him. "I don't want you to say it, James!"

He rushed after me. "Say what?"

"That it's over! I know I screwed up and freaked out, but I don't want to lose you. Can you at least let me pretend that we're still together by not saying the words?"

He grabbed my arm and turned me to face him. "You think I want to break up with you?"

I nodded as tears burst out.

"Cadence, no!" He clasped my face and brushed my tears away with his thumbs. "I'm here because I thought *you* wanted to end it with me. I got a text this morning from Michael saying you were ready to talk and that I needed to come back. But I didn't wanna face you if you were going to end it. Then I thought no, I'm not going to let her end it. I'm gonna go down there and make her listen to me so I can tell her that I love her."

I gasped and my gaze shot up to meet his. "You . . . you . . ."

"Yes, Cadence, I'm madly, deeply, crazy in love with you. There's been no one else to equal you since the moment I laid eyes on you. You're beautiful, and wonderful, and smart, and a complete nut job, but I love you more than anything."

I clasped his wrists as he caressed my face. I gazed up into his eyes. "I was going to tell you the same thing—that I'm in love with you."

His whole face lit up as a wide, relieved smile swept across it. He pulled my face in and he kissed me passionately as his arms wrapped around me, completely encompassing me. It sent ripples through my whole body, warming my soul.

I broke away, but stayed less than an inch from his lips. "James?"

"Yes?"

"Are your parents home?"

He looked down at me, confused. "No, Melanie has a . . ." He paused as his eyes widened. "Really?"

I nodded.

"But . . . really?"

I nodded again.

"Shoot! Come on!"

We ran to his car and rushed to his house. He fumbled to unlock the door and tugged me inside. Once the door shut, he grabbed me and kissed me as he guided me backward toward his room. He shut the door behind him and pulled off his shirt.

"Are you sure?" he asked as he stroked my face. "That's what started all this, and I don't want to—"

"Shut up." I grabbed him by the back of the neck and pulled him back in to a kiss.

He pushed me backward until my legs pressed against his bed, and he hurried to unbutton my blouse. I broke free of the kiss as I watched him and stroked his bare torso.

"James, you're so hot."

He grinned and finally pulled off my shirt. "It's all for you."

I reached back and unclipped my bra, watching his gaze fall. He stared as I became exposed. He shoved me back onto the bed.

"Oh, James." I forced aside the feelings of guilt. Geri was right, I was crazy about James and he was mad about me, so there was no harm in any of it.

"Are you sure you're okay with this?" he asked.

I nodded and took his hand. With a tug, I brought him up over me to kiss me. He slipped on his protection, and he made love to me gently, lovingly. "I love you so much, Cadence."

"I love you, too."

There was a tap on the door. James swore and pressed down over me the second before it flew open. I ducked under him, trying to hide.

"James!" Melanie said in a high-pitched voice.

"Get out, Mel!"

She slammed the door. A moment later, his parents started arguing in the hallway. He jumped off me. "Get dressed."

I hurried to obey. As I pulled my skirt back on, Karen tapped firmly on the door. "Both of you get dressed and come out right now."

"She sounds angry," I said.

He buttoned and zipped up his pants before rushing over to me. "Stay behind me."

"They're going to rip into us, aren't they?"

"Me? Yes. You, they'll probably try to ignore." He pulled his shirt over his head.

My stomach felt like a hollow pit. "James—"

He kissed me. "It'll be okay."

He handed me my blouse. I pulled it on and buttoned it, then he took my hand.

The five steps from his bedroom to the living room were the longest walk I'd ever taken. As we passed out of the hallway and the room opened up, I dropped my gaze to avoid looking at his parents sitting together on the couch. James pulled me behind him as he came to a halt in front of them.

An awkward silence reigned, then John's voice cut through. "Stop touching her, James."

I bit my lip as my cheeks burned. But James's hand tightened around mine, and he pulled me closer until my nose pressed against his shoulder. From my well-protected position, I dared to glance up at them. John sat clenching his fists on his legs, his glare boring into James, while Karen couldn't even look at us.

"Dad, Mum, it's not as bad as it seems."

Karen's head fell into her hands as John launched onto his feet. "How long has this been going on?"

"This was only the second time."

"James!" Karen said from the couch. "I thought you were past all of this."

"I thought *she* was better than this!" John pointed at me accusingly with a hard, tight expression. "I thought you weren't going to have sex until you were married! I thought, for once, James had picked a good girl—"

"Leave her alone!" James yelled at him.

"Shut up, boy! You're grounded indefinitely."

"I'm eighteen! You can't do that!"

"But you still live under my roof." He leaned in closer, staring James dead in the eyes. "This ends right now! You and her are over, since I can't trust you to keep your pants on."

James's arms came back and wrapped around me. "No."

"No?" John turned his focus onto me. "Cadence, you are no longer welcome in this house."

"John, don't go that far!" Karen shot to her feet.

"Karen, I won't have them having sex in my house."

I pressed my face into James's back, feeling more embarrassed by the second.

"Geez, Dad!" James's voice rose to a yell. "It's not like Cadence was my first!"

That drew John's attention back to him. "Excuse me?"

"Yeah, I slept with Carla, Sally, and Becca before I started dating Cadence."

Karen gasped and John stepped back in shock.

"I didn't know you'd slept with Sally and Becca," I said softly.

He glanced back at me and pulled me around under his arm. "But I was Cadence's first, and that's special to me because I love her."

Both his parents stared at me in a stunned silence. My face burned, so I tucked it away into his chest. His arms wrapped around me protectively, and he kissed my head. "I love her more than anything because she's amazing, and smart, and beautiful, and no matter what you do, I'll always be with her."

I couldn't help looking up at his face. He gazed steadily at his father, his jaw clenched defiantly, his chin raised. He would fight them for me if he had to, but I didn't want that. His family was more important than me. I squeezed his waist to get his attention.

His gaze fell to me and instantly he softened. His adoration for me poured out and almost made my heart stop beating.

"James." I touched his face. "Don't fight them."

His eyes widened. "Cadence, I'm not going to let you go."

"They're your family. You shouldn't let *them* go either. Maybe I should just go home so you can talk to them and work things out."

"We wouldn't need to if you hadn't interfered in our lives." We turned at the sound of Melanie's voice. She leaned against the entrance to the hallway with her arms folded. "I knew you'd be bad for him. All your fake 'I'm so sweet' crap never fooled me."

"Mel!" James's voice rose again.

"Shut up, James! You're such an idiot not to see it."

"Melanie! Enough!" Karen said firmly. She looked at me and spoke gently. "Cadence, do your parents know about this?"

I drew a sharp breath. "No."

Melanie scoffed behind us.

John's eyes burned with indignity. "I guess they're about to find out. Both of you get in the car."

I panicked. Dad would kill me. He'd never look at me the same way again. I clung to James as I glued myself to the floor in utter terror. The image of Dad shedding a tear as he raised a glass to Austin flashed through my mind. "I can't tell my dad!"

John glared at me. "Then why did you do it?"

I gnawed at my lip, wishing I could muster my adult way of thinking, but it had long gone as my teenage brain blinded me with fear. I couldn't help myself as I cried.

"Oh, geez," Melanie groaned.

James held me tighter.

Karen rushed over and grabbed my wrist. "John, you stay here. I'll handle this."

"Her parents need to know!" John responded.

"Yes, they do. But I think it would be better if I handle it. You're not in the frame of mind to do this. All you'll do is make matters worse." She rested her hand on my shoulder. "Cadence, sweetie, you know this is very serious and your parents have to know. James and I will come with you to support you."

"Mum!" Melanie groaned.

"Don't coddle her!" John said.

"For heaven's sake, John! She's seventeen years old! I remember what it was like at her age. She has all these feelings and desires and is struggling to deal with them while trying to please everyone. Your son is as much at fault as she is, and maybe we are, too, for not paying closer attention. But she doesn't deserve to be treated like trash for this."

She wrapped her arms around James and me. "I'll take them, and I'll talk with Harmony and handle it tactfully." She encouraged us out the door, and to my relief, John didn't follow.

James slid into the backseat beside me and pulled my head onto his shoulder. "Cadence," he said softly as the car started. "Please don't end it with me. I don't know what I'd do without you."

I gazed into his eyes. He was just as afraid as me. I caressed his cheek, and he leaned down and kissed me.

"James, I love you."

He pulled me closer. "I love you, too."

I rested my head on his shoulder and saw Karen glance back at me. In the brief moment before she noticed me looking at her, I saw she wasn't angry at all. Nervous and concerned, yes, but mostly she loved us, both of us, and saw how much we loved each other. For the first time in a long time, I remembered Austin's mother, Linda, and how she'd looked at me the same way.

We rode in silence as James kissed my head over and over. I sighed, feeling safe with him, even though I knew what we would soon face.

We arrived at my house. The car engine cut. I stopped breathing. Karen stepped out of the car and came around to open my door.

James nudged me. "Breathe, Cadence. I'll be right here with you."

We walked up to the door and Karen knocked. Mum answered.

"Hi, Karen . . ." Her face fell. Her gaze shot between each of us. "Oh, no."

My cheeks burned and I cried again.

Mum opened the screen door and grasped my shoulder. "Come inside and sit down."

James and I sat on the sectional together, and he clutched my hand. He held it so tightly that his knuckles turned white. Karen sat across from us on one of the armchairs, and Mum sank onto the far end of the sectional, facing us. "It just happened, didn't it?"

Karen nodded. "We came home early . . ."

Mum covered her face. "Oh, Cadence."

My heart ached at the pain written all over her. "Mum, please don't be upset. I love James."

"Oh, sweetheart, I already knew that." She shifted beside me and took my hand. "I just hoped you'd wait a little longer. I hoped you'd at least wait until you graduated." She sighed. "Your father isn't going to take this well."

My lip quivered. "He's going to hate me."

She stroked my hair. "You were responsible, weren't you?"

I met her gaze. Dodging my statement and redirecting the conversation only meant one thing: I was right.

"Yes, we were," James said softly.

Mum nodded, but wasn't able to look at him. "Well, that's a start."

"Mum." Tears filled my eyes. "Are you disappointed in me?"

She stroked my cheek and gazed sadly into my eyes. "No. I'll always love you and be here for you. You're my little girl. I just wish you hadn't grown up so fast."

I threw my arms around her and we cried. I felt so glad she wasn't angry at me and understood. It would make facing Dad easier.

Karen stood. "James should stay until David gets home, but I need to go do damage control with my husband and daughter. I'll be back to pick him up at seven." She stepped over and squeezed Mum's shoulder. "Harmony, you're a good mother. As much as this has shocked both of us, I know Cadence is good for my son, and they love each other. At least we have that."

Mum squeezed her hand. "Thank you, Karen. I'm grateful for all you do, too."

Karen left.

Mum turned to us. "Well, Cadence, where do we go from here?"

I wasn't sure myself. I wanted to be with James, but it seemed that level of intimacy involved more people than just us. I leaned against James as I carefully weighed my options. "What do you think I should do?"

Mum shook her head. "I'd prefer if you didn't do it again, but I'm not naive. We'll take you down to the doctor next week and get you on birth control. I'd rather you not run the risk of getting pregnant."

I sat bolt upright. I hadn't even thought about that. I looked back at James as he shifted back into the sectional and knew, by the calm expression on his face, that he had.

He'd been careful both times. I turned back to Mum. "I'm not sure if I'll do it again, but I appreciate that."

She squeezed my hand. "Okay. Why don't you and James go hang out with Dusty so I can talk to your father when he gets home? I think he'll need baby steps for this one."

James and I made our way to Dusty's room.

When we opened the door, Dusty launched to his feet with a grin across his face. By the quick flash of his gaze to me, he sensed our somber mood, but he didn't want to dwell on it. Instead, he focused on the return of his idol into our house. "James! You're back. I was a little worried there for a while."

James grasped Dusty's hand and shook it. "Nah, I'm not going anywhere. I'm stuck on Cadence."

"Well, hotness runs in the family." Dusty plucked up his science exam. "Check it! I totally aced it because of you."

James took it. "Nice, but you did know a lot of it on your own."

"Nah." Dusty grinned proudly. Nothing could be better to him than James's praise. "Come on, let's go out back and pass the football around or something."

He plucked up his rugby ball and we made our way outside.

We played and laughed, even after the sun set. I had so much fun I forgot about having to face Dad. When he came in the gate, I rushed to him and threw my arms around his neck. "Hey, Dad!"

"Hey! I heard you three out here and wanted to see what all the fun was." He kissed my head as he pulled me around. "And James is back."

I hesitated as James hung back, acutely aware of what would come for him. He ruffled his hair and gave a crooked smile. "Hey. Yeah, we made up."

"Well, good. Cadence was pretty mellow without you around."

I wanted to be sick. He wouldn't be making such friendly comments in a few minutes.

"I'm gonna go in and check if your mother needs any help with dinner." He kissed my head again and turned inside.

I rushed over to James and grabbed his arms. "He's gonna kill us."

"It's okay." James pulled me against him. "I'm here no matter what."

Dusty averted his eyes and spun the ball on his hand, in no way oblivious to what was going on.

Suddenly, Dad roared. *"WHAT?"*

James swore and shoved me behind him and Dusty. I darted forward.

"No, I need to face him."

The back door burst open. Dad marched straight to us with Mum bustling along behind him. He stopped in front of us, completely ignoring James. His glare fixed on me. His chest heaved as he stared into my eyes.

I wanted to cower back and burrow deep into the ground under his gaze, but I didn't dare flinch.

"You . . ." he said in a barely audible voice. "Oh . . ." His head fell and he rubbed his eyes. We waited while he rubbed his face and hair. Finally, his gaze lifted to me again and all I could see was a deep, devastated agony. "You've broken my heart."

His words felt like knives cutting deep into me, piercing all my vitals, making me want to die. I'd never disappointed him like that before, and it tore me apart. "Daddy, please—"

"Don't 'Daddy' me!" he yelled, then lowered his voice to a near whisper. "You're not my little girl anymore. I can't even look at you."

He marched back inside.

Tears streamed down my face again. I couldn't move. That was worse than him yelling at us. I wished he *had* yelled at us. The level of disappointment he'd just laid on my shoulders was the worst feeling in the world.

James straightened as he looked down at me, fists clenched. "I'm gonna talk to him."

"No! James, he'll kill you."

James shook his head. "I don't care." Before I could react, he hurried past Mum and back into the house.

Mum stepped beside me as I grabbed Dusty's wrist.

"Get out of my house!" Dad's hollering echoed from inside.

"I won't. I will be heard out," James replied defiantly.

"Heard out? You screwed my daughter! I trusted her with you, and you abused that. The *one thing* I made clear as being off limits, and you went and did it. You disgust me."

"I love her. We didn't take it lightly. We held off for so long because she wanted to respect you and herself, and I've always loved that about her. This wasn't just a thing, it was special. I would never hurt her, and I know that what you just did to her tore her apart—"

"What *I* just did to her?" Dad snickered. "No, you don't get to blame me for that."

"Maybe not, but all I want is for her to be happy."

"I should rip you to shreds . . ." I heard a thump as something hit a wall, probably James's body. "You will never touch her again. You will never come here again. You will never take her out anywhere *again*!"

"I will. She loves me as much as I love her. You can't stop us."

Dusty flinched. "He's just provoking him."

"Shh." Mum wrapped her hand around mine.

Dad's laughter filled my ears. "I can't, huh? Well, Mr. Gordon, you are eighteen, making her illegal for you . . ."

I pulled away and rushed inside. The thought of James going to jail because of me wrenched my heart. I couldn't let Dad do that.

When I burst through the door, I saw Dad had James pinned against the wall of the hallway leading to the bedrooms. James stared defiantly at him with his hands wrapped around Dad's as he held tightly to his shirt. Both of their heads turned as I entered.

"Cadence! Get out!" James said in a tight voice.

But I rushed over and grabbed their hands. "Dad! Let him go!"

Dad's hands tightened and he shoved him harder against the wall. James winced, the drywall cracking, and Dad said, "He'll never come near you again."

"Dad!" I pulled at his hands. "Dad! I love him! Don't hurt him!"

My words caused his head to snap around to me. "What?"

"I love him!"

His hands still held to James's shirt, but he never looked away from my face. "You're seventeen years old!"

"So? I've been with him for two years, and I know how I feel. He's my best friend, and the only person who makes me feel so alive. Don't hurt him, Dad, because all that does is hurt me, too."

Dad turned his focus back onto James as he slowly examined his face. Then, he let him go. "Don't ever touch her again. I mean it. I'll be watching you, boy."

He turned away from James and looked down at me. His hand came up to touch my cheek, but he pulled away, his face full of pain. "I love you, Cadence. Don't break my heart again."

I reached for him, but he stormed to his room, slamming the door behind him.

Chapter Twenty-Five

Geri's knees quivered with her hands pressed between them. She glanced over at Mum, who flicked through a magazine while I waited to go in to the gynecologist. "So he still hasn't even looked at you?"

I shook my head. "I did the one thing he was afraid of, and he won't come out into the house when James is around. I'm afraid he'll never forgive me."

Mum's hand squeezed my knee and she spoke without looking up. "He will. Just be patient."

"Your mum's awesome," Geri said.

I smiled. "I know."

Mum squeezed my knee again.

"Thanks for coming, Geri," I said. "You didn't need to be here."

"Hey, what are friends for?"

The nurse called my name. I stood, heading in to see the doctor. I glanced back, wishing my mum could hold my hand, but knowing the time had come for me to be an adult again.

Melanie tossed a note at my head. I opened it and read, *SLUT*.

I tore it up. She'd turned vicious on me after she found me with James. Worst of all, she wouldn't let either of us talk to her about it.

James's parents soon accepted what happened, although they took precautions to avoid it happening again. James and I were never alone at their house anymore, not that we had any intention of trying again.

"Melanie," I said in a low voice. "Why don't you and I have a chat after class?"

"Ha! No."

Geri growled. She jumped from her seat and marched out of the room. This didn't faze anyone—being eleventh graders had its privileges, and leaving class without asking was one of them. When she came back, she carried a vial of something. She made a beeline for Melanie.

I jumped to my feet. "Geri, no!"

She tossed the liquid in Melanie's face. "Burn, witch!"

Melanie screamed and tried to wipe it off her face. Everyone turned and stared. The teacher rushed over as Geri sank back into the chair beside me. "Geraldine Turner! Detention!"

Geri scoffed. "Whatever."

Melanie rushed to the sink to wash her face as Geri sneered.

"What did you throw on her?" I asked.

Geri shrugged. "$H2O$."

I bit my lip and covered my smirk.

After returning home from Christmas shopping, Mum and I paused when we saw James's car parked out in front of the house. Exchanging concerned looks, we hurried inside.

"James?" I rushed through the house, knowing Dad was home, but not seeing either of them. "James?"

The office door creaked open, and Dad peered out with a stern scowl. "In here."

Mum's hand rested between my shoulders, giving me the courage to face Dad. She followed me in.

James sat facing the desk, his knees quivering. He shot to his feet as I entered, smiling nervously.

"Dad." I looked up at him. "What did you do?"

"Sit, Cadence." He moved to sit behind the desk. I felt like I was about to be interrogated for murder.

As I sat, James's hands rested on my shoulders. Dad smoldered, but kept his head. "James and I have come to an agreement."

I glanced back at James. "What kind of agreement?"

"No more sex." Dad spat the last word out like a foul taste. "I will allow him to keep taking you out on that condition. Do you understand?"

I nodded vigorously. "I don't want to do it again anyway. I don't want to hurt you again. Please, Dad. I love you, and I hate that you won't even look at me."

Tears burned in my eyes as my voice caught.

His gaze shot to me. "Cadence." He sighed, rubbing his eyes. "I love you too, sweetheart."

Standing, he hurried around and pulled me into his arms. Relief washed over me at the comfort of his broad chest and strong arms. Dad had forgiven me, and everything in the world felt right again.

Afterward, I walked James to his car. "Did Dad call you, or . . . ?"

He smirked. "I just came over. I thought I'd try facing my fears."

I giggled, leaning against his car. "Thank you."

"Anything for you." He rested his hands on my waist, kissing my forehead. "Next year will be better than ever for us, I promise. You and I are far from over, and I made that very clear to your dad. Everything will be all right."

I nuzzled up in his arms. We were far from over. He still had me, hook, line, and sinker. But with him going off to university, I thought about my own university options coming up. I met Austin at university, but I'd gone to university clear across the country to start anew because I'd screwed up things so badly with my friends. This time, I had people keeping me where I was. I had Geri, a close relationship with Harper, and of course, James.

I wondered if I should talk to him about me going to Western Australia for university, but as he pulled away and stared into my eyes, I knew that was a conversation for a later date.

I stroked his face. "Next year will be great, James."

He beamed. "As long as I have you."

part three:

decisions

Chapter Twenty-Six

The house was buzzing and jam-packed with people. Tom hosted the New Year's party, so I was one of the few underage people in the house. As a result, I was the designated driver, having just earned my probationary license.

James was tipsy. To my relief, he didn't seem inclined to get totally wasted. He was handsy enough.

"Cadence!" he bellowed across the room.

"What do you want now?" I yelled back.

"Yo mama!" He burst out laughing.

I slapped my forehead. At least he was a happy drunk. I knew he wanted me to join him—I'd been mingling with some girls and felt his keen stare on me the whole time—but I kept my distance to see how desperate I could make him.

When I stepped up beside him, it pleased me to see how well it had worked. He wrapped his arm around my neck and moved in to kiss me, but I blocked him after one whiff of his breath.

"Gross!"

He grinned, plucked some gum out of his pocket, and started chewing. "Having fun?"

"Yeah, everyone has this nervous, excited energy about them. It's making me anxious for my turn."

He kissed my forehead. "I'm looking forward to you graduating too. You should apply for Macquarie so you can be with me."

I dodged his gaze. "We'll have to see if I'm smart enough first."

"Cadence, you're way smarter than me, and *I* got in." He pulled me closer and brushed his nose against mine. "Breath better?"

I sniffed. "Mmm, spearmint."

"Good." He gave me a swift kiss and pushed the gum into my mouth.

I pulled away, leaned over a bin, and spat it out. "You're disgusting."

He laughed merrily and pulled me back in. "That's why you love me."

The countdown began. Ten, nine . . .

"Another year, another kiss." James grinned. "Seriously, I think there's something to this."

I laughed. "Maybe there is."

He waited for the countdown to hit three. On two, he pressed his lips firmly against mine.

One . . .

Freeze.

I expected it that time, so I pulled away from James and walked over to the food table while I waited for the angel to appear. He stepped through the door, dressed once again as Father Time, and leaned against the table beside me. "You're growing up fast, sweet Cadence."

"Again."

He chuckled. "What shall we look at this year?"

I shrugged and offered him some chips, but he pushed them aside. "I dunno," I said. "That's your thing. You know what I need to see."

"Very well." He touched my shoulder and, like the last two times, images and feelings of Austin and Melody flooded my thoughts—when Austin first kissed me, Melody's first step—but I managed to keep my composure and didn't fall back into a sobbing mess. A few tears fell as the pain of their deaths tore through me, but I kept it mostly under control.

The man watched me as I struggled, but when I straightened and met his gaze, he nodded his approval. "You're getting stronger. You're gaining control over your emotions and the teenage hormones aren't so overwhelming. Very good, Cadence."

I smirked. "Thanks."

He rested his hand on the small of my back and led me to the door. As we stepped out, I found myself in a house I'd never seen before. He led me to the center of the small living room.

There was a knock at the door. Brian appeared from the hallway and hurried to answer it. Melanie stood on the other side with a wide smile across her face. She looked beautiful. She'd straightened her shoulder-length hair, and even wore eyeliner and mascara.

"Hey, Brian. I'm ready to go."

"Oh, yeah." He rubbed the back of his neck. "Just a sec, okay? Sit down if you want."

As she entered, the angel and I followed Brian to his room. Inside, a photo of Geri and me rested on his desk. He glanced behind him and slid it between some papers.

"Oh, no!" I gasped. "Is this when he breaks up with her?"

The man nodded, and I found myself in a park as Melanie sobbed beside Brian.

"Mel, don't cry. I'm just being honest," he said. "Why keep at something that isn't working out?"

"I thought we were doing fine," she responded. "I really like you, Brian. I thought I was doing everything I needed to do to be a good girlfriend. Is it because I'm not pretty enough? I can be pretty if you want. Tell me what you like and I'll do it."

"You sound desperate."

She glared at him. "I don't understand. We never fight, and James and Cadence argue all the time . . ."

He dropped his gaze and shifted his feet. She examined his face, her eyes narrowing.

"And Cadence is a whiny baby—"

"Don't talk about her like that."

"Oh my . . ." Her eyes widened. She jumped to her feet and pointed at him accusingly. "So you'd prefer it if I had blonde hair and big boobs?"

Brian shifted uncomfortably. "Mel, you're very pretty."

"But I'm no Cadence, huh?" She pressed her hands against her hips. "I'm such an idiot to not notice sooner . . . but then again, you're an idiot to think she'd go out with you while she's dating my *brother*!"

"They're about to break up. Everyone's talking about it. Your total jerk of a brother is going to dump her because she won't have sex with him!"

Melanie's mouth moved, but no sound came out. Once she had her thoughts in order, she said, "James wouldn't do that. He likes her too much to dump her, so don't talk about him like that! How *dare* you think you can end a perfectly good relationship to pick up the pieces of a girl who's already rejected you! *You're* the jerk!"

Brian jumped to his feet. "If Cadence needs me to mend her heart, I want to be available."

Melanie planted a swift, hard slap across his face. "You're the biggest jerk I've ever met!"

She marched away.

"Melanie! At least let my mum take you home."

She gave him the finger as she kept walking.

"She was so brave," I said as the scene froze. "I felt terrible. I couldn't believe he would do that to her."

The man nodded. "Yes, it was bad luck on your part. One of those choices others make that you can't do anything about. You and Melanie always had a relationship that teetered on disaster, and things like this never helped. You tried hard to keep things going, but she never wanted to believe you were genuine. She just believed you did it for James. But then, when she found you two—"

"Please don't show me that," I said as my cheeks burned. "We haven't done it since. His family freaked out, and Dad has barely started talking to me again. We feel it's safer to leave it alone for a while."

"Wise decision." The scene changed. We stood in Melanie's room with her furious face locked in a motionless scream as she poked angrily at her father's chest. "The pain she felt from finding her brother with you like that— her beloved and truest friend in the world, with the girl she blamed for always getting in the way. This time, you were in the way in the worst way. Her brother loved you more than he could ever love her, and he even threatened to leave her for you."

I stepped across to look into her face. Tears streamed down her cheeks. "But, he didn't leave her."

"No, but his heart did. He proclaimed that he was in love with you, which put her at number two. Everyone seemed to choose you over her, even the one person she hoped never would."

I let out a long breath as I gazed into her angry face. I was *that* girl to her. Where she failed, I was the one who won at everything and stole all her glory.

"This year, I'm gonna have to help her," I said, as images of her slitting her wrists flashed through my mind. "I'm going to give her as much credit and love as I can, no matter how hard she pushes me away."

"That's very noble of you."

The scene melted away, and I stood staring at me and James locked in a passionate kiss outside my maths classroom. By the tears streaming down my face and the abandoned corridor, I knew exactly when it was. "This was the moment he told me he loved me."

"And you him," the man said. "Come and see earlier."

The scene melted into James and Tom sitting in a park with a creek cutting through it. They made themselves comfortable by the shallow water, James resting his head on his backpack with his arm covering his face, while

Tom pulled out a book, his dark, shaggy hair flopping over his forehead.

Without even looking, James said, "You're boring."

"You're not exactly fun lately," Tom answered.

"Then you shoulda stayed home."

Tom grunted and shut his book. "You should just apologize to her. That always makes girls happy."

James scowled and turned his head so he could see him from under his arm. "It's not that simple. I freaked her out, and I have a feeling she might dump me."

"Wow, you musta done something pretty bad." Tom shifted around and opened his bag. "I stole a ton of junk food from the kitchen. I hoped it would distract me from your depression, since you refuse to tell me what happened."

James smirked. "Gimme some."

They ate in silence, until James's phone beeped. He dug into his bag and pulled it out, but stared at it in shock. "It's Michael."

"As in Cadence's friend Michael?"

James looked at his watch. "He was probably just with her." He ruffled his hair. "This can't be good." He opened the text and read it, then tossed the phone to Tom.

"She's done. She was gonna dump me today when I showed up."

"It doesn't say that. It just says she's ready to talk to you."

"Which means dump me."

"Geez, James!" Tom exclaimed with exasperation. "What did you *do* to her?"

James snatched his phone back and grabbed his hair. "We had sex."

Tom leaned back, stunned. "Oi."

"It was all good until she freaked out and ran away afterward. I tried to talk to her, but you shoulda seen the way she looked at me—like I was the scum of the earth."

"That sucks."

"No kidding." James huffed. "Don't tell anyone."

"Nah, man, your secret's safe with me."

James climbed to his feet and paced, running his hand through his hair. "I totally screwed up. I knew she wasn't ready, but I wanted it anyway. So when she relented, I just kinda took it."

He threw his arms in the air.

"I shouldn't have done it! Her dad's probably gonna cut off my manhood if he finds out I took his little girl's virginity. She's probably terrified of him disowning her or something. She'd dump me long before she'd ever stand up to him."

"So you're just gonna avoid her?"

James stopped pacing and looked down at Tom. "Yeah, pretty much."

"James." Tom shook his head. "You can't do that."

"Why not?"

"Because she's a girl. She'll find a way."

James collapsed back into the dirt beside his bag. "I'm done talking about this."

"Whatever."

We fast-forwarded a couple of hours and he started talking about it again. "Tom, what should I do?"

"I thought you got a job at Target—"

"No, I meant with Cadence."

"Oh, we're back on that."

James sat up and faced Tom. "I can't lose her."

"Then fight for her."

"But . . ." James glanced around, his brows furrowed and jaw tense. "How?"

"Don't let her dump you." Tom pulled out a box of Pizza Shapes. "When she tries, tell her that you don't want to, and she's gotta give you a really good reason."

"That sounds stupid and desperate." James flopped back onto his bag.

"Whatever, you know her better than I do. I've never actually had a girlfriend, so what do I know?" Tom tossed a stone into the water.

James looked at his watch. "We should think about packing up soon. Melanie has some karate thing after school."

Pause.

"She better be ready, 'cause I don't wanna risk Cadence seeing me and dumping me."

Tom groaned.

James sat up, indignant. "Hey! She's not just some girl! I'm in lo—" He clamped his mouth shut and turned away with his arms folded.

"James?" Tom asked in a firm tone. "Were you about to say you're in *love* with her?"

"Yeah. So what?"

"Dude." Tom shook his head with a smirk. "Chicks love that crap."

"It's not crap! I've known it for months, but I can't tell her. It would totally freak her out."

"Worse than what she is now?"

James pursed his lips and looked toward the creek.

"Why don't you tell her now? You have nothing to lose, right?"

James's jaw flexed, but he didn't answer. They sat in silence for several minutes before James shot to his feet.

"I'm not gonna let her dump me. I'm gonna wait outside her classroom and make her see that I want to be with her because I love her."

He plucked up his bag and marched toward the car park.

"James! Wait!" Tom hurried to follow.

The scene froze. I turned to face the man, who held his hands behind his back. "The rest you know."

I nodded and looked back to James. "For months? I didn't know that."

The man smiled. "Are you happy with him, Cadence?"

I bit my lip, giddy from the memory of James confessing his love. "I am."

"Then you have a decision to make." The man touched my shoulder and the scene split, showing me the first time I'd laid eyes on Austin. "Will you go to Western Australia again to pursue the love you know is possible, or will you stay and be with the love you already have?"

My stomach knotted as I stared at them both. They looked so different. James was tall, lean, with gray-blue eyes and chestnut brown hair. Austin was shorter, but broad across the shoulders and heavily built, with dark hair and brown eyes. They were equally attractive, and I loved them both.

"I guess I'll have to think about it this year. I mean, a lot will change with James going off to uni. He may even find a girl who is far more attractive and interesting than me, so . . ."

The man chuckled. "You're going to keep your options open."

I bit my lip and wrapped my arms around myself. "No, not really. I just . . . I know where the path I'll take with Austin will lead, and I want that. I want stability and our beautiful Melody. Austin's the best thing that ever happened to me. But James . . . he's an uncertain path."

The man touched my shoulder again. The scene faded back into Tom's house, and I stood facing James.

"You've been taking that risk all along, and he's proven over and over his dedication to you."

His hand released me. I swung around, but he had gone.

I hurried back into James's arms and kissed him, just in time for time to move forward again.

Chapter Twenty-Seven

I hurried into the townhouse and found the A/C. I flicked it on as the first people began carrying the furniture inside.

"Thanks, Cadence!" the three guys yelled.

School would start for me in a week, but university started in just over a month. James, Tom, and Sam were each attending different universities, so they'd chosen a central location close to all the public transportation.

I ran back out, passing Karen and John as they brought in a couch. I found Melanie by the trailer, pulling out boxes. She scowled when I stepped up beside her, but didn't say a word.

"Hey, Melanie."

She rolled her eyes and dumped a heavy box in my arms. "Kitchen."

I struggled to carry it inside, wondering what was in it. James ran over to me. "Why are you carrying this?"

"What is it?"

He lifted it out of my arms. "All my books."

I glanced back at Melanie, who smirked. I pulled the box out of his arms. "Where do you want them?"

"Cadence, this is way too heavy—"

I glared at him.

"Up the stairs and in the room on the left."

I trudged up the stairs and into the room. Inside, his parents worked on setting up his bed. His desk and drawers sat by one of the walls. In the wall opposite the window was a door to a bathroom. I set the books on his desk and turned to his parents. "How did he score the master bedroom?"

"He pays twenty dollars more each fortnight," John answered as he bolted the headboard to the frame.

Karen stood while John finished screwing in the frame. "I can't believe he made you carry his books."

I scowled. "He didn't, I just did."

She rested her arm around my shoulder. "Come on, let's empty that trailer."

When Melanie saw us heading out together, she turned her back on us. I wasn't sure what I could do to get through to her. "Melanie . . ."

She dumped a much lighter box in my arms. "Living room."

"Melanie," Karen said. "When are you going to let go of this resentment for Cadence? She's only ever nice to you."

Melanie sneered. "Yeah, when *you're* around."

"Melanie, I've never been mean to you." I frowned.

"Oh, yeah? So what was with the acid in my face?"

I paused. "Oh! That was Geri, and it was only water."

"Whatever."

"And I distinctly remember you calling me a slut before—"

"Melanie!" Karen swung to her. "You know better than that."

Melanie glared at me and continued unloading the trailer. *That didn't go well.*

Once we had everything inside, Karen and I unpacked in the kitchen. We didn't say much, but I followed her lead on where to put the cookware. While we worked, Melanie put away the DVDs in the living room, and John and James set up the bedroom. Sam and Tom had gone out to buy groceries, having already set up their rooms and arranged the furniture how they wanted it around the house.

I watched Melanie when I could, hoping to find a moment to speak to her again. She worked slowly, looking at each DVD before she set it on a shelf. I felt fairly certain she didn't want James to move out. She'd made a few snarky comments while we packed the truck about him using the townhouse as a brothel and for drug dealing. James ended up angry, and she'd earned a week's grounding.

It grew dark, and James and John came down the stairs, joking and laughing loudly together. As they entered the living room, Melanie jumped up to meet them, but James rushed by and wrapped his arms around me, swinging me around.

"Check this place out!" he said. "Look at how hard you've worked! Cadence, we're gonna have so much fun here."

"Ah, I'm not the only one who worked hard, James."

He set me down. "I know that." He walked over and wrapped his arms around Karen. "Thanks, Mum."

When he turned back around, I motioned toward Melanie with my eyes. He stared at me, gaping, before a light turned on in his eyes. "Thanks, Mel."

I glared at him and mouthed, "*Go hug her, too.*"

He raised his eyebrows. "Ah . . . no. She's been a right little brat all day."

"James!"

"Well, she has." He walked past me to Melanie. "Thanks for your help, but you could have been nicer about it."

She flushed bright red as he walked over to the TV. I went to snap at him again, but Karen intervened. "Say goodbye to your sister, James. We're going to leave now."

He turned back to Melanie. "Bye, Mel. Good luck at school next week."

She slumped. "Thanks."

John embraced him. "We're going to miss you around the house, son. Don't be a stranger."

"I'm sure I'll be back, so Mum'll wash my dirty laundry for me," he said teasingly.

Karen slapped his behind. "You have your own laundry, so don't you dare."

After John pulled away, she wrapped her arms around James.

As his parents headed out to the car, Melanie stepped in front of him. I pulled back into the kitchen to give them some privacy, but could still hear everything they said.

"Bye, James," she said flatly.

"Bye, Mel."

"James?"

"Yeah?"

"You know you're my best friend, right? So you better call and text me every day."

"Mel . . ." He sighed. "You need to detach a bit. Make friends at school with kids your age. You were doing great for a while before you freaked out and turned all bitter again. You should try being friends with Cadence. I know she wants to, and I know you were really happy hanging out with her and her friends. So whatever it is that's making you so nasty, you need to let it go."

I glanced around the corner. Her fists clenched and her face turned dark red. "I'm so tired of hearing about Cadence," she said in a low voice. "It'll be great now that you're gone, 'cause I won't have to see her in my house!"

"Seriously, Mel?"

"Bye, *James.*" She stormed out, banging the door behind her.

He shook his head. I hurried over and grabbed his hands. Immediately, his demeanor changed; his eyes lifted as a wide smile spread across his face. He pulled me against him. "Let's christen the couch."

He grabbed me around the waist and shoved me onto it, climbing on top.

"James!" I laughed as he bit into my neck.

"I just wanna ravage you!"

I slapped his shoulder. "Well, you can't!"

"I know." He shifted up, giving me a firm and intense kiss. I gave in to him as a warm rush flooded over me. His tongue slid in my mouth, stroking my lips and tongue. His left hand caressed my face. He broke away for a second to whisper, "You know I love you, right?"

"I do."

"And do you love me?"

I smiled. "Of course."

He pressed his lips back against mine again as I clung to him, enjoying the feeling of his body all around me.

We must have made out for about half an hour before Tom and Sam walked in.

"Geez, James!" Tom snarled.

"Get a room!" Sam groaned.

James sat up. "Hey, you're just jealous."

"Seriously, James, we talked about this," Tom said. "This is a *public* area. *That* is for *private* areas."

James laughed and climbed off the couch as I sat up, discreetly trying to flatten my hair. "We were only making out."

I blushed when they both looked at me. Sam walked over, carrying in groceries. "Help us out, Cadence."

I jumped up and scurried to the car. When I came back in, I found them wrestling on the floor. *Boys.*

I set the bags down on the counter, and James came up behind me, pinning me in place. His hands rested on my waist. "Are you gonna miss me at school?"

I was going to say no to spite him, but when his lips found my ear, I melted. "Yes, very much."

He chuckled softly. "As you should."

I giggled. "Are you gonna miss seeing me every day?"

"Not as much."

I elbowed him in the ribs. He burst out laughing and I turned to face him with a fierce look. When he stopped, he grabbed my hand and we sat to watch a movie with the guys before he drove me home.

Chapter Twenty-Eight

I kept scanning the corridors for James out of habit. It frustrated me, and I scolded myself mentally every time I caught myself doing it. Geri knew that I desperately missed him being around, so she rarely left my side. When we were in our two separate classes, she'd drop me off and meet me at the door afterward.

The first few weeks passed, but I still couldn't get used to it. One day, I sought out Dusty. He lay on the ground while his stupid friends tried to stand on his belly. I watched with my hands on my hips for several minutes before he looked across and saw me.

He jumped up and ran over with a huge grin. "Hey, Cadence. What's up?"

"I need a hug."

"Ah . . ." He raised his eyebrows. "Seriously? We're out in public."

"I miss James."

"Ooooh." His grin turned into a smirk. "Oh, James. How I miss—"

I slammed my hand over his mouth. "I don't know why I even bothered."

When I moved to walk away, he wrapped his arms around my waist. "There," he said gently.

I squeezed him back. "Thank you."

He released me, wearing a smirk across his face again. "So . . . how's Geri?"

I rolled my eyes. "You're hilarious. I'll tell her you say hi."

Back with my group, Geri rushed to me and wrapped her arm through mine. "Where'd you go?"

"Dusty."

"Oh." She glanced around. "So . . . how was your date last night?"

I grinned and eagerly told her about James. He'd worked all day every day to save up for when he started university, but he'd finished at seven and picked me up. We pretty much spent the whole two hours in the back of his car making out, but I told Geri we'd gone to a movie.

We sat at the table, chatting away like normal, when Brian sat beside me. I tried to ignore him, furious again about how he'd treated Melanie, but he shifted closer to me.

"Hey, I've noticed you've been kinda down lately."

Geri leaned forward. "Hey, dirt bag! I'm *talking*."

"I'm just checking on Cadence," he said calmly. "With James gone, she's been pretty low."

"I'm fine, thanks, Brian," I responded.

He touched my back. "If you need anything, I'm here, okay?"

Geri scowled. "Get lost."

Brian stood and moved away.

I huffed. "Will he ever give up? It's not like I encourage him."

Geri threw him a filthy look before she continued with her rambling.

In maths, Justin sat beside me. I wasn't fazed by it—he often sat beside me—until he leaned back to stretch and his arm rested on the back of my chair. I leaned forward onto my desk, my stomach flipping. Was I just being paranoid, or was he hitting on me?

A quiet murmur spread across the class while everyone discussed their work. Justin's hand pressed against my back and he leaned in.

"Hey, how you doin'?"

"I hate doing these equations," I answered, trying to deflect his focus.

His hand stroked my back. "It must be hard with James moving on, but I'll be here for ya if you need me."

I pushed his hand off. "We're still together."

"Yes, but you're a high school girl, and he's about to start university."

I glared at him. "What are you saying?"

"Well, chances are you'll be single soon . . ."

I slapped his chest. "Shut up!"

"Ouch! Cadence, you've gotta be realistic. There's gonna be a lot of girls there that will distract him. Not that you're not smoking hot, but they're promiscuous—"

I jumped to my feet, marched out of the classroom, and paced the hallways. Unfortunately, he'd raised a good point and brought up fears I didn't want to consider. What if James *did* find someone prettier and more interesting than me?

I gnawed on my lip as tears streamed down my cheeks. I didn't want to lose him, but then again, maybe it would be easier that way and going to Austin wouldn't be complicated. But James . . . I still had almost two years before Austin came into my life.

The bell rang, making me jump. I ran back to my classroom to find the last of my classmates leaving and Justin standing by my bag. I tried to avoid him as I grabbed it, but he caught my arm.

"Cadence, I'm sorry if I upset you. I just care about you. We've been friends for a while, and I don't wanna see you get hurt."

"Justin, I'm okay. I can handle whatever happens."

He glanced around, causing me to do the same. "You deserve better than to be cheated on—"

"That's terrible English."

"—so you should get him first. I could make sure you—"

"Justin!" I tried to pull free.

"Don't reject me again, Cadence."

"I'm still with James!"

"He's going to cheat on you, and then dump you like a piece of trash!"

"Is that so?" James leaned against the door frame with his arms folded. "Cadence is definitely *not* a piece of trash, so, Justin, why don't you let my girlfriend go?"

James walked casually over to us and stared down Justin. They may have been the same height, but James exhibited a definite superiority. Justin released my arm. James nodded and wrapped his arm around my shoulders.

Without looking away from Justin, he said, "You ready to go, Cadence?"

"Yeah."

"Good. Because I have a romantic night of *not* cheating on you and *not* dumping you like a piece of trash planned."

Justin scowled as James turned me around and guided me out the door. I held in a laugh.

James didn't say a word until we stood by our cars—he'd parked next to my silver hatchback. As I reached to unlock my car, he caught me by the waist and turned me to face him. "How long has this been going on?"

"Ah . . ." I wasn't sure what he was talking about, so I answered, "Me driving? A few months now."

He pushed me back against my car. "No, Justin trying to convince you to date him."

"Oh, that."

He scowled. "Don't be so casual about it. I know he tried to date you way back before we were together, and he's had his eye on you ever since."

"Don't be jealous." I kissed his bottom lip. "There's no one here who could possibly tempt me away from you."

He stroked my hair behind my ear. "Good, because there's no girl anywhere who could distract me from you, so don't go listening to any of his lies."

I clasped his face and kissed him. "So, where are we going?"

He grinned at my smooth change of topic. "We'll drop off your car first, so I can charm the socks of your dad, as usual"—he smiled as I giggled—"then I was thinking maybe the drive-in?"

"Oh! I've never done that before."

"Then let's do it."

We drove to my house. Dusty greeted us on his way home from the bus stop. He didn't like riding home with me, preferring the bus so he could talk to the cute girls in the bus bays. Most of the time he ended up talking to Geri, and she'd complain about him harassing her the next morning. He waved as he made his way over, and he and James did their man embrace, pounding much too hard on each other's backs.

We entered the house and Mum smiled at James as he brushed a kiss on her cheek. "James Gordon, you don't need to keep charming me."

"Aw, but I can't help myself. You're the reason Cadence is so beautiful."

She rolled her eyes and laughed.

He followed me to my bedroom and stood at the door, watching me as I picked out my clothes. I pulled out a pair of jeans and he snorted.

I paused and looked at him. "What?"

"I don't like those."

"Really?"

"Mmm. You should wear that paisley skirt with your red tank top."

"That's a bit dressy for a drive-in."

"Fine. How about that denim mini with your black tank?"

I rested my hand on my hip and glared at him. "I'm sensing a theme here."

"What's that?" He grinned.

"Minimal clothing. Not gonna happen."

He laughed. "Fine. Your dark blue skirt—that one goes below your knees—and that white, low-cut shirt."

"Fine, but I'm wearing a jacket with it so you don't get any big ideas." I pulled them out and turned to see him still watching me. I shoved him backward and shut the door.

He tailed me, watching me put on my makeup and pick out my jewelry. When Dad came home and saw him standing by the bathroom door while I straightened my hair, he growled and grabbed him. "Do you really have to watch everything she does?"

James laughed. "Yeah! She's so beautiful."

Dad dragged him into the living room, where Dusty joined them to chat while I finished. I was relieved that Dad was getting along with James again. It took months, but when we both swore we weren't having sex anymore, he'd finally calmed down.

I entered the room and Dad shot to his feet. "Cadence, you look lovely, sweetheart."

"Thanks, Dad." I kissed his cheek.

He wrapped his arm around me and turned to James, whose gaze locked on me. "You better take care of her, boy. If she's in a wreck because of you, I'll—"

"I'll be careful, sir." James reached for my hand. "You know there's no one more important to me than her."

Dad scoffed, but a smile curled the corners of his mouth. "Get out, and since it's a school night, have her home by ten thirty."

"Midnight."

Dad scowled. "It's not a negotiation."

"The movie doesn't finish until ten twenty."

Dad growled. "Fine. Ten forty-five."

James shook his hand. "Deal."

Once in the car and driving, I caught James smirking. I didn't want to give him the satisfaction of asking about it, so I asked casually, "What are we seeing?"

"*50 First Dates*," he said with a shrug.

"Ah, Adam Sandler. Will we ever go see a chick flick?"

But as I sat in the car sobbing, I ate my words. James chuckled at me, apparently mighty proud of himself. I couldn't believe I'd never seen it in the first timeline. I'd been so put off by early Adam Sandler films, I never gave it a chance.

When the movie finished, I looked at my watch. Eight thirty. That explained his smirk earlier.

He drove me back to the townhouse. Tom and Sam sat with fast food strewn across the living room while they played video games. They grunted as we entered, but never looked up.

"I'm gonna take off my shirt," I said to them.

They grunted again and kept playing. James smirked.

"Wow, the graphics are so poor quality," I let slip.

They both swung around in horror.

"Are you insane?" Tom said. "This is the best graphics on any video game out!"

"Oh, so now you hear what I say. An offer to flash you my boobs didn't do the trick, but an insult on your graphics—"

Sam sat bolt upright. "You offered to flash your boobs?"

James wrapped his arm around my waist. "Sorry, you missed it."

"Gah!" Sam pouted and returned his attention to the game.

I sighed at the sight of the mess. It gave me images of cockroaches and mice infesting the house. Before I even realized it, I was picking everything up and dumping it in the trash.

"Cadence!" Tom growled. "You're in the way!"

"Well, you're disgusting."

"We're gonna pick it up."

James grabbed me by the waist and pulled me up the stairs. He closed the door to his room and my gaze swept across a similar mess, but of dirty laundry. I snorted with disgust and started scooping everything into the hamper. "You know, it's not hard to dump your dirty clothes in this."

He laughed. "Cadence, you're not my maid."

"It looks like you need one."

"Cadence!" He laughed again. "Relax."

He shoved me onto his miraculously made bed, and we lay side by side. He grabbed my hand. "Uni finally starts next week."

"I know."

"I'm kinda nervous."

I turned my head to look at him. He had his hand on his forehead as he stared solemnly up at the ceiling. I shifted closer to him to help ease his mind, then nuzzled up to his neck and kissed his jaw.

His hand shifted from his head onto my face as he let out a long breath. "You know just how to make me feel better."

"James?"

"Mmm?"

I shifted over him and kissed him. He stroked my neck and his fingers pushed up into my hair. How I loved kissing him!

He pushed into me as his tongue entered my mouth. It sent shots of excitement through me and I felt myself craving him. I climbed on top of him, straddling him. His lips parted from mine as a soft moan burst from them.

I rubbed against him, feeling his arousal. It excited me. I found myself remembering months earlier, when we'd last been together intimately, desiring the sensations he'd provoked in me. I wanted him to love me.

"James?" I met his incredible gray-blue eyes.

"Yes?" he said breathlessly.

I climbed off him. I rubbed my hand over his crotch. He groaned.

"Cadence, don't tease me unless you plan on following through."

I unbuttoned his pants. "Lock the door."

His eyes widened, then he shot up and rushed to the door. I leaned over and pulled the blankets back as the door lock clicked. I turned to face him and saw a hungry look in his eyes. I bit my lip and backed toward the bed as he eagerly approached.

"Cadence? Are you sure you're ready for this?"

I nodded.

We made love tenderly, passionately. My skin tingled at his touch. My body came alive, aching, yearning. His touch, his kisses, drove me over the edge. Every noise of pleasure I made, he rewarded with more tenderness. I hadn't realized how much I missed him.

When we finished, he looked down at me, searching my face, checking to make sure I wasn't about to bolt or freak out on him.

To reassure him, I touched his cheek. "That was wonderful."

A relieved smile spread across his face and he kissed my jaw. "I know. Cadence, you have no idea how much this means to me. I love you so much."

He shifted onto the bed beside me, but held me tight against him. He turned me onto my side and pulled the blankets over us. Our faces pressed together as we gazed into each other's eyes, exchanging silent expressions of love.

His fingers slowly brushed over my hips and waist, then descended down my back, making long circles. I shut my eyes, completely lost in him and the moment. I softly kissed his lips, causing him to sigh.

Before I knew it, I dozed off.

I awoke to James shaking me. "Hurry up and get ready. It's ten thirty! Your dad is gonna have my hide!"

I jumped out of bed and rushed into the bathroom to freshen up and get dressed. We bounded down the stairs and saw the guys still playing. I thought they didn't notice us at first, until Sam said, "You guys sounded like you had fun."

I whimpered. Had I really made that much noise?

James picked up a pair of socks and threw it at his head. "Shut up!"

He rushed me out of the house and into the car.

We sped home and pulled up at ten forty-seven. Dad stood in the driveway with his arms folded and a deep scowl. James scurried out of the car, opened my door for me, and hurried over to Dad. "Safe and sound, as promised."

I hurried up beside James and grabbed his hand.

Dad looked James over slowly. "You're two minutes late."

"I know, I'm sorry."

Dad rested his hand on my shoulder—the one closest to James—and pulled me away. "Good night, boy."

"Wait!" James grabbed my hand. "I just want to kiss her goodnight."

Dad rolled his eyes. "You have ten seconds."

James planted a kiss on my lips as he cupped my face, but then Dad pushed him back. "Time's up. Cadence has school in the morning."

I smiled at James and mouthed my goodbye as Dad led me inside. As I shut the door behind us, he stood in the driveway, watching me.

Chapter Twenty-Nine

Geri huffed as she flicked through the pages of the enormous book. I stared over her shoulder at the diagrams of cells. The teacher drew the structure on the board as he lectured us in great detail. I knew all of it, so my mind wandered.

James had started university a few weeks earlier, and he loved every second of it. It was right up his alley, with all the hands-on experiments and online notes. Unfortunately, between a full-time class schedule and working, I hadn't been able to see him much, and only on the weekends. I missed him terribly, and his texts between classes only seemed to make it worse.

"Here are the assignments," the teacher said loudly.

I snapped myself out of my daze as he handed them out.

"Your assigned partner is written on the second page."

Oh no! Twelfth grade bio assignment? In the last timeline, I'd been paired with Melanie. Could I be assigned to her again?

He set my assignment sheet in front of me and gave Geri hers. Geri flipped her page over and grinned. "Not so bad. I got Cody." She looked across the room and waved at him.

He smiled and waved back. That's right! They started dating during this assignment. I looked him over. He was slender and an average height, with dark hair and hazel eyes. He hung out in a different group than us, so we didn't interact with him much, but he was a nice guy. She could definitely do worse.

"Who have you got?" She whipped my assignment sheet open and moaned. "I'm sorry, Cay."

I looked down and read, *Melanie Gordon*. I sighed. At least I'd expected it. I looked across the room at her and she turned away.

"I guess we should make some plans," I said.

"You should ask the teacher to change," Geri responded under her breath.

"No. I need to show Melanie it's not just about James."

"But it is." Geri shrugged.

I scowled, but stood and walked across the room. I sat beside Melanie, who clenched her pen.

"So . . ." I said, watching her closely. "I was thinking we could—"

"Of course we're going to use *your* idea," she responded. "Because it will be *so* brilliant, and inspired, and perfect."

I huffed. "I was just going to make a suggestion. What's your idea?"

"It's biology, isn't it?" She glared at me. "Why don't you just set up a camera in James's room and film yourselves going at it?"

"For heaven's sake," I said with a grunt.

"You're disgusting."

I rubbed my eyes. "Okay, let's try to be civil to get this done. I wanna get a good grade and I'm sure you want to as well. So, let's just try to focus on getting our work done."

"Fine."

"Good. So, give me a *real* suggestion."

She made a strange throaty noise before she grunted and explained her idea.

After class, Geri met me and we headed to our group. "So, was she awful?"

I shook my head. "I think it will be okay. How about Cody?"

She shrugged. "He's nice, and actually seems to know what he's doing, which is a bonus."

Since I hadn't been friends with her when she dated him before, I was curious to see how the whole thing played out.

"Do you think he's cute?" I asked.

She scoffed. "Not really, no."

So it wasn't an instant thing.

"Why would you even ask me that?"

I shrugged. "I'm just curious. You haven't mentioned any hotties lately."

"I'm not feeling it. Guys are kinda depressing me. I figure I'll wait until I'm surrounded by a sea of them at uni."

I giggled. She elbowed me and smiled.

I sat in the public library, wondering where Melanie had gotten to. In the other timeline, she'd been held up because James was arrested, and I grew concerned something had happened to him.

I pulled out my phone and saw a text from him. My stomach flipped and I bit my lip as I opened it.

HEY BEAUTIFUL. JUST CHECKING IN AND LETTING U KNOW I LOVE U. CYA SATURDAY. J.

I let out a breath of relief, but still wondered what had happened to Melanie. I sat for another hour before I stood to borrow my books and head home. Just as I headed toward the door, she hurried into the entry and glanced around.

I paused, watching her as she darted to the bathrooms. I slipped my books in my bag and hurried after her.

Inside, she'd locked herself in a stall, sobbing. I froze, not sure what to do. I had to do something. I took a deep breath and gently said, "Melanie?"

She took a sharp breath and cut her sobs short. "What do you want?"

"Mel, come out here and talk to me."

She swore at me and kicked the door.

"Melanie, don't make me climb in there with you," I said in a voice that sounded like when I'd snapped at Melody for eating something she shouldn't.

"You sound like my mother."

I sighed and leaned against the door. "What happened?"

"Get lost, Cadence."

"Okay." I slipped some notes I'd copied out of my bag. "I made these for you. I hope they help." I slid them through the crack in the door.

She sniffed, and pulled them from my hand. "Thank you."

"Do you need a ride somewhere?"

A long pause followed. I thought she had ignored me, so I pushed off the door to leave. It opened behind me. She had red eyes and blotchy skin, with mascara running down her cheeks and her hair draped over her face. "I need to go home."

"Okay. Why don't you clean up a bit first?" Grabbing some paper towels, I ran them under water. I gently wiped the tear stains from her cheeks as she sniffed. I pulled out a tissue so she could blow her nose.

When she finished, we walked out to my car. Once I'd pulled out of the parking lot, she said softly, "Why are you nice to me?"

"Because I want to be. I know you think it's just about James, but I liked you before I started dating him."

She scoffed. "No, you didn't."

"I did. I was just stupid and didn't want to look *uncool*."

"And Cadence must always be cool." I glanced across and saw it wasn't a contemptuous statement. She stared out the window with a long face. "How come everyone likes you and not me?"

"I . . ." I had no idea how to answer that without offending her, so I carefully considered my words. "You do shut people out a lot. People liked you when you opened up."

She dropped her face into her hands. "James said that too. I miss him so much."

"Don't you talk to him?" I asked, surprised.

She shook her head. "I've been . . . he would . . ."

"Why don't we go see him now, while he's at work?"

"No!" Her head shot up and she looked at me with wide, alarmed eyes.

"Melanie! Why?"

"He . . . I . . ." She huffed and her face fell back into her hands. "I'm pregnant."

For the first time in my life, I swore. I pulled over and turned to her. "What?"

"Oh, yes, something else to make you look more wonderful than me." She looked up and met my gaze as fresh tears streamed down her face.

"But . . . what . . . who . . . ?"

Her lip quivered as her gaze fell. "Robbie Cluff."

I swore again.

"Geez, Cadence." A small smile curled her lips. "Twice in a few minutes. How unlike little perfect you."

"But . . . when?"

She shrugged as she stared at her hands. "We dated for a few months. It turned out he was using me . . . like everyone else. He wanted to get back at James by banging his sister. I was such an idiot to believe that he cared about me."

"You *dated*? As in, not anymore?" I struggled to comprehend everything she was telling me.

She shook her head, touching her abdomen. "He dumped me when I told him."

I leaned against my seat, grabbing my forehead. "What are you going to do?"

She looked down at herself. "I'm going to keep it. It's not due until after exams, and since I had no intention of going to uni, being a mum seems fitting."

I bit my lip as she stared down at herself. "Does anyone else know?"

She shook her head.

"You need to tell your parents."

Her gaze shot to me. "No, I don't. I'll . . . I'll run away, find a place of my own."

"Melanie, you're only seventeen."

Her tears burst out again. "I can't tell them! They'll be devastated! They gave James a huge lecture about knocking you up and they like *you*. Could you imagine what they'd do if they found out I . . . and with Robbie?"

I sighed. "Melanie, they love you. They'll want to take care of you."

She shook her head and bit her lip.

My phone rang.

"Just hold that thought." I reached over and answered it.

"Hi, beautiful."

Melanie let out a loud gasp at the sound of James's voice. She swore, then covered her mouth.

"Hey, are you with Mel?" he asked.

"Ah, yeah," I answered.

"No!" She cowered back. "Don't tell him!"

"Tell her I can hear her," he said. "Hand her the phone."

I offered her the phone and she shook her head.

"Cadence, put me on speaker," I heard him say. I pressed the button and his voice came through loud and clear. "Mel, I'm sorry about how I spoke to you last time we talked, and I wish you'd take my calls. Look, I've just finished work, so why don't you and Cadence come over to my place?"

She shook her head.

I nodded and mouthed, "*You should at least tell* him. "

She shook her head more desperately.

I huffed. "We're on our way over."

"No, Cadence!"

"Melanie!" James sounded frustrated. "I'm sorry, okay? Geez, I didn't realize I'd upset you so badly."

"James, we'll talk to you when we get there," I said.

"All right. I love you . . . both of you."

"I love you too, James. We'll see ya soon."

Melanie pouted as she stared out the window the whole way there. I had a sick feeling in my stomach as we drove. What she'd revealed worried me. It was serious, *so* serious; a teenage girl's worst nightmare, and the parents of teenage girls, too.

But what was worse, it belonged to Robbie. How had he managed to convince her to date him in the first place? I understood how easily he could use her like that, but I hated that he did.

We pulled up in front of the townhouse and parked in the driveway. James came out to meet us as Melanie sank down in her seat.

James opened her door. "Mel . . ." He stared at her. "I'm sorry, Mel, really."

She burst into tears all over again.

I jumped out and came around, pushing James out of the way to help her out. We stumbled into the house while James followed with his hand in his hair, completely confused.

I sat her on the couch and glared at Tom until he scurried upstairs. When I turned back around, James sat with his arm around Melanie as she cried.

"Mel, come on, I'm so sorry. I didn't know—"

"She's not crying because of you," I said softly as I knelt in front of her. "Melanie?"

She shook her head.

"You need to tell him."

Her head slowly turned and she told him everything from the beginning: how Robbie had come across her in the street and took her out, how he convinced her to be his girlfriend, and last of all, that he got her pregnant and dumped her.

I couldn't read James's face as he sat back and stared into her eyes through the whole story. His expression fell stone cold with no emotion whatsoever. When she finished, he sat motionless for several minutes, just staring at her.

Finally, he stood. "I'm going to kill him."

"James?" I said hesitantly.

He looked down at me. In his eyes, I saw a deep agony unlike anything I'd ever seen before. "First, he tried to hurt you, then he does this to Mel . . . Cadence, he's out of control."

He pulled out his phone from his pocket.

"What are you doing?" Melanie asked.

"I'm gonna get him arrested. You're underage. I'm gonna get him done for having sex with a minor."

Melanie gasped. "James! No, he'll—"

"He'll what?" James swung to her. "He ran out on you! He needs to start facing the consequences of his actions."

"James, no! If you do that, then Mum and Dad will know."

James's gaze fell to her belly. "They're gonna find out soon enough."

I grabbed Melanie's shoulders. "He's right. What Robbie did to you was wrong. Your parents will know soon enough, but we're all going to be here for you."

James hit call. Melanie sank back and hid her face. Tears of shame ran down her cheeks as James reported the incident. When he hung up, he turned to her. "They'll be over in an hour to get your testimony."

Her chin quivered, but she nodded.

After the police had gone, John and Karen came to collect Melanie. They were heartbroken, but told her they loved her and would look after her no matter what.

As they headed out, Melanie turned and threw her arms around me. "Cadence?"

"Yes?"

"I'm sorry about everything. You're a good friend."

I held her tightly.

Chapter Thirty

Cody smiled at Geri while she talked. I found it fascinating to watch things happening between them. She wasn't aware of his interest, and rambled on like she normally did as he watched her.

I reached over and wrapped one of her curls around my finger, making her pause for a moment before she kept talking. Cody glanced at me briefly with a look that said, *I wish I could do that*, before his eyes darted back to her face.

I looked to Melanie, who sat in front of me, staring down at her workbook. She'd been somber, but I felt grateful that she'd attached herself to me. Geri was shocked when, the Monday after Melanie's confession, she'd come right up to me and grabbed my hand. But when we explained—*we* being me, with Melanie silently standing beside me—Geri instantly took her in and became like a mother hen.

As I looked at Melanie, I saw her sweating, which seemed odd considering the weather was getting cold.

My phone buzzed. I glanced up to check that the teacher wasn't looking, then slipped it out and read the text from James under my desk.

Cops got Rob and r lining him up 4 several charges on top of Mel's. Looks like he's going away 4 a while.

I hurriedly typed out a reply. How do u know?

He responded quickly. I was just at the station as a witness. I've got the rest of the day off so I'll pick u up.

Stunned, I asked, Y were u at the station?

He simply said, I'll tell u later. Love ya.

I put my phone away. Geri was still talking. Apparently, she hadn't noticed my distraction. I looked over to see Melanie gritting her teeth. I stared at her, sensing something wrong.

She looked across at me and forced a smile. "I'm fine."

"Are you sure?"

Geri stopped talking.

"I'm sure," Melanie said breathlessly.

"You look like you're in pain," Geri said.

"It's nothing. I'm just going to go to the bathroom."

She hurried out of the classroom, holding her stomach tightly. Geri and I exchanged worried glances. To anyone else, they'd assume she had period cramps, but to us . . .

We launched to our feet, startling Cody, and hurried after her.

As we rushed toward the bathroom, we heard a blood-curdling scream. We charged in and heard Melanie sobbing. We rushed to the only closed cubicle and banged on the door.

"Melanie! Let us in!" I said.

"No! It wasn't supposed to happen like this!"

"Melanie, please!" Geri slammed her fist against the door.

Melanie slid a bloodied pair of underwear under the door. Geri and I gasped. Geri darted out to get a phone.

I knelt beside the cubicle. "Melanie, what's going on?"

"It's so tiny."

"Oh . . . my . . ." I pulled at the door. "Mel, open up!"

"No, Cadence, I just wanna die."

"No! No, you don't!"

She cried loudly.

"Melanie, please let me in!"

I heard banging and peeked through the gap to see her hitting her head back against the wall.

"Melanie!" I grew desperate. I scrambled into the next cubicle and used the toilet and paper holder to climb over the top. She jumped when I landed in front of her and grabbed her shoulders. "Melanie! It'll be okay."

Her gaze fell into her hand as she lifted a tiny fetus that barely filled her palm in front of me.

Flashes of Melody filled my mind: my pregnancy, her birth, her first tooth, her first step, her first word . . . then her lying limp in my arms.

I jumped back from Melanie, slamming my head against the door. Emotions, suppressed by my teenage state, surfaced—pain, grief, overwhelming love and loss. My whole body trembled and I screamed, "No! She can't die! No!"

Melanie's tears paused as she gazed at me. "Cadence, you can't tell what it is."

Panic set in as she raised it up again. Melody's pale face flooded into my mind, and I scrambled for the lock as I screamed. I stumbled out, scrambled across the tiles, and curled up under the sinks.

Melanie remained sitting on the toilet, her skirt around her ankles, staring at me. "Cadence . . ."

I covered my face and cried. "No! She can't die! I came back so she wouldn't. Not my baby! Not my Melody!"

Melanie stared at me, gaping.

Geri burst back into the bathroom. "Melanie! I got your mum on the . . ."

She saw the door wide open and me cowering under the sinks. She glanced between us, then decided Melanie, being covered in blood, was more urgent. She hurried over to hand her the phone and gasped at the fetus in Melanie's hand. "Mel . . . an . . . ah . . ." She held the phone against Melanie's ear.

As Karen spoke to Melanie, Melanie's gaze fell and she forgot about my strange behavior. But Geri's stare locked on me as I cowered, whimpering, under the sink. I pressed my eyes against my knees, trying to force the feelings back into submission. I couldn't believe they'd flared up right then, becoming so vibrantly alive and searing my heart.

I cried as I whispered, "Angel?"

The soft sounds of the phone conversation fell silent and a hand rested on my knee. "I'm here, sweet Cadence."

I looked up and was met by a pair of dark brown eyes that looked just like Melody's. I covered my face and sobbed loudly.

"Cadence, stand up."

"I can't."

"Melody hasn't even been born yet."

"But she has! And she died, too!"

"Not this time. You can still save her. Her spirit is waiting for you. She is yours when the time comes."

I looked up at him as his words slowly seemed to make the pain ebb. He gazed at me steadily, in a way that seemed to make the world feel . . . better. I wiped my face and took several deep breaths. "Okay."

He smiled. "Now, Cadence, this is a new trial for you. So far, you have succeeded in your choices, but this moment will make all the difference in your relationship with Melanie. Everything in life has its purpose. Melanie's pregnancy has fulfilled its purpose, so the infant has been returned to heaven. The child is happy, and it knows it was loved during its brief time in mortality, so you do not need to worry. But Melanie needs *you*."

He stood and walked out the door.

Time returned to motion and I forced myself out from under the sink. I crawled over to Melanie, and looked up at her. She stared at me, her eyes dull.

"Melanie?"

"Yes?"

"We can get through this. You'll see."

She looked at the fetus in her hand. "What should I do with it?"

"We'll bury it."

She nodded.

I climbed to my feet, and Geri and I helped her stand. Geri had the sense to bring a pad and a clean set of underwear. We helped her clean up, then we made our way to the sick bay, with a piece of toilet paper covering the fetus in her hand in case anyone walked by.

Karen soon arrived, her face already covered in tears. She threw her arms around Melanie and held her tightly as they cried together. Geri and I crept out the door.

We stood in the hallway, just staring at each other in shock. That was easily one of the most traumatic things we had ever seen.

"Cadence, that was awful."

I nodded, forcing the images of Melody out of my mind.

"And you totally freaked out."

I sighed. "I know."

There was a long pause. Then, "It's probably for the best."

My gaze shot to her. "What?"

She bit her lip. "Well, she's only seventeen. I mean, I was so proud she had the balls to keep it, but . . ." She sighed.

"I understand."

She smiled and took my hand. "Let's go get her things."

We stayed with Melanie until she felt well enough to leave with Karen. Once Melanie was in the car, Karen turned to me and kissed my forehead. "Cadence, thank you, again. We all love you so much."

I squeezed her hand. "I love you guys, too."

She climbed into the car, and Geri and I watched them drive away.

"This day sucks," Geri said.

"I'll agree with that."

She huffed. "How are we supposed to go back to class now? We have, like, an hour left."

I looked her over. She slumped, her arms folded and her eyes low. I wrapped my arm around her shoulders. "Geri, have I told you that you're the best friend ever?"

She smirked. "Geez, Cadence."

"No, I mean it." I smiled. "You were on the ball when I just fell apart. You're the Queen of Awesome Friends."

She giggled. "Thanks, Cadence."

We turned to head back to class, while I dreaded the prospect of taking James to see his family that afternoon.

I lay on my belly across James's bed as he sat cross-legged beside me, staring off into space. He'd been quiet since we left his parents' house. Melanie was relieved to see him, and they'd spent an hour alone together in her room. I'd stayed out with Karen and John, who were both somber. At one point, Karen grabbed my hand to whisper, "Thank you for bringing him by."

I smiled at her.

"No one gets through to Mel like James."

"I know."

When we left, Melanie hugged both James and me, and I noticed she looked brighter and happier than when she'd left school. James really had done the trick.

I reached across and grabbed James's wrist to get his attention. "Hey, what's on your mind?"

He sighed and lay beside me. He gazed into my eyes as he stroked my hair. "I feel like what happened with Mel is my fault. If I'd done something about Robbie sooner, maybe—"

"You can't think like that. Melanie can make her own choices, and you weren't to know he'd go after your sister. All this will pass, and we'll be okay."

He pulled me closer and kissed my head. "I saw him at the station. I went down to leave my statement when he was brought in. He tried to attack me. He said Mel deserved it, that she asked for it. I was so disgusted I told the cops everything I knew he'd done right in front of him. He pointed out that I'd done some of those things, too, and because I admitted it, I was given a couple of fines. But he's gonna be locked up for a while."

"Would it be bad of me to say thank goodness?"

He chuckled. "No. A few years ago, I thought Robbie had life dialed in. I thought he was really cool, but now . . ."

I nuzzled up to his chest. "Now, you're the coolest guy out."

He laughed. "Thanks, kid."

"You're welcome, old man."

He pinched my arm and I shoved him. He almost fell off the bed, but caught me and used me to pull himself back up. He climbed on top of me. "Cadence, I'll never hurt you like that."

"I know."

He smiled and kissed me.

Chapter Thirty-One

The application for the University of Western Australia sat on my desk. Beside it lay several others, including one for James's university, which he'd pulled out for me, one for UWS that Geri gave me, and one for UNSW that Harper insisted I fill out. I felt like they tugged me in several different directions.

I slowly filled out each of them, and considered flunking my exams so I wouldn't have to go to any. But I needed to get good enough marks to go to Western Australia, if that's what I decided on doing. I hoped only one of them would offer me a place so I wouldn't have to decide.

I set the applications aside and slipped out my scrapbook. I turned to some pictures of Melody and stared at them. She was such a beautiful child, with her daddy's eyes and the same golden hair I'd had as a little girl. Her personality poured out in each of her photos as she glared, grinned, and pouted at the camera.

I came to a photo of Austin, laughing as she kissed his cheek. In the next photo, he and I kissed while Melody tried to pull our faces apart. It made me chuckle as I remembered how protective she was of each of us. So protective, that in her mind, only *she* was allowed to kiss either of us, and we weren't allowed to kiss each other.

Sweet little Melody.

I closed the scrapbook and sighed. Over the past few weeks, Melanie struggled to recover. Geri and I went out of our way to do things for her. We brought her gifts, had her sit with us in the classes we shared, and went by her house after school to help her focus on her schoolwork.

It did the trick, too. She really picked up her game and even applied to a couple of universities. Her course choices varied drastically, so I knew she didn't have a clue what she wanted to study, but the fact that she considered it meant she'd come along in leaps and bounds.

"Cadence?"

I looked up to see Dusty standing at my door.

"Can I talk to you?"

I glanced at my scrapbook and saw it had turned into a textbook. I patted the bed beside me, and he shuffled over. He sat staring off for a while, then he spoke quietly. "Promise you won't tease me or tell anyone this?"

"Ah, sure."

He let out a long sigh. "You know how I give Geri a hard time?"

I giggled. "Yeah."

"Here's the thing . . . I kinda like her. Is that weird?"

My jaw fell.

He turned his head to look at me and flushed. "It is, huh? She's way older than me and looks at me like her little brother." He huffed. "I knew I didn't stand a chance."

He moved to stand, but I grabbed his arm. "Dusty, you're serious?"

"Yeah."

"Oh my . . . wow!" I couldn't help the smile that burst across my face. When Geri and I split up in the first timeline, Dusty had only been in the eighth grade, so the chance to develop a crush had never been in place, but this time . . . I was speechless.

"Don't look at me like that." He scowled. "I knew I shouldn't have said anything. Just don't tell her, okay?"

I squeezed his hand. "Dusty! I didn't see this coming at all. Sit and tell me what's going on. You know I love Geri, so this is like . . . *wow!*"

His eyes lit up as he turned to face me directly. "It just kinda happened. One day I was like, hey, she's actually really pretty, and from then on, I couldn't help noticing. Do you think maybe I should ask her out?"

I paused. Geri had just started to like Cody, and I knew from the timeline before that she would date him soon. I also knew approximately how long it would last, so I decided to give Dusty a vague time frame. "She's actually kinda seeing someone right now."

His face fell, so I hurried on. "But, you know how high school things go. I'd wait for a few months and see where she is then. She might be hesitant because, as you said, you're younger than her. She might not take you seriously at first because she'll think you're teasing her, but stick to it and I'm sure she'll come around."

He took a moment to contemplate my suggestion. "So, for now, I should date around, see if I can make her jealous—"

I slapped his shoulder and laughed. "Dusty!"

He laughed and wrapped his arms around me.

My heart skipped a beat when I saw James waiting at the end of the corridor. I squealed with delight and ran into his arms.

He stumbled back, laughing, and kissed my ear. "I've missed you, too."

"It's been almost two weeks! I can't believe how hard it's been to line up our schedules."

"I know. Stupid work." He kissed my cheek. His gaze darted over my shoulder and he grinned. "Hey, Mel."

She stepped up beside me. I let him go so she could hug him. I loved seeing the protective expression on his face as he squeezed her. He'd been very conscious of her feelings and what was going on in her life since the pregnancy. Luckily, she'd been more careful, and it helped that she had rejoined my group of friends and felt loved again.

She looked into his eyes. "We've got exams coming up so I need to study, otherwise I'd totally hang out with you guys. Have fun with Cadence." She reached across and squeezed my hand before heading out.

James turned to me, grinning. "My place?"

"Sounds good."

"Awesome."

At his house, only Tom was home and studying with his notes strewn across the floor. He glanced up when we entered and smiled.

"Hey guys." He smirked. "Cadence, super brain, come here for a second."

I stepped over and looked down at his notes. "What?"

"Can you write this essay for me? You seem to know a lot about physiology and such, and your referencing is spot on—even your high school teachers can't fault it."

"Ah . . . no."

"Fine, it was worth a try." He gathered up his notes and slid them into a binder. "I'll go upstairs so I can type something out then."

As he left the room, my stomach growled. James looked at me and raised his eyebrows. "I'll get us some snacks."

We went into his kitchen and I almost threw up. Dishes lined the counters while the dishwasher sat empty. Five bags of trash sat along the wall. "James!"

He spun from inside the pantry. "What?"

I waved my arms around. "Gross!"

"What?" He glanced around the kitchen. "Oh, it's just a little mess."

"There are maggots in this pot!"

He looked into the pot with leftover Bolognese in it. "Oh . . . yeah, that's kinda gross."

"Kinda?" I reached for two bags. "Take these outside right now!"

He moaned. "Cadence . . ."

"I'm not eating anything from here until this place is tidied up."

He growled and snatched the bags from me. "You're such a woman."

I kicked his butt.

"Ouch! Geez, Cadence!" He hurried out the front while I turned to the dishes.

It took us about an hour to clean it all up, and when we finished, James sighed. "Excellent! It's spotless. *Now* can we eat?"

He raided the pantry again and pulled out several packets of chips.

"Why don't you just make dinner?"

He rubbed his neck. "That's such a hassle."

I growled and shoved him out of the kitchen. "Go do something constructive, like maybe some laundry—which I'd bet is piling up."

"Aw, Cadence . . ."

"Go, James!"

Once he left to thump around his room in a huff, I started making dinner. They had very little fresh food, but I managed to throw something together with frozen and canned foods. Soon, I had the chicken parmigiana cooking and the garlic bread ready to go with a pot of mixed frozen vegetables steaming on the stove.

Tom returned downstairs. He sniffed the air, then called, "James?"

"What?" James bellowed down the stairs.

"Is your girlfriend cooking us dinner?"

"Why don't you ask her, genius?"

Tom appeared beside me. "Damn! I don't think I've had a real meal like this in months."

"I really have no idea how you guys stay alive," I responded.

"Pizza and burgers have veg on them." He smelled the food in the oven. "Geez, Cadence, when are you moving in? I can eat like this every night."

I giggled. "Keep dreaming."

"So . . ." He leaned against the counter. "Got any idea which uni you wanna go to? James said you were talking about Macquarie with him."

I sighed and stirred the veggies. "*He's* talking about Macquarie. I've been looking around at all my options."

"Don't wanna go to school with him again?" he said teasingly.

I rolled my eyes, but smiled. "You know that's not it. Geri wants me to go wherever she goes so we can move in together, and Harper wants me at her school so I can move in with her, too. I just wanna get *in* first, and into a uni with a good sports science program."

He let out a quick sigh. "Macquarie *is* a really good uni."

"I know." Which concerned me. If I was admitted, I'd struggle to make a legitimate excuse for *not* going there. "I don't think it really has what I want course-wise though."

James entered and stared at me. "Macquarie is awesome, and we can be together again."

"James, you know it's not about you. UTS, UNSW, and UWS would be much better fits." I didn't dare even mention the University of Western Australia.

"Okay, but you're still applying, right?" He stepped over and pulled the milk out of the fridge.

"Yeah, I sent in the application."

He grinned and kissed my cheek. "Good."

I stared after him in exasperation as he walked out, swilling his milk.

"Cadence," Tom said softly. "He just wants to be with you."

"I know." I turned back to the veggies. "It's just . . . what if I end up at Charles Sturt or one of the unis further away?"

Tom groaned. "Please don't put *me* through that. He's bad enough when he hasn't seen you in a few days."

I groaned and thankfully, the oven beeped. James would make things hard for me, but I didn't want to leave him either. I pined for him after a few days apart, too.

I slipped the garlic bread in the oven to toast while I divided up the chicken and veggies onto three plates. Tom hovered in anticipation, keeping a close eye on the garlic bread. James heard me dishing up and appeared behind me in a flash.

"Mmm. Real food."

"Don't get too accustomed to it. You boys need to make your own food." I lifted two plates and carried them to the table, pushing a pile of clean, unfolded laundry onto the floor to make room.

They both followed me and sat expectantly. Thankfully, they had enough manners for me to return and sit with them before they stuffed their faces.

"This makes me miss Mum a little," Tom said through a mouthful of food.

James grunted.

"Cadence." Tom turned to me with a huge grin. "Can we adopt you?"

James kicked him under the table. "Weirdo."

After dinner—which they completely devoured, leaving none for Sam—James took me up to his room, where we made love.

"This is payment for dinner," James said as he kissed my ear.

"I'm okay with that."

Afterward, he lay on his side beside me as his fingers stroked over my waist and hip. I nuzzled up to him, taking in his scent and warmth.

He stared into my face, examining my features closely. He took a deep breath and sighed. "Cadence, move in here with me."

I shook my head, smiling. "I'm still in high school—"

"I meant after you graduate. Tom and Sam won't mind, they like having you around, and I . . . well, I *love* having you around." He leaned forward and kissed my cheek.

My stomach did somersaults as I thought about my applications, and the one I knew I'd definitely get into—the one clear across the country where Austin would be. The time had come for me to tell him what might happen. "James, what if I don't get into one of the local universities?"

He laughed. "Of course you will. You're brilliant."

"But what if one of the universities further away has a better program, or is the only one that gives me an offer?"

He scoffed and pulled me closer. "You'll get into one of the Sydney unis. Don't even worry about it."

"But . . ." I bit my lip, feeling guilty for thinking about Austin as James nibbled on my neck. "But what if I want to go to one of those universities that are further away? Like, for example, there's one in Western Australia that—"

He pulled back. "Western Australia? Cadence, why are you even looking there?"

I pushed up onto my elbow to meet his gaze. "There's a sports science program over there that's perfect for what I want—"

"And there isn't one closer that fits your needs just as well?"

I dropped my gaze. "I . . . ah . . . I want to get out of Sydney for a while and explore new things."

"You what?" He leapt off the bed and stared down at me. "Cadence, we can go on a trip somewhere. We'll save up and fly to freaking Mongolia if you want. But move clear across the country away from me? Why would you even consider that?"

I stared up at him. His nostrils flared, his brow furrowed, and his eyes filled with fear. How could I leave him and go so far away? But Austin . . . I needed to know what could happen with Austin.

To diffuse the situation, I sat up and clasped onto his hips as I gazed into his eyes. "It's just a backup option. I wanted you to know it's a possibility if I can't get somewhere here. I don't want to hide it from you."

He turned away, ruffling his hair as he gazed out the window. "I don't want you to take it if it comes up."

"What if it turns out to be my only choice?"

He turned on me. "Don't take it! Wait a year or so and apply to somewhere around here as a mature age student. Don't you dare go that far away!"

I gasped and pulled back at his ferocity. "James—"

"No, Cadence, your choices affect me, too. I can't have you going that far away. I need you here with me. I love you so much that I think it would kill me."

I rubbed my eyes, feeling guilty for even bringing it up. "Let's not talk about this."

He climbed back onto the bed and leaned over me. "No, because there's nothing to talk about. You're staying here. You don't have to move in if you don't want, but you're staying here, in this state, in this city."

"James, you're acting really possessive."

His arm slipped around my waist. "I can't lose you."

I gazed into his eyes and saw his desperation. My heart pounded as my love for him swelled inside me. "I love you."

He smiled and pulled me into a tight embrace. "I love you, too."

Chapter Thirty-Two

Dusty rambled on about his Design and Tech project, his arm draped lazily over my shoulder as we walked from the student parking lot into the school. I looked up at him, amazed by how handsome he'd grown. We had matching sandy blond hair and dark blue eyes, but his face was more masculine, with a square jaw and a wide lazy grin. It felt like he'd grown up overnight.

We rounded a corner, and I pulled back.

"Cadence?" My odd behavior turned his attention to me.

"I, ah . . . I thought there was a bee or something," I lied.

"You're so weird." He moved to keep walking, but I kept my feet firmly planted. "Ah, what's up with you?"

"Let's go a different way."

His eyes narrowed and he dashed around the corner. I hurried after him to see Geri and Cody pull apart from their kiss. I looked up at Dusty. Only a flash of pain flicked through his eyes before he covered swiftly by saying, "Oh, gross! You kissed Geraldine Turner!"

Geri turned bright red and slapped him. "Get lost, Dusty!"

He laughed. "Seriously, Geri, you can do better than this, don't you think?"

She swung to me. "Cadence!"

"I got it." I grabbed Dusty's arm and dragged him away.

Out of their view, he pulled away from me and scowled. "I hate that guy."

"You've never met him."

"I still hate him."

I wrapped my arm through his and rested my head on his shoulder. "It won't last much longer. Just be patient."

He chuckled. "You know, James is right. Sometimes you get this mysterious, weird vibe thing going and talk like you can see the future."

I bit my lip. "Ah, well you *know* that's impossible."

"Maybe." He shrugged. "But there really are times when you know things that kinda blow me away."

"Like what?" I forced a laugh to hide how uncomfortable I felt.

"Like, ah . . ." He tapped his chin. "Like you always seem to know which football team is going to win the Grand Final, or at least, you always go for the team that wins."

"That's just good luck."

He tilted his head and looked down at me. "Well, you must have the best luck *ever*."

I glanced around, relieved to see that nothing froze, time hadn't warped. I was safe.

"I probably do."

The middle weekend of the winter break, I stayed with Harper for a few nights while Daniel was out of town. I arrived on Friday, and she spent the day going on and on about how amazing he was. It started to grate my nerves, and I hoped I wasn't like that about James.

We ordered pizza and watched a girlie TV show while we waited. The next day, we'd meet up with James and spend time together in the city, but right at that moment, I focused on Harper. Since her life seemed very similar to what it had been in the first timeline, I wanted to see if I could gain some insight on what I should do once I finished school.

The pizza arrived and, after the delivery boy shamelessly eyed us over, we paid him and slammed the door in his face.

We retreated to Harper's bedroom, and she shut the door behind her. She handed me a plate of pizza and sat beside me on the bed. "Cadence, I have to tell you something."

"Sure, what's up?" I said as I bit into a slice.

"Daniel is incredible."

I smirked. "That's not news, Harper. You tell me that all the time, and you've been going on about it all day."

She glared at me. "What I'm trying to say is . . ." She bit her lip as she blushed. "I slept with him."

My jaw fell. "Really? When?"

"On Friday . . . and Saturday . . . but you can't tell Dad. He'll totally freak out . . ."

"I think he'll be better about it than you think," I muttered, but she didn't notice.

"Just so you know, the first time isn't as mind-blowing as everyone makes it out to be."

"I know."

"It was kinda weird and gross to be honest. But he's talking about having me move in with him, and maybe eventually get married! Cadence, I'm twenty in a month and a half, and I think I've found the love of my life! And he's . . ." She paused. "Wait, did you say that you *know*?"

I shrugged.

"Cadence!" She grabbed my shoulders. "You've been holding out on me! When did you and James . . . ?"

"The first time was just after my birthday, but we stopped for a while."

"But when he moved out . . ." A wide grin swept across her face. "Cadence! Why didn't you tell me?"

"I thought Mum or Dad would have mentioned it— it caused such a huge explosion that Dad didn't talk to me for weeks."

"*That's* what that was about!" She shook me. "Oh, Cay, he's the one for you, I just know it! I can see when he looks at you that there's no one else in this world for him. You should totally get married. We can have a double wedding! Wouldn't that be romantic?"

"I don't think I'm ready for that." I laughed. "I'm not even eighteen yet!"

"You will be soon." She winked at me.

I scoffed. "When did you start gushing? You're kinda freaking me out."

She slapped my shoulder and scowled. "You're such a brat."

"That's better."

She slapped me again, then collapsed onto her pillow and sighed. "Daniel is the best thing that's ever happened to me. I can see myself with him forever. He'll get his bachelor's at the end of next year, so that would be the perfect time to get married, and not just for us. You'll be nineteen, James will be twenty . . ." She winked.

"Seriously, no. I don't think we're gonna be at that point."

She growled. "Whatever. You can't see it now because you're a stupid teenager."

"*You're* still a teenager."

"Technicalities! Cadence, he's been with you since he was sixteen! And he hunted you for months before that! He's yours, and to be completely honest, I've always been a bit jealous of that, especially because he's a great guy."

I stopped chewing. "Wait, did you just say James, as in *my* James, is a great guy?"

She rolled her eyes. "You're so thick sometimes. I've always liked James. Why do you think I'm always so mean to him?"

I laughed and lay beside her, staring up at the blank ceiling. I thought of the painting of our family on her ceiling back at home; Dad still hadn't painted it over. I nuzzled up to her. I loved how close I'd become to her with my second chance. We'd never had a close relationship before, so to have her confiding everything in me felt wonderful.

I curled up beside her as she continued on about Daniel again and slowly fell asleep.

James managed to stay patient with Harper as she told him everything she'd already told me about Daniel, excluding their intimate moments. I watched him as he nodded and responded appropriately, amazed that he'd put up with her endless gushing.

Finally, when we stopped to have dinner and she had a mouthful of food, he changed the topic. "So, I think we should go to a club tonight."

"I'm not eighteen," I said.

Harper grinned. "I still have your fake ID."

I rolled my eyes as they both grinned. "No way! You guys, I don't wanna go clubbing."

Harper moaned. "You're so *boring*."

"Nope. I'm not going." I folded my arms and pursed my lips.

"Sweet, I'll text Tom and Sam to see if they wanna join us." James whipped out his phone. "They seriously need help picking up."

"I said no!"

Harper giggled. "We picked up some cute new outfits today, so let's go get changed into them."

I grunted, knowing I wouldn't win. "Fine! One hour. I don't wanna risk getting caught. Dad will lose it."

Harper scoffed. "Cadence, you're almost eighteen. You need to stop worrying about what Dad will think. Once you're an adult, it won't matter! Not to mention, you're sleeping with *him*, aren't you?" She gestured at James.

He grinned. "She has a point."

I backhanded his shoulder as my face burned.

He laughed. "Anyway, you need to stay to help Tom and Sam pick up. I swear, you're the only girl they talk to."

I sighed, knowing there was no way out.

At the club, Harper and I were probably the most dressed girls in the room. We both wore long tanks—mine pink and hers black—while I wore black dress pants and she wore a denim mini. James kept his arms around our waists protectively to ward off anyone who might try to hit on us on the dance floor.

He glanced between us and grinned. "Sometimes I wonder if one of you was adopted! You look so different I'd never pick you as sisters."

Twenty minutes later, Tom and Sam arrived. They'd ditched their nerdy slogan T-shirts and had raided James's wardrobe for more acceptable attire. So, looking clean-cut in dress shirts and jeans, they approached us.

Harper eyed them over. "When you drop the nerd act you both clean up pretty well." She wrapped her arm through Sam's. "Okay, kiddo, you're my project. Let's see if any girls wanna talk to you."

She dragged him away.

James and I turned to Tom, who looked apprehensive. "I'm no good with girls."

I wrapped my arm through his. "James, go keep an eye on Harper while Tom and I get something to drink."

James nodded and pushed through the crowd away from us. I took Tom to the bar, and he ordered a beer while I asked for water. Once the bartender moved on, Tom shook his head with a grin. "Always the good girl, aren't you, Cadence?"

I snorted. "I didn't even wanna come here, so there's no way I'm going to drink."

He laughed. "No wonder James is such a good boy now." He took his cup and sipped from it. "Speaking of James, you wanna hear something pretty cool?"

"Ah, sure, I guess."

He leaned closer with a smirk. "The other day, I went to meet him after one of his classes. I stood just outside the lecture hall so he could see me, and as he came out, he was being tailed by a huge group of girls."

I grabbed his shoulder. "I, ah . . ."

"No, don't stop me, this is great. James had his head down, finishing up some notes from the lecture, and had no idea they were tailing him—I had to call his name to get his attention. When he came over, I asked him to introduce me to some of his friends because they were hot. He looked around and seemed surprised to find them with him. He had no idea what their names were, but they quickly introduced themselves and talked to James like they'd known him forever. But when he started talking about his girlfriend Cadence, their flirting came to an abrupt end. They walked away, but he didn't care and started telling me about his classes."

I stared at him as a knot formed in my stomach. "Girls are hitting on him?"

I glanced across the room and saw James's presence with Sam wasn't helping Sam at all, as the girls focused on him instead. "Oh, no . . . maybe I should . . ."

I moved to climb off the stool.

Tom grabbed my arm. "No need, Cadence! I think you missed my point. Those girls were *hot*. James blew them off for *you*."

I looked back in time to see James point at me with a proud grin. The girls showed a hint of dejection before turning their attention to Sam. I smiled at James, and he grinned, rushing over to me.

He wrapped his arms around my waist and kissed my head, while I shut my eyes and breathed him in. My heart fluttered at his devotion to me.

"Alrighty, Tommy," James said. "Now Sam's well on his way, it's your turn."

About an hour later, both Sam and Tom had a girl with them and were having a great time. Harper returned to James and me with a huge grin.

"Mission accomplished! Nerds with girls!" She laughed merrily, and then her gaze fell to James's hands on my waist. "Hey, you know what? I'm tired. Cay, why don't you go stay with James tonight?"

His grip on my waist tightened. He'd wanted me to stay the night since he moved in, but he'd never pushed it.

I shook my head. "No, Harper. If Dad found out, he'd—"

"How will Dad find out?" She folded her arms. "Just stay the night and pick up your car and stuff from my place tomorrow. He'll never know the difference."

"I don't think . . ."

She disappeared through the crowd. I hurried after her, but couldn't find her. James was right behind me as I burst out onto the street, scanning everywhere for her.

"Cadence, I could—"

I turned to him, my anxiety spilling over. "I don't know if I could spend the night."

He clasped my face and lifted it so I'd look at him. "Why not?"

I bit my lip as my heart melted from the love pouring out of his eyes.

"I just . . . I don't . . ."

"It's okay, Cadence. I'll take you back to Harper's."

I grabbed his shirt around his waist and pulled him closer. "James . . ." My heart raced. I wanted to wake up with him beside me. "James, let's go back to your place."

Chapter Thirty-Three

Something shifted beside me. I awoke enough to realize someone lay in the bed with me. I sat up, startled. It had been a long time since I'd shared a bed with someone, and even then, the memories of Austin beside me felt hazy and more like a dream.

James didn't notice my movement and continued sleeping. I rested my head back on the pillow and stared into his face. He looked so peaceful and content. I shifted closer to him so I could feel his skin against mine, and his eyes flickered open. His arm wrapped around me before he relaxed back into a light sleep.

I ran my fingers through his hair, amazed at how soft it felt.

"Cadence?" he said quietly, making me start. A grin swept across his face, but he didn't open his eyes. "This is the best way to wake up. You should move in with me."

I smiled. "James, you know I can't."

"Not yet, anyway." He slowly let out a breath. His arm tightened around me, pulling me closer.

I kissed his cheek, and his eyes finally opened to meet mine. "You're so beautiful."

I kissed him as he rolled on top of me.

After we showered, we headed downstairs to eat breakfast. On the way down, I paused at the sound of two female voices in the kitchen. James's hand rested on my shoulder as he chuckled.

We entered the living room. Tom and Sam sat in just their jeans by the table. In the kitchen, two girls chatted quietly as they made pancakes. They were both very pretty, with long, straight dark-brown hair, but that was the only similarity they had—one was a petite Asian girl, and the other, a much taller Greek.

They heard us enter and turned, both smiling at me.

"You must be Cadence," the Greek girl said. "I'm Nicki, and this is Amanda."

"Hi." I smiled shyly.

James's hand pressed against my back, and I couldn't help noticing them eye him over with envy. *Yes, my boyfriend is smoking hot.* I tried to brush aside my jealous, possessive feelings. "So, you're here with Tom and Sam?"

"Yeah." Nicki smiled and touched my wrist. "Tom and I hooked up last night, so I guess I'm his girlfriend now."

I looked over at Tom and winked. "Nice. She's pretty."

Tom shrugged with a grin.

"Unlike you," Amanda muttered.

Nicki shot her a fierce look before she smiled again. "So, you wanna help us finish up here? You know, have some girl time?"

"Sure." I smiled back.

Amanda huffed. "I thought you meant that other girl was the girlfriend. She was way cuter."

James caught my wrist and pulled me back against him. "Hey, Sam, tell your girl to shut up."

Sam stared over, confused, having not heard the exchange.

Amanda rested her hand on her hip. "I would have tried harder if I'd known it was this one. She's not even pretty."

"Amanda, stop it," Nicki said under her breath.

I shrugged. "It's okay. I know my sister is prettier than I am."

Nicki blinked, genuinely surprised. "She's your *sister*?"

James wrapped his arm around my waist. "Yeah, you'd never pick it, huh? We all went to school together, and I didn't even know until most of the way through year ten. Their younger brother, though, could be confused as Cadence's twin, they look so similar."

"How long have you guys been together?" Nicki asked, trying to be friendly. I liked her—she would be good for Tom.

"Almost three years," James answered and kissed my ear.

"She must have grown out of her good looks," Amanda responded.

That time, Sam did hear her. "Hey! That's totally uncalled for!"

She rolled her eyes. "Whatever."

"Amanda, stop it," Nicki said.

Amanda glared up at her. "I wanted that one." She pointed at James. "But I settled because I thought it was that other girl."

"Settled?" Sam stood, pointing to the door. "Get out!"

She folded her arms. "Come on, Nicki. These guys are lame anyway."

Nicki looked across at Tom. "I think I'll stay, but I'll call a taxi for you?"

Tom smiled.

Amanda growled and marched out, pausing to put on her shoes and grab her handbag before she slammed the door behind her.

Sam sank into his chair. "Well, that just sucks."

Nicki bit her lip, obviously conflicted, but then Tom came over and touched her hair, and suddenly, all she could see was him. I was happy for Tom, so I took her hand. "Come on, let's feed them before they eat the furniture."

She chuckled and nodded.

Nicki turned out to be wonderful. She and I got along like we'd always known each other, but I noticed Sam kept throwing icy looks at James. I had no idea what to do, so when James and I returned to his bedroom, I talked to him about it in a low voice.

"Sam's upset with you."

He nodded. "I know, and I don't blame him."

"I can't believe she did that."

"Yeah." He scoffed. "I can't believe she said you aren't pretty. You're the most beautiful girl in the world."

I paused, my heart fluttering. "I can't believe you still think I'm so beautiful."

He clasped my face. "Every day you grow more and more beautiful."

I jumped him, knocking him back onto the bed as I smacked my lips firmly against his—I couldn't help myself. His hands flew up my shirt and pulled it off. As he grabbed my bra to unclip it, my phone rang on the nightstand.

"Ignore it," he said.

I glanced over and saw my dad on caller ID. "Crap!" I shot out my hand to answer it. "Hey, Dad."

James's hands froze and he held his breath.

"Hello, sweetheart," Dad's bright voice came down the line. "I just wanted to see how you girls are doing."

"We're doing great," I answered. James's hands slid off me and he flopped onto the bed. "Harper's living up to her name and harping on and on about Daniel."

He laughed. "Where is she? We need to set up a time to meet this young man."

"Ah . . ." I stared down at James. "She's in the shower."

"Wow, you girls really do sleep late when you have nothing to do. Well, that's okay. Your mother, Dusty, and I are on the way over. We thought we'd spend the day together as a family."

I jumped to my feet. "Oh! Wow! How far away are you?"

"We just barely left, so don't worry—you'll have plenty of time to make yourselves beautiful." He chuckled at himself.

"Sweet! I better go tell Harper to hurry up so I can get in the shower too. I love you, Dad."

"I love you too, sweetheart. We'll see you soon."

I hung up and scrambled to find all my things. James worked at shoving everything into my shopping bags before we rushed into the hallway. We scurried down the stairs, startling the other three sitting on the couch.

"What's goin' on?" Tom asked.

"Cadence's dad!" James blurted out as he burst through the front door.

"He's coming here?" Tom jumped to his feet. "Oh man, he's scary!"

"No," I answered, seeing my shoes in the middle of the living room floor and rushing over to slip them on. "He's on his way to Harper's, where I'm *supposed* to be."

"Wait, why does it matter?" Nicki asked.

"She's still in high school," Sam replied.

"What? But—"

"Cadence!" James started the car.

"Bye, guys!" I ran out.

We sped through the streets to Harper's apartment, and James grew more stressed at each red light.

"Your dad's gonna kill me if he finds out," he muttered every time we stopped, running his hand through his hair.

We pulled up, parked, and then sprinted to the apartment. We pounded on the door, and one of Harper's flatmates answered, looking as if she just woke up. "What the . . . ? Oh, it's you, Cadence."

We shoved past her, hurrying to put my things in Harper's room. Harper sat in bed with her laptop and jumped as we stormed in.

"Geez, Cadence! What's going on?"

"Dad's on his way."

She swore and tugged my things from James's arms. She kicked us out so she could change out of her pajamas. We hurried back to his car, but as he climbed in to leave, they pulled in beside us.

James swore under his breath, but straightened up and smiled as they climbed out of the car. "Hey, David, Harmony, Dusty."

Mum smiled. Dusty grabbed him, and they embraced.

Dad scowled. "What are you doing here?"

"I just wanted to see Cadence before work this afternoon," James answered smoothly.

Dad stepped in front of him and looked him over. "It looked like you were about to leave."

James cleared his throat. "No, I just left something in my car." He bent over and was lucky enough to find one of my sweaters in the seat.

Dad raised an eyebrow, but offered him his hand. "Come on, then."

We headed to the apartment together. Harper grinned as she burst out of her bedroom. "Hey, guys. Oh, James, you're here too?"

I rolled my eyes. Her surprise was far from convincing, and when Dad's eyes narrowed, I knew he suspected something. He pushed into her room, and we all hurried after him. He glanced around the messy room with the air mattress on the floor.

"What's wrong, Dad?" I asked as innocently as possible.

He glared at me before moving some clothing around on the floor. Then he came across Harper's small trash bin. She gasped as he reached for the lid and snatched it away. "Gross, Dad. There's tampons in there."

He snatched it out of her hands and opened it. His eyes widened and he turned on James. "You!"

"What?"

"You promised me you'd stopped sleeping with my daughter!"

James backed out of the room as Dad advanced like a raging bull.

"Dad!" Harper yelled. "They're *Daniel's*!"

Dad froze and slowly turned to her. "Excuse me?"

"Daniel and I are planning on moving in together soon, and we're even talking about getting married."

Dad's eyes widened as his teeth ground together. Mum grabbed his arm and stepped between him and Harper. "Harper, honey, that's wonderful! You must really love him."

Harper smiled warily, her gaze darting to Dad before she responded. "I do. He's amazing, Mum. I can't wait for you to meet him. Cadence has already met him, haven't you?"

I nodded. "Yeah, he's great. Tall, dark, and handsome, and very . . . polite."

Harper threw me a filthy look. "Thanks, Cay." She turned her attention back to Mum. "He'll be back from his trip during the week, so if you want, we can have dinner on Saturday?"

Dad growled. "Marriage? Ha! You're nineteen years old!"

"Wow, Dad, delayed reaction." Harper folded her arms. "But I'm twenty soon, and we aren't planning on getting married until he graduates next year."

"You're still too young!"

Harper pressed her hands against her hips. "It's not like precious Cadence isn't on that track! We all know what's on Jimmy Boy's mind!"

James winced. Dusty grabbed my arm and tugged me out the front door. James followed, shutting the door behind him. Thankfully, the argument became muffled so we could no longer hear it.

Dusty turned to James. "She totally stayed at your place last night, huh?"

I gasped and my cheeks felt like an inferno. How did he figure that out?

Dusty chuckled. "Yeah. Nice cover, by the way."

We paused and listened as the noise died down.

"Who do you think killed who?" Dusty asked in a whisper.

The door burst open, making us all jump. Dad glared directly at James, who stood stiff. "You, boy! Saturday, 6:00 p.m. Are you working?"

"Ah, no—"

"Good. Dinner at our house. Don't miss it, or I'll turn you into a eunuch." Dad slammed the door shut.

James looked at me with raised eyebrows and gritted teeth. The door burst back open, making us jump again, but Dad focused his attention on Dusty.

"And you, son, bring a friend, or a date, or something. Your mouth causes trouble, so I want it preoccupied." He slammed the door again.

Dusty scowled and slumped. James patted his back sympathetically. A few minutes later, Mum, Dad, and Harper emerged. Mum explained that the following weekend we would all meet Daniel at a family dinner. A wicked grin swept across Dusty's face, earning him a backhand across his chest from Harper.

James left eagerly to avoid Dad's burning glare. After I kissed him goodbye, I set out with my family, and, forgetting all the tension of the morning, had a great day. My brother and sister had become the best friends I'd always wanted them to be, and Mum and Dad were happier and loved us more than ever. If nothing else worked out for me in my second chance, at least my family was closer.

Chapter Thirty-Four

I couldn't believe Dusty had the balls to ask Geri to come, but apparently she loved the idea of observing Dad and the two guys dating his daughters all in the same room.

She arrived first. She dragged me straight to my room, where she made predictions on how long it would take Dad to completely lose it. She said Daniel would probably hit the first nerve, not knowing how touchy Dad could be, while someone would definitely say something about James that would provoke him. The last straw would be if someone brought up either me or Harper sleeping with them.

Dusty entered and flicked her shoulder. "Hey, you're supposed to be my date, woman."

"Whatever." She waved her hand at him as she focused entirely on me. "Your mum's gonna end up with a migraine tomorrow from the stress of keeping your dad under control."

I rubbed my temple. "I just hope we still have a roof over our heads by the end of the night."

Geri laughed. Dusty watched her, smiling affectionately. I cleared my throat, and he snapped out of it.

"So, Geri," I said. "How's things with Cody?"

Dusty scowled at me.

Geri sighed. "I don't know. We've done a few things together over the holidays, but I just don't feel like he's what I want."

Dusty's face lit up.

"Why's that?" I asked.

"Well, he's nice and all, but I want a guy who makes me laugh and keeps me on my toes."

"Kinda like Dusty here." I winked at her.

He glared at me.

She giggled, patting his leg. "Kinda, except without the whole brotherly thing. That's just weird."

He huffed.

"Dinner!" Mum called.

Geri and I exchanged confused glances. "But . . ."

Geri nodded. "Yeah. What about James and Daniel?"

We hurried to the living room. They both stood by the wall, their heads down. Dad stood in front of them, his arms folded, legs slightly splayed, looking fierce and dominant. Harper stood back by the entry to the dining room, looking angrier than ever.

James glanced across at me, and his head lifted. "Hey, beautiful."

"Hi, Ja—"

"Hush, boy!" Dad snapped his fingers.

James sighed. "You know, I've done this particular grilling about a hundred times before. I've even had some worse—"

"Shut up!" Dad moved in and met James's gaze. "Then you should know the rules."

James took a deep breath and recited, "No touching of any kind. No hand holding, no footsies, and definitely no kissing. There's to be no prolonged staring, and no whispering."

"Very good," Dad stepped back.

"I'm not finished," James said with a sly grin.

Dad turned to him. "Excuse me?"

I slapped my forehead, dreading what he had come up with.

"You heard me. There's more. There *will* be brown-nosing, begging, pleading, panicking over being a minute late, long lectures—"

Dad growled and shoved James's chest. He turned to Daniel and looked him over. "The last rule: don't be like *him*."

Everyone snickered, trying to hold in laughs. James looked over at me and winked.

Harper rushed forward and grabbed Daniel's arm. "Dad, I think that's enough. Let's just have dinner, okay?"

We all hurried to the table. As we sat, Dad noticed Geri. "Geraldine? What are you doing here?"

"I asked her to come," Dusty said calmly.

"Oh." He stared at Dusty and raised an eyebrow. I knew he wondered whether Geri's presence was to keep her in the loop, already being a permanent fixture in our home, or if he sensed a hint of something more.

The roast was served, and right away, James struck up a conversation with Daniel. I ate, silently observing James's talent for making people like him. Within half an hour, he and Daniel were laughing together like old friends.

Harper leaned across and twitched her eyebrows at me. I rolled my eyes and looked at Dad instead. He watched James and Daniel closely as he ate. Finally, when James had Daniel rolling with laughter, Dad cleared his throat, causing everyone to fall into a tense silence.

"So, Daniel, what are you studying?"

Daniel cleared his throat as he composed himself. "I'm studying engineering at UTS, specializing in computers, telecommunications, and such."

That's right! I'd forgotten that he ended up working as an IT guy at a big company in the city.

"And what do you plan on doing with that?" Dad asked, leaning forward.

"Ah . . ." Daniel obviously believed he'd explained it in layman's terms, but he didn't know Dad. Dad was testing him. "Well, computers are used everywhere now, so I can work on them, do system upgrades and so forth, for companies."

"Is that a good, stable job with a steady income?"

"*Dad.*" Harper groaned.

"It should be, yes," Daniel answered.

"How about debts? How much debt do you—?"

Mum intervened. "So, do we want dessert?"

Dusty and I leapt to our feet to help. While we were in the kitchen, James took hold of the conversation again and had everyone laughing, even Dad. Mum shook her head and smiled. "Cadence, that boy of yours has a knack for getting through to your father."

I scoffed. "Yeah, through to his nerves and irritating him."

She handed me one of the cheesecakes. "No, he has completely defused your father three times now."

She handed Dusty the other cheesecake while she dug out the bowls and spoons.

I set the cake down on the table and James grinned up at me. I always believed Dad thought James was below me, that he didn't approve of him. But as I sat, I thought about what Mum said. When Dad leaned forward to tease

James and they both laughed, I saw something I never expected: Dad really liked James.

James's arm lifted and rested on the back of my chair. Dad saw it and didn't even flinch. Daniel looked over in envy and tried to do the same with Harper. Dad shot him a fierce look, and his arm withdrew. *Sorry, Daniel, you aren't there yet.*

I looked across at Geri, who sat soaking up the whole scene with great delight. It tickled her pink watching Daniel torture himself, seeing Harper grow short-tempered with Dad, all while James seemed to be trying to provoke him.

As we ate dessert, James became bolder than ever. Dad watched him as he leaned over to whisper in my ear.

"You're so sexy, you know that?" He kissed my cheek and sat back.

I glanced across at Dad, who stared down at his cheesecake, trying to pretend nothing had happened.

Harper noticed. She slapped the table. "Oh my gosh, Dad! How can James be allowed to whisper to Cadence, but Daniel can't even touch me?"

Dad's gaze flashed to Harper with a hint of anger. "James knows his boundaries."

"No, he gets away with it because he's gonna marry your favorite child!"

Everyone gasped and looked at me. I froze, my mouth full of food, stunned by what she said.

Geri intervened. "Holy cow, Harper! Cadence is only seventeen!"

"But we all know that—"

"Enough, Harper!" Mum said harshly.

Having Mum snap at her made us all drop our gazes, and an awkward silence fell. After a few minutes, Dusty said, "Ger, have you ever cut off one of your curls to see if it behaves like a slinky?"

Geri scowled while I giggled. "No, Dusty, thank you very much. And don't call me *Ger*."

"Okay, Ger."

She growled and wiped whipped cream across his face.

After dinner, Dad sat Daniel down to interrogate him, with Mum as a mediator. The rest of us retreated to the family room to play a board game. I wanted to talk to Harper, but she remained surly for the rest of the night, only speaking to us if absolutely necessary.

Afterward, when she and Daniel headed out, I rushed to his car and grabbed her arm. "Harper."

She looked into my eyes, and I saw her discouragement. "Cadence, was it this bad for you? Dad was awful."

She leaned against the car. Daniel came back around and stood beside her. "Hey, babe, it wasn't that bad. To be honest, I expected much worse after everything you told me."

He wrapped his arm around her shoulders and kissed her head.

I took her hand. "Dad was so much worse to James, you know that. Oh, and you weren't here the night Dad found out about us . . . you know. *That* was awful."

A smile flitted across her face. "I wish I coulda been here for that. To see Dad rip into James . . ."

"He almost ripped him apart. He shoved James so hard against the wall in the family room, he broke it."

She brushed my hair back from my shoulder. "So it will all be okay? Dad will chill out soon?"

I nodded. "Just be patient. Daniel is way less troublesome than James."

She giggled. "Thanks, Cay."

She turned toward the car, and Daniel hurried to open the door for her.

I patted his arm. "It's good seeing you again."

He smirked. "You too. But don't think I haven't forgotten that twin thing when we first met. I think you owe me something for that little trick. I believed it for months until Harper explained it all to me."

I chuckled. "I'm sure I can work something out."

He climbed into the car, and I waved as they drove off.

The third term of school seemed to drag. With what felt like a million assignments due, our impending graduation at the end of term, and exams during the fourth term, an ominous feeling hung over my peers.

I, on the other hand, felt irritated. My assignments were the same as the first time around, so I aced each and every one of them. It annoyed me, despite how great it was. I had struggled and agonized over them the first time—now, it felt as if I was cheating.

Geri broke up with Cody a few weeks after term started. They ended things very civilly, but he was devastated. Luckily, they'd done most of their assignment and only had individual notes to throw together, so she could avoid seeing him alone.

"He keeps asking me to do things with him," she said quietly one day in Community and Family Studies. "He thinks we still stand a chance, but all he's doing is making things awkward."

"I'm sorry, Geri. I wish I could help. Unfortunately, all I can say is give him time to move on. Maybe try dangling some other girl in front of him."

She sighed. "If you were single, I'd offer *you* up as sacrifice. But alas . . ."

We giggled quietly.

After school, we walked to the parking lot together. Dusty sat on the bonnet of my car, waiting, which surprised me, but Geri surprised me even more when she made a muffled gasp. Out of the corner of my eye, I saw her swallow hard.

"Oh man! Your little brother is here."

I looked across at Dusty, spinning a rugby ball on his hand. "Yeah, it's warmer than the bus."

"He's such a pain."

"Yeah, well, he seems to like you."

I glanced at her as a hesitant pause followed. She bit her lip, but released it straight away. "Yeah, in the *she's-so-fun-to-tease-and-get-under-her-skin* kinda way."

This is a good sign. Dusty's quirky charms are working. I laughed. Dusty heard me and jumped off the car.

"Think quick!" He tossed the ball at me.

My hands flew up and caught it just before it could slam into my face.

"Dusty, I should drive off without you for that!"

He laughed. "You caught it, didn't you? I knew you would, so it's all good." He wrapped his arm around my shoulders and winked at Geri. "Hey, Ger. Looking fine today."

She rolled her eyes and turned toward her car. "Don't call me Ger!"

"Okay, Ger."

She huffed and threw her hands in the air.

"You're beautiful when you're angry!" Dusty called out.

"Stupid kid!" she yelled back. She waved to me as she opened her car door. "I love you, Cay! See ya tomorrow!"

I waved back as she climbed in and drove away.

Dusty squeezed my shoulder. "I think that went well."

I laughed as we walked to my car and climbed in. "Do you wanna know something?"

He shrugged as I started the engine. "Sure."

"I think Geri may have a *hint* of a crush on you."

He swung to face me. "Are you *serious*? Don't mess with me, Cadence!"

I laughed. "I'm not messing with you. She may not know it yet, but there was definitely nervous energy coming from her when we saw you waiting."

"Gah!" He grabbed his hair and flopped back against the seat. "What does that even *mean*? You girls are so complicated!"

I chuckled at his reaction. "It means keep trying, Dusty. Just remember how long it took James, and we're doing great."

An evil grin swept across Dusty's face. "Oh, I'd love to be *that* great with Geri."

I slapped his shoulder. "Hey! That's my best friend!"

He laughed. "I love you, Cay."

Chapter Thirty-Five

Like I did for his graduation, James sat outside waiting for me. When I received my diploma, I rushed straight out the door into his arms and kissed him.

"I'm so proud of you," he said. "But how did you *not* get dux? Second place in your grade? Cadence, that's just not acceptable."

I giggled. "I'm sorry, I'll just have to try harder next time."

But I knew he was proud of me, and I felt the same. The first time around, I'd ranked around the middle of the grade, but this time, I deliberately held back. I didn't feel I deserved that honor since, in a way, I cheated.

He came with my family to a celebratory dinner that night, along with Geri and Daniel. Dusty spent the night teasing Geri mercilessly, and her quick and snappy retorts fascinated me. I couldn't believe I hadn't seen it earlier, but they were perfect for each other.

Daniel was far more comfortable with the family the second time around, and to Harper's delight, Dad even wrapped his arm around his shoulders while they talked.

The next day, after having a fantastic day trashing the school and water bombing the underclassmen with my fellow graduates, James picked me up for a date.

Like all our dates, he made it low-budget—a fast-food picnic by the river—but his company mattered the most to me. We ate, he joked, and I laughed. I loved how his gaze always lingered over my face to watch my reactions to everything he said.

Once we'd finished eating, I lay back, resting on my elbows as I looked up at the stars. I sighed, feeling melancholy wash over me. My second chance was flying by, and I soon faced a time I didn't want to change in the slightest, but happily wanted to live over again.

When James lay down beside me and kissed my ear and neck, I felt my apprehension rise. Could I choose to go so far away from him? Could I hurt him like that? He'd become my world, my rock, and I loved him so much.

His hand slid under my shirt and ran over my belly. His skin on my skin made me forget everything except him. He intoxicated me. Within moments he had me in his car, and we hurried back to his place to make love.

When we finished, I lay with my head on his chest as he stroked my hair. "James?"

"Mmm?"

"You make me so happy."

He kissed my head. "I'm glad, Cadence. You are *my* happiness."

I turned my head so I could look into his eyes. "When I was fourteen, and you were bugging me to date you—" a grin swept across his face "—I never would have seen this coming. I can't believe we've been together for almost three years."

"Well, for me, it's been longer than that." He ran his thumb down my cheek. "I've been counting it from our first kiss at that school disco. I considered myself taken right then, and told everyone I was your boyfriend, but you just didn't know it yet."

"You dork."

"You know it's true. We made out a lot considering we weren't actually a *couple*."

I giggled and rested my head on his chest, listening to his heartbeat as his fingers stroked up and down my back. I shut my eyes and sighed.

I sat up, dazed. I'd fallen asleep, and so had James. I glanced around at the digital clock, and its bold red numbers read 5:27 a.m.

A small screech escaped my lips. I was so dead! I checked my phone. Eight missed calls from Dad! Oh, I was *so* dead!

Then I heard the noise that had dragged me out of my sleep—loud banging on the front door. James sat upright and stared at me, his eyes widening as it dawned on him what had happened.

"Oh, no . . ."

The banging became louder the third time, and Dad bellowed, "James Gordon!"

James swore, yanked on his pants, and grabbed a shirt as he burst out of the room. I hurried to dress as well, knowing Dad would be up the stairs as soon as James opened the door.

As I pulled on my jeans, I heard the door click open. "David, I can explain—"

"Shut up!" I heard a thud. "Cadence!"

I pulled on my shirt, but felt too frightened to go down and face him.

"Cadence!" His footsteps pounded up the stairs.

Tom and Sam's doors clicked open, and Tom exclaimed, "Mr. Anderson!"

"Where's my daughter?" Dad said fiercely, a moment before I heard another thud.

I backed away from the door, pinning myself against the wall. My heart pounded wildly as I stared at the door-knob, waiting for it to turn. The door burst open and Dad stood, his glare boring into me.

He rushed toward me. I whimpered and raised my hands instinctively. He grabbed my wrist, yanking my arm as he pulled me out of the room. "Cadence! You . . . oh, you're gonna get it, girl!"

"Dad! Please don't—"

"You *knew*, Cadence. You *knew* this was off limits."

"Dad . . ."

We marched down the stairs. James slammed the front door, locked it, and held his ground in front of it.

Dad paused, his grip on my wrist tightening as his whole body tensed. "Get out of my way," he said, slowly and deliberately.

"You said once she graduated she could move in if she wanted," James responded calmly.

"But she hasn't moved in. She's still seventeen and still lives under my roof. She's not your fiancée yet, *boy*. In fact, I'm considering taking back my permission for this!"

My heart jumped into my throat as I stared at James. James's eyes widened with panic, his lips pulled back in horror. His gaze flashed to me and pain filled his eyes as I realized my own expression must have reflected my own shock and horror.

"Fiancée?" I said breathlessly.

"Cadence, I know you're not ready for this yet—"

"But you're ready to screw her again!" Dad snarled. "She's grounded until she's eighteen, which means you can't see her until then!"

"That's two months away!" James's voice rose, filled with tension.

"Good."

"Dad!" My eyes burned with tears.

"No, Cadence! You're still legally a child and under my care." He pulled me around and grabbed my shoulders, staring firmly into my eyes. "I'm trying to protect you. You're lucky I don't call this in, because you're underage! But for now, I'm calling a time-out for you two so he can cool down."

"I don't want to cool down!" James yelled. "I *love* her! Nothing you can ever say or do can keep me away from her."

Dad stiffened and turned so slowly it was agonizing. "How dare you speak to me like that," he said in a hushed voice.

"How dare *you* keep her from me!" James stood taller and folded his arms.

"She's not your wife yet, boy!"

What was all these fiancée, wife, and marriage references they kept throwing around? I pulled away as it all hit me. Dad said he'd revoke his permission, that there had been an agreement for me to be with James post-graduation. James planned on marrying me, and had been laying the foundations for quite some time.

I turned to James, my feelings torn. I loved him so much, and I wanted to marry him, but all my memories of Austin flooded through my brain. Then, the most powerful memories of all hit me—Melody.

"Wife?" I said quietly.

James swore, and, ruffling his hair, turned on Dad. "She's not supposed to know yet! She's not ready. Now she's freaking out."

Dad let out a sinister laugh. "Good. You betrayed my trust. You broke our promise. You don't deserve her."

He grabbed my arm and, with one swift movement, shoved James out of the way.

He unlocked the door and threw it open. As he pulled me outside, James grabbed me by the waist and pulled me back. He spun me around and clasped my face. "Cadence, I love you."

Dad shoved him away, but he pushed back and caught my face again. "You love me too, right?"

"James . . ."

Dad pulled me away.

"Cadence!" He ran after me and caught my arms. "Don't freak out on me! Please trust me. I wasn't going to ask you until you were ready. I know we're both really young, but it's always been you."

Dad shoved me into the car and slammed the door in my face. He turned on James and grabbed him by the shirt. "Go take a cold shower. You sound desperate. Two months isn't going to kill you."

He dragged James to the front door. I chewed on my lip. I had to say *something*. I threw the door open. "I love you too, James!"

James's face lit up and he stopped struggling against Dad. "Cadence, everything will be okay, I promise. I'm going to fight for you no matter what."

Dad shoved him inside and slammed the door. He marched back over to the car and glared at me until I sank back inside.

We drove in silence most of the way home. I had disappointed and hurt Dad. I pressed my forehead against the window as I stared out. My mind buzzed with thoughts and feelings all trying to outdo one another. Marry James? But I was supposed to marry Austin. I wanted to marry James . . . but I also wanted to marry Austin again.

I glanced across at Dad, who noticed and glanced back at me. I huffed and looked back ahead.

"Cadence," he said sternly. "Don't be like that with me."

"I'm not being like anything, Dad."

"Yes, you are! You are seventeen years old! You don't have a grasp on what it is to be an adult. What he's asking—what you were *doing*—are adult things."

He sighed and softened his tone. "I don't want you jumping into them and looking back five years from now and regretting your choice. I promise you this: Between now and the time you are twenty-five—twenty-one, even—you will grow and change so much. You're about to go off to university and start working, and will suddenly be faced with bills and debt and choices so new and incomprehensible to you that you'll wish you were a teenager again.

"James . . . he does care about you, yes, but if you choose him now and next year, when you go to uni, you find that you've grown and changed and suddenly he's not keeping up, you won't be able to easily move on. I understand you've been together for a very long time, but high school and the real world are two very different places."

I sighed. "I know, Dad."

"Do you, Cadence?"

I looked into his eyes. He was worried about me. His concern didn't come from sex or marriage, but from how much he cared about me. I was his little girl, and he only wanted the best for me. Images of his face as he gazed steadily into Austin's eyes filled my mind. He'd always thought Austin was the best person for me.

I rested my hand over his. "I'm not going to rush into anything. First things first—go to uni. I know I need to grow up more before I commit to something like marriage, no matter how much I love James."

He took a deep breath and slowly released it. "Cadence, I love how levelheaded you are. It eases my mind to know you think big choices like this through."

I squeezed his hand and rested my head back against the window. "Two months, huh? That's pretty harsh."

Dad chuckled. "It'll be good for you. You're coming up to exams anyway, so it will help you focus."

"You have a good point." I leaned forward to grab my phone to text James, but found I'd left my handbag behind. "Crap."

"What?"

"We have to go back."

He scowled. "Why?"

"I left my handbag behind with my wallet and phone in it. I need those."

He sighed. "Your mother can go get it later."

I sank back into the seat. "Okay."

Chapter Thirty-Six

James sent me texts every hour. He didn't dare call me if he thought Dad would be around. But, despite how much I missed him, Dad was right about one thing: I could focus on studying for my exams.

I studied hard, too, determined to do much better the second time around to prove that I could. In the end, I came out of each of my exams feeling like I'd aced them.

Melanie and Geri grew envious of my calm demeanor. They had me study with them, not only because they thought I knew everything, but to try and have some of my serenity rub off on them.

Geri decided to stay over the night after the exams finished, to relax and have a girls' night. We covered each other in the traditional goop—face masks, nail polish, lotions—and ate pizza and ice cream while watching chick flicks.

Halfway through a bowl of ice cream, Geri said, "I haven't seen the brat at all tonight. It's kinda weirding me out."

"Who? Dusty?" I asked.

She scoffed. "Um, yeah. The other brat doesn't live here anymore."

"He's in his bedroom," I responded. "His exams start this week."

"Oh."

"Why do you ask?" I winked.

She rolled her eyes, but blushed. "Gross, Cadence, don't even."

I laughed. "Hey, Dusty!"

Her blush deepened. "Don't call him out! We're covered in . . ." She stopped as his head popped around the corner.

"What?"

She covered her face with a towel. "Ew! Send him away!"

Dusty rushed over and sat in front of her with a wide grin. "I wanna join in."

He picked up my jar of mask, poked his finger in, and wiped it down his cheek. "Oh! It tingles."

Geri smacked him with a pillow, but kept the towel up over her face. "You're such a girl."

He grabbed her knees. "Come on, Ger, we look the same now." He tugged the towel out of her hands.

She screeched and tried to cover her face. "Give that back! And don't call me Ger!"

"Aw, look at you. You're so pretty."

She slapped his shoulder. "You're a jerk."

He laughed and reached to touch a patch on her face that hadn't dried yet. I stared in amazement at his boldness, even more amazed that Geri allowed him to do it. But then, she slapped his hand away. "Geez, you're weird."

Dusty laughed again and covered his face with the mask.

At six in the morning on my birthday, the doorbell rang. It woke everyone except Dad, who was already up for work. I sat up in my bed, wishing to sleep longer since I had nothing to do that day, until I heard Dad talking in a stern voice.

A few moments later, footsteps rushed through the house and my door burst open. I shrieked with surprise and pulled the sheet over myself. A body knocked me back onto my bed as a pair of lips planted themselves over mine.

I stared up in shock at James. After just over two months apart, I melted into his kiss, completely losing all sense of reason as he caressed my face.

"Hey!" Dad's voice came from the door.

James jumped back with a wicked grin. "I missed her so much. Two months just about killed me."

He looked into my face and leaned in again.

"Out!" Dad pointed to the hallway.

James leapt to his feet. "Okay."

Dad glared at him as he rushed by and shut the door with a bang. I hurried to make myself decent and scurried into the shower.

When I finished and slipped on my robe, I opened the bathroom door a crack to make sure James wasn't around. On seeing and hearing nothing, I dashed back to my room and shut the door behind me. I let out a long breath and untied my robe.

"Oh, yeah."

I jumped and swung around. James sat in the corner. "James! Dad will kill you—"

"Your dad left for work. Keep going with that thought."

I pulled the robe tight around me. "Get out!"

He jumped up and wrapped his arms around me. "You have no idea how much I've missed you."

His fingers slipped under the robe and found the skin on my hip, making me break out in goose bumps. "Every inch of you, every part of you. Calls and texts weren't enough. I craved your kisses, I ached to touch your hair, to see your face."

"Who even talks like that?" I said breathlessly.

He chuckled. "I've got to have you, Cadence. Right now."

His arm wrapped around my bare waist as he bent down to nibble on my neck. I moaned, feeling my own need to have him awaken, but it wasn't right—not in my house with Dusty in the next room and Mum nearby.

I pushed him off. "James, please get out."

He chewed on his lip as his gaze lingered over my lips. He groaned. "Ugh! Fine."

He slipped out of my room.

I dressed and stepped out to find James and Dusty locked in an intense battle of . . . something. I stared at them—Dusty in his blue and gray school uniform, and James in his black and white work uniform—just staring at each other with their arms entwined.

"Um . . . should I leave you boys alone?" I asked.

"Shh, Cadence!" Dusty replied.

I sighed and walked by them to get breakfast, then sat to watch TV. After a few minutes, Dusty roared and James cheered. Sounds of a tussle followed, which James apparently won. Dusty groaned and appeared in search of his school shoes.

James flopped onto the sectional beside me and sighed. "It's so good to be with you again."

"So you've made very clear," I said through a mouthful of food.

He sat up and glared at me. "You seem pretty nonchalant about it."

I giggled at his stern face. "I'm sorry, it's been a crazy two months for me with all my exams, and studying, and Dusty trying to pick up Geri—"

"Wait, what?" James's eyes widened.

"Cadence!" Dusty rushed into the room. "Shut up!"

I laughed, and Mum appeared around the corner. "What was that?"

"Nothing, Mum!" Dusty grabbed her arm.

"Dusty likes Geraldine? This is interesting." She pushed by and sat on the armchair.

Dusty groaned. "Cadence! That was our little thing! It was just supposed to be kept between you and me."

"Oh, ah . . ." I locked eyes with him as he stared at me. "I was just kidding?"

Dusty huffed. "Fine, now everyone knows. But don't tell Dad. I see how he is with you and Harper, and I really don't want him on my case about girls."

He marched out of the room.

James changed the topic. "So, I have a couple of hours before work. Let's go do something."

I scratched my head, thinking about all the lazing around I'd planned to do for my birthday. Then, I remembered our three-year anniversary and panicked. I'd been so distracted by my exams that I hadn't bought him anything, or for his birthday either. The worst part was that by the look in his eyes, he'd gone all out like usual.

"James, what would you like to do today?"

He grinned. "I might have something planned before my shift at one."

I looked across at Mum. She laughed. "You're eighteen now, Cadence. You don't need my permission. As long as I know where you are, I'll be fine."

James shot to his feet. "We'll just be at some shops, then my place. I'm keeping it simple."

"Okay. Be safe."

I rushed to my room to grab my handbag, then James dragged me outside to his car. As we drove away, I asked, "So, what are we going to do?"

He grinned. "Have sex."

I slapped his shoulder. "No! Come on!"

He laughed. "No, you'll find out."

We stopped at the mall and, as we walked, I discreetly searched for something to buy him. I felt like the worst girlfriend in the world as he paused at jewelry stores and asked me if I liked anything. He also bought me a bunch of flowers and a teddy bear.

"To add to your vast collection." He grinned.

I rolled my eyes.

As we passed the pet store, he stopped. "Hey, check out that puppy!" He stared inside at the puppy trying to kill a toy in its mouth. "Ha! Dogs are hilarious."

I had an idea. I'd have to check with Tom and Sam first, but I would buy him a dog. I bought a card while he bought a giant bag of caramel popcorn, filled it out, and slipped it in my handbag for later.

Back at his house, only Tom was home. He greeted me excitedly and gave me a hug. "Long time, stranger. That morning . . . oh, man! Your dad is scary!"

I smiled. "I know. I couldn't believe James stood up to him like that."

"Me either. So, on that topic, when are you moving in? I cleaned the bathrooms and everything."

My face fell. "Oh . . ."

James interjected. "I bought cake."

While he banged around in the kitchen, I asked Tom if dogs were allowed under their rental agreement.

"Yeah," he answered. "Why are we whispering?"

"Because it's a surprise for James, if you guys are okay with it."

Tom grinned. "A dog, for us? That's awesome! But it has to be less than twenty kilos."

"Okay. How about this weekend we go to the shelter and he can pick out one you can all deal with?"

He grabbed my face. "Gah! I could just kiss you!"

"Hey! Hands off!" James glared at him with a hint of a smirk as he set the cake on the table. "Only I'm allowed to kiss her."

We all sat around the table and James cut the small chocolate cake into three pieces. He handed Tom his and sent him away. James tilted his glass of milk at me and said, "Happy birthday and three years."

As he went to dig in, I whipped out the card. "I'm going to give you this right now."

His smile widened as he plucked it from my hands. He opened it, read it once, then again slower. His eyes widened and he burst out laughing. "Are you serious?"

"Yeah. Is it okay?"

"Yes! Cadence, you're the best." He leaned over the table and kissed me. He sat back and gestured for me to eat my cake.

We ate quietly, until I felt something metallic click against my teeth. I spat it out and found a white gold ring with five princess-cut diamonds on the top. I stared at it, completely baffled, before James's hand rested on my leg. I looked down and saw him kneeling beside me. "Cadence."

I gasped and tossed the ring onto my plate. "No, no, no! James, no!"

His face fell. "Cadence, but—"

"I'm eighteen! I'm barely out of high school!"

"So? You love me, don't you? I love you, and after two months apart, I know now more than ever that I need you in my life. We'll go to uni together, you'll move in here, and everything will be great."

"James . . ." I caressed his face. "No, not yet. I'm not ready for this. I'm still just a kid."

"Legally, you're an adult."

"No, I mean I still have so much growing up to do."

"Then do it with me. Cadence, we've practically grown up in each other's arms, and there's never been anyone but you since the moment I laid eyes on you."

I stroked his hair, marveling at the richness of its chestnut color. I loved him so much, but I couldn't marry him. "I know, James. But just . . . not yet."

He grabbed my hand in his hair and gazed up at me, his eyes pleading. "Cadence, I'm not going to give up on you."

I nodded and rubbed my eye as a tear fell. "I know, but please understand."

He grabbed the ring and slipped it onto my right hand. "I understand. I've always needed to be patient for you, so I will continue to be patient." He leaned forward and softly kissed me. "I love you so much, Cadence."

I smiled and caressed his face. "I love you, too."

Chapter Thirty-Seven

Geri stared at my right hand on the steering wheel. "You're crazy, you know that?" she said for about the umpteenth time. "Saying *no*? I wish some hot guy would propose to me."

"Geri, we've been through this."

"I know, I know. You don't feel ready, blah, blah, blah." She reached across and lifted my hand off the wheel to look at the ring. "Wow, it's so beautiful. You better say yes *eventually*. This thing is gorgeous! And the fact that he just *knows* your ring size is like, insane, you know that? What normal guy knows his girlfriend's ring size?"

"James is far from normal." I pulled my hand away and rested it back on the steering wheel.

"Duh! Which is why you're totally crazy!"

I sighed, done with this particular discussion. I'd had similar ones all week. Harper pretty much yelled my ear off, Dusty didn't talk to me for several days, Melanie hung up on me when she called to ask if we would be sisters soon, and Geri just kept nagging me to change my mind.

Mum and Dad seemed to be the only people to support my decision. Dad, predictably, told me he was proud of me, agreed with my reasoning, and supported my decision. Mum just touched my arm, smiled, and said, softly, "You do what you feel is right, sweetheart. You're so thoughtful that, no matter what you choose, I know it will be for the best."

I loved Mum more than ever.

We pulled up in the parking lot at the shelter and found James, Sam, and Tom already waiting for us.

Geri jumped out and rushed to James. "Hey, James, I want to apologize for my friend's stupidity. I want to tell you yes for her because she has no idea."

I rushed over and pulled her away. "Geri!"

James ruffled his hair with a look of confusion in his eyes. "Ah . . . okay." But then his gaze flashed to my right hand and he grinned. "Come on, I want my dog."

He rested his arm around my shoulders, and we all headed in. We followed James up and down the aisles, examining each dog closely. Tom and Sam said no to some of his favorites, reminding him of the size limit. Finally, he ended up tossing up between three—two puppies, and a scruffy little mongrel. He rushed up and down between their cages, trying to work out which one he liked best.

Tom took the opportunity to talk to me. "Cadence, you know you crushed him, right?"

I huffed. "Oh, here we go again."

"Hey!" He grabbed my arm and turned me to face him. "It was a big deal to him. After he came home from work that night, he just went to his room without saying a word. You know that's not like him."

I stroked the hair resting over my shoulder. "I'm just not ready for that yet."

Tom sighed and paused as James rushed by us. "Could you at least move in with us? I'm sure he'd appreciate that more than anything."

I watched James as he squatted down in front of one of the puppies. "Maybe after Christmas and New Year's. I should be at home when my HSC results come through."

Tom nodded. "That sounds fair."

James rushed back to us, his eyes alight. "I want *that* puppy."

New Year's was quiet. Harper and Daniel managed to score a harbor cruise, Mum and Dad were invited to a party, so just Dusty and I stayed at home. I invited Geri and James to come around, which satisfied Dusty.

The four of us talked endlessly. I couldn't believe how lucky I was to have them. During New Year's in the first timeline, I'd ended up home by myself; Dusty had gone to a friend's house over staying home alone with me. It had been depressing, and I'd cried into the New Year. I'd hoped more than anything to get into UWA so I could escape and start over.

But this time, as I looked around at my three best friends who I loved more than anything, I doubted whether I wanted to leave them. I felt so happy, I didn't know if I could move away.

James ran his fingers through my hair and I shuddered. He chuckled softly and leaned forward to whisper in my ear. "Another year with you."

As the countdown began, Dusty shifted closer to Geri. Before I could see what happened, James turned my head and, with a quick smile, kissed me. Time froze, and I pulled away with a sigh. I looked into his face and stroked his cheek.

"Cadence."

I looked over to the door and smiled. "Hello, Angel."

He stepped up beside me, adjusting his Father Time robe. He tilted his head toward Geri and Dusty. I turned to face them. Dusty had his hand on Geri's neck as he leaned in, their lips barely touching.

"Did you anticipate this?"

I giggled. "At the beginning? No. But I couldn't ask for anything better."

He touched my shoulder. I gasped as my memories and feelings flooded over me. As images flashed through my mind, I stared at James, my internal conflict rising. I ran my fingers through his hair as a tear ran down my cheek. I loved him as much as Austin—that was clear to me as my memories came back, so how could I possibly choose one over the other?

The man sighed. "Sweet Cadence, do not be afraid to choose him. He does love you."

I shook my head. "How can I when I know what Austin can give me? How can I possibly choose one and break the other's heart?"

His voice grew deep. "Austin hasn't even met you yet. You wouldn't be breaking his heart at all."

I chewed on my lip and forced myself to turn away from James. I looked up into the man's dark eyes. "But *I* would know."

The man gave me a sympathetic smile. "Come. Let us review the year and make plans for the next."

I shook my head. "No. I'm thinking clearer than ever, but everything seems even more confusing as a result. I can't make plans like this."

"Very well." He stretched out his hand for me. "Let us review and see what was done differently."

We started with James moving out, then we saw Melanie's pregnancy and miscarriage, followed by her growing friendship with me. I smiled as I watched her keep in close contact with me, even if she simply kept me in her line of vision. I'd become her safety blanket.

Then, in contrast, I watched Melanie slitting her wrists in the other timeline. It broke my heart, but the worst thing was when James found her laying on the floor in a pool of her own blood. He stared at her unconscious body, too wasted to respond.

Karen found them. She shoved James aside and grabbed Melanie's wrists as she wailed, "Don't die, Melanie!" between her sobs. Once she'd wrapped Melanie's wrists with some shirts, she called an ambulance. Melanie spent several days in the hospital on suicide watch.

James didn't seem to notice.

Tears ran down my face. "I'm so glad that didn't happen this time around."

The man nodded. "Yes. Robbie's need to try to force James back into his old ways may have caused the pregnancy, but the love Melanie felt for the child, and the friendship you and Geri gave her, along with her brother fighting to protect her, showed her that her life did mean something."

He turned me around and I found us standing by the bus bays, watching Dusty and Geri talking. I'd missed out on these exchanges because I drove home. I moved closer as she giggled.

"When was this?" I asked.

"A few weeks after she and Cody started dating. She didn't want to admit to herself that she liked a tenth grader, and of all people, her best friend's brother. It was what you kids call 'social suicide,' especially when Cody was so interested."

"But she dated Cody in the other timeline, too."

He shrugged and the other timeline appeared beside us. "In this timeline, she'd never had a boyfriend before, and his keen interest grabbed her attention. She wanted to know what it felt like to be kissed, to have someone who showered her with attention, to feel beautiful."

"But Geri *is* beautiful."

"Yes, she is." He waved his hand and we appeared back in my living room in front of Geri and Dusty. "He makes her feel that way, even though she's hesitant to be with someone younger than her."

"What should I do?"

He brushed my hair back and a strange electricity sent a chill down my spine. "Encourage her feelings to the surface. She shouldn't be afraid to love."

His hand withdrew and I realized I'd been holding my breath. I released it and turned to see he had gone. I dashed over to James, just as time started moving again.

Five options. My offers were much better the second time around. I had three Sydney schools, one rural school, and of course, my offer from Western Australia. Now, what to do?

Talking to anyone about it would be pointless. They'd all want me to stay nearby and try to convince me to pick a Sydney university. I knew of only one person I could talk to, if I could even call him that. "Angel?"

A moment passed before a hand rested on my shoulder. "Yes, sweet Cadence?"

I looked up at him, smiling at his familiar, calm countenance. "I . . . I need guidance."

"With what exactly?"

"With which school to choose."

He sat on my bed. "That's not exactly my area of specialty."

"But it is." I shifted forward in my seat. "How do I choose between Austin and James?"

His face fell and sadness crept into his eyes. "I cannot advise you on that."

I groaned. "This is insane! James doesn't want me to go so far away, but I'm drawn to the life I had with Austin. It's the reason I did all of this. I can't just give it up, no matter how much I love James. I have to know if what I had with Austin was real or not, and if I can get it back."

A smile curled at his lips. "Well, Cadence, you sound like you already know what you want to do."

I turned back to the letters on my desk and stared at the one from Western Australia. When I turned around, he had gone.

I scrambled onto the floor and pulled out my scrapbook to look at Austin. He stared at his own offer from the university with a look of excited awe on his face. My heart fluttered. It would be about a year before we met, as we would be doing different courses, but the thought that we would be at the same university, on the same campus, sent waves of nervous energy through me. I wanted to do everything exactly how it had been the first time. I wanted to know if he could love me all over again.

I reached over, picked up my letter, and filled out my acceptance.

Chapter Thirty-Eight

Dad wasn't happy with me moving in with James. He helped me pack my room, but he refused to come help Mum and Dusty move me in.

Dusty was confused. I'd packed most of my things in boxes and stored them at home, bringing only a few essentials.

"Are you guys gonna find a place of your own soon?" he asked.

"Ah . . . maybe." I didn't want to answer with the truth. Telling everyone I'd be living in the townhouse for only two months before I left would go down like a lead balloon.

As we were about to leave, I turned to Dad. He stood stiff as a board and refused to make eye contact with me. "Dad?"

"Yes, Cadence?"

"I love you."

His gaze fell and tears welled up in his eyes. He wrapped his arms around me and kissed my head. "He better take care of you, or I'll tear him limb from limb."

I clung to him, burrowing into his chest. The time for these moments, in the safety of his arms, had ended. I'd enjoyed having them a second time, and it saddened me knowing they would rarely happen now I'd be out on my own.

He didn't want to let go of me, not that I pressed him to. His hand clasped the back of my head as he kissed my forehead over and over. "Why did you have to grow up so quickly?"

I nuzzled into his chest. "I'll always be your little girl."

His grip on me tightened, and I felt warm tears in my hair. "I'm always here if you need me."

He kissed my head again before finally letting me go.

I walked to the car, my own emotions swelling up inside me. I bit my tongue hard to stop myself crying. As we drove away, I waved to Dad, who waved back, but I knew his heart was breaking.

I stared out the window, remembering when I'd left for Western Australia the first time. Dad came with us to the airport, and he'd held me tightly, like he just had. I'd turned back just inside the gate to see him and Mum both in tears, arms wrapped around each other, as they watched me leaving to go out on my own. I sighed and fought back my tears.

When we arrived at the townhouse, James burst out with his puppy right behind him. He came over and opened the door for Mum, making her laugh and shake her head. He rushed around to the back.

"I expected a few more things than this, like some furniture, or . . ." He opened the tailgate and stared. "Ah . . . I thought you were moving in?"

"I am." I came around and looked at my two suitcases.

"Um, where's your mirror, and your books, and your stuffed toys?"

I shrugged as I pulled out one of the suitcases. "I packed them up."

"But . . ." He grabbed the other suitcase. "I rearranged everything so you had plenty of space. I even bought a new set of drawers and a bigger bed."

Dusty made a gagging sound.

"I'll need those," I answered as the puppy bounced around under my feet. "Hey, Cane."

The chocolate-brown, lop-eared puppy, which James had given the very "original" name of Canis, bounced and yipped as we dragged the suitcases inside and up the stairs. We dumped the suitcases in his room—our room—and headed back downstairs. Dusty browsed through the DVDs while Mum examined the living room and kitchen.

"Mum?" I said.

She swung around and smiled at me with tears in her eyes. "This place looks nice, and it's in a great location for wherever you decide to go to school." She ran her finger over the freshly cleaned countertop. "But I'm going to miss you at home with us."

I rushed over and threw my arms around her. "I'll miss you, too."

"And me." Dusty wrapped his arms around both of us. "Dad's going to be completely focused on me and on my case about everything now."

We laughed.

"So," James said from behind us. We turned to face him and saw him standing with his hands in his pockets, staring right at me. "Which uni did you decide on?"

I dropped my gaze. "I haven't yet."

"You better hurry up, sweetie," Mum said, stroking my hair. "Deadlines are coming up."

"She'll pick Macquarie, won't you, Cadence?" James grinned.

I shook my head. "No, I don't wanna do that course."

His face fell slightly. "Then UTS, and you can travel with Tom," he said smoothly.

"Maybe." I stepped over to him and grabbed his hand. "Let's not talk about it right now. I'm feeling emotional enough about moving out without adding to it."

He caressed my face. "Okay."

After some very emotional goodbyes, where even Dusty fought to hold back his tears, James and I were left alone. I made my way back into the living room and gazed around. It felt strange. Even though I'd been there plenty of times, living there would be another thing entirely.

"Are you okay?" James asked as he headed into the kitchen to make lunch.

"Um . . . yeah. I think I might go and unpack."

He turned to me. "You know, there's nothing wrong with feeling weird about this. Take your time to adjust, but don't block me out, okay?"

I smiled. "Okay."

"All right. Well, I'll make you something to eat while you unpack."

"Thanks."

"You're welcome. I love you, beautiful."

Canis followed me to the room. He ran around, trying to jump up onto the bed to get my attention while I stood staring at my open suitcases. My thought process came to an abrupt halt, and I felt numb.

I reached in and pulled out my five response letters. I needed to mail them, but I was so afraid. I set them back down, pulled out my jewelry and makeup, and then slid my suitcases into the corner.

I caught Canis and lay back on the bed with him on my chest. I shut my eyes, trying to force all my thoughts and feelings aside and just relax. Canis's little body felt warm and comforting on my chest, and his rough little tongue occasionally licked my hand. I giggled and looked into his large amber eyes as they gazed down at me. They definitely called them puppy eyes for a good reason.

A soft tap came from the door. I sat up as James entered and set down a sandwich for me, then sat beside me on the bed. "Cadence, are you freaking out?"

I giggled. "Yeah, a bit."

He plucked up Canis and shut him in the bathroom. When he came back, he climbed on top of me and kissed me. I moaned at the taste of his lips. His hand stroked my cheek and neck as he laid me flat on my back underneath him.

He broke away and softly kissed down my chin and neck. "I'll take care of you. You don't need to worry about anything."

I shut my eyes as his hand stroked down my leg, exposed by my shorts. He drove me wild as his lips moved onto my collarbone, but he pulled away and sat on the bed beside me to eat.

I stared up at him, gaping. He grinned and continued eating. I slapped his leg. "What was that?"

"What? I'm hungry."

"You're such a man."

He raised his eyebrows. "A man, huh? I've been promoted from guy. I like that."

He set his food aside and rolled back on top of me, making me giggle.

That afternoon, James and I headed to the store to buy some decent groceries. I refused to eat instant noodles and frozen pizza every day. I also slipped my letters into my handbag while he wasn't looking, determined, albeit afraid, to mail them.

We perused the store, where I made him pick out fresh fruit and veg, and he insisted on steaks. As he waited for the checkout, I went to the bakery to pick up some bread. While I walked through the shopping center, I found the post office. The red mailbox sat out in front of it, beckoning but tormenting me with its mere presence.

I stood frozen for several moments, trying to build up the courage to mail the letters. Then, I took a deep breath and surged toward it.

Glancing over my shoulder, I slipped the five letters in the mailbox—four declines, and one acceptance to Western Australia. I hadn't told anyone which one I'd chosen. My parents didn't even know I'd applied for an out of state school.

I knew how it would go with James, and I dreaded telling him. He would have been disappointed if I didn't choose Macquarie, but would have accepted it. This would send him into a fit of rage.

I stepped back from the mailbox, wishing I could jump inside and take the letters back. Those letters were on their way to tear James's heart apart, and I didn't know if I could live with that.

"Hey, where's the bread?"

I jumped and swung around at the sound of James's voice.

"Oh, I . . ." I hurried to the bakery.

In the car, he asked, "So were you mailing your acceptance letter back there?"

I bit my lip, not wanting to answer.

"Cadence." He sighed. "You've been kind of closed off lately. I hope it's not because I freaked you out when I asked you to marry me. I get that you're not ready, so I'm not going to push you, and if you don't feel ready to live with me, I understand that, too. I'm not going to make you do something you're not comfortable with."

Loud sobs burst free from me. How could I do this to him? How could I just leave when he was so wonderful?

He kept looking at me with concern as I cried the whole way home. I needed to tell him. He needed to know I would break his heart more than I already had. Maybe he could come with me? But the whole point of going out there was to see Austin, so how could I test those waters with my boyfriend in tow? What was I even *thinking*? I still had a boyfriend, and I was thinking about another guy whom I hadn't even met yet, technically.

James, Austin. Austin, James. I played a dangerous game, and it hadn't even started yet. I didn't want to end it with James. I still loved him, but I couldn't get the memories of Austin and the love we'd shared to die down.

I began to reason and make excuses. Maybe with the distance, James would end it with me, which would remove my guilt about Austin. Then again, I'd be devastated if James broke up with me, and more than anything, I didn't want that.

Everything was so messed up.

When I drew myself out of my thoughts, I realized James had me in his arms, carrying me up the stairs to our room. I drew a shaky breath and nuzzled my head into his shoulder. I loved the way he smelled, and his warmth encompassed me. It gave me comfort, and I relaxed as he placed me on the bed.

He knelt beside me, clasping my hand in his, and softly kissed my fingers. "Cadence, you know I love you, right?"

I rolled onto my side to look into his amazing gray-blue eyes. "Yes."

"Then talk to me. I hate seeing you like this."

I sighed and closed my eyes as his fingers brushed my cheek, tucking my hair behind my ear. "I don't want to hurt you, James."

His breath caught, and a flash of fear crossed his face. "How could you hurt me?"

I clasped his hands tightly as I stared at them, unable to look him in the eyes as I dealt the crushing blow.

"I accepted UWA."

"UWA?" He hesitated, then pulled his hands from mine and launched to his feet. "*What*? Are you insane?"

"I told you it would hurt you," I said softly.

"Yeah, it does! How could you do that? You could have stayed right here, but you chose to go clear across the country? Is it because I asked you to marry me and you're freaking out?"

I pulled my knees up as my tears fell. "No. I just needed a fresh start."

"A fresh start from what? Your family? You can have that right here!" He waved his arms around the room. "From your friends who love you? Or no, you're running from me, right?"

My head shot up. "No!"

He backed away from me, grabbing his hair as his face twisted with pain. "Then why? Why would you run so far away from me?"

I sat up to face him. "I'm not running from you!"

"I don't understand. What about *us*? What will I do without you? You know I love so much I want to marry you and have you with me every day, so you go somewhere so far away that I'd be lucky to see you every few months? You're killing me!"

My face fell into my hands as my heart broke from the pain I'd inflicted on him. "I'm so sorry. But this decision has nothing to do with you. I still love you so much, but I have to do this. I have to learn who I am on my own. We've been together so long that I've become lost in you. I can't pick out my own thoughts and feelings from yours. I can't seriously consider marriage until I know who I am and know I can stand on my own two feet."

I dared to look up at him. He stood stiff, his hand in his hair, staring down at me with a horrified expression. Our eyes met, and his hand slid down over his face. "I didn't know you felt so lost. You've always been so with it and in control."

He knelt in front of me and grasped my knees. "If that's how you feel, I'm not going to stop you. I love you, and more than anything, I want you to be happy. I guess I've been so focused on trying to manipulate circumstances so you'd marry me, I'd forgotten to pay attention to what you need.

"Am I hurt by this? Yes." He stroked my cheek. "But watching you cry like that in the car was far more painful. You're my world, Cadence."

I sobbed and pulled him in to kiss me.

Dad barged in, startling me as I cooked dinner. He marched across the room and shoved his finger in my face. "*Western Australia?*"

He then went on a twenty minute rant about it, only stopping when James came home and hollered, "Hey! Don't yell at her."

Dad swung to him. "You let her do this!"

"I didn't even know about it until after it was done."

"So you're not even going to fight for her or try to make her stay?" Dad scoffed and folded his arms. "You don't deserve her."

"Of course I'm going to fight for her!" James advanced on Dad and met his gaze. "But I'm not going to force her to stay. She needs to do what she needs to do, and I'm not going to stop her."

I smiled at James, loving him more than ever.

Dad looked at me and I stopped smiling. "At least she won't be living here with you."

James raised his chin, but didn't respond.

Dad turned back to me. "Cadence, if you leave, you better be back for your breaks so we can see you."

"Of course," I answered.

"Good. Well . . ." He glanced between me and James uncomfortably. "I'll be going."

"Dad!" I rushed over and wrapped my arms around him. "Thank you for looking out for me."

He stroked my hair. "Oh, Cadence, you make it so hard for me to be angry at you."

He kissed my head before he left.

As I closed the door behind him, James stepped up behind me and flicked the lock. "Wow, your dad is so indecisive. One minute it's 'fight for her, boy,' and the next it's 'how dare you live with my daughter.'"

I giggled, but stopped abruptly as his hands slid under my shirt. "So, Tom is with Nicki tonight, and Sam is at his sister's birthday . . ." He lifted my shirt and unclipped my bra. "And I was thinking we should take advantage of that."

"Dinner's in the oven. I don't want it to burn," I responded softly as he pulled off my shirt.

"We have a few minutes, then we'll eat, and then fool around some more." His hands ran up over my waist and ribs. I shuddered. He chuckled and wrapped his arms around me. He had complete control of me.

Much later, we lay in bed with the bedside lamp on. He lay facing me, propped up on his elbow as his other hand stroked down my face, neck, and shoulders. I shut my eyes and sighed, completely content.

He softly kissed my lips. I smiled. "James?"

"Mmm?"

"I'm going to miss you like crazy."

His fingers paused their motion and lifted to clasp my face. I opened my eyes and found him staring down at me. "Well, you'll have to come back to me whenever you can, because I'm going to miss you like crazy, too."

I wrapped my arm around the back of his head and pulled him down to kiss me.

Chapter Thirty-Nine

The morning of my departure arrived. I awoke to James kissing my shoulder. I smiled and leaned back into him, pulling his arms tighter around me. His lips found my ear, making me giggle, and his leg wrapped around me. "If only I could never let you go."

I relaxed into him. "I wish that, too."

The door cracked open, and a little brown furball dashed across the room and up onto the bed.

"Cane!" James sat up and grabbed the puppy as he licked at our faces.

Sam chuckled in the hallway and shut the door again.

James jumped out of bed and tossed the puppy into the bathroom. He turned back to me.

"I'm not ready to . . ." He eyed me over in my sports bra and short, striped pajama shorts. "I think I just died and went to heaven."

I grabbed the sheet and pulled it back over me.

He rushed at me and knocked me back. "Oh no! You're not getting away with that!"

He tickled me. My screeching made Canis yip at us while James laughed menacingly at me.

He attached himself to me all morning. I couldn't even take a shower without him right there beside me. He watched me dress, do my hair, eat my breakfast, and brush my teeth.

"Can't you leave me alone for one second?" I asked as I put on my mascara.

"No. I want to absorb as much of your beauty as possibly before you leave me for several months." He stepped forward and rested his hands on my hips. "If you have a problem with that, then too bad."

I turned to face him. "I'll be back for winter break, and that's a whole month, maybe even more depending on when my exams are. I'll let you know my flight details as soon as I get them."

He softly kissed my lips. "You'll stay here for that time, won't you?"

"I thought I'd give my parents and Dusty a week, but yes, I'm planning on staying here with you."

He grinned and kissed me again. "Good. I want to spend every moment I can with you."

He drove me to the airport. The whole ride remained dead silent. I could feel tension emanating from him so I was afraid to speak, in case I made him lose control and break down.

At the airport, we met with my family, including Harper and Daniel. James greeted Daniel warmly, and Dusty gave him a knowing nod. We knew James would break down once I'd gone, and I felt glad he would have someone there to support him. But I felt nervous while we waited after my check-in. I clung to James's hand as the family chatted together. I wanted to wait until the last minute to go down to my gate so I could be with the people I loved.

I rested my head against James's shoulder and took a deep breath. He shifted his arm around my waist and gave me a firm squeeze. He would hold on until the last moment.

"Cay-Cay!" An abundance of long, loose curls sprang on me. James managed to hold onto me as Geri squeezed me as hard as she could. "I'm so glad I didn't miss you! The trains were all running late, and I thought you'd be gone for sure!"

"Why didn't you come down with my family?" I asked.

She glanced back at Dusty uneasily, and he dropped his gaze. "I didn't think about that. But it doesn't matter because I made it!"

"Barely." Harper pointed at the boarding screen. "Cadence, they're calling for your flight to board."

James pulled me tightly against him. His breathing became shallow, and his whole body tensed as he whispered, "It's too soon. I'm not ready."

I glanced around and saw everyone turn away. He brushed his hand over my cheek, turning me to face him. He fought back tears and did a very good job of it. "I'm gonna miss you, Cadence Anderson."

My own tears burst out, and I lunged in for a kiss. His arms wrapped tightly around me as I ran my fingers through his hair, taking in as much as I could so I could carry him with me for as long as possible.

When I pulled away, he said, quietly, "Don't forget how much I love you."

"I won't." I caressed his face. "I love you, too, so I'm relying on you to keep an eye on these miscreants while I'm gone."

He cracked a grin as our eyes met. "You should go now."

It took a moment, but I pried myself from his arms. I gave everyone a quick hug and whispered to Geri, "Don't be afraid to like Dusty. He likes you, too."

She gasped as I let go and winked at her.

As I walked away, I glanced back to see Mum and Dad hand in hand, just like the first time. Tears ran down my cheeks as I felt my love for them burst out of me, and as my gaze fell on everyone else who came along this time, I knew I was so blessed. I truly had done it better the second time around.

To be continued . . .

About Katie

Born and raised in Australia, Katie's early years of day dreaming in the "bush", and having her father tell her wild bedtime stories, inspired her passion for writing.

After graduating High School, she became a foreign exchange student where she met a young man who several years later she married. Now she lives in Arizona with her husband, daughter and their dogs.

She has a diploma in travel and tourism which helps inspire her writing. Katie loves to out sing her friends and family, play sports and be a good wife and mother. She now works as an Acquisitions Editor to help support her family. She loves to write, and takes the few spare moments in her day to work on her novels.

Acknowledgements

The road to publication has been a long one for Cadence. The story came to me through piecing together a string of what-if's in my own life. Because of this, the novels became a labor of love, and the characters took lives of their own. So first of all, I want to acknowledge the hints of people I know that filtered into the pages. To those moments from my own life that helped fill the plot with genuine emotion, whether embarrassing, hilarious, or sweet. I hope the people who helped form the characters will see themselves and know they touched my life.

Next I'd like to thank my family, my wonderful husband, **Landon**, especially for his patience with me. Although my books are a little too "girly" for his taste, he puts up with me telling him about them and does what he can to support me when times for edits and marketing come around. I'm also grateful for my daughter's understanding that mommy needs "quiet time" to work.

I'd also like to thank all my writer friends who read these drafts for me. I feel like there were so many readers I can't possibly remember all of them. But I'd like to mention **Stacey Nash**, **Anabel Gonzalez**, **Darci Cole**, and **Summer Wier**. They each went beyond a critique and helped me with discussions regarding the plot, and encouraged me to keep going when I kept being told Cadence wouldn't fit anywhere, or didn't work, or whatever other obstacle was thrown in my path. Summer even helped me line things up and connected me with REUTS, which I am so incredibly grateful for.

Last of all, a huge thank you to **REUTS** for taking a chance on Cadence. The team fell in love with the story and saw it exactly as I intended it to be. Every step of the way I've felt nothing but support. **Kisa Whipkey** helped me enrich the plot, **Michelle Hoehn** patiently put up with me biting at the bit through edits, **Ashley Ruggirello** made an absolutely stunning cover that is so perfect, and **Summer** who never stopped supporting me through the whole process.

Of course, I can't forget to say thank you to all my **readers** who have followed me along since my debut novel, or who found me somewhere along the way and stuck around. Readers keep me going, and give me faith in myself to try despite the ridicule all authors face.

I am truly so blessed!

www.ingramcontent.com/pod-product-compliance
Lightning Source LLC
Chambersburg PA
CBHW072008020726
47501CB00006B/1732